The Sentence

ALSO BY LOUISE ERDRICH

FOR CHILDREN

Grandmother's Pigeon

The Range Eternal

THE BIRCHBARK HOUSE SERIES:
The Birchbark House,
The Game of Silence,
The Porcupine Year,
Chickadee,
Makoons

NONFICTION

The Blue Jay's Dance

*Books and Islands in
Ojibwe Country*

The Sentence

A Novel

Louise Erdrich

HARPER LARGE PRINT

An Imprint of HarperCollins*Publishers*

THE SENTENCE. Copyright © 2021 by Louise Erdrich. All rights reserved. Printed in the United States of America. No part of this book may be used or reproduced in any manner whatsoever without written permission except in the case of brief quotations embodied in critical articles and reviews. For information, address HarperCollins Publishers, 195 Broadway, New York, NY 10007.

HarperCollins books may be purchased for educational, business, or sales promotional use. For information, please e-mail the Special Markets Department at SPsales@harpercollins.com.

FIRST HARPER LARGE PRINT EDITION

ISBN: 978-0-06-315715-6

Library of Congress Cataloging-in-Publication Data is available upon request

21 22 23 24 25 LSC 10 9 8 7 6 5 4 3 2 1

To everyone who has worked at Birchbark Books,
to our customers, and to our ghosts.

From the time of birth to the time of death, every word you utter is part of one long sentence.

—SUN YUNG SHIN, *UNBEARABLE SPLENDOR*

Time in Time Out

EARTH TO EARTH

While in prison, I received a dictionary. It was sent to me with a note. *This is the book I would take to a deserted island.* Other books were to arrive from my teacher. But as she had known, this one proved of endless use. The first word I looked up was the word 'sentence.' I had received an impossible sentence of sixty years from the lips of a judge who believed in an afterlife. So the word with its yawning *c*, belligerent little *e*'s, with its hissing sibilants and double *n*'s, this repetitive bummer of a word made of slyly stabbing letters that surrounded an isolate human *t*, this word was in my thoughts every moment of every day. Without a doubt, had the dictionary not arrived, this light word that lay so heavily upon me would have crushed me, or what was left of me after the strangeness of what I'd done.

I was at a perilous age when I committed my crime. Although in my thirties, I still clung to a teenager's physical pursuits and mental habits. It was 2005, but

1999 was how I partied, drinking and drugging like I was seventeen, although my liver kept trying to tell me it was over an outraged decade older. For many reasons, I didn't know who I was yet. Now that I have a better idea, I will tell you this: I am an ugly woman. Not the kind of ugly that guys write or make movies about, where suddenly I have a blast of blinding instructional beauty. I am not about teachable moments. Nor am I beautiful on the inside. I enjoy lying, for instance, and am good at selling people useless things for prices they can't afford. Of course, now that I am rehabilitated, I only sell words. Collections of words between cardboard covers.

Books contain everything worth knowing except what ultimately matters.

The day I committed my crime, I was sprawled at the skinny white feet of my crush Danae, trying to deal with an interior swarm of ants. The phone rang and Danae fumbled the receiver to her ear. She listened, jumped up, shrieked. Clasped the phone with both hands and screwed her face shut. Then her eyes waterbugged open.

He died in Mara's arms. God, oh god. She doesn't know what to do with his body!

Danae flung the phone away and vaulted back onto

the couch, howling and thrashing her spidery arms and legs. I crawled under the coffee table.

'Tookie! Tookie! Where are you?'

I dragged myself up onto her cabiny moose pillows and tried to soothe my deranged dear, rocking her, clutching her frowsy yellow head against my shoulder. Though she was older than me, Danae was spindly as a downy pre-woman. When she curled against me, I felt my heart surge and I became her shield against the world. Or maybe bulwark gives a more accurate picture.

'It's all right, you are safe,' I said in my huskiest voice. The harder she wept the happier I felt.

'And don't forget,' I said, pleased by her needy snuffling, 'you're a big winner!'

Two days before, Danae had scored a once-in-a-lifetime casino win. But it was too soon to talk about the beautiful future. Danae was clutching her throat, trying to tear out her windpipe, banging her head on the coffee table. Filled with an uncanny strength, she smashed a lamp and tried to gouge herself with a shard of plastic. Even though she had everything to live for.

'Fuck the win. I want him! Budgie! Oh Budgie, my soul!'

She rammed me off the couch.

'He should be with me, not her. Me not her.'

I had heard this rave for the past month. Danae and Budgie had planned to run off together. A complete overthrow of reality. Both had claimed they'd stumbled into an alternate dimension of desire. But then the old world clobbered them. One day Budgie sobered up and went back to Mara, who was not such a bad person. For instance, she'd got clean and stayed clean. Or so I thought. For now it was possible that Budgie's effort at getting normal again had failed. Though it is normal to die.

Danae was howling.

'Doesn't know what to do with his body! What, what, what is that about?'

'You are amok with grief,' I said.

I gave her a dish towel for the crying. It was the same dish towel I'd tried to kill the ants with even though I knew I was hallucinating. She put the cloth to her face, rocked back and forth. I tried not to look at the crushed ants trickling between her hands. They were still twitching their tiny legs and waving their fragile antenna stalks. Some idea stabbed at Danae. She shuddered, froze. Then she twisted her neck, blared her big pink eyes at me, and said these chilling words.

'Budgie and me are one. One body. I should have his body, Tookie. I want Budgie, my soul!'

I slid away to the fridge and found a beer. I brought her the beer. She knocked my arm away.

'This is a time to keep our heads crystal clear!'

I chugged the beer and said it was the time to get wrecked.

'We are wrecked! What's crazy is that she, who wouldn't give him sex for a year, has his god-given body.'

'He had an ordinary body, Danae. He wasn't a god.'

She was beyond my message and the ants were fire ants; I was scratching my arms raw.

'We're going in there,' Danae said. Her eyes were now flaming red. 'We're going in like the goddamn Marines. We're gonna bring Budgie home.'

'He's home.'

She pounded her breast. 'I, I, I, am home.'

'I'll be leaving now.'

I crept toward the broken door. Then came the kicker.

'Wait. Tookie. If you help me get Budgie? Bring him here? You can have my win. That's a year's salary, like, for a teacher, honey. Maybe a principal? That's 26K.'

I froze on the sticky entry mat, thinking on all fours.

Danae felt my awe. I reversed progress, rolled over, and gazed up at her cotton-candy upside-down features.

'I give it to you freely. Just help me, Tookie.'

I had seen so much in her face. Seen the sparkle glow, the tinfoil Ferris wheels, and more. I had seen the four winds travel the green wide-woven world. Seen the leaves press up into a false fabric, closing out my vision. I had never seen Danae offer me money. Any amount of money. And this amount could set me up. It was disturbing, touching, and the most consequential thing that ever happened between us.

'Oh, babe.' I put my arms around her and she panted like a soft puppy. Opened her pouty wet mouth.

'You're my best friend. You can do this for me. You can get Budgie. She doesn't know you. Mara's never seen you. Besides, you have the cold truck.'

'Not anymore. I was fired from North Shore Foods,' I said.

'No,' she cried. 'How come?'

'Sometimes I wore the fruit.'

I'd put melons in my bra and that sort of thing when I delivered groceries. Cukes in the trou. Well, was that so terrible? My thoughts spun out. As always when I held down a job, I had copied the keys. When inevitably fired, I gave the old keys back. I kept my key copies in a cigar box, clearly labeled with their use. Souvenirs of my employment. It was just a habit. No thought of mischief.

'Look, Danae, I think you're supposed to have an ambulance or hearse or something.'

She stroked my arm, up and down in a pleading rhythm.

'But Tookie! Listen. Clearly. Listen! Clearly!'

I focused elsewhere. The stroking was so nice. Finally she coaxed my gaze to her and spoke as though I was the unreasonable child.

'So, Tookie honey? Mara and Budgie relapsed together and he died. If you wear a nice dress? She'll let you put him in the back of the truck.'

'Danae, the trucks are painted with plums and bacon, or steak and lettuce.'

'Don't let her see the truck! You'll hoist him up and load him in. He'll be . . .'

Danae could not go on for a moment. She gagged like a toddler.

'. . . safe in a refrigerated condition. And then the money . . .'

'Yes.'

My brain revved up with money-sign adrenaline and my thoughts came on furiously. I could feel the neurons sparking. Danae's voice went sweet and wheedly.

'You're big. You can heft him. Budgie's on the slight side.'

Budgie was measly as a rat, I said, but she didn't care what I said. She was beaming through her tears, because she could tell I was ready to do her bidding. At that point, the job I currently held took over. Reader of contracts. That's what I was at the time. A part-time paralegal who read over contracts and defined the terms. I told Danae that I wanted the deal in writing. We'd both sign it.

She went straight to the table, wrote something up. Then she did a better thing. Wrote the check out with zero after zero and waved it in my face.

'Put your dress on. Fix up. Go get Budgie and the check is yours.'

She drove me to North Shore. I walked up to the warehouse. Fifteen minutes later, I was pulling out in a delivery truck. I was wearing heels, a painfully tight black cocktail dress, a green jacket. My hair was combed back and sprayed. Danae had swiftly applied my makeup. Best I'd looked in years. I carried a note-book, a file from Danae's daughter's stack of school-work. There was a pen in my purse.

What was Danae going to do with Budgie when she got him? I asked myself this question as I swiftly rolled along. What on earth is she going to do? Answer there was none. The ants came up under my skin.

Budgie and Mara lived just west of Shageg, the casino town, over the border between Wisconsin and Minnesota. They inhabited a slumping gray cottage. I parked in the street, where the truck wasn't so conspicuous. A collapsed pit mix in a chain-link enclosure just beside the house lifted its head. It didn't bark, which chilled me. I'd had run-ins with the silent surprisers. However, this one slumped back. Its colorless eyes rolled up as I pressed the doorbell, which must have been installed in better times. From inside there came a civilized *doodly doo.* Mara fumbled at the door and threw it wide open.

I met her puffy red eyes with extractive sympathy.

'I am so sorry for your loss.'

We reached out and clutched fingers, the way women do, transmitting emotion to each other via our ragged nails. Mara was interestingly cogent for one who did not know what to do with a body. She tossed her retro Joan Jett shag. It turned out she had her reasons.

'Sure, I thought of calling the fire department,' she said to me. 'But I didn't want the siren! He looks so peaceful and contented. And I don't like funeral homes. My stepdad was an undertaker. I don't want Budgie pumped full of preservatives and looking like a wax museum. I just thought I'd put it out there . . . to the universe . . . make some calls. . . .'

'Because you knew the universe would answer,' I said. 'Giving back to nature is a natural thing.'

I entered the house as she stood aside. She blinked unknowing hazel greens at me. I nodded at her with sage sympathy and went into selling mode, where the things that come out of my mouth are all intuition for what the buyer truly wants. Partly, my rugged face makes me trustworthy. Partly, it makes me very good at trying to please people. Mostly, homing in on another person's deep needs is my best skill. I took my cues from Mara's questions.

'What exactly do you mean, giving back to nature?'

'We don't use chemicals,' I said. 'It's all biodegradable.'

'What then?'

'A return to the earth. As our psycho-spirituality intended. Thus our name: Earth to Earth. And trees. We surround the loved one with trees. So that a grove springs up. Our motto: Graves to Groves. You can go there and meditate.'

'Where's this place?'

'In the fullness of time, I will take you there. For the present, I need to assist Budgie in beginning his journey. Can you show me where he reposes?'

I cringed at the word 'repose'—over-the-top smarm? But Mara was already showing me the way.

The back bedroom in Mara and Budgie's house was stuffed with unwrapped merchandise—looked like they had a problem I could help with—but I left that for later. Budgie lay slack-jawed on stained pillows, squinting in perplexity at the stack of plastic containers in one corner. It was like he'd been mildly puzzled to death. I gave Mara forms. They were permission forms for Danae's daughter's class field trips, which I'd grabbed off a counter top. Mara read them through carefully and I tried to hide my panic. Few people read official forms; it sometimes feels like I am the only one, due of course to my current employment. Then again, sometimes people read them for show, with their eyes and not their brains. Mara was doing this. She winced as she entered Budgie's name in the first blank. Then she signed the forms at the bottom with an air of miserable finality, pressing down hard on the sticks of the *M*.

That earnest gesture got to me. I am not heartless. I went to the truck and rummaged behind the dairy coolers to where I knew there would be a tarp. This I brought in and laid out beside Budgie's body. He was still somewhat pliant. He was wearing a long-sleeved T under a ripped fake vintage Whitesnake shirt. I rolled him into the tarp and was able to straighten his legs and fold his arms across his chest as if he were, say, a disciple of Horus. I closed Budgie's inquiring eyes and they stayed shut. While I was accomplishing all of this I thought, *Do now. Feel later.* But brushing my fingers down to shut his eyelids got me. Forever not to see the answer. I needed something to hold his chin. All I had in the truck was a bungee cord.

'Mara,' I said, 'would you prefer I go out to my vehicle and get professional bindings, or do you have a scarf you could gift George as a token of your love in the next world? Non-floral if possible.'

She gave me a long blue silky scarf with stars on it.

'My anniversary present from Budgie,' she said, very quiet.

I was surprised, because to my knowledge Budgie was cheap. Perhaps the scarf was an *uh-oh* gift from a guilty returning spouse. I wrapped George's head in the scarf to pull up his jaw, stood back. Wondered if I had a calling. Suddenly he had a wise preternatural look. It was as though he'd only pretended to be an asshole in life but was really a shamanic priest.

'It's like he's . . . all knowing,' said Mara, impressed.

We twined our fingers again. All of this began to take on a shattering significance. I nearly broke down and left Budgie there. Now of course I wish I had. But my ever reliable sales persona took over and kept things moving.

'All right, Mara. I am going to start Budgie on the next phase of his journey, and usually it goes better if the bereaved one has a cup of tea and meditates. You don't want to hold him back.'

Mara bent over and kissed her husband on the forehead. Then she straightened, pulled in a deep breath, walked into the kitchen. I heard water rush, presumably into a teakettle, and I rolled Budgie into firefighter carry position. While Mara was making her tea, I lugged him through the door, past the depressed pit mix, and deposited him in the back of the truck. I had to kick off my heels and jump aboard to pull him in. The adrenaline helped, though my dress ripped. I rolled in behind the wheel and drove him to Danae's.

She was waiting on the front deck. I got out of the truck. She came rushing at me, but before I gave her Budgie, I wiggled my fingers. She took the check out of her back jeans pocket, unfolded it, but said she had to see his body first. She licked her pulpy lips and smiled. It was like turning over a rock.

My love for Danae sloughed off me like an old skin. Sometimes a person shows you something. Everything. Budgie had attained a reflective dignity. Danae was freakishly eager. I could not put these two things together. We went around to the back of the truck. I reached in and tugged back the tarp, but restrained myself from looking at either Budgie or Danae. She handed me the check, and then she climbed in beside him. I made sure the check was properly signed. Then stepped away from the truck in relief. From what I did next, you can tell I am no professional body snatcher, as was later alleged. I left. I threw the keys in the truck's front seat and got into my little Mazda beater. I was out of there in two tails. I mean, I should have helped her bring Budgie into the house. I should have sneaked back the truck. Wait. I shouldn't have taken Budgie's body at all. But leaving the body in the refrigerated truck actually did me the most harm in the end.

That, plus not looking in his armpits. However.

It was still only midafternoon, so I went straight to the bank and deposited the check. Minus the cash amount that my account would cover before the check cleared. Sixty dollars. With those twenties in my purse, I drove along and distanced myself, telling myself to breathe, to not look back. I went to the steakhouse/ bar I used to frequent when I was flush. It was a few miles down the highway, in the woods. At Lucky Dog, I bought myself a whiskey and a fancy rib eye. It came with a green salad and a twice-baked potato. Delectable. My senses opened up. The meal and the money cured me. The whiskey killed the ants. I was a new person, one whose fate would not be to end this life squinting at a stack of tubbies. One whose destiny had been forged during unusual circumstances. I mulled over my creative burst. The business I'd thought up on the fly, Earth to Earth, could go places. People were looking for alternatives. Plus death was recession proof and could not be easily outsourced to another country. I knew there would be laws and hurdles and regulations, but with this grubstake of Danae's, I could get a life.

As I laid out my promising future, he slid into the booth across from me. My nemesis. My alternate crush.

'Pollux,' I said. 'My Potawatomi conscience. Where's your cute Tribal Police outfit?'

Pollux had once been a keen-eyed boxer. His nose was mashed, left eyebrow dented. He had a false tooth. His knuckles were uneven knobs.

'I'm off duty,' he said. 'But I'm here for a reason.'

My heart lurched. I feared that Pollux was here to provide a special service.

'Tookie,' he said. 'You know the line.'

'We've got to stop meeting like this?'

'I knew it was you when I saw the truck. Innovative.'

'A thinker, I am that.'

'The tribe didn't send you to college for nothing.'

'Yes they did,' I said.

'Tell you what. I'll buy you another whiskey before we go through the hoopla.'

'I was going to start a beautiful business, Pollux.'

'You still can. In twenty years, max. You did a good job, really. Eyes were on your friends. If only they hadn't gotten all hysterical and started bragging you up.'

(Danae, Danae! Other coin of my heart.)

'You're kidding about the twenty. Woooo, I'm scared. Did you talk to Mara?'

'She praised your service, your compassion, yes, even after we told her Danae was behind it.'

'Oh really?' I was pleased even under the circumstances. But he hadn't admitted he was fake-intimidating me.

'Pollux, give your ol' pal Tookie a break. And hey what, twenty?'

'I'm hearing things,' he said. 'You could be . . . I mean, with your past record. You never know. It could go double.'

Now I was trying not to hyperventilate. Yet there was something missing. A crime.

Pollux gave me the eye—the dark sad eye from under

his scarred brow. He was staring into the nervous slush of my heart. But I saw now he was struggling.

'What is it? Why the twenty fucking years?'

'It isn't my place to figure out if you know or don't know what Budgie was carrying.'

'Carrying? What he usually carries, tragic bullshit. You haven't answered my question.'

'You know the routine. But it would help if you would not deposit that check.'

'I'm not stupid. Of course I deposited it.'

He said nothing. We sat some more. His damaged brow lowered. He sipped at a whiskey and wondered sadly into my eyes. While in some lights I am striking in a Hell Girl way, Pollux might be considered definitively ugly under any light. But as a man, a fighter, it doesn't lose him many points. Rugged, he is called. He looked away. I knew it was too good to last, him staring at me.

'Now tell me,' I said. 'Twenty?'

'You finally went big-time, Tookie.'

'It was a substantial check. I was thinking charity, you know? After business expenses . . .'

'Not the check, although that will enter into it. But Tookie. Stealing a corpse? And what he carried? That's more than grand larceny. Plus the truck . . .'

I nearly choked. I did choke. Tears even welled up. I

had not even considered what I was doing to be a crime. Grand larceny has a swell ring, unless you're looking at the time.

'Pollux, I wasn't stealing! I was relocating a body. Doing a friend a favor. Okay, and so I borrowed a truck. What was I supposed to do when she screamed out, *Budgie, my soul?*'

'Yeah, Tookie. But you deposited the check. Also, the truck was refrigerated. Like maybe you did it to harvest body parts.'

I couldn't speak.

Pollux bought me that drink.

'You're one of a kind,' I finally said. 'Plus a Potawatomi. Tribal kin.'

'And kith,' said Pollux. 'We surely go back an eon. We evolved together on Turtle's Back. Oh Tookie, my endless . . .'

'Endless what?'

He didn't answer. I asked again. 'We'll get it reduced,' he said. 'I'll weigh in on your behalf. Maybe some kind of deal. I don't think body stealing should be that big a crime. And you didn't know . . .'

'Right on. Why's it a crime? It's just Budgie.'

'I know. And the body parts thing . . .'

'It's stupid. He wasn't near fresh enough to sell.'

Pollux gave me a serious look and told me not to say that in court.

'Tribal won't be involved,' he went on. 'This goes federal. People in that system don't know your sense of humor. Your charm. You'll just be a big mean-looking Indian like me.

'Though also—' He was going to amend. I butted in.

'Only you became a tribal cop. Wise choice.'

'You could be anything,' said Pollux. 'You make my brain boil. You make my heart [he delicately touched his chest] flip over. Twist in a knot. It's like you never learned that our choices get us where we are.'

Truer words were never spoken, but I could not respond. My thoughts were barging around in my skull.

We stared into each other's eyes. I rolled up the sleeves of my green jacket and slid my arms across the table. That's when he pulled out the cuffs and arrested me. Right there.

※

I'm not much of a TV watcher, so as I waited for the trial in jail, I used my call to ask Danae to drop off books. Her number was disconnected. Later I called Mara, same. To my surprise, it was my seventh-grade teacher in the reservation school who came to my rescue. I'd always thought Jackie Kettle had been nice to me because it was her first year of teaching and she was very young. But it turned out she kept track of her students. She found out I'd been jailed, went to a rummage sale, and bought a dollar box of tomes. Mainly, they were inspirational, which is to say, comical. But there were two or three seemingly tossed in from forced freshman college reading. Yesteryear reading. They let me have an old *Norton Anthology of English Literature*. It got me through. I didn't have many visitors. Pollux came once, but I think he may have started to cry, so that was it. Danae had got me hauled in with her story, which made what I did into a special thing and all—she wasn't thinking. I forgave her, but I didn't want to see her. Anyway, the anthology blurred the time and soon enough I had to see L. Ron Hubbard. Indeed, our tribe had a defense attorney who was a Scientologist. This is what happens to the stewards of the land. But his name wasn't really L. Ron Hubbard. We just called him that. His real name was Ted Johnson. Ted and I were meeting in the same dreary little room we always had before. Ted Johnson was the most nondescript person ever, sad-sack in baggy Men's Wearhouse suits, floppy 1980s ties, a half-bald pate sprouting hair just at the ear line, a curly swatch he kept tucking back. He had a round bland face with perfectly opaque green eyes and pinhole pupils cold as drill bits. Unfortunately he was not covering up a preternatural shrewdness.

'Tookie, I'm surprised.'

'You're surprised, Ted? I'm surprised. Who made this a crime?'

'It is body theft!'

'It was not theft. I didn't keep the body.'

'Good. I'll use that. You did, however, accept payment of over twenty-five thousand dollars, which under statue etc.'

'Under statue? Aren't you missing the *t*?'

'Yeah, like I said.' Ted didn't flinch. I was in trouble.

'The human body itself is worth ninety-seven cents,' I told him. 'Boiled down to its minerals and so on.'

'Good. I'll use that.'

He paused.

'How do you know that?'

'My high school chemistry teacher,' I said. Then it occurred to me what a ditz Mr. Hrunkl had been and also that, on some black market for body parts, Budgie would possibly have been worth a lot more. I felt cold, kept talking.

'Look, Ted. The money from Danae was a coincidence. I took it for safekeeping. I was afraid in her grief that she would do something stupid with the money, and I am her best friend. I was keeping that money for her. As soon as you get me out of here it will go back in her account where no doubt she will squander it.'

'Of course. I'll use that.'

'So what's our strategy?'

Ted looked at his notes. 'You didn't keep the body, which boiled down is only worth ninety-seven cents.'

'Maybe lose "boiled down." And probably it's a bit more now. Inflation.'

'Okay. The money from Danae was for safekeeping so she wouldn't spend it while she was stupid with grief.'

'Out of her mind with grief. And I'm her best friend. Write that down.'

'Yes. We're going to be okay here! I'll get you off!'

He looked like he needed a nap. But before he nodded off he whispered something odd.

'You know what was taped on the body, right?'

'I suppose a tag of some kind. Like D.O.A.'

'No, beneath the shirt.'

'His Whitesnake shirt. Classic. Old cassette tapes?'

Ted's face creased in an effort to study my meaning. He looked side to side in a paranoid fashion, then shook his head. 'It's too risky for me to say. You'll get a visit from the DEA or somebody like that. I don't know, maybe just the locals. There's more to this than you know. Or maybe you do know. I'm not part of this.'

'Part of what?'

He got up and hastily stuffed his papers back into his plastic briefcase.

'Part of what?'

I stood up and yelled after him. 'Get back here, Ted. Part of what?'

⚜

Ted came back a few days later, even sleepier. He kept rubbing his eyes and yawning in my face.

'So,' he said. 'Danae and Mara finally broke down.'

'They were stricken with grief, each in a different way,' I said.

'Not broken down like that. No, I mean they started talking.'

'That's good! They should talk through their loss. Good thing they have each other now.'

'I'm beginning to think you really didn't know.'

'Know? That he OD'd? I knew that.'

'It's more than that. You were questioned.'

'Yeah, but I had no part in it.'

'Tookie,' he said, too gently, 'you moved a human body with armpits full of crack cocaine from Wisconsin to Minnesota. That's across state lines.'

'Well, look, Indigenous people don't recognize state lines. And why would I check his armpits?'

'Danae and Mara already talked and made a deal. Thing is, they swear the drug transport via armpit was your idea and the money you accepted was your cut against future profits. Tookie, I'm sorry.'

'Like I'd cash a check for advance drug profits? How stupid do you think I look?'

It unnerved me that Ted didn't answer.

'Oh for godsakes, Ted, nobody's listening to me! I had no idea!'

'Everybody's listening. It's just that you're saying what everybody says. *I had no idea* is kind of overused as a defense.'

❊

There was a period of time like the blank pages in a diary. I can't say what happened. Then I was hauled over for further questioning. From this interview came the evidence that put me away. My downfall was duct tape. This time it was a steely-eyed man wearing bronzer and a ripped woman with a lipless grin.

'Your friends say you masterminded this idea.'

'What idea?'

'Transporting crack taped onto a dead body. Dishonoring this poor fellow. You'd drop him at your little blond friend's house. She'd pay you for the delivery. Give you a cut of sales later. She'd remove the contraband and call the funeral home to pick up Budgie.'

'Crack? There wasn't any. I hauled Budgie's body for Danae. She was in love with Budgie. Theirs was a blessed love, ordained by the gods, see, and she wanted him with her. Why the hell, I don't know.'

'There was crack cocaine. And duct tape.'

Duct tape. Smart-ass me, I asked if it was gray duct tape. My interrogators had the swaggery exhausted cynicism of high school football coaches. They looked at each other poker-faced and then one gave the other a significant eyebrow twitch.

'What?' I said.

'You asked about the duct tape.'

I told them that I didn't know how to react to the information they'd given me. Therefore I'd asked an irrelevant question.

They told me the question about the duct tape was not irreverent.

'I said *irrelevant*.'

'Have it your way. Can you guess why?'

'Maybe the tape wasn't gray?'

'What color was it?'

'No idea.'

'Are you sure?'

'Why else would I ask?'

'It's a very strange thing to ask.'

'I don't think so. I think it's a normal thing to wonder. They make duct tape in different colors now.'

Again the significant eyebrow twitch. 'Different colors,' said one. And then the question that terrified me.

'If you were to pick a color, what color would that tape be?'

'I don't know. Suddenly my mouth is very dry,' I said. 'Do you think I could have a drink of water?'

'Of course, of course. As soon as you answer the question.'

I was in that room for a very long time. And they didn't bring me any water. I was hallucinating when they came back. My tongue was so thick I couldn't fully close my mouth. There was a foul brown crust over my lips. The woman had a Dixie cup. She poured out the water in front of me and I lunged.

'Did you remember the color of the tape?'

I'd had time to scheme. What if I picked a color and I got it right? I'd pick all the colors. Yes. That way I couldn't possibly get it right.

'It was all the colors,' I said.

They nodded, gave me a sharp look of approval, and together said, *Bingo*.

Who even knew they made rainbow duct tape? And why for no reason had Mara used it to tape the moon rocks in Budgie's pits?

On the day I was sentenced by Judge Ragnik to sixty years, there was consternation in the courtroom, but as for me I could not get the puzzled look off my face. I wore the same expression as Budgie. However, many in that courtroom were not surprised. Federal sentencing is harsh. Crack cocaine inflated everything to a crazy degree. And finally, the judge had leeway— stealing Budgie was an aggravating circumstance and this judge was fervently appalled by what I had done. He spoke of the sanctity and holiness of the dead, how helpless they are in the hands of the living. How this could set a precedent. The ridiculous contract had come to light—damn my smart-ass. Also, I quote statistics. I was on the wrong side of the statistics. Native Americans are the most oversentenced people currently imprisoned. I love statistics because they place what happens to a scrap of humanity, like me, on a worldwide scale. For instance, Minnesota alone imprisons three times as many women as all of Canada, not to mention all of Europe. There are the other statistics. I can't even get into those. For many years now, I have asked myself why we are at the bottom, or at the highest worst, of everything measurable. Because I know we have greatness as a people. But perhaps our greatness lies in what isn't measurable. Maybe we were colonized, but not enough. Never mind casinos, or my own behavior, most of us do not make money our one fixed star. Not enough to wipe clean the love of our ancestors. We're still not colonized enough to put us in a dominant-language mind-set. Even though most of us don't speak our Native languages, many of us act out of a handed-down sense of that language. That generosity. In our own Anishinaabemowin, it includes intricate forms of human relationships and infinite ways to joke. So maybe we are on the wrong side of the English language. I think that's possible.

Still, the history of an English word eased my despair. At the jail where I stayed before I was transferred, they x-rayed my dictionary, removed the cover, poked around in the stitching, ruffled through the pages. Ultimately, I was made to earn it for good behavior, and I did so. Bad behavior had vanished when the sentence was pronounced. At least if I could control it. There were times I couldn't. I was Tookie, always too much Tookie. For better or worse, that's a fact.

My dictionary was *The American Heritage Diction-ary of the English Language,* 1969. Jackie Kettle sent it to me with a letter. She told me that she was given this dictionary by the National Football League as a prize for an essay she had written about her reasons for going to college. She carried this dictionary to college; now she was entrusting it to me.

> **sentence** n, 1. A grammatical unit comprising a word or a group of words that is separate from any other grammatical construction, and usually con-sists of at least one subject with its predicate and contains a finite verb or verb phrase; for example, *The door is open* and *Go!* are sentences.

On first reading this definition, I marveled at the italicized examples. These were not just sentences, I thought. *The door is open. Go!* They were the most beautiful sentences ever written.

❈

I was in a decrepit jail for eight months because there was no room anyplace else. There were too many women in Minnesota making, as my coun-selors liked to say, bad choices. With this uptick in

female incarcerations, there was no room in the Sha-
kopee women's prison, which didn't even have a real
fence around it at the time. I wanted to go there.
But anyway, I was a federal prisoner. Waseca, now a
minimum-security federal women's prison in south-
ern Minnesota, hadn't yet started taking women. So
I was transferred from Thief River Falls to a place
out of state I'll call Rockville.

It was the transfer that got me into further trouble.
Transfers happen at night. I would find the only times I
was personally awakened in prison were the rare times
I was having a happy dream. One night, still in jail,
I was just about to bite into a giant piece of chocolate
cake when I was blown out of sleep. I was told to put on
a paper shirt and pants, then shuffled off to a van bus
wearing paper slippers. Each prisoner was shackled
in a cubicle. When I saw that I was supposed to enter
this tiny cage I collapsed. I was deadly claustrophobic
at the time. I had learned about St. Lucy, whom God
made so heavy she could not be lifted. I tried to make
myself that heavy and tried as well to tell the transport
goons that I suffered from claustrophobia. I begged like
a maniac, so they treated me like a maniac. Two men
sweat, strained, pummeled, pushed, and dragged me
into the cage. Then Budgie came in with me, the door
shut, and I began to scream.

I heard them talking about getting a shot of knock-out juice. I started begging for that. But there wasn't a nurse to administer the shot in the middle of the night. We took off, me screaming, Budgie gloating, the star scarf still tying up his jaw and knotted floppily atop his head. The other women were swearing at me, and the security guys bellowing at us all. As we rolled along, things got worse. Once the adrenaline of a panic attack hits your system there's no stopping it. I've been told that the intensity of a panic attack means it can't go on forever, but I'll tell you, it can go on for hours, as it did when Budgie started hissing through his rotten teeth. During those hours I have no memory of what I did, but apparently I decided to kill myself by tearing up what I could snatch of my paper clothes, wadding up bits of my pantalets and sleeves, stuffing my nose and mouth. When I went silent, I'm told, everyone was so relieved that nobody wanted to check on me. So I could have died of blank paper if one cop hadn't had a conscience. If there had been words on the paper, would my death have been a poem? I would have a lot of time to ponder that question.

Once landed, I was confined to the segregation unit, or seg, for a year. Because of my attempt at death by paper, I was allowed no books. However, I discovered that unknown to myself I had a library in my head. Every book I'd read from grade school to college was in there, plus those I'd been obsessed with later on. My brainfolds held long scenes and passages— everything from the Redwall books to *Huck Finn* to *Lilith's Brood.* So passed a year in which I somehow did not go mad, then a couple more before I was transferred. This time, on the way to Waseca, I was shackled but not confined to a cubicle. Anyway, my time in seg had cured me of claustrophobia. I did seven years in Waseca and then one day I was called into the warden's office. By then, my tune had drastically changed. I was keeping my head down. Taking college courses. Doing my job. So what the fuck had I done? I stepped into the office expecting to hear some disaster, only to hear sentences that stopped my heart: *Your time here is over. Your sentence was commuted.*

Then quiet like a thunderclap. Commuted to time served. I had to sit on the floor. I'd be out once the paperwork went through. I didn't ask questions in case it turned out they had the wrong person. But I later learned that I had totally underestimated Ted Johnson. He had not given up. Yes, he'd had me apply every year for a pardon, I knew that. But I didn't think it would go anywhere. He'd filed appeal after appeal. He'd brought my case to a group at the University of Minnesota. I got attention because of Budgie and the judge's extreme beliefs. Ted Johnson had also acquired confessions from Danae and Mara, who, now that they'd served their short exclamative sentences—example, You assholes!—saw no use in blaming me and admitted they'd set me up. He'd pressed my story everywhere possible.

I wrote to Ted Johnson, thanking him for giving me a chance at a free life. My letter did not reach him because he was in a world with no addresses. He had died of a massive heart attack.

The night I found I was going to walk free, I couldn't sleep. Although I had dreamed of this moment, the reality filled me with a combination of terror and euphoria. I thanked my tiny god.

Once, when I was in isolation, sitting on my bed in a fugue state, a tiny spirit had visited me. In Ojibwe, the word for 'insect' is manidoons, tiny spirit. One day an iridescent green fly landed on my wrist. I didn't move, just watched as it stroked its jewel-like carapace with eyelash arms. Later, I looked it up. It was only a greenbottle fly, *Lucilia sericata*. But at the time it was an emissary of all I thought would never be mine again—common uncommon beauty, ecstasy, surprise. The next morning, it was gone. Back to garbage or a carcass, I thought. But no. It was smeared on the palm of my hand. I'd slapped it to death in my sleep. I was fucked. Of course I'd lost all sense of irony because I lived in a cruel cliché. But in the despair of routine any aberration is a radiant signal. For weeks afterward I fervently believed that this little spirit had been a sign I would someday walk free. And here I'd killed it.

Yet the gods had mercy.

I left in a pair of sunflower-print overalls, a white T-shirt, and men's work boots. I still had the dictionary. A transition house took me in until eventually I found a place to live in the shadow of I-35.

Between 2005 and 2015 phones had evolved. The first thing I noticed was every other person stared into a lighted rectangle. I wanted one too. To get one, I needed a job. Though now I could operate an industrial sewing machine and work a printing press, the most important skill I'd gained in prison was how to read with murderous attention. The prison libraries had been deep in crafting books. At first I read everything, even knitting instructions. There were occasional windfalls of donated volumes. I read every single Great Books of the World, every Philippa Gregory and Louis L'Amour. Jackie Kettle sent a book, faithful, every month. But I dreamed of choosing a book from a library or a bookshop. I took my so-called resumé, filled with lies, around to every bookstore in Minneapolis.

Only one store answered, because Jackie now worked there as buyer and manager.

The bookstore was a modest little place across from a brick school building in a pleasant neighborhood. The sheltered blue door opened into a sweetgrass-smelling, scuffed-up eight-hundred-square-foot space stuffed with books, with sections labeled Indigenous Fiction, History, Poetry, Language, Memoirs, and so on. I realized we are more brilliant than I knew. The owner was sitting in a narrow back office with high windows that let through scarves of mellow light. Louise was wearing vintage oval eyeglasses and had piled her hair in a beaded clip. I knew her only from early author photos. Age had broadened her face and nose, plumped up her cheeks, grayed her hair, and given her a general air of tolerance. She told me the store was losing money.

'I might be able to help,' I said.

'How?'

'By selling books.'

I was at my most intimidating then and spoke with my old sales confidence. After I ditched the sunflower overalls, I cultivated a brutal gorgeous look—thick black eyeliner, cruel slash of lipstick, weightlifting arms, and thick thighs. My go-to outfit was black jeans, high-top black Stompers, black football jersey, nose ring, eyebrow cuff, tight black bandanna headband to keep my hair in place. Who would dare not buy a book from me? Louise took it all in and nodded. She had my resumé in hand, but she didn't ask me a single question about it.

'What are you reading now?'

'*Almanac of the Dead.* A masterwork.'

'So it is. What else?'

'Comics. Graphic novels. Uh, Proust?'

She gave me a skeptical nod and sort of scanned me over.

'This is a dark time for little bookstores and we probably won't make it,' she said. 'Would you like a job?'

I started with a swing shift and added hours. I reconnected with Jackie Kettle, who had read everything ever written and taught me how to run the store. The old Tookie had her ideas about the opportunities in retail. But I resisted the temptation to pilfer the till and I resisted the temptation to steal credit card info and I resisted the temptation to filch our sidelines, even the best jewelry. Sometimes I had to bite my fingers. Over time, resistance became a habit and the urge diminished. I worked my way into getting a raise, then another, and there were always perks, including discounted books and advanced reader's editions. I lived on the cheap. Window-shopped. Roamed. After work I rode the bus here and there, stop and start, all through the Cities. Things had changed since I was a kid. It was thrilling to be carried along the streets, scant notion where I was going, into neighborhoods inhabited by surprising people. Women in billowing fuchsia robes and purple head scarves roamed the sidewalks. I saw Hmong people, Eritrean people. Mexican. Vietnamese. Ecuadorian. Somali. Laotian. And a gratifying number of Black American people and my fellow Indigenes. Store signs in languages with flowing script and then mansion after mansion—spruced up, decaying, chopped up, gated under floating canopies of trees. Then abandoned areas—train yards, acres of paved fields, dystopic malls. Sometimes I'd see a tiny restaurant I liked the look of so I'd get off at the next stop and go inside, order soup. I took a tour of world soups. Avgolemono. Sambar. Menudo. Egusi with fufu. Ajiaco. Borscht. Leberknödel suppe. Gazpacho. Tom yam. Solyanka. Nässelsoppa. Gumbo. Gamjaguk. Miso. Pho ga. Samgyetang. I kept a list in my diary, with the price of the soup next to each name. All were satisfyingly cheap and very filling. Next to me in a café, once, I heard men order bull penis soup. I tried to order it from the waiter, also, but the waiter looked sad and said they only got one penis a week and the soup went fast.

'They got some,' I said, gesturing at the table of skinny, potbellied men.

'They need it,' he said, sotto voce. 'It's good for hangovers and you know.' He cranked his arm from the elbow.

'Oh, that.'

'Their wives send them.'

He winked. Instead of winking back, I gave him the kill stare. I wanted him to buckle at the knees. He didn't, but the free soup was excellent.

One day, I got out by the Hard Times café and back-tracked to an outdoor supply store on Cedar Avenue and Riverside in Minneapolis. Midwest Mountaineering had a chain-link back enclosure filled with kayaks and canoes. They were bright—blue so blue it glowed, happy red, sale-tag yellow. As I was walking toward the back entrance to look for an on-sale parka in August, I felt eyes on me, turned around.

Those broad shoulders. That square head. He stood out against the crayon pack of self-propelled boats. His legs were skinnier and he was wearing a pair of glowing white runners. He was a black cutout with the sun behind him. His shadow was crooked and hurt, from way back, even before the boxing and the tribal copping. He entered a patch of sun and lighted up. Flat assed, goofily smiling, homely. Pollux hugged me like a big kid, stepped back. He narrowed his eyes and stared at me with strange force.

'You're free?'

'Let's just say I'm on the outside.'

'On the run?'

'No.'

'Then say it.'

'Say what? How's my Potawatomi conscience?'

'No, not that.'

'Then what?'

'Say you'll marry me.'

'You'll marry me?'

'Yes.'

The door *is open. Go!*

Now I live as a person with a regular life. A job with regular hours after which I come home to a regular husband. Even a regular little house, but with a big irregular beautiful blowsy yard. I live the way a person does who has ceased to dread each day's ration of time. I live what can be called a normal life only if you've always expected to live such a way. If you think you have the right. Work. Love. Food. A bedroom sheltered by a pine tree. Sex and wine. Knowing what I know of my tribe's history, remembering what I can bear to remember of my own, I can only call the life I live now a life of heaven.

Ever since I understood this life was to be mine, I have wanted only for it to continue in its precious routine. And so it has. However. Order tends toward disorder. Chaos stalks our feeble efforts. One has ever to be on guard.

I worked hard, kept things tidy, curtailed my inner noise, stayed steady. And still, trouble found where I lived and tracked me down. In November 2019, death took one of my most annoying customers. But she did not disappear.

Story of a Woman

NOVEMBER 2019

Five days after Flora died, she was still coming to the bookstore. I'm still not strictly rational. How could I be? I sell books. Even so, I found the truth of this hard to accept. Flora came in when the store was empty, always on my shift. She knew our slow hours. The first time this happened, I had just learned the sad news and was easily rattled. I heard her murmuring, then rustling about on the other side of the tall bookshelves in Fiction, her favorite section. In need of good sense, I picked up my phone to text Pollux, but what to say? I put down the phone, took a deep breath, and queried the empty store. Flora? There was a gliding shuffle. Her light-heeled, quiet step. The material she'd worn was always of the sort that made slight noises—silk or nylon jackets, quilted this time of year. There was also the barely perceptible tap-clink of earrings in her double-pierced lobes, and the muted clatter of her many interesting bracelets. Somehow the familiarity of these sounds calmed me enough to go on. I didn't panic. I mean, her death wasn't my fault. She had no reason to be angry with me. But I didn't speak to her again and worked unhappily behind the counter while her spirit browsed.

Flora died on the second of November, All Souls' Day, when the fabric between the worlds is thin as tissue and easily torn. Since then, she has been here every morning. It is disturbing enough when a regular customer dies—but Flora's stubborn refusal to vanish began to irk me. Although it figured. She *would* haunt the store. Flora was a devoted reader, a passionate book collector. Our specialty is Native books, of course, her main interest. But here comes the annoying part: she was a stalker—of all things Indigenous. Maybe stalker is too harsh a word. Let's say instead that she was a very persistent wannabe.

The word isn't in my old dictionary. It was slang at the time, but it seems to have become a noun in the midseventies. Wannabe is from *want to be*, as in this phrase I've heard many times in life. *I used to wanna be an Indian.* It usually comes from someone who wants you to know that as a child they slept in a tipi made of blankets, fought cowboys, tied a sister to a tree. The person is proud of having identified with an underdog and wants some affirmation from an actual Indigenous person. These days I nod along and try to sell a book, although people who tell that story rarely buy a book. I put Paul Chaat Smith's *Everything You Know About Indians Is Wrong* into their hands anyway. Wannabe. At its most fervent, this annoying impulse, *I used to wanna be an Indian*, becomes a kind of personality disorder. It turns into a descriptive noun if this fascination persists into adulthood. Over time, Flora disappeared into her earnest, unaccountable, persistent, self-obliterating delusion.

Flora told people that she had been an Indian in a former life. That was her line at first, anyway. No form of argument could disabuse her of this notion. Later, once she absorbed the fact that 'Indian in a Former Life' was a much ridiculed cliché, she changed her tune. She suddenly discovered a shadowy great-grandmother and showed me the photograph of a grim woman in a shawl.

The woman in the picture looked Indianesque, or she might have just been in a bad mood.

'My great-grandma was ashamed of being Indian. She never spoke about it much,' said Flora.

This shamed-out grandma was another common identity trope. I asked about the tribe, and Flora was vague. Ojibwe or Dakota or Ho-Chunk, she was still doing research. I was pretty sure that Flora had plucked the photo from a junk-store bin, though she insisted it was given to her, and changed that to 'passed down.'

I thought of questioning this, but for a long time she had been doing the work of the angels. Flora fostered Native teen runaways, raised money for a Native women's refuge, worked in the community. So what if she needed, however fake, a connection? She showed up at every powwow and protest and gathering. She would even show up on the doorsteps of her favorite Native people, unannounced. And the thing is she always had a gift—books, of course, or a bag of pastries, a coffee-maker she'd scored at a yard sale, ribbons, fabric. Also, she was nice, good-natured, not just friendly, but ready to help. I mean, she would do your laundry. Why did her niceness grate on me? She would buy meals, loan money, help sew quilts for ceremonies. And she always had tickets to movie previews, new plays, artists' re-ceptions, usually with some Indigenous connection. At every event, she'd stay to the bitter end. She'd always been that way, or so I'd heard. The last to leave.

So in death as in life. She couldn't take a hint.

One morning at the store, I lost my patience and said what apparently no one ever told her in life—that she had overstayed. I spoke to the air. Time to go! She fell silent. Then her footsteps began again, sliding and sly. A picture of her stealthy resentment formed. I had trouble catching my breath, a bit afraid, as though Flora might materialize right in front of me. She had been a striking woman in her indeterminate sixties, comfortable in her body. Her face was large featured and vivid—a bony nose, jutting cheekbones, a pink pouf of lip. She wore her whitening blond hair in a messy updo. Flora was a pretty woman, used to being gawked at, unable to let that go. She'd been pursued by Native men, but somehow she'd never married one. Flora loved powwows, had made herself a traditional dance outfit of buckskin and purple beadwork. She had plenty of acquaintances who believed in her grandma picture or indulged her because she was helpful. She smiled in delight as she bobbed around the dance circle.

Flora had a foster daughter she'd informally adopted as a teenager—Kateri—who was named for the Lily of the Mohawks, Kateri Tekakwitha. The original Kateri was canonized in 2012 and is the only Indigenous saint in the Catholic Church. This contemporary Kateri had come to the Cities as a runaway and she still had family in Grand Portage. About a decade ago, she became the focus of Flora's life. After high school Kateri started college at the University of Minnesota. She was now working on her teaching degree. When she had called with the news about Flora, I didn't ask many questions, except about the funeral. Kateri told me that there would be an autopsy, no funeral. She would let me know about a memorial. I had begun to wonder when this commemorative service for Flora would take place. For I hoped a decent memorial might satisfy my ghost and take care of the problem.

A week or so after she'd called me, Kateri walked into the store. I thought that she had come to deliver an invitation to her mother's memorial, which I expected to be held at the American Indian Center. (If she could have, I know that Flora would have brought a casserole from the other side.) Kateri is an imposing young woman. Athletic, a bit fierce. Her long hair was chopped brutally short—an act of grief among Native people. Her clothing was simple—a lightweight black windbreaker and jeans. She wore no makeup, not even a hint of lipstick. Her eyes were shadowy and tired; her face was calm. Maybe she was already cultivating calm for her work. Kateri would be a high school teacher, someone who supposedly cannot be fooled. Although I imagine that, to most people, she lacks a warm manner, I find her coldness reassuring. She is single-mindedly professional. She has a disciplined bearing and a sharp presence. If she'd been a CO, I'd have steered clear. I wondered what type of book I might be able to sell her under the circumstances. But she was already holding a book.

'I thought you should have this.'

She handed the book to me. Flora's extensive library included rare editions of old books, manuscripts, local history. She was also fond of keeping the advanced reader's editions of her favorite novels, and we sometimes tracked them down for her online, as a courtesy. As she did for all books she collected, Flora had used her own cover paper—cream, archival—to protect the original jacket. The cover bore the imprint of Flora's specially embossed stamp. She had never been in favor of see-through protective plastic film. I had seen her collection often. The eggshell white bookshelves in her Navajo white house filled with dove white books embossed with Flora's nearly invisible stamps made me crazy.

Kateri explained. 'My mother died around five a.m., in bed, with this book splayed open beside her.'

'Splayed!'

She died instantly, said Kateri, implying she'd not had time to use a bookmark. Kateri said that one of our bookmarks was found in the bedcovers. Flora's daughter had lifted the book carefully from the bed, saving her mother's place. She had inserted our blue bookmark to signify the last page upon which her mother's eyes had rested.

I thought Kateri's impulse to mark those last words was morbid. However, if anyone was morbid, it was me, experiencing those disturbing visits from the other world. I found myself gazing at Kateri too fixedly, and turned away. Kateri didn't linger. It was rumored that she would move into her mother's stone-trimmed cottage in South Minneapolis, and I imagined she had a lot to do.

Left alone, holding the book, its protective jacket slivered but otherwise pristine, I felt strongly the presence of its owner. I used to bend toward Flora across the counter. Her voice was often heavy with dismissed hope. For all her generosity, people rarely made her happy. But books did. I was unconsciously leaning over now when I did, I am sure of it, hear her voice. The words were unintelligible but the voice was Flora's. I was so startled that I cried out, and then was glad no customer was in the store. I rocked back, still holding the book. It was an oversized book and seemed a well-made object with a pleasing heft and warmth. It had the dry, subtle scent of well-cared-for old paper. I did not open the book. I was conflicted by the sudden joy I'd felt hearing Flora's voice when her living presence had so annoyed me. When she wasn't throwing herself into Indian lore, Flora had been devoted in an almost mystical sense to literature. Omnivorous and faithful, Flora had followed literary series to the end. She bought hardcover copies of her favorite authors and was also discriminating about paperback editions. We exchanged excitements and argued about them all. I missed that. I missed how she kept up with what books would appear each season. Her pre-orders were a sign we should increase our own. A couple of times, when ill or indisposed, she'd asked us to deliver an order. I had always been the one to bring the book, and if Flora was being herself, not deep in some Indigenous obsession, I often sat down for tea or a glass of wine. We had talked. How we had talked books!

You don't have to leave, I whispered, and added in a surge of longing, *The Tokarczuk, what did you think?*

I put Flora's book high on the shelf where we display Ojibwe baskets and decided to take the book home that evening. As I was the one on duty when she visited, I thought that perhaps I should keep it. Besides, she'd spoken to me. Me alone, apparently. I have experienced the creepiness of aural hallucinations. Also, as I was finding, this dimming season sharpens one. The trees are bare. Spirits stir in the stripped branches. November supposedly renders thin the veil.

RAGGED BOOKSTORE ROMANCE

An hour or so after Kateri left, one of our young staff members breezed in wearing a pair of ragged black palazzo pants and a black bookstore sweatshirt with the hood thrown back. Most everyone who works here has an alternate life, and Penstemon Brown is an artist and a writer. Her rimless blue-tinted glasses were clouded with fingerprints and her hair was slicked into a sumptuous bun. As always, she wore an enviable pair of boots, black lace-ups with a metal Red Wing label. Most of the time she notices nothing. Once in a while she notices everything. Today, she critically examined the books on our large front table. Pen is one of a mass of young Native people who have book-crushes and a rich book life, a true Indigerati. Pen proselytizes for books, maintains our staff-picks display, meticulously receives books, and makes sure our windows and front table invite browsing. A friend of the store constructed the front table from the poetic remains of a smashed sailboat, and Pen has high standards for what she places on it.

'Why don't we have Clarice Lispector out?' asked Pen.

'You fell in love with her eyes, remember? You took it.'

'There was another copy. We sold it. But you're right. I think mine is still in my backpack.'

Pen had started working here because she developed obsessions with female authors, alive and dead, and was having a May-December romance with Isak Dinesen's stories. In the beginning, she told me that she intended to get a Mount Rushmore–style tattoo of her favorite female authors on her chest. Clarice, Octavia, Joy. She was debating between Isak Dinesen, Zitkala-Ša, Susan Sontag. I thought this was a ridiculous idea so I confused her by extolling Marguerite Duras. Would she choose Duras's young face from *The Lover* or her sexy ravaged face from thereafter? At last I told her the whole thing would make sex uncomfortable. Who wants to be confronted with five pairs of eyes in bed?

'You're not going to have sex at all with grandmas peeking up over your dodooshag,' called Jackie from the office.

'What makes you think I have sex on my back?' said Pen.

'And think about what time does to the bosom,' I said in a prim voice. 'By the time you're sixty they'll all look like *The Scream*.'

'Oh my god,' cried Pen, 'will you aunties leave me alone?' But she was laughing too.

Actually, Penstemon is desperately romantic, deeply tied to her traditions, and I worry for her paper heart. Recently, she took off on one of her mysterious spiritual quests. Or maybe she's in love yet again and keeping it a secret. Every time Pen falls in love she falls hard. Today, from the state of her clothing, she looks like she landed in some garbage. There were chalky smears on her sweatshirt, a bright ribbon of ketchup on her cuff. Her eyes were hollow with lack of sleep.

'Did you go home last night or is this your bookstore persona now?' I asked.

'A ragged persona.' She cocked her leg up and regarded the cuffs of her drapey pants. 'I met a guy.'

'Here?' I asked.

She nodded and looked around the store as if to make sure we were alone.

'He's white,' she whispered.

'Is there anything else wrong with him?' I was being sarcastic, but Pen took me seriously. She is a sucker for doe-eyed versions of Jesus Christ.

'He doesn't like hot pepper,' she said, and kept working with a solemn, distracted air. 'But he has a beard and long brown hair.'

'Here we go . . .'

Small bookstores have the romance of doomed intimate spaces about to be erased by unfettered capitalism. A lot of people fall in love here. We've even had a few proposals. Penstemon stomped back to the office to haul away signed books and restock the shelves. A customer came in, lunging hungrily toward the sailboat table. After meandering about for a while, the person came to the counter and asked if I was Louise. I don't look the least bit like Louise. She's years older. But every woman, and even some guys, who work here gets that question. I gave my standard answer, which was usually true.

'You just missed her.'

'Oh well, I'm here for the Clarice Lispector,' said the customer. 'I could have bought it on Amazon, but I said to myself—although I live miles away, other side of St. Paul—I said to myself that I really should support the little independent bookstores. So I drove all the way here and you know it took me an hour because I-94 is down to one lane again?'

'Just a moment,' I told the self-congratulating customer, to whom I was nevertheless grateful. 'That book is probably in our warehouse.'

I went into the office and interrupted Pen, who started guiltily. She was reading the Lispector.

'Did you crack the spine?'

'Of course not. No, no. I hardly opened it.'

She examined the book. 'It's perfect. Listen to this. *Out of a whole lifetime, by God, sometimes the only thing that saves a person is error, and I know that we shall not be saved so long as our error is not precious to us.*'

My error. My precious error. I'd think about that quote later.

'It's from the story "Mineirinho." An interior argument about justice. Such a good story!'

'I've got a customer who drove all the way here from St. Paul and wants it.'

'Let's give her a discount, since I opened it and all. Can I bring it to her?'

Nothing makes Penstemon happier than handing a favorite book to someone who wants to read it. I'm the same. I suppose you could say this delights us although 'delight' is a word I rarely use. Delight seems insubstantial; happiness feels more grounded; ecstasy is what I shoot for; satisfaction is hardest to attain.

CUSTOMERS

I was hardened when I first started selling books. I resented those who came into the store, disturbing my communion with the books on the shelves. But the people who love books softened me. Customers, I suppose, but when I use the word it means much more. When you recommend a book and a customer buys it, they are taking a chance, trusting you. Trust makes me nervous. I might laugh too loud or awkwardly crash into the sailboat table. It is hard to maintain self-control because underneath it all I think, *If you knew me, you'd run out the door.* But nobody flees. The best thing is when a customer comes back and praises the book you recommended. I can't get enough of that.

Boy: *I saved my lawn-mowing money to buy this book.*

Me: *I had no idea that kids still did this.*

Boy: *Kids still pull up the couch cushions too. For change. See?*

He held up a baggie of coins and small bills.

Me: *I'll be hornswoggled.*

Teen Girl: *Are you still open? Oh, thank god. I ran here. I promised myself.*

Me: *Promised yourself what?*

Teen Girl: *This book. It is my birthday and this is my present to myself.*

She holds up Joan Didion's biography.

For the rest of the week I enjoy this moment.

Woman in Tracksuit: *My son is a teenager and he wants to know how to be a feminist. Can you recommend a book?*

I hand her Chimamanda Ngozi Adichie's *We Should All Be Feminists*. I wish I could know if he liked it, but I never hear from her again.

Woman: *It has taken me years, but I've read all of Proust. I need something complicated.*

Me: *Have you read the Russians?*

Woman: *My god, has it come to this?*

Young Woman: *What do you suggest for someone who needs to gird her loins? I mean, so to speak.*

Me: *Does this involve a special occasion?*

Young Woman: *Yes. A family reunion. And most of them are angry with me.*

Me: *If you don't mind my asking . . .*

Young Woman: *They are pressuring me to break up with my fiancé. They want me to marry someone who isn't . . . It's racial. They don't say so, but it is.*

Me: *I would suggest* Sea of Poppies, *by Amitav Ghosh. It contains a rad romantic scene in which lovers banned to each other deprive a funeral pyre of its widow and elope from fire across water . . .*

PAPER TOWELS

After Kateri gave me the book and I brought it home, our resident spirit kept to her routine. But a short while later, I began to suspect that she was also coming in at night. When I entered the store in the morning, I found piles of papers and books askew, as if someone had searched through them. An odd thought came to me—maybe Flora was trying to find her book, the one Kateri had given me. I dismissed the thought. But the gentle ransacking did not stop. I grew used to straightening and restacking in the morning. Asema Larson was scheduled to open the store.

Asema is twenty-two years old, a history and Ojibwe-language major at the University of Minnesota. She is mostly Ojibwe, her grandfather part Sisseton Dakota, and the rest of her is Norwegian and Irish. She'd parsed all of this out one day when we were parsing out me. Yesterday she'd called in sick.

'My bloods are at war with each other again,' she had said.

'What are you talking about?'

'Historical determinism. As physically manifested,' Asema went on. 'I have severe cramps. I'm sorry, can you cover my shift?'

I did, and today she was back in.

'How's your historical determinism?' I asked.

'A little better,' she said. 'I drank raspberry leaf tea all day yesterday.'

'Good, I missed you.'

'Awww. You're so sentimental.'

'Thanks. Actually, I was swamped. The store was busy. Don't you young people know about Midol?'

'Hey, if I was really traditional, maybe I'd be isolated in a moon lodge somewhere, scratching my back with a long stick so I didn't pollute myself.'

'Don't get me started.'

'Haha,' said Asema. 'You know my take on that.'

'How was your language thing with your elder?' I asked.

'Crazy good. Me and Hank rode around the community on a golf cart bringing meals on wheels.'

I noticed an inked outline on her wrist. 'So what's Ojibwe for tattoo?'

Asema looked alarmed. 'I have no idea!' She muttered possibilities for a while and then texted Hank. She stared at her phone for a moment.

'Mazinizhaga'ebii'igan,' she said.

'That's a lot longer word.'

'Everything's a lot longer in Ojibwe.'

She gave me a significant look, which I ignored. In terms of tattoos, Asema is way ahead of Penstemon. On her left shoulder she has a tattooed hawk, diving down to chase blue swallows to her wrist. She is saving money to have the blue swallows fly up her right arm to feed their nestlings at the top of that shoulder. That way when she clasps her hands she will wear a story of escape. Her long brown hair is tied in two childish tails above her ears. She is a merciless critic. Of everything. Not only books, but history, political bombast, local figures, music, white people, other Indians, and also of the store's operations. In some hope, I waited for her to mention the daily a.m. disorder, for she'd opened a few days ago, but she did not. When I asked whether things were in place when she came to work, she said that as always I'd left things tidy the night before.

So this ghost had the power to read the schedule, and for some reason I was its object of attention in this too.

'Our shelf talkers are a mess,' Asema said, putting away the books we had just received into our system.

'Pen was working on those,' I told her.

'I'll finish.'

Although Pen is our most meticulous staff member, Asema is always irritated by how things seemingly go downhill every other day.

'Plus we need a better vacuum cleaner,' said Asema. 'I hate it when all the flies from summer die and then in winter their eggs hatch and they die too and we get that buildup.'

'Dead fly buildup. I know what you're saying.'

'We need a little handheld vacuum cleaner,' Asema said. 'Our store's got dust issues.'

'It thrills me when a young person such as yourself speaks of dust issues!'

'Oh, Mama Bear.'

'Don't call me that!'

'Plus the window glass. Grossness.'

Asema spritzed vinegar water on the windows, rubbed them clear, then started on the bathroom.

'Shit!' I heard her say.

'Literally?'

'No, it's the paper towels again. Somebody keeps doing that thing where they tug too many towels out of the dispenser and they fly all over the place.'

'Wait.'

I went into the bathroom to help her. The cheap brown paper towels were scattered across the floor just the way in her careless rush Flora had always left them.

ROSE-FLESHED TROUT

Along with losing Flora, we lost the light. With the end of Daylight Saving Time our schedule had tipped backward, which I always find unsettling. The mornings were again brighter, but night came on at a disheartening hour. The sky was black when I closed the store at six and walked home, hungry, the scent of pistou broth having leaked for the past hour through the walls from the restaurant next door. The windows in the houses I passed were like small stage sets, lighted in mellow gold. At first, Pollux and I could not bear walking past the glowing windows of houses at this hour. Once, in this city, we were children and we were hungry. But now we had moved to an inner-ring suburb and become accustomed to glancing in upon small dramas and scenes of comfort. A woman gestured to a child craning over the banister of a staircase. A man stared into the screen of a computer. A boy came in, turning from side to side to admire his pants. Heads on a couch were visible before a bright screen of moving images. These little tableaux are often visible only at this hour—before people button down for the night. Snow had not yet fallen, for it was still unseasonably warm. Already, passing through these tranquil streets, I experienced nostalgia for the present, a sense of dreamy disturbance, then despair over how climate change is already altering our world with supple ease and toppling what is precious, normal. The act of walking down a beautiful November street, comfortable in only a thin sweater, was an infected sort of pleasure.

Our house is one of the few small cottages left on

our street. A few broken elms still shade the boulevard, and we have our tangled old-fashioned yard. The house has one full bathroom upstairs, and another attached to a tiny office/guest bedroom behind the kitchen. We've built in another tiny water closet under the stairs—you duck in and crouch to use the toilet. Pollux is too big to use it. His builder uncle bought this house when the market was down, in the late 1990s, because he wanted to live near a lake. The front door opens into a cozy expanse for living, with the kitchen divided off by a heavy old mahogany table that we bought at one of the many estate sales that occur around us. We even have a handmade dollhouse replica of one of the houses, dignified with two-story pillars. Our house is furnished with the contents of nearby houses that empty out continually as people downsize, move, or die. The roving chairs, the endless carousel of display cases and the carved bedsteads, the couches and well-used desks make their rounds, life to life, only acknowledging their former owners with a chance orca whale sticker, a dog's gnaw marks on a table leg, or, like my own desk, a postcard of Buddha and illustrated CPR instructions taped into a drawer.

Pollux and I were pretending that we'd both had a taxing day and needed to collapse on either end of the couch. Having dealt with the uncanny presence, and kept it to myself while shelving books, checking inventory, ringing up customers, I knew that I'd had a somewhat taxing day. But I'm pretty sure that Pollux hadn't. He'd gone fishing. After his mother died, my sleepy-looking silver-ponytailed Potawatomi was raised by his hell-raising, much loved Nookomis, his grandmother. Noko. Because his father left him alone in their apartment for a week. Because his father left him in the woods. Left him in a shopping mall. Left him with a friend who had a heart attack and died while Pollux was cradling the guy's feet. Noko took custody of Pollux and they moved to northern Minnesota. She married an Ojibwe. Things got better. Pollux went to a regular high school, then started his career as a boxer. Once he quit boxing, he started working as a tribal police officer. Right after my arrest, he quit policing and moved back to the Cities. Pollux's uncle brought him into his construction company, then left it to him along with the house. In early 2008, before the crash, Pollux sold the construction company and two new houses. With the proceeds he bought stock when the market plummeted. What kind of Indian plays the stock market? I once asked him that question. He just said, 'White man crazy. Me take advantage.' The stock regained its value and more.

Now we have a modest income. He makes designer furniture in his garage workshop. He uses the money from his furniture to buy supplies for his ceremonial rattles and eagle feather fans. In fact, he'd applied and now was waiting for the U.S. Fish and Wildlife Service to send him an eagle. He'd been waiting for most of a year. Pollux attends lots of Ojibwe ceremonies as oshkaabewis, or helper. We can—almost—afford for him to gallivant around with his hand drum and for me to work at a bookstore.

We don't have children of our own but inherited a niece from Pollux's brother. Traditionally speaking, the children of same-sex siblings are really close to their aunts or uncles. Pollux calls her daughter and she calls him dad.

'I heard from Hetta,' said Pollux.

My heart jumped. I'd become attached to Hetta too and also think of her as our daughter, though she doesn't like me. He saw the look in my eyes.

'Don't panic, she's fine. She didn't take the part.'

'Ah, thank god, it sounded so sketchy.'

Hetta dropped out of Institute of American Indian Arts and waits tables in Santa Fe. She's often asked to be in movies or videos, especially when the city is flooded with artists and collectors at Indian Market. I'm afraid for her because she's impossibly vivid, headstrong, more than a little wild. She's friends with Asema.

'I doubt it was anything like a porn film. Anyway, she spurned it! Don't worry. If she'd taken the part I would have gone down and dragged her home.'

Hetta hasn't spoken to me for nearly eight months, but at least she talks to Pollux.

'I know you would have. I'm a terrible mother.'

'Now don't you start.' Pollux wagged his finger at me. 'I caught six trout.'

Fall had been so warm that a few streams were still open. He fished with a pal about an hour away in Wisconsin and generally brought home gutted eleven-inch trout in Ziploc bags. The fish were always so perfect that I suspected he visited one of those touristy fish-stocked trout ponds, but he swore they didn't. He asked what had happened at the store. I told Pollux about the book club of cardigan-wearing women with sensible haircuts who had bought Marlon James's *Black Leopard, Red Wolf* and were determined to exist in its aura of fever-dream storytelling. They read passages to one another in hushed excitement.

'Anything else from Hetta?'

'Nothing.'

I knew that couldn't possibly be true. Still, I leaned back and shut my eyes. Our agreement is that Pollux cooks meat and I cook fish. We alternate specialty soups. I shoved everything out of my mind except how I would cook the fish. I would go out into the garden and pick a huge amount of parsley, oregano, tarragon, rosemary, which should have frozen dead by now, but instead has flourished under a light blanket of pine needles. I would chop these herbs finely, stuff the fish, add garlic, sauté the fish in butter. Sea salt, wine. How delicious they would be, the rose-fleshed trout still gleaming like the river.

And it turned out to be so.

After dinner, we took a walk. My head lamp's stark beam cut through the foamy gray of city dark. It was a lesser, human darkness, not like the heart-shredding blackness of the north. Behind the bedroom our yard sloped down past a towering white pine. The yard ended in a dead-end alleyway, no more than a dirt trail. Down the trail and across a parkway, an unexpectedly mysterious forest of ash, Siberian elm, maple, box elder, hackberry, buckthorn, and burdock dropped to a land of hidden beauty. A bicycle and walking trail cut through a waving canopy of popple and birch, then swerved off into a swath of restored prairie that gave off grass light and hummed all summer with insects. Down there, a bumbling freight train passed in the night. To get into the woods, we crossed a construction zone. The city had decided to run a light rail through a leafy bike trail. One day, our streets of houses, many of which had been boardinghouses, would become condos and apartments, our tangled woods tamed and landscaped.

Or perhaps in time it would become even more abandoned.

This area is Dakota homeland, the territory of Cloud Man's people. Their village lay somewhere near Bde Maka Ska, White Earth Lake. Wild rice grew here when this was watery marshland. Dakota cornfields were patched in neatly. Moose waded in the sloughs. Maybe wolves denned in what is now our yard. Bears shuffled through the oak savanna, gorging on acorns. Tonight we walked along quietly, listening for owls.

In the whispery dark, I wondered about Asema's people, the Dakota on her father's side. They had fled from here in 1862, when the state of Minnesota offered volunteer scouts twenty-five-dollar bounties for Indian scalps. Perhaps before the Dakota War, her ancestors were connected to this spot of earth, or to the ground beneath the bookstore itself. I peered into the trees, the slender branch tips scraping in the slight wind. The brush around us was alive with scratching stealthy noise. Many books and movies had in their plots some echoes of my secret experiences with Flora. Places haunted by unquiet Indians were standard. Hotels were disturbed by Indians whose bones lay underneath the basements and floors—a neat psychic excavation of American unease with its brutal history. Plenty of what was happening to me happened in fiction. Unquiet Indians. What about unquiet settlers? Unquiet wannabes? According to Penstemon, the earth's magnetism directs many actions in an unseen world. Maybe the bookstore itself was located on some piece of earth crossed by mystical lines. These invisible runes had touched during what . . . a shift, perhaps cosmically . . . a solar storm—something had jostled reality. Perhaps Cloud Man's relatives were annoyed with me because I was sleeping with a Potawatomi.

I gripped my husband's hand and asked if he knew who the traditional enemies of the Potawatomi had been.

'We were fire makers,' he said, 'so people liked us.'

Boodawe, which perhaps became Potawatomi, means to start a fire, in the Ojibwe language. Some elders refer to them as the fire-making people.

'Maybe your people were arsonists,' I said. 'Otherwise why would you have been known for doing something that everybody could do?'

'Oh, we were special. We could start fires with our bare hands.'

He stopped, rubbed his hands hard, cradled my face in his hot palms. We were on a little patch of ground right beside the walking trail. My head lamp shone straight into his eyes. I put my hand up and pressed the off button. We stood in the sighing dark of the city and I leaned against him. I let myself flow into Pollux. I felt his heart beat at my breast, felt my way along the paths inside of him, lightless. If I stepped off a cliff in that heart of his, he'd catch me. He'd put me back in the sun. I thought of Pollux standing in the glowing colors of the kayaks outside Midwest Mountaineering, his outline and the shadow inside.

'Do you believe in ghosts?' I asked.

'You know I don't. Or you know what I think, anyway.'

'I was hoping you'd changed your mind.'

'No.'

'Well if you did change your mind, and there were ghosts, who would they visit? Would they visit normal people? Good people? Or would they visit people like me?'

Pollux snapped on his head lamp, gripped my shoulders, and stood me there. I shielded my eyes.

'Turn that off, okay?'

'I just want to see who I'm talking to. What's this "people like me"?'

'People who dishonor the dead.'

'He was already dishonored,' said Pollux.

'I know. He was a ferret. But I still regret things I did. Mostly, I regret not checking Budgie's armpits.'

Pollux took my arm and we began walking home in silence. I knew he thought that people who saw ghosts had permeable mental boundaries. They believed in all sorts of other things that annoyed him. Evil fireballs, for instance, or beings he didn't even think it was appropriate to discuss. I couldn't bear that Pollux might see me as cracked, in this way anyhow.

When we got in the door and were shedding our coats and mittens, he spoke.

'You've gotta stop thinking this way, Tookie. You are not the same person who shanghaied ol' Budgie. You are an intelligent bookish nerd who knows a thousand ways to cook a fish.'

'Thanks, ninaabem,' I said. 'But what if? What if I was bothered by a ghost?'

Pollux gave me the annoyed look I was dreading, but then he softened.

'Not me saying this, okay? But if that ever happened, my grandma would tell the person to talk to a ghost, ask it not to bother him, smudge the place down with sage and cedar, put out tobacco, give the poor ghost some comfort, make peace.'

'Okay,' I said. 'Thank you. I'm going to bed early.'

Pollux kissed my hair and closed the bedroom door. He knew that sometimes I needed to retreat. I crawled naked into our king-size bed with the foam topper and the mattress pad pulled down over the foam. With carefully chosen pillows from the discount pillow store. With cheap white, but ever so white, sheets and pillow-cases. When I creep into our bed, there is the joy and relief of a person entering a secret dimension. Here, I shall be useless. The world can go on without me. Here I shall be held by love.

Still, quite often, in this perfect shelter, my con-sciousness refuses to surrender. Jackie, an insomniac, has told me that the same thing is true of her. She says that she is hypervigilant and resists losing conscious-ness. I lay awake thinking about Flora. I would smudge the store. I would note her habitual route in the store. For it seemed to me that a pattern existed. Eventually Pollux rolled in next to me and immedi-ately dropped off. I didn't fight my sleeplessness. I listened to my husband breathe until he fell into an absolute slumber and droned beside me. The freight train slow-galloped across the parkway and woods. Owls talked, a fox barked. People passed laughing drunkenly in the street. There were distant sirens. For a short time the wind rose in the white pine, my favorite sound. I began to feel that lonely intensity, that shiver of being-non-being. At last I began to worry about money and my brain gave up.

MIIGWECHIWIGIIZHIGAD
(The Day We Give Thanks)

Our annual pre-Thanksgiving-pre-Christmas strategy meeting. We dragged together all of the chairs in the store and sat cozily between the Young Adult shelves. Our buyer, all-seeing web guru, tech guy, and troubleshooter was on speakerphone. Nick works remotely.

'Here it is again,' he said.

'The star approaches from the east,' said Louise.

'The money star,' said Asema.

'Our make-or-break star,' said Jackie.

Jackie wore a pair of silver feather earrings, the kind we sell, and had on her serious, intimidating, Native-Woman-of-a-Certain-Age-in-Charge look. Every year we made most of our operating expenses for the whole year during Christmas. Or there were times, hard times, when we didn't.

'So far we're down,' said Jackie.

'Because it hasn't snowed,' said Asema. 'Only snow

gets Minnesotans to reach for their wallets. The first snow triggers a mini panic.'

'I hate Christmas,' I said.

'So say we all. But that's retail.' Pen sighed, as in a world-weary drama.

'You're watching *Battlestar* again, aren't you. Did you break up already?' Jackie gave her the sharp eye.

'He didn't work out,' said Pen.

'Quick turnover.'

'He cut his hair off and shaved the beard.'

'Let's get back to Christmas,' said Nick. He gave a sensible detailed report on all that mattered, and signed off.

Everybody looked at the phone. Pen waved.

'Can we all do more hours?' asked Jackie. 'Gruen?'

Gruen, who is Asema's friend, was our part-timer last Christmas, but it worked out so well that he became practically full-time. Gruen is a German student who came here on an exchange program and fell in love with the Indigenous languages. He is studying to be an Ojibwe-language teacher, which Asema both resents and appreciates. We plotted out our hours and worried that we would not be able to fit all of our customers into our little space during the rush, and we also worried that we might not have enough customers. We stopped worrying and ate the cookies Jackie brought. Oatmeal raisin spice. We drank warm cider and discussed our complicated postage protocol and even setting up another gift-wrapping space, though it might block the bathroom door. There was a long examination of whether we could use the children's play area for book storage.

I was somewhere else. I hadn't followed the shipping problem even though I'd originally brought it up. Something to do with timing on book orders? I looked around at my friends. They fell silent, waiting for me to speak. The cookies were soft and chewy. Oh what the hell, I thought, and spoke to them all.

'It's about Flora.'

Jackie leaned back in her chair. Pen clasped her hands and looked down, praying or upset. Gruen was trying to make sure he'd heard me correctly. Asema slowly opened her wide brown eyes and touched Louise's shoulder to get her attention.

'What?' said Louise.

'Flora,' I said.

Gruen looked expectant. He would be interested in whatever I said. It would be one of those Indigenous perspectives. I gathered myself to say, *I swear she still comes in and visits me every day. . . .*

'You're right,' said Louise. 'We should get together a memorial tribute. Sign a card for Kateri. Maybe a large donation of Native books somewhere in her honor.'

Asema reached over to the rack and pulled out a Carly Bordeau wolf card.

'Was she of the wolf clan?' asked Gruen.

'She was raccoon clan,' said Asema, passing a pen along with the card to Penstemon, who already had her own purple fine point out. She hunched over to write her message.

'Raccoon clan? That is interesting?' Gruen looked expectant but Asema ignored the question in his voice.

'She's pulling your leg,' Jackie said. 'There's no raccoon clan.'

'That you know of,' said Penstemon, handing on the card. 'I bet there's a tribe with a raccoon clan. They're kind of like omnivorous little tricksters.'

'Flora was omnivorous,' said Asema. 'I mean, an omnivorous reader.'

'She was my most annoying favorite customer,' I said. 'In fact, Flora was here so often that I can still, I mean *still*, hear her come in every day at the same hour, looking for a book.'

My heart thumped. I'd just told them the truth. But the way I'd told them was far too plausible. I hadn't used the words haunting, or ghost, or spirit.

'Oh, Tookie! Damn.'

Louise has lived with a ghost in her house for many years, but it is a helpful presence. Nobody she has known. In fact, as it manifests most often in her attic writing office, she thinks it might be helping her write.

Jackie shook the cookie plate in front of me and said, 'C'mon, take two.' It was her way of offering solace, and it usually worked.

Asema got out the abalone shell we keep under the counter and rolled up a little ball of prairie sage. Gruen passed his lighter to her and the sage flared up and smoked. The shell with the burning sage came around, we each brushed smoke onto ourselves, and then Asema walked about the store, waving the smoke into the corners. While she did this, I decided to talk to the ghost, like Pollux's grandmother would have advised.

'Flora, it's time you moved on,' I said out loud.

My colleagues' eyebrows went up, but they didn't seem particularly alarmed. I waited. This time, there was no response from Flora.

'Whatever you're looking for, it's not here,' I called. 'Did you hear that, Flora? It's time you moved on.'

Asema turned away from Fiction and a book fell from the shelf with a harsh smack. Every one of us jumped in our chairs and were held there, frozen, our eyes glancing back and forth, our mouths open.

'I knocked it down! Don't freak!' said Asema. She

broke the spell but her voice was squeaky. She hadn't been anywhere near the shelf that the book had dropped from. The smack had sounded angry to me. It sounded like the times that instead of talking my mother threw something at the wall or down on the floor. I walked over and picked up the book that had fallen. It was by Lily King. *Euphoria*. I replaced the book upon the shelf. Tapped it.

'No big deal!' I called in a strangled voice. I tried to laugh, but my heart was pounding against my ribs. 'It was face out, ready to fall.'

Which wasn't true.

BOOK TRAILS

A bookseller's awareness often travels with a browsing customer. Throughout the day, maps of the customer's movements form and collect in a corner of awareness. When the day is finished, books left out on chairs, sills, or askew have to be reshelved. I always know where each book came from. I know which customer carried which book. I know which book was discarded by which person, who picked up yet another book to leave on a chair or shelf.

As with other customers, Flora's ghost left a trail.

After rustling around in the confessional, she always started in her favorite section, Fiction, then slipped to Nonfiction and Memoirs, and conducted her hushed investigations along Indigenous Fiction. She investigated the sailboat table if my back was turned. Then she slid along Poetry and Cookbooks. Eventually more rustling noises would occur in the confessional. Then silence. Flora had been an extremely devout Catholic and maybe the confessional, now labeled a Forgiveness Booth, gave her comfort.

One day, Flora threw down the Lily King book again. She damaged the book in what seemed a fit of pique, and I began to feel the stirrings of pity. For unless with her ectoplasmic eyes Flora was able to read books without removing them from the shelves, she was browsing without the power to open a book and scan its pages. Maybe she could scatter paper towels and nudge books off shelves, but she did not have the power to heft a book, get the feel of it, weigh it in her hands before opening it to look at the words. The thought of our bookstore revenant passing her hands through the books, grasping uselessly at the pages, bothered me so much that I began to leave books open, if they were heavy enough to stay open. The pages never turned. That same night, I opened a book for her to read and anchored either page with one of the smooth basalt stones we keep like pets. The book was a handsome edition of *Flora and Fauna of Minnesota*. I chose the book because it was large, and supple enough to be held open by two rocks. Later, though, I thought perhaps this book had actually been chosen by Flora, for me, because her name was in the title.

THE SECOND NATURE OF PENSTEMON BROWN

Pen is an attenuated person. You have the impression that instead of growing she was stretched slowly out by an artist. A gifted artist who made her arms, legs, torso, neck perfectly proportional and slender. She looks but is not in fact particularly graceful. Pen moves with a childish eagerness, jerkily, especially when excited. And she was excited about Christmas because she loves anything with rites, angels, make-believe, chocolate, or gifts. She glowed these days as though lighted from the inside by a Yule log.

'What's your Christmas ritual this year?' I asked.

'I'll communicate with angels,' she told me. 'Seraphim, especially. Also spirits of the snow.'

Penstemon was in tune with a raft of otherworldly beings. She was an eclectic collector and investigator of all meaning—related to her own tribal background and others. Now she started talking about past holiday rituals and told me that this Halloween she'd dressed entirely in black (which she often did anyway; today she was wearing a black T-shirt, pencil skirt, black anklets, and heavy-soled walking shoes). She had dressed for invisibility and driven to a special place on the Mississippi. There, she crept into the under-growth. Once nobody was around she dug small holes with a trowel. She buried the quarters of a CD she'd snapped. It was a mixtape for a boyfriend previous to the one she had whispered to me about, the boyfriend called the Moaner. Pen always gives her boyfriends a nickname. She had just broken up with Post Jesus Heat Wimp. Also, on this past Halloween she deposited pebbles she picked up all year. Covered them with dirt as she chanted in several languages and added for good measure the Lord's Prayer in Latin. What the stones represented and for what reason she'd selected them she didn't specify except to say, 'I'm getting rid of things I don't like about my second nature.' After this ritual, she went home and ate as much chocolate cake as she wanted.

One of the reasons I loved Pen was that she included chocolate cake in her sacred rituals.

'Was it red velvet cake?'

'What do you mean?' For some reason, she looked guilty.

'Back on Halloween. Just wondering.'

Pen looked at me, nodding up and down.

'What are you, psychic?'

We worked in silence for a while, then we had some customers who wanted their books wrapped in our favorite birchbark wrapping paper. I'm not the fastest wrapper. Maybe tape triggers my PTSD. With my poor taping skills I always affix a finger or stick my hands together. But selling? It's still my game. A customer entered and I rushed to the front. I live for the human algorithm part of the book business, where I ask what our customer likes to read and then run titles through my web of associations. It's an art that I unknowingly prepared for in seg, when I created the library in my head. This customer liked the mystery writer Louise Penny, so I gushed about Donna Leon. But she also liked history, so I handed over Jacqueline Winspear and John Banville. A little questioning changed the trajectory. I extolled Kate Atkinson and P. D. James, suggested *Transcription*. She mentioned liking *Children of Men*. I mentioned *The Handmaid's Tale*, which of course she had already read, then I catapulted over to my most special lady, Octavia Butler. One of my all-time favorite characters is bitter, angry, tender Lilith, who has lots of transcendent sex in a ménage à trois that includes a human and an extraterrestrial ooloi. For the sake of transparency, I'll add that during a period of hallucination I lived that experience. At last I passed along Olga Tokarczuk's *Drive Your Plow over the Bones of the Dead* and became a little giddy ringing up the books stacked on the counter.

'It's as if you like saying that title,' said Pen when our customers had left and we had the store to ourselves.

'I kind of do like saying it. The rhythm gallops. It's from William Blake.'

'I should have known that. What kind of bookseller am I?'

She fell silent, took her phone out, gazed into its crystal muttering about the marriage of heaven and hell, and began to sigh. I sensed an inner struggle. A couple of times she took a deep breath and, I thought, nearly said something, but withheld her thought.

'Pen, what is it?' I finally asked.

'Okay!' she exploded. 'I do have red velvet cake. I brought some in my lunch. Okay! I'll share.'

'I wasn't asking . . . I didn't know. . . .'

'This is not about you. It's about me and the cake and my traditions. My grandma always said if you're Sioux you give 'til it hurts. Well . . .'

'I don't want your pain cake,' I said. But she was

already back in the office. She came out with two paper plates bearing slices of luscious cake.

'I don't care. You have to eat it. I've won my inner battle.' She grinned and held out a plate and fork. So I took it just to please her.

'From scratch?'

'Yuh,' she said, her mouth full, a tear in her eye.

Was it that good? Yes.

THE CONFESSIONAL

The confessional is from an architectural salvage store once located near the Mississippi River. It has some touching details, like a small electric fan set into the priest's box. Occasionally, it seems, the priest would overheat. There is also a box and set of frail tin headphones, labeled the Confessionaire, used to enlarge the sound of whispered sins for the priest's dim ears. The confessional is ornate and not badly damaged. Once it was installed in the bookstore, Louise apparently regarded the holy box as the basis of an obscurely motivated art project, and hired Pen to make a collage. From time to time Pen would paste scraps of paper on the inside walls. Usually, this happened after she had finished a painting and was casting about for the next idea. Sometimes she worked on the collage after plane trips, claiming that in hurtling through the stratosphere she'd lost brain cells. She couldn't shake the conviction that pieces of her mind were scattered about in the sky. When she came down to earth, she had the urge to glue things together.

The next day was Penstemon's day off, but she came in shortly after I opened the store. She dragged a plastic bucket of art supplies into the confessional and sat down.

'What's up? How come you're not out snagging a new man?' I asked.

'I got one already.'

'Of course.'

I left to help a customer. All morning, Pen sat in the priest's booth under the one dim bulb, using a pair of miniature scissors to cut shapes and figures from the bits of paper she'd collected. The sound of her snipping and her occasional muttering began to irritate me. I stepped up to the booth to look at her work and was assailed by the reek of rubber cement.

'Oh my god. Are you all right?'

'There's someone in here with me,' she whispered.

Penstemon started laughing. Silently laughing. Which horrified me. I yelled at Asema to open the outside door. Cold air swirled in. I wrenched the confessional gate open and Pen staggered out of the priest's booth. She sprawled on the floor by the Nature section, spinning her arms.

'Who was with you?' I asked in a low voice.

'Nobody. Somebody. I really like it in there,' she said.

Asema dragged her up.

'This has to stop. Put the cap on the glue,' said Asema. 'You need something for the fumes.'

'No, they help,' said Pen.

I dragged her out the door. She sank down on the steps, in the fresh air. I left Asema to get rid of the glue, and I put Penstemon's coat over her shoulders. It was a puffy black down coat with a lining of burning red Chinese brocade. She was wearing a ridiculous pair of moon boots that she'd picked up at a thrift store.

'What did you mean "nobody, somebody"?'

'There was a voice,' said Penstemon. 'It was a scolding voice. I couldn't make out any words. Maybe it was a leftover penance from the priest. More likely, there was somebody in the basement. A voice bleeding up through the floor. I feel strange.'

'Can I call somebody. Maybe Pollux can take you home?'

'It's all right. He's probably aware.'

'Of what?'

'Collage can be hazardous,' said Pen.

'If you huff the glue, for sure,' I said.

'No, I don't mean that. Too many images. Too much paper.'

'And voices.'

'The voices, I can handle. It's the paper. Would you believe that I have paper from the streets of Berlin? I wanted foreign litter and on his last visit home Gruen brought a few tickets and candy wrappers. I asked him to pick up whatever was in the gutter, but he said the gutters were almost always clean. He picked the papers out of trash cans, which really embarrassed him. I glued them to the confessional's walls just now.'

She put her arm around me. I patted her knee.

'Italian lotto tickets,' she said confidingly, as if revealing the existence of a great treasure. 'Copies of interesting steel-cut engravings of fossils. Matchboxes from obscure pubs in Ireland where Asema ended up on the floor when she went to visit her native turf. And matchbooks from a couple vanished southside bars, where at least I was able to crawl out onto the sidewalk.'

'Pen! Did you really drink that much?'

'Only sometimes. Did you?'

'You know I did stuff. But I'm okay now.'

'Yes, we're okay, aren't we?'

All of a sudden we were clutching each other's knees and she was staring into my eyes. Her voice rasped out.

'How did Flora die? What happened? Wait. I can't know. Don't tell me.'

Pen bent over and rested her head in her hands.

'The glue got to me. I'm sensitive to substances. Sorry to upset you.'

'Listen!' I was shaken. 'You heard a voice. Maybe it was Flora. We all have a history with Flora. Please. I need to know about your friendship.'

'Friendship? It was an annoyship.'

'So a kind of relationship.'

'Based on annoyance, yes. But disturbing.'

'You know I won't be upset. Pen! I was serious at the meeting. Please believe me—she is really visiting me every day. I hear her clothes rustle, even heard her voice once. You heard it too, in the confessional. She is haunting the bookstore.

'*Haunting*,' I said again, sternly, to make sure I got my point across.

Pen gave me a furious look, threw her head down in her hands, and gave a short cry.

'Why can't she leave us alone?'

When Pen said that, just accepted it was true, an unspeakable sense of relief washed through me.

'She drove us nuts,' said Pen. 'I shouldn't be surprised that she won't leave us alone even now. That's entitlement for you. Native people are generally polite, patient people. She took advantage. Sucked away precious energy to feed her needy soul.'

I spoke tentatively, slowly. 'You know, Penstemon, that's harsh. But I'm grateful. Most people would not believe me.'

'That she's here? Maybe right now? I believe you. And I hope to God she heard me.'

'She's dead now, Pen.'

'Yes, and she took it with her.'

'Took what?'

'Never mind. Ask Asema. Anyway, I feel better, Tookie. The leaves have stopped spraying around in the sky.'

It was a windless day and the leafless branches were perfectly still.

'Good.' I patted her hand. 'I'll be the one driving you home.'

THE SENTENCE

Two nights later, I finally opened Flora's book, which turned out to be nothing like its calm white cover. The book inside was an antique bound journal with hand-printed marbled endpapers, swirls of dark red, indigo, and gold. I eased the book from its flaps and turned it over. The cover was scuffed and worn, but the smooth amber leather was in very good shape, considering it was over a hundred years old. The folios were stitched, not glued into the binding. The old paper had aged elegantly because of its high rag content. The spidery swirl of handwriting was unfaded, but it was very difficult to read the writer's rushed eccentric jabbing script. She or he didn't dot *i*'s or cross *t*'s—perhaps the notebook was written in a hurry, or in secret. I looked more closely. The ink was gray-blue. But the notebook was definitely old. I recognized this sort of book because I'd done research in college. There was also a short stint at the Minnesota Historical Society—shamefully cut short by the chemical configuration $C20H25N3O$. There was a sort of title page:

THE SENTENCE

An Indian Captivity
1862–1883

It was hard to make out the rest of the words on the title page. The names were blurred. The dates were light stains. I put the book to my face. Pollux mumbled as he turned away from the concentrated beam of my head lamp. I patted his back and examined the packed, fast-flowing script. I made out a few more words. But the narrative, which seemed to pick up in the middle of an entirely different narrative, was confusing. The age of the paper told me that the journal indeed probably had been written in the late nineteenth century. The title interested me because it sounded like the opposite of most early New England captivity narratives, which were popular, shocking, pious accounts of the experiences of white women kidnapped by Indians. This seemed the opposite. A captivity narrative by a Native woman. The novelty of that idea interested me very much. I was also stuck on the title. *The Sentence.* Perhaps this was a boarding-school narrative or an account of a Dakota woman's incarceration after the Dakota War, although I'd noticed the word Pembina, a town on the Red River. During that time, Pembina was populated by my own ancestors, the Chippewa and Métis. A line popped out, *sentenced to be white.*

Because of the date, it would have made sense for the writer to be Dakota. After the Dakota War of 1862, over sixteen hundred Dakota people, mostly women and children, were confined under deadly conditions at Fort Snelling, only feet away from the place their world began, Bdote. Minnesotans now hike and cross-country ski over ground where so many in the camp died of cholera. Knowing of the unspeakable interest white people had in collecting their bodies, many buried their loved ones directly beneath the tipis and slept on their graves to guard them. In the aftermath of the Dakota War, Dakota fathers, brothers, relatives of the confined Dakota women and children were tried on hearsay and with no advocates. 303 were found guilty. President Lincoln reduced their number to 38. These Dakota men were hanged the day after Christmas in 1862. Those who lived, including Christian converts, women, children, were either imprisoned or exiled to drought-stricken Crow Creek.

Like every state in our country, Minnesota began with blood dispossession and enslavement. Officers in the U.S. Army bought and sold enslaved people, including a married couple, Harriet Robinson and Dred Scott. Our history marks us. Sometimes I think our state's beginning years haunt everything: the city's attempts to graft progressive ideas onto its racist origins, the fact that we can't undo history but are forced to either confront or repeat it. The thing is, our customers have given me faith that we can do it.

I closed the book. I mean, I closed it as gently as possible, but in fact, I wasn't reading it anymore.

Alongside my bed there is always a Lazy Stack and a Hard Stack. I put Flora's book onto the Hard Stack, which included *Being Mortal*, by Atul Gawande, two works by Svetlana Alexievich, and other books on species loss, viruses, antibiotic resistance, and how to prepare dried food. These were books I would avoid reading until some wellspring of mental energy was uncapped. Still, I usually managed to read the books in my Hard Stack, eventually. On top of my Lazy Stack was *Rebecca*, by Daphne du Maurier, which I was reading again because I liked Rebecca—bad Rebecca—better than the goody-goody shrinking narrator. But in spite of the lush descriptions of Manderley, which had been my sinister dream place while in prison, I soon threw down *Rebecca*. I didn't need Manderley anymore. I had Minneapolis. I berated myself for being a coward about Flora's book and steeled myself to read a little further into the text of *The Sentence*. I even reached toward the book, but then my hand dropped away. I was afraid of the sorrows that book would hold. Even the thought of her narrator's incarceration made my pulse jump. So I left Flora's book on my Hard Stack, but it turned out I was a fool to think I could avoid it. The book had its own volition and would force me to reckon with it, just like history.

SO GRATEFUL!

Thankgiving, I mean thankstaking, week remained warm. The day before the feast, I was talking to Asema just outside the store when a woman wearing a floppy blue hat and a floppy blue coat, both the same color as her wide, lashless, staring blue eyes, approached us.

'I have to tell you a story,' the woman said.

'Just a minute. I am talking to Tookie here,' said Asema in a pleasant voice.

'Listen,' said the woman. She edged between us and gave me a shoulder shove. At one time, I would have checked her. But this was right in front of my place of work.

'Oh, by all means!' I gestured with a contemptuous politeness that the woman, who was in her fifties and had just emerged from a sleek blue sports car that matched her eyes and clothing, didn't notice.

'It's about my great-great-grandfather,' she said to Asema. 'This story is handed down!'

'Oh really,' said Asema, shooting a glance at me.

'So, way back when, he walks into his place on Lake Calhoun, okay?'

'Not okay,' said Asema. 'It is now Bde Maka Ska.'

'What? This was back when this area was vacation

homes. He walks in and there were Indians right there in his living room! In front of the fire! Just standing in his house!'

Now Asema was staring at the woman in a way that made me step back. We are often approached by the owners of lake cabins in Minnesota. The cabin and its nearest towns are often the only contact that white Minnesotans have with Native people. Why? Because the cabins are situated on the most valuable land on the reservations, the lakeshore, which is always in various ways stolen land. Which is why Asema, whose family has no lakeshore property but is from Leech Lake, has told me that she hates being approached by cabin owners with Indian stories.

'Anyway,' the self-fascinated woman went on, 'it turned out that the Indians were very hungry. Like, starving or whatever. So my great—'

'Don't tell me,' said Asema, smiling in a totally fake way. 'He gave their land back!'

'Oh, no.' The woman laughed. 'But listen. He had his chauffeur drive back to town and pick up provisions, and then he gave the *food* to the Indians!'

'His what, his *chauffeur*?' I muttered in outrage.

The woman grinned into Asema's face, waiting. But Asema's face had gone stiff with wrath.

'So *then* he gave the land back, right?'

'Nah,' said the woman. 'But one year later those same Indians came back and they gave him a real birchbark canoe. They wanted to thank him for getting them through the winter with food. They were so grateful!'

The woman beamed at us. *So grateful!*

Asema waved her hand and tried to turn away. But the woman raised her voice. 'Listen! There's more! Also my great-aunt, behind her home on Lake Minnetonka there were these mounds filled with artifacts. People were always digging them up.'

Now I thought Asema might choke. Or the historian in her might choke the woman. Alarmed, I put my hand on her arm in case she grabbed for the woman's neck. Remarkably, the woman just kept on talking.

'My great-aunt though? When she dug up two skeletons from a little hill behind her house, she put the bones together with wires. She showed them in the science section at the Minnesota State Fair and won a blue ribbon!'

My mouth dropped open but I had no words.

Asema and I were both paralyzed. There was a sliding sensation. Like when you see the car driving along in front of you slip on ice and proceed across the roadway sideways. It is something that an Indigenous person often feels as they listen to non-Indians appreciate an unbelievably dense dealing with Indians.

The woman continued. 'After the blue ribbon, my great-aunt didn't know what to do with the bones! I mean, what do you do? So she kept them under her bed.'

Asema croaked, 'Wha . . .' and then shifted closer to the woman, speaking at an uncomfortable proximity.

'Did she give the bones back? And the land?'

The woman suddenly understood that Asema wasn't in her thrall. Her expression flattened and she snapped out of her complacency. 'That's not gonna happen.'

Asema smiled politely. 'I hear these stories all of the time. If you don't give what is ours back at the end, then I just have to say fuck your story.'

The woman's eyes flickered to me in alarm, but I was smiling now. I've been told that sometimes my smile makes people uncomfortable. The woman in the blue hat quickly crossed the street and got into her matching car. We watched her drive away.

'That's a waste of blue,' I said.

'I was afraid you'd attack her.'

'Me? What about you?'

'Oh, I'd never do that. We're used to it. I'm used to it. We serve a purpose. I guess you'd say that listening to something like that, no matter how outrageous, is part of our mission. Actually, I'm very sorry. I should not have lost my temper. And surely, you know, she meant well . . . ?'

Her voiced weakened. Regret after anger is a thing I share with Asema.

'She's been wearing out that story for years. About time she got pushback.'

'People need a place to bring their stories and questions about Indians,' said Asema. 'But her shoving you aside like that.'

'Yeah. I guess I'm just one of those places too.'

I thought of a few questions I'd been asked at the store.

QUESTIONS FOR TOOKIE

Can you direct me to the nearest ayahuasca ritual?

Can you sell me some vine of the dead?

How do I register to be an Indian?

How much Indian are you?

Can you appraise my turquoise necklace?

Can you sell it for me?

What's a good Indian name for my horse/dog/hamster?

How do I get an Indian name?

Do you have an Indian saying about death?

What's a cultural Indian thing that would fit into our funeral service?

How do I find out if I'm an Indian?
Are there any real Indians left?

REAL

'I'm real,' I always say. 'Real as you're gonna get.'

Even though there are times I do not feel real. I rarely get sick—maybe I have a preternatural immunity acquired as the descendant of the one Indigene in five or ten who survived all of the Old World diseases that descended upon us. My lucky-gened ancestor may have bequeathed to me this resilience. At the same time, losing everyone else you love is obliterating. And some believe that trauma changes a person genetically. I don't know if that's possible, but if it is, along with the rude good health I have an inherited sense of oblivion.

Once in a while I encounter that oblivion in the form of an unreal me. This unreal me is paralyzed by one bottomless thought: I didn't choose this format. I didn't choose to be organized into a Tookie. What, or who, made that happen? Why? What will happen if I do not accept this outrage? It isn't easy to stay organized in this shape. I can feel what it would be like to stop making that effort. Without constant work the format called *me* would decay. I close 'my' eyes and meet Budgie's puzzled gaze. There was no struggle on his face. Just a question. *What is this? What was this?* They are the questions I ask the gauze curtains.

THE ARMY MEDICAL MUSEUM

My intention to dismiss the captivity narrative did not work out. I began to feel an irritating buzz of awareness. I could feel the swish of my thoughts as they passed through my mind and circled back to the book I was afraid to read. The thought that I should read the book even though it might be painful popped up when I let my guard down. I definitely did not want to go back into history. I was not only lazy, I was scared. Then I started thinking about the lake-cabin woman's story, the 'so grateful' story, and I realized that although Ho-Chunk and Ojibwe people also roamed the area, the 'grateful' Indians and the Indian bones she was talking about were probably Dakota people. By not addressing what had happened here, I was not much different from the bone lady. I was an avoider. This all had to do with Flora. If I wanted to get rid of my ghost, I'd have to find out what was keeping her here on this side of the veil. I'd have to open up and read the book that had killed her.

I opened the book that night. I swear I was about to read it. But again I got sidetracked by bones.

Asema's name appeared on my phone. I couldn't believe it. Was she calling me? Pollux gets calls from Hetta, but I have never had a phone call from anyone under the age of thirty. Scenes flashed. Had she been abducted? Run out of gas on a lonely road? I picked right up.

'Are you okay? What's wrong?'

'I've gotta read you something from my senior project research. I'm working on the problem of human remains in Minnesota. Of course I started with Dr. Mayo. Do you have a minute?'

I was irritated, as if I'd been fooled.

'No, I'm trying to read *Rebecca*.'

'That's about bones, ultimately.'

'The bones of a woman murdered for having sex and being strong.'

'Whatever. So. I found this newspaper clipping from 1987—pre NAGPRA—about the Army Medical Museum at the Smithsonian from the 1860s to the 1890s. The surgeon general and staff at the museum were doing a racial study on Indians—men, women, children. Let me read you some stuff.'

'Do you have to?'

She ignored me. 'Army surgeon B. E. Fryer in Fort Harker, Kansas. In 1868 he waits three weeks for a

Kaw man wounded in battle to die. He thinks this guy is a really good specimen and keeps watch like a ghoul. The man's family knows and they hide his grave. Fryer conducts a search and digs him up but laments that his body would have been more valuable fresh. . . .'

I held the phone away from my ear and looked wildly around the bedroom.

'Then there was surgeon G. P. Hackenberg. What an apt name. He's working out of Fort Randall in what's now Iowa. In 1867 he's thrilled to outwit a Lakota family and wrote, "Believing that they would hardly think I would steal his head before he was cold in his grave, I early in the evening with two of my hospital attendants secured this specimen." Later, Hackenberg sends in a skull that he'd kept "on account of the beautiful teeth she had." He says, "I had a lively adventure which is perhaps partly on that account I held onto it as long as I did, as a trophy."'

'Stop, I'm having a panic attack.'

'I'm sorry. But maybe that woman coming to us with her story about our Indigenous relative's skeleton winning first prize at the Minnesota State Fair was not an accident. I mean, it pissed me off. This lady thought it was okay. She didn't even think we'd take it personally, Tookie.'

'Your point?'

'Chill please.'

'Look, Asema. Maybe I'm no better than Hacken-berg. I body-snatched a white man.'

'I know. That's my point.'

'Point taken. Goodbye.'

'Wait. I didn't tell you my point. Do you think you're maybe experiencing PTSD? Maybe Flora's death trig-gered you.'

'No! Flora's real. I mean, she's a real ghost. I might believe Budgie sent Flora back to haunt me. He was big on getting even.'

'You didn't send him to be put in a display or kept in a museum drawer.'

'No, but respect was lacking. I tied a scarf around his head and loaded him up with some crates of toma-toes. And there was celery.'

'Wow, Tookie. I didn't know the details.' Asema paused. 'Did he like celery?'

'Does anybody? Come on.'

'Okay, but look. Think how white people believe their houses or yards or scenic overlooks are haunted by Indians, when it's really the opposite. We're haunted by settlers and their descendants. We're haunted by the Army Medical Museum and countless natural history museums and small-town museums who still have un-claimed bones in their collections. We're haunted by—'

'Asema. You're forgetting. A people who see them-selves primarily as victims are doomed. And we're not doomed, are we?'

'Fuck no.'

'So get a grip. I have to go now. A dump truck just fell out of the sky and landed in my yard.'

'Very funny. . . . Wait. . . .'

SLEEPY SUNDAY

There is Thankstaking, Black Friday, Small Business Saturday, and at last there is Sleepy Sunday. On that day, I sleep in and recover from one day of heavy eating and two days of heavy retail. For which I give thanks. We've had a small but steady increase in book sales for the past two years. Asema thinks that people's Kindles broke. Louise's daughter Pallas affirms that but mentions also the great de-Kindling, which started when people realized their e-readers were col-lecting data on their reading habits, like what page they stopped on. Jackie thinks people miss turning real pages. Gruen says it's note taking, marking up the books, that people miss. Penstemon's conviction is that people miss the scent of paper, so clean and dry and pleasant. She even wears a perfume called Paperback.

I don't wear perfume. But sometimes I spritz perfume into the air on Sleepy Sunday.

I've only got two more Sleepy Sundays left this month. Our daughter will return. Hetta will come back on December 19 and stay through Christmas. She'll spend New Year's Eve back in Santa Fe, because the plaza is wonderful that night, heated by piñon bonfires with cozy places to drink hot chocolate and hot buttered rum and eat biscochitos. She wants to live down there forever, or until the water runs out, at which time she plans to move up to Lake Superior.

'You won't be able to afford it, just the way you can't afford Santa Fe now,' I said to her when she told us.

Why I said that is apparently because I am a prime bitch. I don't blame Hetta for answering my comment with that observation. I don't blame her because I do not understand myself around Hetta. I don't know how she manages to press all of my buttons and pluck every string of my guitar. She actually does throw lettuce in my deer-meat stew, use all my dishwashing soap, splinter my wooden spoons, curdle my gravy, and she stained my sheets—not with menstrual blood, which would be understandable, but with French's yellow mustard that when high she squirted out in patterns that she thought were meaningful.

She is so much like me.

Which is why I am the way I am around her, Pollux thinks.

But now back to Sleepy Sunday.

Pollux was off on an adventure where he would learn a new song. A song, he said, to keep the world turning. I was glad. Because it seemed like the world had stopped. The sky was so gray it matched the cool bark of the trees. Steamy fog rose off the lake. The sun was also gray, as was my blood, if there was blood inside of my body. I felt there wasn't. Instead of blood, there was agar, restrictive to all but gray cells. I couldn't even feel my heart beating. A ghost. I had awakened as a ghost. It was Sleepy Sunday so nobody was expecting me anywhere, in the entire universe, human or inhuman. It was a day that made no claims upon me. I was free to disintegrate.

Or to read.

I chose the Hard Stack. Why I did that, when I wasn't even planning to make the effort to stay organized in a recognizable shape, I do not know. Maybe I forgot, which ordinarily would be a good sign. Sometimes I can forget myself and win the struggle with oblivion. Anyway, I didn't stop my hand. It went searching out the hardest book in the stack. *The Sentence.* This time, because the gray was colonizing my agar heart and because I felt, surprisingly and reassuringly, a slight panic for my own preservation, I started reading line by line. Which meant I began to form a picture of the person speaking to the person writing. I was surprised to find that she looked very much like the picture of Flora's fictive grandmother. She was a young woman with a look of guarded misery in her eyes. She was afflicted. Inhabited. By exactly what I didn't know yet. The woman whose story was being written down had the look of a woman enduring a very long sentence. It was the look I had worn upon my own face.

Still, I began to decipher the book. I figured out several sentences:

Once I entered those doors I determind that for all
they would try to change me it would not sackseed.
No matter what they died to me, it would still be a
'life sentence' to be a white woman in the rong skin.
sentenced to be white was my fate. But as it came
about this was far from my worst triall to sufer

Then I made a mistake. I looked ahead. I decided to turn to the page that Kateri had marked, the last page that Flora's eyes had rested upon before she died. I felt pulled there and quickly flipped forward. The writing on the marked page was even more illegible. I tried to puzzle it out, letter by letter. Once I had a word, I muttered it out loud. Tried to make sense. Formed the next letters with my mouth. Then tried the next word. I remembered the words briefly, going forward, but I don't remember them now. I became so completely absorbed in this task that my heart began to pound. I heard a whistle outside, but it was not the train whistle. It was something different, a low and intimate sound, right by the window. I had heard this sort of whistle before. A not-good thing had followed it. I startled—then it happened. I felt my body disintegrating in a cascade of cells. My thoughts bleeding into the obliterating gray. I saw my atoms spinning off like black snow into the air of my bedroom. I watched myself on the bed, and found that I was looking from different perspectives—at the walls, and out the windows. I had become kaleidoscopic. I was many-eyed, all-seeing. The cells flew from my body faster and faster until, pop, I was gone. There was nothing for a long time.

Slowly, much later, I was back in bed.

As soon as I could move my fingers, I closed the book.

Black Snow

NEVER

I was trying to burn a book. I am a bookseller—this is an identity, a way of life. To willfully burn a book, and a one-of-a-kind book at that, an original piece of writing, is something I would only consider under desperate conditions. However, I was driven to imagine that this book contained a sentence that changed according to the reader's ability to decipher it and could somehow kill. I didn't want to find out if my terrifying idea had any merit. I just wanted to destroy the book. After my near death experience, after I'd dropped the book earlier that day, I had apparently fallen directly into a profound slumber that lasted all night. While I was asleep, Pollux returned and climbed into bed beside me. I am usually a light sleeper but didn't stir at all. That night a violent storm rose and toppled the 102-year-old elm tree in our backyard, missing the house by only a few feet. The next morning I looked out into an upside-down world full of branches. Had I completely read the sentence, would the tree have fallen directly on us, pierced its great branches through the roof, killing me, pinning Pollux, killing both of us, perhaps, with its shafted arms? Was that sentence the continuance of narrative I had luckily missed? I was not going to find out. No investigation was required, no further questions. This book had sentenced my most irritatingly faithful customer to death. It had tried to kill me too. On the back patio was our hibachi grill, and in my hand a can of lighter fluid.

It is horrifying when you cannot burn something so obviously flammable. Books of course are notorious for burning at Fahrenheit 451. I lit coals and tried to grill the book. I tried to torch it directly, but the creamy dust jacket and good paper were immutable. I was almost too exasperated to be scared. At last, having failed, I sat on the steps and stared at the book, barely even scorched. Perhaps at that moment, I would have fetched Pollux for help, but early that morning he had gone to Lake Nokomis because of his grandmother. It was where he went walking to think about her. I stared at the book and stared some more.

The ax?

Or hatchet. We had a small one for camping. I pushed the book off the grill and with the sharpened blade proceeded to hack. The book withstood it. Hardly a dent, not a mar, a streak of dirt, or singed paper. I had never in my life encountered an object that went against the laws of nature. So I began to swear, up and down, back and forth, every swear word I knew or could invent. Then I got a shovel, dug a hole in the part of the yard behind the vast downed tree. I spent the rest of the morning digging as deep as I could, put the book into the hole, and shoveled all of the dirt I'd taken out back in. Of course there is always dirt left over when you dig a hole, because it loosens up. I spread this extra dirt around the yard as neatly as I could and then I collapsed on the couch with some books by Mark Danielewski. There was a sort of athleticism to the act of reading his books that might take my mind off what had just happened. I turned on my reading lamp. I called Jackie to exchange a day with her and I planned to thaw a block of frozen oxtail soup. I did leg lifts and crunches between bouts of reading Danielewski's inverted texts sideways, forward, and back while exercising. You cannot really tell that I'm strong, though. No matter how many crunches, I still have the softly thickened waist of a middle-aged woman. It is infuriating. Maybe it's the beer.

102 YEARS

Over a century of growth, and my favorite tree was now flung down right next to the house, missing us as if on purpose. Its expansive crown of intricate bare branches filled the windows. I stroked the lichen-flecked, grooved bark. It was very unusual for the tree to have toppled without the dragging weight of leaves, and when the ground, if not frozen, was at least firmer than during summer downpours. Yes, I definitely blamed the book. The base of the tree, uptipped on the boulevard, was fascinating and upsetting, both. Because the roots had snapped and ripped beneath the ground, the support system seemed sparse, but when he came home Pollux assured me that the tree had grown a root system that mirrored its crown. The roots ran below the streets, under the sod, into my yard, perhaps surrounded my house.

'As above so below,' I muttered.

We stared at each other.

'The world below feeds the world above,' he said. 'It's simple.'

Pollux talked about the bricks of the house down the street, the pillars of a stone gate, mentioned gas tanks and roots, hidden aquifers, metals.

'All that is from the earth, right? We've drawn life from below for too long,' he said.

'You're going to start talking about fossil fuels any minute.'

'Sucking out oil and digging up minerals.'

'Here we go.'

'Things will improve when we start living on the top of the earth, on wind and light.'

'Are you done?' I didn't want to get into the weeds with my husband. Instead, the tree. He'd fixed mugs of coffee and we climbed up to sit. The light was clear, the air now watery and warm. The morning's frost had melted in the startling green grass. We edged into the crown of the tree, so graceful and powerful, so inviting even cast down on its side. I suddenly felt—though I was bereft about my tree—overjoyed to be sitting there, in the crown of a 102-year-old elm, drinking not just coffee, but an Ethiopian coffee Penstemon had given to me, claiming its scent was dirt made of flowers. She was right. Pollux made himself comfortable against a branch and closed his eyes.

Asema came over because I had texted her about my tree and its estimated age. She is a tree lover. She leaned on the trunk.

'I wish you could just leave it here, as it is.'

I glanced at the spot where I'd buried the book, and was pleased to see that the ground looked undisturbed and the place was almost impossible to detect. I wondered if the book would look the same if I dug it up. Would the cover have buckled, the finish disintegrated, would moisture have fused the pages, making the lethal sentence impossible to read? An image of the pale book popped into my mind. I shook it out of my head, and leaned against a branch with my hot coffee, closed my eyes.

'Your tree is beautiful like this, so friendly. Like a giant put its hand on the earth to cradle a mouse.'

The image of the book was in my thoughts again, the pages slowly flipping up and turning, as if in the wind.

'Maybe we shouldn't sit here,' I said.

'Yeah, we should,' said Pollux. 'You afraid our neighbors will think we're weird? Don't worry. They already know.'

It wasn't that. I was uncomfortable about the way the image of the book kept entering into my thoughts, and wary of my proximity to the burial spot.

'Oh, forget it,' I said.

I began talking about the store. Which books were selling, which we needed to buy. Asema climbed into the branches and began to touch the cracked limbs, pick up slabs of sloughed-off bark, and scramble about alarmingly under the precariously poised limbs. Pollux closed his eyes for a snooze. Soon, I found that I was talking to myself and Asema had disappeared. I jumped up in alarm, and saw that she was staring down at the very place I had buried the book. It happened in a flash. By the time I approached, she'd scuffed up a bit of the earth and then tamped it back down with her shoe.

'What were you doing?' I asked.

'Nothing,' she said.

'What made you stand there, right where you are, and scuff up the ground with your shoe?'

Asema frowned at me in surprise.

'I was lost in thought,' she said, 'or not even thinking. Sorry I messed up your grass.'

'That's not it. What I mean is, what made you stand in that exact place?'

'What's wrong, is someone buried there?'

'Yes,' I said. 'No. A dog.'

'Whose dog?'

'A stray dog.'

'You buried a stray dog?'

'It died in the yard one night.'

'You never told me that.'

'It wasn't a big deal. Sad though.'

'Then why are you so worried about its grave? Is it like, a Cujo dog? Is it a Pet Sematary dog?'

'Kind of,' I said. 'I keep dreaming about it.'

'Poor puppy,' said Asema, suddenly upset along with me.

As Asema was leaving, Pollux woke and I suddenly

found myself dragged along as he hugged me and walked me back into the house. He sat me down, and told me not to move until he made me a fried egg sandwich with green chilis. He would make it on an oversized toasted English muffin. So I obeyed. I couldn't tell him that my oppressive ideas and murky dreams were about a ghost and now a book. He had known me under circumstances in which these sorts of ideas would have been inspired by my addiction to all sorts of interesting drugs, including the vine of the dead. This would sound like a major relapse.

'You lost your tree,' he said, bringing the sandwich on a pottery plate. 'It's been your shelter and your friend.'

'Yes, that's it. My tree. My lovely soul.'

Pollux put his hand on my shoulder, squeezed in sympathy, then took his hand away. After I'd finished the sandwich, he seemed to remember what he'd heard in his sleep and blurted out, 'Buried a dog? What was that about?'

'Asema was getting on my nerves,' I said, full and happy now. 'She's overzealous. There was no dog.'

'She was just standing on our so-called lawn,' said Pollux. 'What was wrong with that? Why would you make up a dog?'

'No reason! Let's live in the moment!'

'I've never heard of anything so crazy.'

'What's crazy is how good this sandwich was,' I said, staring at my empty plate.

'Split another?'

'It would be my honor. Let me help you by talking to you while you make it.'

BLUE

In spite of the fact that I'd buried the book, Flora continued to visit. We were starting to get holiday busy, but there was usually a pre-lunch lull. Flora was still punctual. Eleven a.m. sharp and I'd hear the slide of bracelets on her wrist in the Fiction corner. Now it seemed she was wearing her long slippery down coat, for it rasped faintly along the sailboat table. An old Mexican blanket draped over a chair in Memoirs often ended up on the floor. Flora had always said we should get that chair reupholstered. She rustled in the bathroom but rarely managed to dislodge the paper towels, and then as always she seemed to slip into the confessional without opening its low gate.

When this space was renovated, the friends of the bookstore put sacred tobacco, sweetgrass, cedar, and sage in the walls. Then they painted the front and back doors blue to keep out malignant energies. All over the world—in Greek villages, in the American Southwest, among the Tuareg—blueness repels evil. Blue glass bottles on windowsills keep devils out, and so on. Thus the front door, painted spirit blue, and the vibrant blue canopies above the windows.

Which blue? There are thousands of blues.

I had come to know the bookstore as a place where, in addition to droves of readers, annoyance did occasionally wander in. But no evil, as far as I could tell, had ever made it past the blue door. Flora was a busybody of a spirit, restless and irritable. Still, the blue door should have kept her out. Perhaps she'd squeezed in through a floor crack. With the exception of the one instance I'd told her to leave, and received a zinging sense of her resentment, I told myself again and again that she was harmless enough.

Not so, of course, the book.

The book lay beneath my thoughts, submerged like an old grief or an anger unresolved. It was down there, like something terrible that was done to you in childhood. Sometimes the thought of the book came again and again, like an annoying tune you can't shut off in your head. I longed for snow to fall, hoping that the cold white shield would help me. For I had the uneasy sense, ever since I'd sat in the tree, ever since I'd watched Asema go straight to its grave, that the book itself was not an inanimate thing. I had buried something alive.

One morning when the store was empty but for the slide of Flora's skirt along the edge of the sailboat table, I asked, out loud, if it was the book that had killed her.

'Flora?'

I could feel her listening.

'Did you read the sentence through the end? Was that what happened?'

I sensed an immediate focus. Earlier, when the book had actually been in the store, I thought I'd heard Flora's voice. Although the possibility that she might speak was unnerving, my distress about the book was worse. I needed an answer. And I could feel Flora's need to answer. I could feel the attempt right there, the sensation of Flora's will pushing at the thin divide between us. Living and dead, what was that? We seemed so close. I could hardly breathe. I threw from my body some assisting force toward Flora. We were locked in the effort to communicate across the charged air above the featured books. Waves of force between us pushed and receded and began again. Then a customer walked in.

DISSATISFACTION

Dissatisfaction is a hunched, sinewy, doggedly athletic Black man in his seventies. We see him running slowly around the lake and yet when he enters the store his tracksuit is immaculate. Today he wore the navy blue one with orange stripes, plus a black parka over the thin jacket. These were casual clothes, but he wore them well. As always, he presented an air of elegant outrage.

'What's new?'

He stood in the entryway, glaring, belligerent. I glared back at him, furious that he'd interrupted my communication with Flora. *Beat it! I'm talking to a dead customer!*

But I didn't say that. I relented. By way of the fact he was impossible to please, Dissatisfaction was one of my favorite customers. Also, I didn't want him to tell me again that he had only a decade or so left to read. He was always in a hurry and wanted me to drop everything. He is one of the cursed, a Tantalus, whose literary hunger perpetually gnaws but can never be satiated. He has read everything at least once. As he began reading capaciously at the age of six, he is now running out of fiction. I love the challenge of selling books to him and tried first, as usual, to interest him in history, politics, biography. I knew he would not accept anything but fiction, but this was a chance for him to vent anxiety over what he might read next. He snarled and swatted aside my factual offerings.

Asema walked in and tried to help.

'All right,' she said to him firmly, 'you should really read this.' Before I could stop her, she handed him *The Narrow Road to the Deep North*, by Richard Flanagan. An anguishing read about prisoners of war worked to death in order to build a highway through impassable jungle. He didn't just wave it off; he lifted his hands and fended it off.

'Too much,' he said.

'Well, what about this?' She held up *Every Man Dies Alone*, by Hans Fallada.

'It's more World War Two history,' he said, thrusting it back at her.

'Yes,' said Asema, 'but it's something we should all know about, right?'

He peered at Asema, then spoke with incredulous contempt.

'Are you kidding me? *Honey, I was there.*'

Asema looked at him with a burst of intensity.

He nodded back at her and flared his eyes.

She returned the flare.

'There how?'

'My dad was a G.I. My mama was German. They fell in love. I was born, rode her back as she picked through rubble after the war. Eventually he married my mom and we moved here. Happy now?'

'Pretty much,' said Asema, subdued.

It isn't that he wants fiction with happy endings. He hates happy endings. He turned back to me, dismissing Asema with a flick of his fingers. Dissatisfaction wears thick glasses, has brilliant young brown-gold eyes, a long angular face with a broad jaw, grim line of mouth. His hair is thick, gray, cut close to his skull. His hands are singular—long and narrow with tenuous wrists. When he picks through books with avid purpose, his fingers are nimble and hungry. He holds his breath and either lets it out explosively after reading the first page, a signal of disgust, or with no sound at all turns the page. Generally, if the first pages satisfy, he will read the entire book. He will not quit even though he may come to hate it.

Now, I stood beside him ticking through the past few months of success and failure. Toni Cade Bambara and Ishiguro, yes, all of Murakami, yes, Philip Roth, James Baldwin and Colson Whitehead (Get out. Read these a hundred times). Yaa Gyasi, yes, Rachel Kushner, yes, and W. G. Sebald, but no more mysteries because he complains that he becomes compulsive. A month ago, I gave him Denis Johnson's *Angels*, which he liked well enough. He tried *Tree of Smoke* and excoriated Johnson for enervating him with the evidence of hard research, although, he said, he could see where in fact the book was pretty good. I had then pressed *Train Dreams* into his hands. He came back and faced me, teeth gritted.

'What else you got by this guy?'

Which told me he'd been extremely moved. This lasted a week. He has now finished all of Johnson. We are in trouble. If I sell him a book he dislikes, my favorite customer will return with an injured air, his voice cheated and tattered.

What shall it be?

I pull *The Beginning of Spring*, by Penelope Fitzgerald, off the shelf. He grumpily buys it. Much later that day, just before the store closes, Dissatisfaction returns. *The Beginning of Spring* is a short book, after all. He shuts his hands violently on a copy of Fitzgerald's masterpiece, *The Blue Flower*, and bears it away.

THE MIX-UP

Kateri called me at home, on my day off. Our landline is unlisted, but that was the number she called.

She probably found the number in her mother's telephone list. As I was learning, there is no small talk with Kateri. But her immediate urgent intimacy was a surprise.

'Something's up,' she said.

'You must have the wrong number.'

'No, this is Kateri. Something's up.'

'Hello to you too,' I said.

'Hello. Something's up.'

I was silent.

'It's Mom.'

'What about her?'

'I'm not sure yet. I'll tell you when you get down here.'

'This is my day off and I am busy. Here at home. Which you know because you called my unlisted number.'

Kateri paused, readjusting her attack.

'Look,' I said, 'I'm gonna help you out. When a person who works retail is off duty, we don't do nothing for nobody—unless that person asks nice.'

'Wow. You could never be a high school teacher. I'm sorry to be so abrupt,' said Kateri. 'It's not like me to be upset, but I am very upset by something. It has to do with Mom. And I know you and she were best friends.'

'What do you mean "best friends"?'

Silence from both of us. The notion filled me with alarm, and was simply not true. For me, anyway. I only connected with Flora over books.

'She said . . .'

Kateri stopped. Her voice registered distress.

The worm of guilt twitched. What if Flora really had thought of me as an intimate? What if she was still trying, as an awkward ghost, to stay friends?

'Look,' Kateri said. 'Books meant everything to my mother. She lived in her books! And you have that same . . .'

'It's not that bad,' I said. 'But it is pretty bad. We were immersed in *Swann's Way* when . . .'

Kateri didn't answer.

'You still there?' I asked.

'Yeah. You sounded like her. I miss her so much. Please, can you come?'

I didn't want to, but I couldn't say no, not when she talked about the books, not when she asked that way. There was a note of pleading in her voice that was utterly unlike the person I had first met and the woman who had first called me.

'All right, I'll be there. But where are you?'

'Fifth Precinct Headquarters.'

'For godsakes, no.'

'I had to talk to the police. Now I'm too upset to drive home. You'll see me right when you walk in the door.'

While she was giving me the address, which I already knew, and where I did not want to go, I looked out the window. My dying tree reached toward the sky from its back down on earth. Its branches were like beseeching arms. It takes a while for life to leave green wood. I felt the helplessness, the lack of agency, the frustration of the tree. Severed from its roots, unable to taste the starlight.

The building was an innocuous brick and glass box, the strip-mall-type doorway strung with all-faith white holiday lights. Kateri came forward to greet me. I was extremely unhappy to be at a precinct house, but she didn't seem to notice. She took my arm. I noticed the desk behind her. Its surface was neat, the decoration spare, one framed photo of a dog and a cheap clear glass vase, stained at the base and still bearing a brittle brown rose. I am superstitious about keeping dead flowers.

'Thanks for coming to get me. Really, I mean it. I need to tell this to someone. And when I tell you, you'll understand why this had to be in person.'

My heart began to twist. My hands sweat. Okay,

Tookie, I thought, at least now you know you are still physically allergic to standing in a police station.

'Just tell me,' I said.

Kateri bit her lip. She put both hands on her heart and took a deep breath.

'Okay. Well. First of all, they mixed up her ashes. I got the wrong ashes.'

Now I was getting dizzy.

'Then as if that weren't bad enough, her body turned up yesterday at the county morgue.'

'How could—'

'I know. The wrong body was brought to the crematory. The morgue attendant for the funeral home was having a bad day. She apologized. Sometimes, well, quite often, they have bad days. She'd gone into an overheated apartment to remove a large body that had apparently been there for some time and then, what they call decomp juice, it splashed all over her when her colleague let go of the feet. A lot of bodies came in that day and the ashes I've got are apparently a portion of that big man. The autopsy never happened. I'm sorry to tell you all of this. The attendant went into way too much detail the way I am doing now because I'm terribly, terribly . . . Ah, my heart is wracked!'

Kateri put her shorn head into her hands. All of what she'd said was too much, and then that last sentence. It was so oddly Victorian. But then, Flora also sometimes used odd, anachronistic turns of phrase.

'I've just gotten back from identifying my mother. And I don't know how to say this. . . .'

Now Kateri gripped her head with both hands and did not finish whatever she was going to tell me.

'I don't know how I got back here,' she said. 'I'm afraid to drive alone now because I'm shaking. See? It's starting to hit me.'

Kateri put her hand out. But her hand was steady.

'Well, anyway,' she said. 'I guess it's all inside.'

I was nearly overcome by the effort to withhold my own thoughts. My jaw began to ache.

'Let's go,' I managed to say.

She got up and followed me out the door. I pulled out smoothly and got onto the street in spite of the interior quaking sensation and high-pitched singing in my head. Breathing slowly, I managed to calm myself enough to feel that I was driving safely. Mindful breathing, I kept telling myself. It didn't work. I took the long way, easy streets. The drive had an aura of unreality. At the door to Flora's stone-trimmed house, I had to physically restrain myself from talking by putting my fist against my teeth. This was obviously not the time to tell Kateri about her mother, but there was now an actual sensation of illness inside of me. And when I tried to close off all thoughts of it the pressure became worse. I truly felt that I might go foaming mad if I kept it all in much longer. However, Kateri preempted what I might have said by asking me a question.

Have you ever heard of someone's body looking younger after death? I mean, not just smoothed out, but much younger?

I looked at Kateri when she asked this astonishing question and noticed that terse new lines had formed around her mouth, framing her lips like parentheses. She got out of the car. As I watched her walk unsteadily up the path, I bit my knuckles so hard I tasted my own blood.

SCORCHED CORN SOUP

'What happened?'

Pollux held my bandaged hand. He poked at the bandage. I hardly wanted to tell him that I was a mad dog biting myself for sympathy.

'Ow!'

'Oh god, I'm sorry!'

'I bit my own hand.'

'Again? Oh my girl.'

He lifted my hand to his lips and kissed the bandage.

It was a Finding Nemo bandage, from the bottom of the bandage drawer.

'Poor little Nemo,' said Pollux.

I hugged him too tightly and he took the cue, held me, and stroked my hair.

'What's this all about?'

I quickly filled Pollux in on Kateri's vexing news about her mother's body. He went still, and when he looked into my face his eyes were wide. Besides ghosts, Pollux has an extreme aversion to anything connected with death. He also has fixed views on the afterlife. He is certain that after we die we get whatever heaven we believe in—he has constructed a complex world to come. I haven't, but the one he believes in includes me, so I am covered. His assurance in this matter gives me a surprising amount of peace. He had barely begun to react to the news, however, when Jackie knocked.

I went to the door. Maybe I looked annoyed, or distressed.

'Was this the night?'

Pollux called out. 'I'm making your scorched corn soup recipe, remember?'

I pulled her in and told her everything I'd just told Pollux. Her dog, Droogie, followed. She was a lumbering, lazy, deeply affectionate, brown rottweiler-poodle-husky mix. Jackie hauled in a large sack.

A friend of hers had finished processing his wild rice, or manoomin, and the bag was for us. The rice was nicely cleaned, a rich green-brown. I plunged my unbandaged hand into the bag. The feeling of the rice, the cool laky scent, was calming. We took some out and admired the length of the grains. Native people around here have a specific ferocity about wild rice. I've seen faces harden when tame paddy rice, the uniformly brown commercially grown rice, is mentioned, called wild rice, or served under false pretenses. People get into fights over it. Real wild rice is grown wild, harvested by Native people, and tastes of the lake it comes from. This was the good stuff. I sealed the bag, already feeling better. When I offered to pay, Jackie said it was a perk. Bookstore perks are random. One time, the bookstore bought a farm-raised lamb and we had to divide up the tiny chops and shanks. Another time, it was homemade pickles. Jackie's dog dislikes wooden floors. Droogie loves our house because the rugs start right at the front door and there is never any danger of finding herself trapped, surrounded by a sea of floor, because the rugs run all through the house. So Droogie had entered happily, and now she assumed an alert down-sit, watching us. She followed our conversation with her eyes, interested in the tone of our voices, perhaps waiting for one of us to drop a string of words she knew. Droogie has a large vocabulary.

For the past year, Pollux has been perfecting my favorite soup of those that saved me—it is a corn soup. First he caramelizes fresh-cut sweetcorn, toasting it slowly in a heavy pan, adding onions. Then cubed potatoes tossed lightly in butter, to set a crisp. He adds all of this to a garlicky chicken broth with shaved carrots, cannellini beans, fresh dill, parsley, a dash of cayenne, and heavy cream. The scent was making me delirious. Still.

'I have to talk about Flora some more,' I said.

Jackie and her dog cocked their heads and at the same angle, making the same expression. The effect was comical, but I didn't laugh.

'Go ahead,' said Jackie. 'A while ago you said there was supposed to be an autopsy. I thought it was a stroke.'

'No, it was her heart.'

'She had no heart,' said Jackie.

'Hard words,' I said, after a moment.

'I begged her to return something very important,' Jackie said. 'Actually it belonged to Asema. She refused.'

It seemed unlike Jackie to hold a grudge against a dead person.

'No autopsy, huh,' Jackie muttered. She looked at me and frowned. 'What were you going to tell me about Flora?'

I told Jackie more about how Kateri got the ashes back, but then how Flora's actual body turned up. So they weren't her ashes, obviously.

Jackie nodded. Surprisingly, she was not surprised. She folded her arms, stared out from under her eyebrows at her dog, who gave her a long look in return and then sank down, head on paws. Jackie looked so forbidding that I didn't feel like breaking into her thoughts. At last, though, she spoke.

'I thought it was too simple.'

Now I gaped at her. Really? *Too simple?* It already felt too complicated. My head began to ache.

'Some people are slippery,' Jackie went on. 'They are difficult to deal with after death. They don't behave like dead people. They are death resisters.'

I took a deep breath. So, there was an explanation? My thoughts expanded in such relief that when she immediately moved on to talk further about the wild rice and Pollux called from the kitchen, I didn't ask questions. I just enjoyed feeling sane.

Wine, soup, bread, salad, later, Jackie said that the scorched corn had attained perfection and she had to go home. Her teenage granddaughter had a girl-friend over. They were studying, but, said Jackie, they needed her because she was an irksome yet comically reassuring presence.

'Uh-oh, they're texting. Making ramen again. I've got to get back before they burn the pot.' Infuriatingly, she up and left.

After Jackie was gone, I decided that the only therapy possible would be to put on my blue rubber gloves and do the dishes. I slipped my hands into the super-hot water and scrubbed. I used lots of lavender-scented dish soap. Because this is my job when Pollux cooks, I have decided to make the chore more sensual, which may seem absurd when applied to scrubbing pots. But Pollux likes to put his arms around me when I stand in the foam and steam at the sink.

'Hey baby.' He breathed in my hair. 'Your rubber gloves are so sexy.'

'You're interesting,' I said. 'But not the way you think.'

I turned around, flicked water off my stubby blue fingers. 'Is that a leer?'

'Do you want it to be?'

'I keep reading about men's leers. They're always

leering in books. I've always wondered what a leer looks like.'

'Maybe you should take your gloves off. Then I'll give you a leer.'

'I think you're leering right now. Quit leering at me.'

'It's just an expression,' said Pollux.

'Expression of what?'

'Hope. A sad, manly sort of hope.'

'Sad for sure. Anyway, I've always wanted a man who would not express his lust on his face, but use his hands instead.'

'Like this?'

'More like this.'

'Oh.'

And later. 'Would you take the gloves off? Would you take the gloves off, now, please?'

'Are you sure?'

'God! Wait. Okay. Leave them on.'

And still later:

I burrow into the pillows. Comforted by Pollux, I shape myself around him. The agitations of the day, Kateri's strange behavior, the dreadful persistence of Flora, those questions, and the book, always now the book. These were in my thoughts. Then I felt it. The earth held its breath. There was a slow release and then a soft downsifting silence. I turned my lamp off and my thoughts dimmed. It was starting to snow. At last, the pure and fragile snow was falling upon us, separating off the air from the dirt, the living from the dead, the reader from the book.

Solstice Fire

HETTA

Pollux drove to the airport to fetch Hetta, and while he was gone I whipped up a batch of oatmeal cookies. 'Whipped up' makes me sound like a cookie expert. The truth is the only thing I do not do in the kitchen is bake. I consulted the back of a Quaker oatmeal box, squinted, frowned, tried to smash cold butter, poured the oats on my feet, and put double or maybe triple brown sugar in the bowl. We had no raisins so I used dried cranberries and chipped a prehistoric bag of white chocolate chips out of the freezer. I threw the frozen chips into the bowl, then realized some were stuck in clumps. I used a hammer on them. Oh well. I started the oven and spooned the cookie dough onto the cookie sheet, pinching and poking at the dough mounds to make uniform sizes. I slid the cookies into the oven, then I sat down to wait. About five minutes in I set the timer. I wanted to pour myself a glass of wine but didn't want Hetta to get a whiff of my breath and think I was a lush. I just sat there, staring at nothing, in dread. To be haunted and also have Hetta in the house seemed an unfair stroke of ill fortune, a joke, and I, plaything of the fates, seemed destined for these sorts of unpleasant visitations. I called Jackie, who knew my history with Hetta.

'Boozhoo, teacher.'

'Uh-oh. You always call me teacher when something's wrong.'

'You got me. I am sitting here waiting for Pollux to pick up Hetta, you know, for winter solstice, which she celebrates instead of Christmas.'

'Solstice is day after tomorrow, the twenty-first, right?'

'I just whipped up a batch of cookies.'

'Are they in the oven?'

'Yes.'

'Did you set the timer?'

'Of course.'

'Don't of course me. Remember the time you set the oven on fire?'

'Yes. Now I know you put the brandy on the fruit-cake after you broil it.'

'Bake it.'

'Okay. I'm not much of a baker but I've learned that much. It wasn't a question of the timer.'

'Never mind. How may I help?'

'Talk me down.'

Silence. At last she said, 'Your reaction is perfectly appropriate so why should I talk you out of it? Hetta is a monster. Well, I will amend that, she sometimes can be a little much.'

'A little much.' I laughed. 'Predictions?'

'She will say something sarcastic about your cookies within, oh, three minutes of walking in the door.'

'A sure bet.'

'She will be dressed in something skintight covered by something transparent.'

'Noted.'

'She will talk only about herself, never asking about you.'

'Of course.'

'She will be sweet to her father in order to get money.'

'That's always painful to watch.'

We fell silent.

'Let's start laughing again,' she said.

'There's nothing funny. I can't take it.'

'All right, let's be philosophical. You have Pollux, you love him, he loves you. Rare. She's the fly in the ointment. And by the way, what an odd figure of speech. Just a second. I'll look it up in my slang dictionary.'

I heard her put the phone down and her footsteps squeaking away on her old wooden floor. In order to get points in the carceral system, I'd attended a Bible study group. I'd practically memorized the King James so I already know it was Ecclesiastes 10:1: 'Dead flies cause the ointment of the apothecary to send forth a stinking savour.' This made me think of my cookies. They were ready, sending forth a heavenly savour. I put the phone down and rushed to the oven to take them out. Ah, and oh, they were perfect! I set the pan on a rack to cool. Wait, I'm going to say that again because again it makes me sound like I know how to bake. *I set the pan on a rack to cool.* When I picked up the phone again the line had gone dead. I still felt triumph. Maybe I can do anything. Maybe I'll take up knitting, I mused, or learn to play the recorder. Maybe I will eat a cookie. I picked one up, broke off a bit, let it cool a little more, then popped it into my mouth. My teeth ached before my sense of taste kicked in. Triple sugar. Damn. But I swallowed the bite anyway because I heard Pollux drive up. I wanted to appear welcoming, so I rushed to the door and opened it. As I waved, I realized that I should have scraped the cookies off the pan into the garbage. Too late.

And here came too much.

The two of them emerged from the car. Pollux eyed me from the driver's door, gave a feeble wave that sank my heart like an iron ball. Something extra was up. Hetta had gotten out of the passenger's door and was leaning into the backseat. Before I could take a breath, she turned around. She had lifted a sort of basket from the backseat and now she held it in the crook of her arm as she came up the walk. I welcomed her in and saw with suspicion that she'd used a baby carrier to haul in, I assumed, some sort of contraband. But then she pushed the blanket off the carrier and revealed a bundle shaped like— No, it was *an actual baby*. My brain froze. I nearly shrieked. But the sugar closed my throat. I choked, coughed. My eyes teared up. Thus, as Hetta turned, my glistening eyes and the tears sliding down my cheeks gave her reason to think that I was moved.

'Wow, Tookie. Thought you were badass. You've gone all mushy,' she sneered. But her sneer was half-hearted and this comment was so mild and toothless that I glanced at her in surprise. She had removed her heavy silver septum ring and was only wearing one pair of earrings. A moment later, she said, 'Are those cookies? It smells like someone's trying to act all maternal. Speaking as the only person here who's had a baby using her own body, I'd say . . .'

Hetta walked over to the cookies, picked one up, and took a huge bite. Then another. Her face glowed with surprise.

'. . . that you succeeded! These are delicious!'

She grabbed two more cookies, informing us that

she was nursing and needed sustenance. Pollux went to the refrigerator for milk. You need milk to make milk, right? I could feel his thought. He filled a glass and brought it to his daughter. Hetta sat down, still munching, and unveiled the wonder in her arms.

I peered at an alarmingly new baby. I couldn't remember when I'd seen one so tiny. He had a marvelous thatch of dark brown hair. His features were bold, I thought, for a baby. But what do I know? He seemed to have a lot of hair for a baby. I said so.

'Yes, he does,' said Hetta, doting. She rewrapped the baby tightly and set him on her lap to admire. 'His father has such thick hair.'

I looked at Pollux. He twitched his lip and raised his eyebrow. Thereby telling me he had no idea who this father was, hadn't yet asked or hadn't yet got an answer. As I am Tookie, I immediately jumped right in on the mention. I tried to make my comment into a compliment and a query. I was also uncharacteristically hospitable.

'He must be pretty special, this guy with great hair. Is he coming too? There's plenty of room.'

What was this? Hetta was looking at me with an expression I had never before seen cross her face. Her eyes were warm, lighted up specially for me. I looked at her more closely. Maybe it was smudged eyeliner.

Or the wonder of sugar. If only I'd known. The hard edges of the geometric tattoos on her hands softened as she stroked and rocked the tiny bundle with a slight jiggle of her legs. There was about her a sense of both fatigue and joy. There was also melancholy. I'd never seen her feelings so openly displayed, except of course as rage, cynicism, resentment, and so on. Everything about her was altered, even her strictly tended details. Perhaps caring for a baby gave her no time to suffuse her hair with product, for it fell naturally to one side in a glamorous sweep, the ends hennaed a soft orange. As much as seeing the baby, her next words shocked me.

'Thank you,' she said. And then, flooring me completely, 'How are you, Tookie? What's happening?'

Later, after Hetta had devoured a turkey reuben and a bowl of ginger ice cream, the baby began to stir and she made her way to the back bedroom she always used, ordinarily the office space for Pollux. I hauled a large duffel along behind her. As she entered the room, she sighed and said, 'It's good to be home.'

I looked over my shoulder at Pollux and pretended to bang my head in amazement. Again, had I really heard this? He shrugged suspiciously and walked away. A second later, I asked the question I should have asked in the beginning.

'I suppose you told your father, but I was so excited I forgot to ask. What is your baby's name?'

'Jarvis,' she said. 'Named for his great-grandfather.'

'It's a classic,' I said. It was also a very adult name. Hard to pin on a baby.

I stood awkwardly in the doorway, nodding and trying to look affable. Hetta asked me if I would hold the baby while she got ready for bed. When I told her I didn't know how to hold a baby, she arranged my arms and gave me the baby anyway. She went into the bathroom and there we were. Jarvis and me. I was nervous, intensely so, trying to control my ragged breathing, conscious of how I'd hunched over in a way that seemed unnatural. I heard the shower running. Hetta took such long showers that she always used up all the hot water. Knowing I would be holding Jarvis for a long while, I tried to unhunch myself and sit down.

'Sorry, little fellow,' I whispered, shifting my weight.

Jarvis opened one tiny, dark, defiant eye. He stared hard at me, without cracking a smile, but without crying either. What a cool character, I thought. He was studying me. I was unnerved by this, but also I was intrigued to have such a finely modeled intelligence in my arms. Maybe he did have the bitter dignity of a Jarvis. Let me say without reserve, Jarvis was exquisite. He was what, three weeks old? He hadn't plumped out. His features were drawn with a 003 Micron marker. The distinct curve of his upper lip, the swoop of his eyebrows, so fine! The point of his nose was impossibly aristocratic, precocious for a baby, I thought, uncertain. This was the first baby I had ever been privileged to study. He didn't blink, like the leader of a prison gang. He didn't change his expression. So the study was mutual. He stared holes through me. He saw straight into my heart and didn't seem to care that it was riddled with cowardice, hubris, stupidity, regret. Those things meant nothing to him. He saw that what was left of my heart was good and loving. He trusted me not to scare him, not to drop him. I blinked to keep the raw tears back. He became restless and his face squeezed shut, alarming me. I felt my arms move automatically and realized that I was rocking him, not with big Tookie swings, but tiny movements, to suit his needs. His face uncreased and his eyes drooped shut. He was sleeping again, making kitten noises. How much could my heart stand? Much more, apparently, as Hetta's shower was just beginning.

Later still, middle of the night in fact, I lay awake listening to high disconsolate squalls from below. Hetta had told me that her baby's father was originally from Minneapolis, or a suburb, and that he was already in the Cities. He would live at first with his parents, but he had an apartment already picked out. He'd put down the deposit. It was even close by, in the part of the city bought up by multinational development corporations. They were building giant boxes of expensive apartments and condos and not replacing the trees they killed. Our city was ever more boring, treeless, generic, but I'd become fond of this city anyway via soup. I am loyal. Hetta said the apartment they'd move into was behind one of the new boxes, near Hennepin, on a side street in a fourplex. They would have only one roommate, who was 'cool with the baby.' We'd meet Jarvis's father soon, she said, he just had to finish his book. She winked and refused to tell me his name.

'He's a writer?'

Hetta nodded.

'A famous writer?'

'Not yet. He's writing a novel.'

'Is there a plot?'

'Sort of.' Hetta smiled at the baby and shook her hair. 'Young man meets girl with a piercing while tattooing her hands. They fall madly in love. She becomes pregnant and has his baby, which they sort of keep a secret from her family until at last she brings the baby home for solstice.'

'Autofiction?'

'No. He can't stand that stuff. It's hard to describe his book. I don't think there's a category that fits it.' She waved her ornate hands and laughed the low musical burbling laugh that used to seem incongruous, coming from the forbidding tigerish girl she was, but perfectly fit the young mother she had become.

DECEMBER 21

Pollux and I are phobic about the season of good cheer. We have an aversion to red and green decorations, carols piped into the streets, though not so much the colored lights and frosted cookies. People actually come around caroling in this neighborhood, and if we hear them we turn off our lights and hide. The only way that we are comfortable with this holiday is sitting in front of the fire and exchanging gifts. We agree. Gifts are nice. And special food, we'll eat that. We were cool with celebrating the solstice all the short day long. In fact, I would have liked to but those of us who work in retail bear the onslaught of the season and ride the wave. I was exhausted. On solstice night, I was prepared to put my feet up after work and accept sympathy. However, as I walked home along the crunchy snow, I was flooded with tenderness. Baby Jarvis was at our house and I couldn't wait to hold him. I wondered how he'd progressed that day, if his fingernails had grown, how far his eyes could focus, if he was seeing the world in color, if his eyes had subtly darkened, if there was any way that he would possibly smile.

Hetta was wearing the baby as she danced around the room. She was playing old LPs from Pollux's collection. Prince albums were scattered around the turntable. One was propped up. Prince in his original beauty. I put my hand to my heart like I was pledging allegiance—maybe to everything in our home. There was a delicious scent. Pollux was browning chunks of squash with onions and garlic. Maybe he would make some sort of spicy curry. I took my coat off and began to dance, whirling, punching at the air. I am a lousy dancer, maybe dangerous, but Hetta called out to encourage, not to mock. I spun like a pinwheel and bunny-hopped until my face flushed. When my heart was beating like crazy, I sat down, laughing. Hetta unlatched the baby carrier and put Jarvis in my arms.

'You can call him Cubby,' she said. 'Dad nicknamed him.'

Sometimes Pollux's diplomatic skills amaze me.

However, I found that I was stuck on the name Jarvis now. Holding him in the crook of my elbow, I put my feet on a stool and sank back into the pillows. Hetta went into the kitchen to help or just encourage her father. I watched the baby for as long as I could, then banked my arms with a rolled blanket and closed my eyes. How could I possibly have stepped into such a golden life?

Later on, we made a small solstice fire. We usually make the fire outdoors, but because of Jarvis we stayed in and used the fireplace. Hetta laid the fire using birchbark and strips of kindling. Nothing made by humans could touch the pagan fire, she said. Her fire was expert, caught easily, and blazed cheerfully upward. I asked if Pollux had taught her the Potawatomi way to make a fire.

'He taught me to make a one-match fire in the driving rain,' she said. 'We got massively soaked. But we had a fire to dry us out.'

The pleasant crackle of the small branches and pinecones she had used settled into a comfortable lapping as the fire took the logs. I wondered what sort of solstice ritual Penstemon was observing. I texted her. She answered.

'I usually have interdimensional sex on the solstice, but Crankyass is still sulking,' she wrote.

I guessed this was her new boyfriend, but didn't ask.

'I'm having a premonition,' she wrote.

'That's nice.' I signed off. I wasn't altogether glad I'd gotten in touch because I don't like premonitions. When are they ever good?

⁂

The cold finally came, and it was true cold. Maybe not the -40 in real numbers that we used to get, but -20 with the cheat of the windchill factor. Yes, it was cold, and our house was cold, but I thrive in the cold, love to bundle up. Hetta had a few days left of her visit. Pollux bashfully mentioned a longer stay.

'There is nothing I'd like better,' I said. 'Hetta should stay.'

He tried to hide flabbergastedness but failed. His mouth hung open.

'Nothing's gone wrong.' I shrugged. 'Not an ill or insane word had been spoken.'

Not only that, but Hetta hadn't badgered Pollux for money or dished out anything but weak sarcasm. Which at some point she apologized for. How could I not forgive her? I hoped, however, that she hadn't entirely lost her edge to motherhood. At least she was wearing red tights, black biker shorts, an old Veruca Salt T-shirt, and an attenuated plaid flannel. It made

me happy that she always wore smoldering black eyeliner, often a shade of bold purple lipstick, or made pin
curls with Xs of bobby pins and left them in for three
days. I was reassured by her outfits. They made her
other changes seem real. And even more, I helplessly
adored everything about her baby.

Maybe we'd have gone on this way, but then I started
worrying. The worry made me interfere. I began to
have thoughts about the father of Hetta's baby. One
day when we were having a perfectly nice breakfast, I
asked her if she'd heard when he was showing up.

'Pretty soon, I think.'

'Did he give you a date?'

'No, not really.'

'So he's just sort of being a writer?'

'I guess.'

'While you take full-time care of his baby?'

'What the fuck is it to you?'

Hetta stink-eyed and hit me with a poison sneer. She
put down her toast and turned away from me, jouncing
her baby on her shoulder. One of his eyes was squeezed
shut. He gave me a piercing stare from the other as he
audibly burped.

'That's my boy,' crooned Hetta. She stood up and,
keeping her back to me, took Jarvis away, into her
room. My heart plunged. She kicked the door shut

behind her. So that was that. I'd ruined the visit. And just by asking about the baby's father, just by pointing out that she was giving the baby full-time care while the father frittered away his own time somewhere writing what was probably a lousy, self-important novel.

What was wrong with me? Why had this blue bolt of concern seized me? Why even now did I think Hetta needed to eat? Why did I meekly sidle toward the slammed door, bearing Hetta's toast on a plate, and why did I give a pathetic little knock and say, in a ragged tone, *I'm sorry. Here's your toast.* And why did I walk away without flinging the toast at the door when from inside Hetta shouted, 'Fuck off, you old sow!'

Why? Because I guess I loved Hetta and was enraptured by her baby. I would do anything to hold him. And here I'd gone and wrecked my chances by asking the wrong question. And this had occurred because doing the wrong thing in general was my nature. I would be Tookie, now and forever, amen. Or at least I would be Tookie for a few days, until next year, when I could start out as a better person who used diplomacy, tact, and wasn't shadowed by a needy ghost.

Bonne Année

A WARM NIGHT IN JANUARY

Turtle Mountainers are big on New Year's and we were having open house at Louise's. The day would be celebrated with a meatball soup called boulettes or bullets, and small bites of frybread called bangs. If the night was warm, we'd sit around an outside fire. Pollux made the bangs because he knows how to work with hot grease, while I'm an expert on cold grease. I brought Old Dutch potato chips. The picnic party box, double bags in the red and white cardboard, still made me feel rich. Hetta was still using the monosyllable treatment on me, but she'd made a chocolate cake with Penstemon, so I didn't care. Soon I was sitting by the fire with a bowl of bullets and a bang to dunk in the broth. Behind us, people crammed Louise's creaky house. I was going for a second helping, but a friend of the store walked over with a Crock-Pot of avgolemono. My favorite. I decided to wolf down the boulettes and follow that Crock-Pot. There was also wild rice on the inside table: wild rice soup, wild rice hot dish, wild rice salad—all different sorts of wild rice. Asema sat next to me, her plate heaped with these offerings. She took a bite.

'The rice in the salad is from the Northwest Angle,' she said critically. 'Red Lake.'

'How is it?'

'Holds up well. But the Fond du Lac rice is nuttier.'

'I disagree,' said Penstemon. 'White Earth has the nuttiest rice.'

'I believe I have the most discriminating palate at this party,' said Pollux, whose plate was also heaped with six kinds of wild rice. 'I bought the rice in the soup from a guy in Sawyer.'

'Overprocessed,' said Penstemon.

'It's soft, kind of fading into the broth,' said Asema.

Pollux ate sullenly, deflated. I didn't like to see Pollux challenged. More than that, a wild rice argument can wreck friendships, kill marriages, if allowed to rage. I had to interfere. I meant to calm things down, but I am crap at de-escalation.

'You critics are so wrong,' I said. 'I'd call the texture silken. And what kind of experts are you and Pensty anyway? You two will eat anything. Wild rice egg rolls? At a powwow? Old grease? I was there. Nothing worse and even so the two of you were chowing down.' My voice was loud, challenging, and thus inevitably I raised the conversation to the level of an argument.

'Sad you'd resort to an ad hominem attack. I take issue with that,' said Asema, standing up. 'I never in my life ate a wild rice egg roll fried in old grease.'

'Saw you.'

Pollux nudged my ankle. Then he flung me the sideways waving peace sign, our sign that means *You're hot, let's get it on.* I grinned. Brushed my shoulder. *Nothing sticks on me. Later.*

'Moreover, Tookie,' said Penstemon, 'I've seen you eat the old standby many times—pot of overcooked wild rice, crumbled hamburg, Campbell's cream of chicken.'

'Oh really? What's wrong with that?'

'I think it's disrespectful to the rice,' said Asema. 'I'd never eat that. However,' she paused, thinking, 'it isn't bad if you use cream of celery. Plus it's a feast dish so often. What I really disapprove of is paddy rice.'

'Oh, tame rice, I guess we all can agree on that.'

'Wait a minute,' said Gruen, who had joined the conversation. 'I believe what you call paddy rice, this dark rice you get in the store bag, is very good. Extremely nutty. What's wrong with it?'

'People, let's drop this!' I was alarmed by the introduction of paddy rice. Next we'd get to genetic modification and the Line 3 tar sands pipeline shoved through treaty territory. All hell would break loose, and the party would be over. But the argument was already beyond my control. Jackie had entered the fray, insisting that Wisconsin rice was far superior to all. Pollux threw up his hands and said, 'Canadian,' in a scared-straight way. The uproar grew more heated, ranging from false advertising to, yes, theft of wild genome, detailed enumerations of what was wrong with the brown stuff from California that masqueraded as wild rice. Gruen wasn't moved by the arguments, and Asema in an unexpected turnaround declared that not every Native had tribal connections, a ricing license, or could afford the real thing. She called us a bunch of in-digelitists, and accidentally knocked Penstemon's plate of rices, mostly eaten, out of her hands.

Penstemon went for Asema, yelling, 'Let's duke it out!'

'My fucking pleasure,' said Asema with a deadly glare. They squared off. I'd have pulled them apart but they were both wearing mittens. Asema's were Hello Kitty and Pen's were Spider-Man.

'Meow,' said Asema.

'I'll web you,' said Pen.

'Hetta's cutting the chocolate cake,' I said, ending the grudge match.

I sat down between Asema and Gruen to eat my piece of cake. It was the dense flourless kind of cake that I loved. There was even powdered sugar sifted on top.

'She's a sitting duck,' said Asema, glancing over me at Gruen. 'Let's hit Tookie up.'

She started telling me how she was gathering donations for fabric. She and Gruen were sewing banners to protest banks investing in Line 3, which meant disaster for wild rice beds in wetlands and lakes.

'So it always comes back to wild rice,' I said, stuffing my cake down in order to get away.

'Every world-destroying project disrupts something intimate, tangible, and Indigenous,' said Asema. 'Wild rice isn't just a cultural issue, or a delicious niche food, it is a way of talking about human survival.'

'I'll pony up if you'll shut up,' I said.

She grinned and held out her hand.

By the time everyone was gone, except for the diehards, the fire had developed a luscious set of coals and the dry, dense logs were burning with an even radiance, throwing heat. This was the delicious part of sitting by an hours-long outdoor fire. When you sat close to the lambent coals whispering as they cracked, throwing a magical heat that wrapped around you but might scorch your knees. When you backed your chair up, the temperature was lovely in front but your back and ass were ice. There was a constant shuffle of chairs and booted feet. Some of us started talking about the travels we'd taken in our late teens and early twenties, when our bodies had been more resilient and tough than we had realized. Pollux had driven Hetta and Jarvis home. Now he settled himself again.

'Riding the dog,' he said. 'Godawful sometimes, but also interesting. Once, there was this lady who sat down next to me. She was wearing a jean jacket, cut-offs, sexy boots, and a deep brimmed hat. A black veil came down all around it so you couldn't see her face. The landscape got boring, so we started to talk. After a while she told me she was a movie star, traveling in-cognito. I asked her why she wasn't riding in a jet. She said that she was gathering material for a movie part. I asked about the part. She told me that she was doing a remake of *Midnight Cowboy*, only it would be *Midnight Cowgirl*. I asked her name and she lifted her veil. By golly, it was her.'

'Who?'

'Kim Basinger. She was . . . I can't describe it.'

'I can,' Asema said. 'I watched her old movies. She was deliriously beautiful.'

'She was wearing a huge puffer coat down to her

knees, a thick beanie, Cree mukluks.' Pollux leaned forward. 'She was hard to look at.'

'How so?' I asked.

'It was like the sun got in my eyes.'

'Blindingly beautiful, then.'

'Maybe,' said Pollux, 'but at the same time I wouldn't have wanted to be her. She couldn't go anywhere without people staring at her.'

I knew the feeling. Sometimes I have felt a signal admiration for the out-and-out nerve of my presentation, though when I wished to be I was invisible.

'That movie wasn't made, was it? I never heard of it,' said Pen.

'Maybe the backers pulled out,' said Pollux. 'I kept waiting to see the movie. I hoped she wasn't playing Ratso.'

'Of course she wasn't playing Ratso,' said Jackie. She was wrapped in a plaid wool blanket, wearing a knit hat with a pompom, and drinking hot cider. 'Kim could only be the cowboy. The Jon Voight character. Anyway, good story. Where did she get off?'

'I got off first. She was going all the way across the country. I guess she made it. I would have heard if something happened, I suppose. But there was something *otherworldly* about her.'

Jackie and I exchanged a glance over Pollux saying 'otherworldly.' What could it mean? We shrugged in wordless agreement—let's let Pollux have his fantasy.

'Riding a bus has really been useful to me in terms of sleep,' said Louise. 'You know how intolerable it is, how awful you feel, after a night or two of sitting up to sleep on a bus? Your feet prickle, yeah, and the back? Agony.'

'Everything hurts,' said Pollux.

'That's what I think about when I really can't sleep. How desperately I wanted to stretch out on the floor in the middle aisle. I would not have cared how gross it was. Nothing. I'd have done anything just to stretch out. After I think about how cramped and desperate I was back then, I usually fall asleep.'

I was about to say, in my usual Tookie way, 'At least you had a bed to go home to,' but then I realized that in fact I had slept in some fabulous beds in my life. I considered making My Favorite Beds the next topic of conversation, but didn't for obvious reasons. We were entering that lucid buzz of weariness when the wine has worn off and we have perhaps dozed a bit, then startled awake.

'There is something in me that aches to do the wrong thing,' said Louise. Her voice was muffled by a knitted shawl across her face. 'That's what being so very good as a child can do to a person. I almost always resist, but I understand when other people don't. The urge is very strong.'

'I have a different urge,' said Penstemon. 'I don't like heights because I'm instantly seized by the urge to leap. L'appel du vide. The call of the void.' Her voice was fake-wise. She nodded at Asema.

Jackie hadn't given me a dictionary for nothing. I spoke up.

'There's a word for your impulse, Louise. Cacoëthes,' I said to her. 'The urge to do something somewhat wrong. Not something unspeakable or horrific. Just something you know is a bad idea.'

'Like eating paddy rice, apparently,' said Gruen.

'There must be a malady related to Louise's other affliction,' said Asema, looking at her phone. 'I've got it. Cacoëthes scribendi. An unbearable need to write. Lots of people have it.'

'I don't,' said Jackie. 'By the way, everybody, Tookie's right. The whole building is haunted. I was working in back the other day and I heard some scratching. Too regular to be a rodent. So I sat in the confessional after the store closed the other night. I wanted to see if Flora would visit.'

I was subtly horrified by the thought. My voice came out low and creaky.

'What happened? Did she?'

'There were noises outside the box, scratching, skittering, probably mice. Then I heard voices. But they were loud and I could tell they were arguing about wine. Of course, the restaurant's wine cellar is right below. After the voices stopped, a cold breeze came from nowhere and I felt the touch of a spectral hand. . . .'

'Goddammit, Jackie.'

'Sorry. You know I believe you.'

I snapped a few sticks in my hands and hurled them into the fire. Pollux stretched. 'I'll be going back into the party now,' he said, although the party was over. He ambled off. I knew he was going to take care of the leftovers by devouring the dishes he liked best. Most everyone else followed him.

'He won't tolerate talk of ghosts and supernatural business, will he,' said Jackie.

'He said "otherworldly" so he's on guard against himself,' I said. 'He won't talk about that stuff, but he'll talk about the next life. He's setting one up for the both of us.'

'You've got a good husband. How does he go about setting it up?'

'He's pretty much using songs and stories, maybe some work with pipes and feathers.'

'He's a sort of spiritual carpenter.'

I poked the fire with a stick, set my stick ablaze, tapped the sparks off, or let it burn. When my stick got too short, I found another stick and started over. I had edged too far away from the coals and I was cold to the bone, becoming miserable. Jackie's children had grown up to be kind, successful, and reasonably happy, so I thought of her as a source of maternal knowledge. I edged closer to the fire, put a blanket on my knees, and prepared to interrogate my teacher.

'In your experience, can becoming a mother change a person from a monster into a human being?'

Jackie opened her mouth, uttered a syllable, then shut her mouth and frowned. At last she spoke.

'I assume you're talking about Hetta.'

I indicated this was true. Jackie tipped her head from side to side.

'I suppose these feelings are new to Hetta. I suppose they seem transformative.'

'At first, she was shockingly agreeable.'

'A newborn baby has a powerful effect on character. But so does a toddler. A child. A preteen. A teenager. A mother changes with every stage. Some stages are within a mother's skill set. Some stages are like being told to scale a cliff using a rope attached to nothing.'

'As usual, I screwed up though. Now she won't talk to me. How do I make up with Hetta?'

I described the short exchange over Jarvis's father and how Hetta had slammed me out.

There was a long, long silence. I thought Jackie hadn't heard me, or paid attention.

'I've been in this dimension so many times,' she finally said.

'What, you mean reincarnation or something like that?'

'No, I mean your quandary. An iffy dimension where I'm afraid for or worried about one of my daughters, like you, where I cross a boundary and then she gets pissed.'

'So you're saying what happened is normal?'

'I think so. It's easy to overstep out of worry. It can infuriate them, though sometimes they understand later on.'

I was struck with the thought that nobody besides Pollux would be willing to violate a boundary and risk my anger in order to help me. I told that to Jackie. She told me she already had, long ago, when she sent the dictionary.

'That crossed a boundary?'

'You could have taken it the wrong way. As a prod

to become more literate or something. Anyway, it's a teacher thing, also a mom thing. What about your mom? I mainly dealt with your aunties. You never talk about your mom. You never talk about your father.'

'Because he was totally absent. And while I was up in tribal school my mother was down in the Cities. We went back and forth. She wasn't snoopy, or controlling, or demanding. She was hardly ever super-angry, or mean.'

'What, then?'

'She wasn't anything. She was always working on her own thing, which was being wasted. She treated me like an adult as soon as I could shit in the right place and get my own food. She tolerated my comings and goings because she wasn't half there anyway. Someone else, usually one of my aunts or a neighbor, got me clothing and put me in school. You helped me after a while. But I wandered around a lot.'

'I know you did,' said Jackie.

'I don't even know where I got the name Tookie.'

'Didn't realize that is your nickname,' said Jackie. 'What's your real name?'

I shifted around, got my feet closer to the fire, turned to look at the door hoping Pollux would come out and save me.

'I can't remember. Maybe I saw it on some official forms a few times,' I said. 'But do you know, I've blocked it out? I guess that's weird.'

'Wait. How'd you register for school? How come I didn't notice? I don't get it how you've gotten away with being Tookie.' Now Jackie was using her teacher voice.

'I went to school my whole life as Tookie. I got my Tookie driver's license. My tribal ID says Tookie. I used my card to get my passport, which I got when I was really young because one of the teachers got me into a summer program in France. But of course I was too stoned to go. Then my old passport was the thing I used to get my new passport and at some point I memorized my Social Security number and had lost my card anyway. So, well, I'm just Tookie.'

'But you have a last name,' said Jackie, 'it must be on your paychecks.'

'I have direct deposit.'

'You'd think I would remember. Want me to look up your real name?'

'No.'

Jackie was now staring hard at me from under her pom-pom. 'I really can't believe this. Just Tookie. Don't you know anything about your real name?'

'My mother named me for somebody who helped

her out, really saved her I guess, when she was pregnant. That's what I've heard.'

'And your mother, is she alive?'

'I don't know if she was ever truly alive,' I said. 'And now she's definitely dead.'

I was troubled by the last part of the conversation and Pollux was inside listening to Asema sing. I could hear 'Blackbird' in her high, sweet voice. I left and took a detour down to the frozen lake, nearly sleepwalking in the dark cold. I revisited the first part of that conversation, about failing as a mom, and it helped switch my gears. I understood that I was doing the opposite of what my own mother did—totally ignoring me. I was intruding. Hetta hated it. I was challenging her autonomy in some respects—she obviously knew that she was acting as a single mother. I was noticing and interfering. I was being a mom. Only I was doing it as a buffalo mom—banging my head on my calf, trying to stomp out a place for her, butting her along whatever path I thought would keep her safe or get her somewhere. I was being awkward and aggravating. I had no finesse. But I had love. Always had. I loved Hetta and her baby. I loved the people I worked with. I'd been in love once in prison. Before that, I'd loved Danae so much that I'd stolen her dead boyfriend for her. And as for Pollux, whom I loved more than any-body in the world, I had built him a life. I was there when he needed me and let him go when he had to go. I worked hard to make things normal and comfortable and bright. I had even been known to make him hot cocoa, but I didn't put in those tiny marshmallows. I didn't mom him. I rarely went over a certain line. And he didn't either. Oh, he fussed sometimes, and wor-ried, and maybe got so mad that it came to the tip of his tongue. He knew. He'd arrested me. He'd married me. And I knew that he knew. But he never said my real name.

Tender Sasquatch

COWBIRDS

The first snow of the new year lifted my burdensome thoughts. The snow brightened and cleaned and filled the air with oxygen. I breathed euphoria all the way to work. I was cheerful even though it was inventory day. And there would be cowbirds. That's what I call the unexpected books that we find here and there in the store during inventory. Throughout the year we are busy feeding the cash register and we do not notice it when people sneak their books onto our shelves. Sadly, we can't accept these books—home-copied, self-published, even occasionally handwritten—because they are a logistical nightmare, tangling our system. I suppose they are also cowbirds because we are providing them expensive shelf space and nurturing them for free, but the authors leave the works as gifts. I like presents. Because it is much easier to digitally self-publish now, the cowbirds increase every year. Culled from the shelves, they fill a box. Our store is so tiny that it amazes me there are so many. I feel for them. Cacoëthes scribendi. Who doesn't have a book in them?

These books are signs of life. The opposite, I thought, of the book buried in my yard.

In the beginning, as I've heard, the first inventory involved taking every book off the shelf to count and catalog. Then the books had to be returned to the shelves. By the end of the week there was weeping, job quitting, Xanax, a stack of pizza boxes. The floor was littered with hopelessly disordered stacks of books. Now, with our handy bar-code zappers, and concerted effort, we can do inventory in one or two strained, super-concentrated days. This time, we were done by seven p.m. and I lugged home a box of cowbirds. It wasn't heavy, but I put it down periodically just to enjoy the end of inventory. I carried the box through the door, stowed it by the couch, and made myself some nachos. Then I settled down to sort through them.

I'm always curious about these authors. There are personal memoirs that depict life in little-known times and places. Many of the books are about loss—brutal, endless, unfathomable loss. Others are about the foibles of adopting a houseplant. Still others are probably about people having sex while wearing blue rubber dishwashing gloves. There are stories of miracle household cures that Big Pharma wants to silence. Everybody seems to have within themselves a collection of poems. There are several books with purple flowers on the gray, lavender, milk white covers. Curiously, they do not have flowers in the titles. *Girl* this or *Girl* that is still popular. A few years ago *The Whatever's Wife* or *Daughter* was a favorite. This is a Bone year. *Bone-bone, BoneyBone-Bone, Daughter of the Bones, Bone Blues, Silver Bones, Coughing Up Bones,* and *Happy Bones,* which I decide to read. There are a couple of novels about cryptids. *Tender Sasquatch* is a love story about 'rough encounters' that ends, the cover tells me, in 'amazement and hope.' I put that aside for Pollux. There's a memoir of working in the Minnesota Department of Natural Resources, one about an owl at the University of Minnesota's Raptor Center, which I keep for myself. There is a book written in a private language that looks like the tracks of shorebirds. This one, I remember from last summer.

The author, a wiry young man with vigilant dark eyes and a thick shock of hair the color of burnt wheat, had been browsing in the store. When the other customers left, he took a few of his own books from his backpack and offered to give them to us in order to contribute their sales price to the store. I really hated to decline. He was one of those beautiful souls who wanders about the lakes, fuzzy chinned, floppy sandaled, thrift shop clothed, an innocent. The book was handmade, the cover a rich rust red, stitched with sinew. The text was unintelligible. He told me how since childhood he had been studying words and grammatical structures in a dead language he'd discovered.

'Hold on,' I said. 'You're saying that during your childhood you discovered a dead language?'

He nodded and his thatch of hair flopped forward.

'This language, how and where?'

The boy waved my questions off and frowned. The language, he said, had a beautiful orthography but no definite articles, no present, no past. Verbs had to be coughed or sung in different pitches. There were a vast number of nouns that completely changed according to whether the object was visible, partly visible, or completely invisible.

'It is a language that really makes you think,' he said.

'I'll bet.'

The writing in the book was sparse, and arranged in graceful paragraphs bounded by wide margins so that you noticed the texture of the paper.

'It's a lovely poem,' I remarked.

'It is fiction,' he shyly said.

He added that it could also be called a family memoir and there was no key to the language, no dictionary, no instructional papers. Yet he didn't think his work would be hard to decipher were the writings to be found in a few thousand years.

'After all, I did it,' he said.

He told me that the writings had come to him line by line while he was hammocking. Perhaps I'd seen him, in fact, swaying among the grove of crab apple trees, perfectly spaced for hammocks, at the park. I had a spasm of maternal feeling. I almost wanted to take this kid home and let Pollux cook for him. He left the store. But he'd slipped this book onto our shelves and now I was quite pleased to have it. I opened the book and was trying to find some pattern in the flow of bird-track marks when Pollux came home. He kicked off his giant runners at the door and walked over to my cozy setup. He sat down next to me.

'What's that? It's weird.'

'It is ancient Potawatomi. Don't you read your traditional language?'

'You speak'um like smug asshole.'

'Funny you should say that. Actually, this book is pretty hot. Did you know that *Fifty Shades of Grey* was actually first written in cuneiform? Ancient clay tablets have been unearthed.'

'Here, you're reading it upside down.'

Pollux turned the book over and gave it back to me.

'Oh, gosh, I now see that this book is actually about the history of the missionary position.'

'I'd like to banter with you, but I'm hungry.'

'How about you make popcorn? Today was inventory. Can you bring me a beer?'

Pollux brought me a beer, and soon he set a huge bowl of popcorn between us. I gave him *Tender Sasquatch*. He said something about Sabe, the Ojibwe hairy giant. Hetta had fixed her car seat into our car and taken Jarvis on a drive to get some organic fast food. It was warm. She planned to eat outside, bundle Jarvis underneath her coat, and walk down to the skating rink with Asema. We were alone. Pollux tapped his computer, pulling up one of his unaccountable playlists—this one Johnny Cash, Tribe Called Red, peyote music from the Native American Church, Cowboy Junkies, Nina Simone, chamber music, Prince. We read for a while, eating the popcorn, sipping the cold Buds. He got up for another beer, putting down the book.

'A tour de force.'

'Oh, you like it?'

'Female Sasquatch carries feeble urban misfit to her lair, teaches him to tend to her needs. Well, she enslaves him, really, but . . .'

He rummaged around in the fridge, came back with a bowl of petite baby carrots.

'But what?'

'I mean it's a great book if you like hairy women. He

writes how he has to part her fur to find her "dugs."
I've never used that word for breasts, you know?'

I had given up on my box and was reading a damaged
copy of *Cool for You*, by Eileen Myles. The book had
arrived with a chapter that was puckered—like maybe
a boy from the institution they were writing about had
carefully scrunched and straightened out the pages. We
are scrupulous about damaged books and when we call
one in we send it back—but Soft Skull Press had sent
us a new copy and told us to keep the old one. 'Did you
ever eat commodities?' I asked Pollux.

'You know I did. My grandma had a closet of commodities that people traded to her. Everybody wanted
the cheese and the peaches.'

'Listen to this. It's from *Cool for You*. *Is there a
recipe book for everyone? In America, when it comes
down to that: here's something for everyone, a book or
a cup of coffee, a bowl of oatmeal . . . food that anyone
would eat when they had finally been determined to
be in that position that they would eat anyone's food. I
don't mean eating from the dumpster. I mean the me-
chanical lunches you got in school. Those vegetables
no one wanted because you could see they had been
prepared for anyone. Extra food. To think you might
wind up eating it one day, looking around, the day you
forgot who you were.*'

'Whoa,' said Pollux after a minute. 'That's heavy. "The day you forgot who you were." Wait up. Let me see.'

He read the passage again.

I'd read this part several times already, because it was like that with me. At first, I refused to eat the food at the corrections facility. Then, one day, I ate the food I most despise—mashed rutabagas. I wasn't starving, but I ate them anyway. After that, I ate greedily. I drank the weak black acid from Styrofoam cups, too. A lot of women had money for commissary snacks, but I didn't. I could feel the coffee and the rutabagas doing something to me that was a lot like eating commodity food—only until I'd read this paragraph I didn't know what that was. These were the foods of forgetfulness and I was soon overtaken by an oblivious calm.

'The day you forgot who you were,' said Pollux.

'I did lose my scalding wit. As you know, my first lockup was in Thief River Falls. At first, it was hard to embrace the irony.'

Pollux leaned over to hug me.

'It wasn't just thieving. It was grand larceny plus,' he said in his soft rumbly voice. 'Gotta respect that.'

'Good ol' Ted. I was touched that he tried to get it reduced to petty.'

Pollux looked serious, thoughtful.

'You're not a petty person,' he said at last. 'Anyways, we underestimated Ted.'

'I sure did. He was a hero, but addicted to McDonald's fries, which probably killed him.'

Ted always tried to eat his fries within thirty seconds of purchase, when they're the best. Then he'd buy another bag and slam it too. I was still sad about his death. A lesson for the ages.

'In contrast, I have wabooz,' said Pollux, 'the kind of food that tells you who you are. Traditional.'

'Where'd you get a rabbit?'

He put his finger to his lips.

'Did you snare it in the backyard?'

'I fought a lady sasquatch for it.'

'If you say dugs, I'm sleeping in the attic.'

'That word's not a turn-on for me. I am going to fricassee, which is kind of a sexy word, but don't watch. Green salad. Those crispy potatoes you like. Now put the book down. Pick up a light read, huh? Enjoy yourself. Watch TV!'

'No thanks. Did you ever forget who you were?'

'The powdered eggs confused me,' said Pollux. 'But you know when she says that thing about everybody in America having a recipe book? I like that. We ate government commodities, sure, but we had our recipes. We made that stuff ours. And we had food, which is the thing. If we could get there, I mean, to the warehouse, we could get the food. I know you did too. And later, it wasn't like we were in jail like you had to be, honey. Noko grew squash, corn, all that. We had a garden.'

Pollux's grandma was the biggest thing I envied him for. I had aunties and some cousins. But my mother's addictions had cut us off from even our own people.

'Your grandma.'

'My grandma.'

Pollux was the child of an American Indian Movement charismatic apostle man who preached the cause to his mother when she was sixteen years old. His mother had not survived the 1970s, and his grandmother had brought him up like an old-timer. I love the ohhhhhlllllld wayyyyyyyzzzz, he liked to say, drawing it out like he had some special sage knowledge, nodding all wise-eyed and serene.

'Can we do it the ohhhhlllld wayyyyy later on?' I asked him.

'Maybe we can do it right now, right here. Keep the instructions open,' he said, taking the unreadable book from me and propping it against a pillow.

'That's okay. I'm really hungry.'

Pollux got up, dusting his hands against his pants.

'I got that covered, Tender Sasquatch,' he said, walking to the kitchen.

LAURENT

One day we had every kind of snow. First there was a gorgeous slow downdraft that turned into a whiteout ground blizzard when the wind came up. Then the sun blazed out above the ground blizzard and provoked a strange reflective intensity. The wind died down and now the snow was big lolloping masses that built up on every surface. At last the snow ceased and the world was white, deep, radiant. Now at last, with snow sealing the book into the earth, I thought maybe I'd be able to put these events in order.

I was constructing a mental bulletin board with clippings, photos, strings making connections like in detective shows. I intended to map it out for real, but things got complicated at the bookstore. Early the next afternoon, I came on second shift, and saw the author of the unreadable book, the hammock youth. He was back, and deep in conversation with Asema. I have to say, she'd chosen a striking look for the day. Her hair was in Princess Leia coils. She wore a dark red knit baby-doll dress, very short, with indigo leggings. Her beaded mukluks. A large sky blue chunk of turquoise dangled from one ear. Perfect with her round symmetrical face. The young author's winter gear consisted of a bristling fur hat, vaguely Russian. He had a large nose and his dark eyes fixed on me for a moment with that strange innocence I'd noticed before, as if he were a visitor flung here from a different time. He didn't remember me. His tawny hat startled me. Before, he'd been an ordinary dreamer. But today the fellow looked like a beautiful animal with its tail curled on its head. He was also wearing an oversized tweed greatcoat and construction boots. His sensitive fingers poked from his frayed black knitted gloves. The two stopped talking when I walked in. I could tell that they wanted me to pass by without chatting so that they could resume their interaction. As I shelved the books that had been received into the system, I couldn't help hearing little snatches of their conversation. Asema was talking.

'White people can't be decolonized, I mean, as the historical colonizers you can't claim that for yourself too! Come on!'

'Don't you see past skin? I'm Métis. Or French. And also Irish. We were colonized by the British.'

'Do you speak Gaelic? Is that book Cree syllabic? Michif? The one you gave me with the really intense geometric shapes?' Asema paused, slapping a book down. 'Are you actually from Ireland or did you grow up Métis? Did you grow up immersed in any of your probable cultures?'

'Define "immersed."'

'You know, like you're in it all the time. From the beginning. Did your parents come from Ireland?'

'My great-grandparents. There was a famine. You ever hear of that?'

'Sure. Maybe. But I don't know if you can call your-self Indigenous unless you have personally suffered from colonization.'

'I remind you, I'm Métis,' said the young man.

'You sounded iffy on that,' said Asema.

Fur Hat shrugged. 'What about you, do you speak Dakota or Ojibwe?'

'I'm not fluent, but yes.'

'What about your name?'

'I have three names, Dakota and Ojibwe, and English.'

'Which one is English?'

'Asema, of course.'

I sneaked a glance at her because that wasn't true. Asema is the Ojibwe word for 'sacred tobacco.' She was heavy into her interrogation, opening her mouth with another jabbing question. But he tried to turn the tables on her.

'So what's up with you? Are you actually from the reservation? Did you grow up with both of your cul-tures? Immersed, as you say?'

'I grew up here. There's tons of culture in my family. So shut up.'

The two poked around for a while murmuring about books, opening and shutting them, and in a while she asked his name.

'My mother named me Laurent. My dad wanted me to have his father's name.'

'What was that?'

'Jarvis.'

I loomed out of the Young Adult section to take a closer look at the fellow who had mentioned my wee idol.

Jarvis?

'I think Laurent's okay,' said Asema with an offhand shrug but a sideways glance.

They continued to meander around the store until in some undetectable way it seemed they had agreed to meet again, and he left. For a while I worked alongside Asema, silently staring into the computer screen and, between customers, responding to online orders. Jackie came in, paced across the floor, vanished.

'What do you think?' Asema finally said.

'Of?'

'Laurent.'

'Not much. Turns out I have one of his books.'

'I hoped it was in Gaelic or syllabics, but no. It's this language he says is much older than Gaelic.'

'He told me it's fiction. Did he tell you the plot?'

'He said it's about a boy who admires a girl working

in a bookstore but he's too shy to approach her. When he finally does it turns out that she liked him too.'

My heart jumped. I gave her a sharp look. I was gripped by instant fury.

'What a line.'

'I kind of liked him up until that.'

'You still like him,' I said in a way that made Asema step back, adjust one of her headbuns, and say, 'So?'

I was in a stew. I was sure the foxlike boy was the nameless father of Hetta's baby. The secretive hammock boy. I'd been drawn in by his innocence, which I now suspected was fake. When looking at Asema there was an avidity in this fellow's eyes, a sense . . . I tried to tell Pollux later . . . not only had he mentioned Hetta's baby's name, Jarvis, but he'd also sketched out a flirtatious plot synopsis tailored for Asema the way Hetta's had been for her. Now everything about him disturbed me, even the fur hat.

My husband had come by to pick me up. I'd stayed after hours to fill online orders. Pollux and I left the car at the store and walked the night's snowy streets. Halos of frosty air hung around the streetlamps.

'In addition to those coincidences, which, I must say, couldn't possibly be coincidences, I don't think he's safe,' I said. 'This Laurent was waiting for Asema to get off work. He was waiting outside. When they were in the store, he followed her in a certain way. It seemed to me that there was something lurkish about him. But maybe I'm reading too much?'

'Oh, being lurkish. It's perfectly normal,' said Pollux with fake concern. 'I'm just sorry you had to witness it.'

'No really, it was sort of vulpine, I mean it wasn't "curious cute animal" like you think is normal. It was more *animal*.'

'I don't know how to take that. And you're acting like a mom. So suspecting.'

Pollux raised his broken eyebrow and even started to shake his head.

'Don't tut-tut me, husband.'

He stopped. 'You probably have the best intentions.' I nodded in agreement. 'Sometimes they do the worst harm.' I thought immediately of Flora.

'Okay, I'll try to pull back.'

⁂

Pollux and I planned to visit Lyle's, one of the last great dive bar/restaurants left on Hennepin Avenue. Lyle's was being encroached on by artisanal shops and fine-dining establishments. On the way back to the car, we could walk off a Saturday night drink if we had a Saturday night drink. It was about 12 degrees, warm enough for Minneapolis. We wore parkas, fleece hats, padded gloves, Sorels. But we still got chilled enough that it was pleasant to reach Lyle's and walk inside. We got our favorite shiny red booth, against the wall, where we could see the rest of the night crowd. Pollux ordered cheese curds and breakfast. Me the spicy grilled cheese with bacon and jalapeños. Pollux ordered a rum and Coke.

'Gross,' I said.

I asked for hot tea and the waiter gave me a solicitous *of course*.

'When you don't order booze here, it means you're an alcoholic,' said Pollux.

There were a good number of young people from the 1940s-era brick apartment buildings and condos behind the restaurant. They were wearing interesting retro clothes and were tattooed or had gauged ears, pastel blue or violet hair, string bracelets, piercings. Laurent entered, wearing the fur hat. He walked over to a group of women by the arcade games.

'Look'—I nudged Pollux—'it's the fox boy.'

The young author, a book in one hand, tried to talk to a woman with a scarlet mullet and shiny black lips. She elbowed him aside. He nearly lost hold of the book but he tried again, and this time she shoved him hard enough to make him lose his balance. He stumbled backward, grabbed a chair; the book spun across the floor. He didn't lose his hat, didn't seem to be drunk, and he didn't get angry, but he didn't leave her alone either. He stood up, retrieved the book, and began to speak to her. He showed her the book, riffled its pages, tipping his head from side to side. I caught a glimpse of the title. *Empire of Wild*, by Cherie Dimaline.

'Maybe we should hire him,' I said.

I liked his salesman's passion; his taste in books was excellent, but he was still suspect.

Our food came. The waiter obscured the drama, arranged our plates of fried stuff, eggs, and sausage, the ketchup bottle. When the waiter left, I saw that all of the young people in that group had disappeared.

'Should I say something about fox boy? I mean, to Hetta? Or maybe to Asema?'

Pollux gave me a critical stare. 'Weren't you just going to hire him? Besides, you agreed to lay off this fellow.'

'I said I'd be tolerant, that's all. And if we all sold books that way we'd be shut down.'

Pollux shrugged and shook his head over the cheese curds.

'Stale grease.'

'The fox boy's stale grease.'

'Loser gibe,' said Pollux. 'Keep your nose out of it.

It's not like he got engaged to Asema, right? And if he was Jarvis's father he would be staying with us.'

'Why do you even think that? Obviously he's avoiding his responsibilities. He's slinking around.'

I said this because the way he moved gave off that ready-to-pounce vibe.

'Slinking around promoting literature,' said Pollux. He made a sound.

'Was that a snort of disdain?'

'No,' said Pollux. 'It was a grunt of exasperation.'

I laughed. 'You are a grunter, true.'

'A proud grunter.'

I picked up a cheese curd. Put it down.

'You okay?'

I started eating so he wouldn't ask that. The grease tasted fine to me. Keep your nose out of it. Pollux was right. I thought of my failures with our daughter. What made me think that I could suddenly become a person trusted by twenty-somethings, even useful to them in any way? Besides, there was a young person who had actually asked me for help. I switched focus. Kateri had tried to get in touch with me right after Christmas and I'd just let the phone ring. I knew that I had to talk to her. I had to tell her about her mother's persistence. But our last conversation had so unnerved me that I dreaded talking to her again. So I had procrastinated, avoided. With Pollux in full eating mode I sneaked a glance at the transcribed voicemail message she'd left. There had been no news of a memorial, just *Kateri here, call me back*. I hadn't called, nor did I answer her one later text—*Call me*—ostensibly because I was so busy with inventory. But then inventory was over and I still didn't answer. There was no excuse. A bereaved young woman had reached out to me and I'd ignored her.

Pollux and I finished eating, lingered in the satisfying raucous, seedy, happy atmosphere, then walked back. The cold was deeper, the dark blacker, the hard air reassuringly Minnesota. We held hands although no warmth passed between our clumpy ski gloves. As I walked, I resolved that tomorrow I would call Kateri.

Still, it took me all morning to choke back dread. We were busy at the store after Sunday brunch next door, then there was an unavoidable lull. It took until late afternoon for me to dial Kateri's number.

She answered.

'It's you.'

'I'm sorry . . .'

'No need for that. Glad I don't have to track you down. Tuesday's the day.'

'For?'

'What do you think? They're going to cremate her

and I've insisted that I have to watch her body go in. Just to make sure.'

'No!'

'You're coming.'

'I . . .'

'You're coming.'

'I'll pass out. I can't be around stuff like that.'

'Tough shit. I need you.'

I wasn't Kateri's mother, I wasn't Kateri's mother's best friend. And as for Flora, I wasn't sure cremation would cramp her style. She'd been in the store that very morning, rustling around in Poetry. I really had to talk about this with Kateri.

'Listen. Can we talk?'

'We are talking.'

'I think we should meet in person,' I said. 'Maybe before the . . . before Tuesday.'

'Why?'

'God! You're irritating. But okay, you asked for it. Here's what I want to say. Your mother's ghost has been hanging around the bookstore, coming in every morning and browsing around, just like she used to when she was alive.'

It seemed that now Kateri had nothing to say, so I went on.

'No, I'm not crazy, not even creeped out anymore.

Flora comes in every morning. I don't actually see her, but I hear her. I know exactly what she sounds like. She was even in this morning, shooting my hopes that she'd decently quit once—'

'She told me about your stupid jokes. This isn't funny. Stop lying. Stop being a jackass.'

I tried my best not to hang up on her, or to apologize. But it was true. I used to tease Flora by setting her bogus tasks. She once cleaned out my garage trying to find a lost sacred scroll. A birchbark scroll that did not exist. For that, I would probably go to Ojibwe hell. It occurred to me that I was in it—haunted by a wannabe ghost. I finally said, in a placating tone, that I hadn't wanted to tell her about her mother's spectral presence on the phone. I had been worried this would upset her, and what could I do?

'You can come with me to get her cremated,' she said, in a slow sad voice to which it was impossible to reply with any word but yes.

PURGATORY?

Pollux had gone off to a ceremony taking his pipe, his drum, his eagle feathers, his medicine bundle, and two large pots of cooked wild rice. He had left me a foil-wrapped container of wild rice, which I ate standing over the sink. Both nutty *and* silky, I thought. This sort of eating was demoralizing. I'd seen my mother do this and it was a sign to me of desolation. It made me feel crummy and lost like *the day I lost myself.* At least Hetta didn't see me. She was exhausted, always taking naps with Jarvis, staying in her room a lot. Maybe just avoiding me.

Our job reviews are casual, mostly a chance to catch up. Louise had asked me over to her house about a week ago, so I went over. Anyway, I did not want to be alone with the prospect of tomorrow's cremation. I texted her that I was on my way, but she didn't answer. I expected her to come out of her mysterious warren of office rooms with that tense DWW—Disturbed While Writing—look on her face. But when I knocked on the kitchen door, I heard a muffled biindigen! and entered. All I could see of Louise was the top half of her that was not in the cabinet under the kitchen sink saying 'Fuckity fuck fuck fuck!' I waited. She emerged, an old sock in her hand. She threw the sock away, thrust her fist up, and cried, 'As God is my witness, I will never hide Halloween candy under the kitchen sink again!' She dropped her fist and looked at me, still a bit crazed. At last she focused and laughed. 'Sorry, that was an epic amount of mouse shit, Tookie. What's up?'

'You invited me over.'

'Oh yeah. Of course. C'mon in.'

I shuffled off my boots. I wore thick wool socks because in spite of the many rugs her floor is always cold.

'How's the job?' she asked at once.

'Let's leave that for later.'

'I'll make a fire,' said Louise.

There was a bank of votive candles in the fireplace. Once lighted, they flickered up into the tiles. It wasn't a real fire, but I didn't want a long explanation about why she didn't build real fires in her working fireplace, so I said nothing. The candles were pleasant and at least gave the illusion of warmth.

'I should have one of those little tin boxes with a coin slot,' she mused. 'The kind they have in old churches to pay for the candles. Get somebody out of purgatory.'

'Maybe Flora,' I said.

'Think she's in purgatory?'

'It's possible, if by purgatory you mean the packing station at the store. I often feel like I'm stuck there. But no. She's in a crematory and tomorrow I have to go over there with Kateri and make sure all goes well.'

'That's good of you. I'll make tea.'

She went to boil some water and then we sat in the drafty living room drinking ginger lemon as the light went blue. My heart was weakly sinking because I'd mentioned Flora. I tried to rally. Now was the time to talk to Louise about the rest of it. Everything: the book—the killing sentence. How Flora was still there. We were rational, alone, solving no big crisis. There was calming tea. But of course I found it daunting to launch such a conversation. At last I decided there was no choice.

'So . . . I've never talked about my past to you. But I think Flora might be haunting me because of it. I went to prison because I stole a deceased person's body. A guy named Budgie. My original sentence was sixty years. And please don't tell me that was a stiff sentence.'

Louise had opened her mouth, but looked embarrassed and only said, 'That's a lot of years for stealing a body.'

'There were factors involved,' I went on. 'I moved him across state lines. And the kicker, he was wearing drugs.' I began immediately to babble. 'But I mean, the more I found out people's sentences, the more random I realized sentencing even is. There were baby killers who only served seven years and women who killed abusive, kill-or-be-killed husbands who were in for life. There was a woman who bought a gun for a guy who used it in a murder. She got a longer sentence than the guy who pulled the trigger.'

I paused because something had turned on in Louise, and she was listening. Not in a normal way, but with the offhand efficiency of a goddamn human tape recorder. And I don't know what it was but the times she did this I could not stop talking. It was an effort to pull back and remember there was something I needed to ask her.

'So Louise,' I said. 'I want to ask you about why some people are trouble even dead, why they refuse to leave. Jackie referred to people who resist death.'

'That's most of us.'

'It's more than that. Flora won't stay dead, can you please tell me why?'

'Oh god, *this*. Oh well. Okay. You've heard of a rugaroo.'

'No.'

'It could be a rugaroo sort of thing. I'm not saying this is what's happening, but there are Michif people who have told me about the rugaroo.'

'Michif? Like Métis? Mixed-bloods?'

'Yes. I remember hearing the rugaroo is a wolf person who keeps coming back to life and who returns to certain places,' said Louise. 'I don't exactly know where. I suppose they were places where it hadn't finished some wolf business?'

A wolf person sounded more like Hetta's fur hat fellow. But returners sounded more like my ghost.

'Flora definitely has unfinished business at the bookstore,' I said. 'There's this book that she was—'

Louise struck her forehead.

'She wants the book she ordered! Oh, Tookie! She wanted *In Mad Love and War*. It finally came in—but of course I took it from behind the counter.'

'You think she came back from the dead . . . for a book?'

'Not just any book.'

'Wait. Seriously?'

Louise brooded into the flickering lopsided candles.

'It bothers me that Flora could have died reading poetry and here I was selfish and took the book just when she needed it most.'

'Forget that.'

'I've been such a hog about books, about everything really, with Flora. But she betrayed history . . .'

'Stop it, Louise! She died from reading a book. A book killed her.'

'People die from reading books, of course!'

'What I'm trying to say . . .'

'Books aren't meant to be safe. Sadly, or heroically, depending on the way you look at it, books do kill people.'

'In places where books are forbidden, of course, but not here. Not yet. Knock wood. What I'm trying to say is that a certain sentence of the book—a written sentence, a very powerful sentence—killed Flora.'

Louise was silent. After a few moments she spoke. 'I wish I could write a sentence like that.'

1,700 DEGREES

Flora had squirreled away money to be immolated at the crematory at Lakewood Cemetery. Not knowing this, Kateri had chosen the first crematory, the one that mixed up Flora's ashes, from an online ad. 'So much for Yelp,' she'd said disconsolately. Now, Kateri said, it was like her mother knew and refused to go there. I suppressed my reaction. It turned out Flora had loved to walk in Lakewood—I knew nothing about it. Kateri said the place was set up to be nonprofit but getting buried there cost a pile. The proceeds of the cremation went to keep up the acres of calm trees and meditative roads that wound up and down the gentle snowy hills and among the dramatic monuments of the last century. Flora probably liked the massive granite headstones and stone statues, calm and melancholy now against the snow and snow-dusted trees. The whole place was very cereal-baron Minneapolis, so maybe for Flora, getting cremated there was aspirational. That, or old cereal-baron Minneapolis was her true and actual heritage. Of course, she also may have known that the Dakota leader known in English as Cloud Man is said to be buried nearby.

We entered an eccentrically beautiful rose-stone chapel. The ceiling was high, with recessed lighting, craftsman-style pillars. It was all right angles and careful colors. Not comforting, but not awful. We sat on one of the couches and waited for Flora's body to be brought out.

'She'll be in a plain wood box. It was what she wanted. Mom once mentioned that she wanted her ashes strewn in the lake, but she didn't say which lake. Another time, she said she wanted to be buried in the roots of a tree.'

'Graves to Groves,' I mumbled, remembering my impromptu business idea. 'I'm getting dizzy.'

'So am I. But this place is super-normal, right?'

'For a crematory.'

'And yet we're still dizzy.'

The attendant wheeled Flora's body into the viewing room. Maybe this was unusual, but Kateri needed to make sure. I got that. We followed. He removed the lid of the box and set it on a table. Then he stepped away and put his hands behind his back. He stood against the wall. We stood by the box. Kateri lowered her gaze to her mother's face.

'It's not so bad,' she said. 'You can look.'

I glanced down, but unfocused my eyes, so that Flora was a harmless blur. This was not a time I wanted clarity.

'Am I crazy,' Kateri asked in a low voice, 'or does she look younger?'

So then I had to look.

Flora's large, soft, pretty face had lost its eagerness. Of course. She was hardly looking forward to what came next. She did not have Budgie's otherworldly severity. However, she seemed to have gathered herself, prepared for what was to come. The immolation, the pulverization, the being poured into a much smaller wooden box, the being carried away from this place. Her inanimate bravery squeezed my heart. Did she look younger? I tried to tell Kateri that it was the way death relaxed all tensions. For she certainly did look younger, remarkably younger, in spite of the long refrigeration.

I stepped away in a fizz of mental disruption. Kateri stood beside Flora, staring at her mother in stricken silence, moving only her lips. She was praying, I thought. This suspension went on for some time. Finally, Kateri gave a nod to indicate that the attendant should take her mother away. Thank god. I averted my eyes from Flora's disturbingly youthful face. Kateri followed the attendant out the door. I had no idea whether the actual cremation happened there, or somewhere else, or how long I had to wait.

Alone, I had to get out of my surroundings the way I used to in prison. There, I had learned to read with a force that resembled insanity. Once free, I found that I could not read just any book. It had gotten so I could see through books—the little ruses, the hooks, the setup in the beginning, the looming weight of a tragic ending, the way at the last page the author could whisk out the carpet of sorrow and restore a favorite character. I needed the writing to have a certain mineral density. It had to feel naturally meant, but not cynically contrived. I grew to dislike manipulations. For instance, besides the repetitive language, my problem with (my now beloved) Elena Ferrante was her use of the winking cliffhanger. Sometimes I wanted to weep when I detected both talent and abused talent in a writer. The life of the writer cannot help but haunt the narrative. Because of the force of the gift, I went along with certain novels. *Tender Is the Night.* Or the work of Jean Rhys. Talent abused sometimes beams off the page with generous humility. Now I wanted to read books that make me forget the elegant cellular precision of a baby vs. the entropic flow of human flesh toward the disorder of death. I want to read books that make me forget the $1.43 breakdown into our component parts.

But the story I read at the crematory was about a birthday party for a very old woman. The story, which was by Clarice Lispector, ended with the unavoidable line: Death was her mystery.

I liked that. After the detailed description of the birthday party—the cake, the intent children, the tablecloth soiled with spilled Coke. After the old woman's refreshingly dark disdain for her family. Death was her mystery.

About forty-five minutes passed, and then Kateri returned. She stood next to the couch, slumped, drained of will. She had slicked back her hair but it had rebelled and stuck out in stiff tufts. Her clear and regular features were distorted, her eyes were puffy from weeping.

'I saw Mom go in. She's safe. I'll get the ashes in a couple of days. You drive.'

DIVINATION

Next morning at the bookstore, no Flora. Eleven a.m. passed and still, no Flora. It was such an intense relief that I could feel my heart lift. All day, I pulled the sweetgrass-smelling quiet around me like a magic blanket. Perhaps the fire cleansed or satisfied. I hoped so. With each day that passed, I began to feel more like myself. She didn't appear and she didn't appear. She didn't appear! During those January days, cold, gray, and dull, I was happier than I'd been since before Flora's so-called death. The cold air was delicious. The gray calm. The dullness soothing. My heart was buoyant. I woke up each morning with the feeling that something special had happened. When I remembered that my haunting was lifted, I sat up and stretched my arms like a young movie ingenue in white, sex-rumpled sheets.

But then, but then. On the fifth day, as I puttered cheerfully along, there was a rustle, a footstep, a gloating clink of bracelet charms. I froze. Then began the sound of meddlesome rustling and the subtle scuffing sounds of Flora's thin-soled fashion boots. I sagged behind the counter. A physical disappointment came over me and I slumped. Such heaviness. My eyes teared up in weariness, in frustration. To be haunted is worse than one can imagine. Although I was alone, I was never *alone*. I was under Flora's eye. Now, again, with a grinding sense of woe, I listened for her whereabouts. As the day wore on, it also seemed to me that her noises were bolder, more emphatic, as if going through the fire had enlivened rather than destroyed her. I thought of her body, her spectral acquisition of youth and vitality. I could tell from the sweep of her clothing and her footsteps the outfit she had chosen. Those fashion boots I mentioned? She had been wearing them on her trip through the 1,700-degree fire.

I concluded there was no stopping her.

Sometimes I utilize a form of bibliomancy, or dictionariomancy, to give me a clue as to what in the foggy blue hell is going to happen next. My method is this: I make myself a pot of Evening in Missoula tea, pretend that I'm in Missoula, where I've never been. I light a wand of Nag Champa incense, pretend that I'm uncountable, which is the meaning of Nag Champa. I light whatever candle is handy. I am alone when I do this, not only out of respect for Pollux's sensibilities. I would be embarrassed for anybody else to know that this is how I make rational decisions. It was a warm winter day, so Hetta and Pollux were out strolling with Jarvis, who was bundled and wrapped like a tiny mummy. The time was now. In an aura of ceremonial gravity, I set the dictionary down on the coffee table. I cleared my mind. I closed my eyes, opened up the dictionary, and let my finger drift until it touched down on a word.

Divination n. 1. The art or act of foretelling future events or revealing occult knowledge by means of augury or alleged supernatural agency. 2. An inspired guess or a presentiment. 3. That which has been divined.

My source confirmed my instinct and my finger landed on exactly what I was doing. My augur told me that something was coming. But I was annoyed. I thought the dictionary got it wrong because that something, the wraith of Flora, was already here. I was wrong. Something else was definitely on its way.

THE END OF JANUARY

I was setting the till up with banknotes from the cash-box the next morning when a very different, confounding, even disturbing note came to my hand. People stow things beneath the cash drawer—checks, lists of duties for opening and closing the store, random addresses, and unfulfillable requests. This piece of writing was very different. For one thing, it was typed on a real typewriter, and not an electric typewriter but a manual one. I know because Jackie used to have a manual typewriter in her classroom to show us that there was a form of technology between handwriting and a computer keyboard. The typewriting imparted character to the writing on the sheet and also made it look like an artifact from another age. I probably wouldn't have bothered to read what was written except for that, and the connection between the title and last night's dictionary word.

Foretelling

by weights, by strangers, by the texture of hair. by shade, by clouds, by itches, by piss. by the shapes in smoke, by things accidentally heard or felt but unseen. by the bites of spiders and geometry of webs. by the scratching of squirrels, by the grass in birds' nests, by the promptings of your soul. by snakes and cheese. by wind and rats. by striations burned in bark and the shapes of lightning. by ashes, by buttocks, by boxes on steps. by the bones of animals, burnt straw, marks on skin. by skulls and beetle tracks. by the shuffle of your

playlist. by the moon and worn-out
shoes. by the riddle of bird shit.

　　by sleep.

　　by fire.

　　by stars and feral pigs. by
needles, by dust, by the accidental
formation of circles and spheres.
by fingernail moons and fingernail
clippings. by the guts of roosters,
soot and scars. by salt, by scales,
by flight patterns of bees. by breath,
by arrows, by the trilling of spring
frogs. by bowls of brass. by wax,
by noises of nameless origin. by
scattering old keys. by leaves. by
sprouting onions, by dripping blood.
by saints, by stones, by water, by
the yowling of cats. by the knife,
by the lines in your face, hands,
wrists. by the soles of your feet
and scribbling in the dark. by daily
numbers and useless coins.

　　by horse.

　　by flower.

　　by computers when they quit, when
they can take no more. by balloons

```
when they burst. by tears, the
words of children, wrinkles formed
in cloth. by the tiny explosions of
breath in mice, by the exertions
of ants. by moonstones, by metal,
by teeth. by shadows, by sneezes,
by what's in a thought. by your
nose and eyes. by who you are. by
science.
    by what's outside the window.
    at the door.
```

I placed the typewritten page carefully back in the drawer, fit the tray over it, counted the bills and coins into the till, and resolved not to think of it again. Fat chance. I thought about it all day and found myself worrying about who had or hadn't written it and what it meant. After I found Foretelling, it seemed to me things started moving faster. The effect of that barrage of typed words was odd—I felt I should be doing something to get ready for something I could not define. The foretelling was a divination, and a warning.

Let Me In

FEBRUARY 2020

'**You have** to see this,' I said to Jackie, lifting the divided tray.

I riffled through the papers, but Foretelling was gone. I described what I'd seen to Jackie, but she only gave me a troubled look.

Of what I should do, there was no hint. It reminded me of what Pollux said once about owls. That when you are approached by an owl, when you don't seek it out but it flies to you or perches on your fence, say, the owl is telling you to prepare yourself. Prepare yourself for what? That sort of warning can drive you crazy. Impossible to know how to avoid something when you don't know what it is. I half-suspected someone in the store of setting up a prank, but dropped that idea because nobody came forward to gloat. I even thought that maybe Louise, who was always full of forebodings before a book tour, had written and retrieved it. I called her to ask.

'Did you write a poem and leave it in the till?'

'Why would I do that?'

'How would I know? I found a poem that provoked a lot of uneasiness in me. Then it was gone.'

'Uneasiness. When I have these feelings, I update my will,' said Louise. 'Shall I leave you the bookstore?'

'No.'

I asked Louise when she was leaving.

'March 1. Yeah, I'm gonna update my will.'

'God, Louise. Relax. It's February 15. What can happen in a couple of weeks?' I said.

'So much,' she answered.

Before she left on her tour, Louise read at Plymouth Congregational Church, standing at a pulpit lectern overlooking people seated side by side in the light-filled space. After the reading, she hugged people, held their hands, hugged again. As always after a reading she looked stunned and flustered. Penstemon and I were selling books at the book table. Jackie had baked stacks of oatmeal spice cookies to make things festive. There was also wine, cheese, crackers, the works, all laid out on another table. Louise's daughters were sitting with her. They were trying to keep people from reaching out, crowding in. If nobody else was, they were worried about the rumors of a novel virus. Afterward, they made Louise wash her hands. Emerging from the church into the cold, she gave me a blank, troubled look.

'Onward,' I said, handing her one of Jackie's cookies. She smiled at the cookie and took a bite.

I asked her to text me from each stop.

On the day of the first coronavirus death in the United States, she flew out with a plastic bag of bleach wipes from her sister, a public health doctor working with the Minneapolis Indian Health Board. Louise texted me from Washington, D.C., to say that the reading at Politics and Prose had been as usual perfectly run with a madly intelligent crowd. 'They made an announcement,' she wrote. 'No touching the author. And counters at hotels are sprouting bottles of hand sanitizer.'

March 5. San Antonio. '11 cases off a cruise ship. They say it is contained. Half the people at this conference bowed out. Buffet dinner at an outdoor patio—LaFonda. I've never eaten such good Mexican food, and I was in the most charming company. But I had such a strange sensation as I looked around the soft-lighted patio and people were laughing as they ate together. It all seemed to be happening in an old photograph. We need sanitizer at the store. Can you and Jackie get some?'

March 8. Dallas. 'Walked into an empty hotel. Desk staff in a trance, staring at the doors. Bartender and waitress watching a soccer match. They keep bringing food I haven't ordered because I'm the only customer. Another madly intelligent crowd. Why is there a picture of a giant padlock on my wall?'

She sent a picture of the giant padlock. I texted back, 'Empty hotel. Should we worry?'

'I'm wiping down absolutely everything,' she answered.

March 9. Houston. 'Jovial people at reading. High spirits. Man in book line with harrowing cough. At hotel elevator—guy with soul patch, case of Colt 45, woman in red designer ball gown on each arm. I wanted to get in and find out their story. But the skirts were huge and maybe it was obvious.'

March 11. Lawrence, Kansas. 'Known for John Brown's raids and first case of 1918 influenza on American soil.'

For Native people it is known for Haskell Indian Nations University. A Historical Indigenous University. It had started as a government boarding school. Every tribal person had someone who went to Haskell or was going there now. Louise was excited to read at Haskell. This was the high point of the tour. Her great-aunts had been educated at Haskell and done well in life. Her grandfather had run away from the place when he was a child. He made it all the way back from Kansas to the

Turtle Mountains of North Dakota, just under the Canadian border. 'How, I wonder?' she texted. The book she was touring for was about her grandfather, Patrick Gourneau.

After reading on the campus in a historic gym covered with hand-painted Native-inspired art deco designs, after a prayer fire, after meeting her new friend, Carrie, the librarian, after the smart, funny, sharply beautiful students and teachers, and Raven Books, Louise checked her phone. There were texts from her sisters and there was a text from one of her daughters that said, *Please come home*. The never used words startled her into packing that night. By the next day it was clear that death was in the air.

MARCH 14

Pollux and I went through our jumbled drawers in the bathroom cabinet looking for whatever can kill a virus. Found half a bottle of hydrogen peroxide, which Pollux said only killed bacteria. There was also a quarter bottle of isopropyl alcohol, and a full bottle of Hetta's favorite vodka.

'I thought she'd stopped,' said Pollux.

'I did stop,' said Hetta, happening in on our bathroom-foraging scene. 'That's from before, when I'd hide in here to get wasted.'

'You sure you stopped?'

Hetta glared at him. Her eyeliner intensified her resentment so it burned me too. Pollux gave her the dad-eye. I knew that neither would back down. I must mollify.

'Vodka's great for cleaning,' I said.

'It's great for all kinds of things,' said Hetta. Her voice was wistful.

'It won't kill a virus, but it's good for washing windows,' said Pollux. 'I'm proud of you, Hetta, you sobered up for Jarvis. You'll always be his hero.'

'Right now I need a drink, though,' said Hetta. 'This whole thing sucks. I'm trapped here with you guys.'

'What could be worse,' said Pollux. 'Oh dang. I meant to say *It could be worse*. It could be!'

Hetta looked shaken at the prospect of living with us for an unknown amount of time. I too was shaken. However, there was no way I'd have Jarvis around without Hetta, so I offered to make cookies. They ignored me.

'Maybe we should sit down,' said Pollux, sitting down on the edge of the bathtub.

'And talk about it? In the bathroom? I don't know

why,' I said. 'I just offered to make cookies. What else is there to say?'

Hetta and I hadn't had a conversation in ten weeks. With the baby to absorb the awkwardness, it had been easy. She would bundle Jarvis up and hand him to me. I'd hold on to him until he needed her.

'We don't need cookies. We need to talk,' said Pollux.

'We do need cookies,' said Hetta.

She slid a glance at me. You got it, triple sugar, I nodded. The two of us stared defiantly at Pollux.

'I'm not scared of you ladies,' Pollux said. 'So quit putting your hex on me.'

Hetta and I groaned at the same moment and Pollux laughed at us.

⁕

Soon the terrible stories started: how you suffocate while the doctor's back is turned, or turn blue and die in your chair waiting for an ambulance, how this, how that, how your lungs turn to glass. One day I woke up with a sore throat. This is it, I thought. I lay in bed feeling every sensation.

'Stay away from me,' I said to Pollux.

He was bumbling around the room, picking up my

socks, which I could never manage to take off and roll together. I always tossed them off my toes.

'Don't pick up my socks,' I said. 'They might have the virus on them.'

Pollux dropped the socks and asked me what was wrong.

'I have a sore throat.'

Pollux gave me a glass of water from his side of the bed. I drank it and felt better.

'I guess I'm okay. That was close.'

'It wasn't close,' said Pollux. 'You're scared, like everybody. First we hear it's nothing, then it's incomprehensibly lethal. Hard on the nerves.'

'What to do?'

'The opposite of whatever orangey does,' said Pollux.

We had agreed early on not to give the prez too much space in our heads. We hardly ever referred to him. But talk about being haunted. He was an ache in the brain.

Outside in the cold late winter air things were normal, although normal was beginning to feel like I was being stupid, like I'd relaxed my guard. People were hoarding, that was to be expected, so I went out shopping for things to hoard. I had taken two hundred dollars out of my savings and felt flush. I went to Target. Against medical protocol I wore a flimsy blue mask from Pollux's tool stash. Of course, the things that other people were into hoarding were gone. Bleach, beans. For some reason, nobody was hoarding taco shells, so I bought five boxes. I was confused about all the ways the virus could get into your body. And whether macro or micro droplets lingered in the air or fell straight to the filthy floor of a big box store. I read where one doctor said that a single virus could kill you. What you touched could be lethal. So I meandered around in the vibrant litter trying not to touch anything extraneous to my purpose and of course not to touch my face. I wondered if I could make a mask out of a cabbage leaf. For some reason, nobody was hoarding cabbages. There were ten of them in the produce section, for cheap. I bought six. I went over to the pet aisle and remembered why I'd never kept a dog for comfort. Look at all the things they need! I bought the last box of tissue and a pair of cheap black sneakers. Back in the canned goods aisle, someone had restocked a patch of beef stew and there was a single can of SpaghettiOs. I reached a hand toward the SpaghettiOs. Another hand slipped beneath my hand, tore the can away. It was a woman wearing a floral scarf tied over her mouth. Her eyes darted around. She continued down the aisle, throwing every can she could reach into her cart. She was an ace hoarder, but I was not going to take up the challenge. I let her get all the chocolate in the candy aisle, but she left the chewing gum. I bought some of that. Think shelf life, Tookie, I counseled myself. A tube of frozen cookie dough. A box of frozen corn dogs. Off-brand shredded wheat. It was time to check out. The jittery focus, the devastated shelves, a couple of fights breaking out over paper towels, a swarm descending on an employee trying to restock toilet paper, madness in people's eyes—it was like the beginning of every show where the streets empty and some grotesque majestic entity emerges from mist or fire.

⁂

'Mmmm, roughage,' said Pollux, peering into my bag. We were out in the garage and had decided to let everything we didn't need right away stay there until the viruses on their surfaces gave up.

'Were there organic diapers?'

Hetta asked Pollux so as not to ask me.

'No,' I lied, upset that I hadn't even thought of diapers. And organic? I thought only food came in organic. What kind of stepgrandma was I?

'I'm going back out,' I said as I turned and went through the door. Thus did I make a wide-flung search for organic diapers, which I found in the exurb of Maple Grove. I took out more money and overfilled one of those giant red shopping charts with Jarvis's current size and the next size up. It seemed like the virus would pass in about a month, but he would need them in the long run anyway. We could store them in the garage too. Hetta would be comforted and we might again be friends.

HETTA'S MIDNITE HAUNTING

When she thought how weak, how careless, how drunk, how selfish, how unknown to her true self she had been, Hetta's door slammed down. It was like a heavy garage door. In fact, it was the heavy garage door she wished had never opened—but it had opened. Again and again Hetta saw that door rising, at the press of a button in slow time, inexorably, rising upon the cameras and the cheap chairs and poker table of the crappy western set and the flimsy swinging door and frosted saloon glass and the bed. A brass bordello bed anchored to the floor with cinder blocks. Surrounded by red velveteen curtains. It was to be the last scene they would shoot. Already they had done the blowjob scene on the bus. They were supposed to be riding back from the dirty East Coast but were in a parking lot with guys off the street hired to rock the bus. After that they'd done the scene in the clean desert where she tamed and seduced a wild mustang which actually was, horrifyingly, a taxidermied horse, and now there would be the cowboy in the bordello bed. She would end with a horsewhip wearing only buckskin chaps that weren't even buckskin, just vinyl. Hetta drank six of the mini vodkas in her purse and used her whip with such liberation that the whole thing became way too real. The baby-faced cowboy had tried to get away but she'd chased him down and went full on freaking out of her mind.

Now, she had to slam the door down every single hour of every single day. She was somewhere else but she was here. It would kill Pollux. Just kill him. She couldn't bear it if her father knew.

TOOKIE'S BUBBLE

Jackie had come in early and was already at work when I arrived. I was relieved, for it seemed to me that after Flora came back from the crematory, a slightly scorched smell emanated from her favorite corner. Not only that, but Flora left that corner more often. She scratched about in areas of the store she'd once ignored.

And she seemed angry now. Who wouldn't be? Consigned to fire, crushed, crumbled, poured into a box. Once, she kicked a stack of books over so violently that they slid the length of the store. Another time, she stamped the floor so hard a display of hand-painted earrings rattled. I felt her rage as a low-pressure system that drained goodness from the air. So I was glad when Jackie brought Droogie, who was old and loved to sleep. When not asleep she'd stand beside me, never asking for attention as she knew I was not a petter of dogs, but selflessly guarding me just the same. Flora never approached.

We hadn't yet figured out whether we'd stay open, in fact, and business was of course dragging. People needed diapers and whiskey, not books.

We improvised masks and took shallow breaths around one another. Penstemon had once worked in a craft distillery mixing artisanal cocktails and she scored a jug of alcohol. She even found a spritz bottle. So far that day, we'd had five customers. They didn't wear masks or anything, but they had all nervously sanitized their hands. We still didn't know—did you get it from handling mail, handling books, touching surfaces, from sitting on a toilet seat, from turning a faucet on or off, from breathing? Maybe from sneezing or coughing. What was it? Where was it? Anything and everything might kill you. Spectral, uncanny. Deadly but not. It was terrifying. It was nothing.

Around the time that Flora made her usual rounds, Droogie groaned and got to her feet. She walked over to the Fiction section and sat, looking up expectantly. I knew immediately that Flora must have gotten hold of some dog treats. Don't ask me how that works when you're a ghost, but Droogie only sat like that when someone was holding up a liver snap.

'Hey, Droogie,' I called. 'Come!'

We had a bowl of treats for dogs that came with customers. She knew about it but ignored me. Kept staring expectantly at the air.

'Look at Droogie,' I said to Jackie.

'She's old. Slipping a little. Sometimes she just stares into space.'

I didn't want to argue but I knew better. Flora was trying to buy Droogie off. I pumped a little sanitizer on my hands and wrapped another book.

To our surprise, a few people showed up, orders trickled in. Gruen made a T-shirt mask. Asema came in wearing a purple bra cup over her nose and mouth. Somehow, she made it cool. Jackie pulled up a neck warmer. Pollux wore a red bandanna like an outlaw. I had a torn-up pillowcase.

The new rules for being alive kept changing. Pollux and I went on furious long walks to break down our anxiety. At least I could calm down by holding a tiny citizen. For Jarvis, I wore a blue paper mask, a flimsy yellow and green flowered bathrobe tied in back, and purple nitrile gloves from a box that Hetta scored from Walgreens. Jarvis was beginning to use his gummy little smile on me. Sounds, too, long sacred vowels. His favorite consonant was a drawn-out *nnnnnn*. He said ohm a lot, which transported me to a higher plane. He had improved his dauntless stare and took a faintly critical joy in my face. His eyes roamed over my features then lighted up as though he found something about my face extremely pleasing. Sometimes Hetta gave me a bottle—her own milk; she was that good a mother—and I fed him. His eyes rolled as the milk hit his tiny stomach and sometimes . . . he fell asleep. When a baby falls asleep in your arms you are absolved. The purest creature alive has chosen you. There's nothing else.

The reports kept saying that those who died had underlying health issues. That was probably supposed to reassure some people—the super-healthy, the vibrant, the young. A pandemic is supposed to blow through distinctions and level all before it. This one did the opposite. Some of us instantly became more mortal. We began to keep mental lists. One morning we started figuring the odds.

'You get an automatic point for being a woman,' said Pollux, 'plus ten years younger. That's two points.'

'I think we both get a point for having blood type O. I've heard type A is more susceptible.'

'Really? I'm not sure. I'd question that.'

'We have to subtract those points anyway for both being a teeny bit overweight.'

'Okay, let's cancel those two factors out.'

'Asthma?'

'I lose a point for having asthma,' said Pollux. 'You get a point for not having it.'

'Although now they're saying it might not make a difference. But I'll give you the point.'

'Thanks. Lung strength? Is that a factor?'

'Sounds like it should be. How do we measure it?'

'Wait here. I've got this thing they gave me when I had an attack.'

I knew where it was—the peak flow meter.

We both blew the marker into the yellow zone, so called it even.

In spite of asthma he ended up having a few more points, so we handicapped the odds by parsing out how long the illness would last. Hospital, no hospital, oxygen, no oxygen. But when we got to the ventilator, we broke. We grabbed each other and held on tight.

'No,' I cried, 'no way, baby. Don't get sick on me!'

'Don't get sick on me either. And if I get it, let me go.'

'How could I do that? My fucking god!'

Pollux held on to me and we gripped each other, rocking back and forth.

Once our mutual panic attack was over, we lay on our bed, purified and still. I stared up at a tiny crack in the ceiling. Pollux was getting dressed, said he'd fix me a chili dog for breakfast. The ceiling crack wavered. It grew sharper, darker, longer. The thing I knew was that if anything happened to Pollux I would die too. I would be happy to die. I would make sure that I did.

EAGLE DELIVERY

While we were parsing out our vulnerabilities, the doorbell chimed. We were too deep in the throes to answer it. But Hetta had answered. I heard her down in the kitchen.

'Package from U.S. Fish and Wildlife,' she called.

I jumped up. It was the eagle that Pollux had applied for. He carried the package outside and unwrapped the frozen bird, lifted it from the bed of dry ice. Hetta put two blankets around Jarvis and came out too. Pollux arranged cedar fronds outside on our picnic table and placed the eagle on top of them. He burned sage and sweetgrass and put tobacco on its heart. This was an immature eagle with mottled feathers.

Hetta jiggled her baby. I put my hands up my sleeves and shivered. The eagle stared into its death with blinded eyes. Pollux sang and we regarded its foiled magnificence.

OUR LAST CUSTOMER

We were getting ready to close the store for what we thought might be as long as two months now. I was looking over the day's reports when Dissatisfaction came into the building. His fingers roamed along the spines of the books, sometimes tracing one, pulling it out to read the first line. Since he'd read *The Blue Flower*, by Penelope Fitzgerald, he and I had compiled a list of short perfect novels.

SHORT PERFECT NOVELS
   Too Loud a Solitude, by Bohumil Hrabel
   Train Dreams, by Denis Johnson
   Sula, by Toni Morrison
   The Shadow-Line, by Joseph Conrad

The All of It, by Jeannette Haien
Winter in the Blood, by James Welch
Swimmer in the Secret Sea, by William Kotzwinkle
The Blue Flower, by Penelope Fitzgerald
First Love, by Ivan Turgenev
Wide Sargasso Sea, by Jean Rhys
Mrs. Dalloway, by Virginia Woolf
Waiting for the Barbarians, by J. M. Coetzee
Fire on the Mountain, by Anita Desai

These are books that knock you sideways in around 200 pages. Between the covers there exists a complete world. The story is unforgettably peopled and nothing is extraneous. Reading one of these books takes only an hour or two but leaves a lifetime imprint. Still, to Dissatisfaction, they are but exquisite appetizers. Now he needs a meal. I knew that he'd read Ferrante's Neapolitan novels and was lukewarm. He called them soap opera books, which I thought was the point. He did like *The Days of Abandonment,* which was perhaps a short perfect novel. 'She walked the edge with that one,' he said. He liked Knausgaard (not a short perfect). He called the writing better than Novocain. *My Struggle* had numbed his mind but every so often, he told me, he'd felt the crystal pain of the drill. In desperation, I handed over *The Known World.* He thrust it back in outrage, his soft voice a hiss, Are you kidding me? I have read this one six times. Now what do you *have*? In the end, I placated him with Aravind Adiga's *White Tiger*, the latest Amitav Ghosh, *NW* by Zadie Smith, and Jane Gardam's Old Filth books in a sturdy Europa boxed set, which he hungrily seized. He'd run his prey to earth and now he would feast. Watching him closely after he paid for the books and took the package into his hands, I saw his pupils dilate the way a diner's do when food is brought to the table.

It seemed right and proper that Dissatisfaction was our last customer. When he said goodbye, I clung to the sound of his voice. I didn't know him, or maybe I knew him better than anyone. I suppose I was desolate. I decided he was my very favorite customer and I rushed to the door to tell him so, although he would have scoffed. His car was pulling away. I yelled *You're my favorite customer* as he turned the corner. It was March 24. I switched off all lights except the blue lamp in the confessional, set the alarm, walked out the door, and turned to lock it. I tried not to feel too much at that moment. Still, as the lock clicked and the alarm fell silent, it seemed that I was turning my back not on dry paper but a living assembly.

Of course, as I often do, I forgot something inside.

Without thinking, I walked straight back in through the dark store. I had to pass through the stacks to get to the lights in the office.

Halfway in, I knew this was a mistake. She made a slithery sound right behind me. I ran for the lights, reached into the dark office for the switch.

There was already a hand on the switch.

Somehow, someday, I always knew there would eventually be a hand on a switch I reached for in the dark. My brain seized up. My first reaction to fear is to lash out. I slapped the hand away and hit the switch. Instant light. Nothing. Nobody. No sound. But the touch lingered like a paralyzing bite. I wrung my hand, grabbed my bag, and left every fixture blazing as I walked back out and locked the door. Halfway home, my legs buckled and I sat down on the curb. The touch was real, and not gentle. She was beginning to manifest. Something in the diseased air, something in the trauma of the greater conversation, something in ache of the unknown, something in the closing down or her trial by fire, was giving her more power.

✳

The day after we closed the bookstore, everything shut down. That night, Pollux and I drove to Eat

Street to pick up Chinese food at Rainbow, a place we'd been going to for years. It was only six p.m. but it felt like three a.m. Shop windows were hollow blurs. The parking lot was clear except for an ominous, idling Humvee. I slid out of our car to get the food. Had the urge to tiptoe or sneak. Two young people sat in the Rainbow's entryway talking on their phones about a party. One of them said, *Nah, I'm young.* The owner, Tammy, brought the order and said thank you in a tone I'd never heard. I took the order to the car and put the bag on the rubber mat next to my feet. The complex smell of Chinese food seeped up like a drug. I glanced down at the stapled paper bag on the floor. Soft circles of oil from the takeout containers had soaked into the brown paper. I thought they were beautiful. Honey walnut shrimp, crispy tiger beef, garlicky green beans. I reached over and held Pollux's wide hand as we slowly drove along. There was a slick of rain on the empty, peaceful streets.

'Why can't it always be this way?' I asked Pollux.

He gave me an odd look. I turned aside. The empty street swished beneath the tires. Perhaps I should have been ashamed. Why was it that I felt this was the world I'd always waited for?

Louise was the opposite, so despondent after we'd closed the store that she kept sending out long garbled emails that were supposed to buck up our spirits but did the opposite. The store was nearly twenty years old. That's a big chunk of life. Jackie, especially, had been through some lean times with her and knew she would be casting frantically around for a solution. But how to find a solution when we didn't yet know the shape of the problem? I also knew in these times Louise relied on something else. She had this weird sense of destiny about the store. It was more than a place, it was a nexus, a mission, a work of art, a calling, a sacred craziness, a slice of eccentricity, a collection of good people who shifted and rearranged but cared deeply about the same one thing—books.

One morning Louise called, jubilant.

'We got essential worker status, Tookie.'

'Yeah?'

'It means we're essential.'

'Okay.'

'It means we can stay in business. Not open our doors, but keep selling. It means our state considers books essential in this time. I'm surprised we got word so soon. It was practically the day after we applied.'

I was silent.

'Essential,' she gloated.

'Well, yeah, we're doing school orders.'

'I know but we didn't say that. We just applied as a bookstore. It means books are *essential*, Tookie.'

'I guess.'

She hung up on me. I know that this meant something huge to her, but to me it just meant more uncertainty and jiggered-together adaptations. I wanted to stay in the shuttered serenity that Pollux and I had traveled through on our trip to the Rainbow. Going to work meant I had to go back to a place where a ghostly hand might beat me to the light switch. Or someone might kill me by touching or breathing on me. Or worse, I might touch, shout at, talk to, and kill somebody else. No, I really didn't want to adapt, unless it meant staying in bed. If life had to go on, I wanted life before a ghost, before the light switch, before this virus, before the buried murder book that infected my dreams.

To avoid exposing the entire staff to the virus, we decided that one person at a time would work the entire day shift. One person, alone in the store, sounded pleasant to most of us. We were by and large introverts. But I knew that for me this so-called isolation would be far from peaceful.

THE HAUNTING OF TOOKIE

Once I turned a certain corner and the marsh end of the lake came into view, I tried to concentrate on the ringing solos of the male blackbirds, their epaulettes flashing as they threw their wings out in effort. As I walked along the lake path, entering each bird's realm, the air resounded. But the city was so quiet that I could still hear my footsteps. Past two memorial park benches dedicated to departed customers, the asphalt path abruptly sheered left. I took the path all the way down to the picturesque Lutheran church, made of soft golden Kasota stone. Last winter, I had seen a great horned owl launch, lit white from below. I thought a lot about the owl. I know I shouldn't have, according to the traditions of my people. But I have always been drawn to owls. The sidewalk was cracked at a tilt beneath my spongy shoes. I hooked the elastics of my dusty mask behind my ears, glanced at the glass door of the Little Free Library by the church, askew and open. I pushed the door shut with the side of my arm. No touch! Slow and smooth, I told myself. Keep your breath calm and relaxed.

I always stopped at the school across from the bookstore. I loitered by the school's lunchroom door, from which the janitor used to emerge to have a smoke off school property. He'd cross the street and lean against the side of our building, gray faced and morose. He stared back at the school the way I now stared at the store I loved. A bleak stare. Knowing I had to go back in there.

It was worst in the morning, when she'd had the place to herself all night. I turned the key and pushed open the blue door. The air was heavy with her resentment. I walked through the Young Adult section toward the beep-beep of the triggered alarm. The sense of her—in the dim shadow of the confessional, turning toward me in longing and despairing anger—trapped the breath in me. By the time I reached the office, hit the right buttons to turn off the alarm system, by the time I frantically slapped up all the switches on the ceiling lamps, my heart was ready to burst. I swear, if she'd poked her head around the corner right then and said *Boo,* I'd have dropped like a shot, dead like her.

If I died, I would be saddled with her ghost anyway. She'd be my ether pal. I laughed, walked back out into the empty-personed store, and yelled, 'Fuck you!'

Which you shouldn't say to a ghost. You should never challenge them. They have two realms to walk in and would get you going or coming. But I was too far gone.

A few hours into my day, I saw a shadow, a blur, an edge. I thought she'd made herself visible, for just that instant. Later, I thought she was hiding behind me, peeking over my shoulder. How clever she was! Nimble enough to stay just beyond my peripheral sight. She moved when I moved, took amusement when I whipped around. Once, I heard her cry out. *Wheeee!* I shook my head from side to side, glaring. *Wheeee!* I thought I'd solve this by walking into the bathroom and looking at the mirror, to catch her out. I stood before the mirror but looked down, into the sink, my chin frozen to the top of my collarbone. I couldn't lift my head. I knew, beyond a doubt, she was there. I felt her staring at me from the glass.

FLORA'S MISCHIEF

The hours crept, the days fled. The afternoons were jumbled by the constant ringing of the phones. Early one day while I was working alone, I received an order for one of our most sought after titles, *Braiding Sweetgrass,* by Robin Kimmerer. We never let ourselves run out of stock. But the order was late, and we were down to three copies. I fetched one copy to wrap and put the order sheet inside the cover. Put that book in my ready-to-ship pile. That was in the morning. Around four that afternoon I got a phone order and went to pull a second book for a curbside pickup. No *Braiding Sweetgrass*. I stared at the gap on the shelf where the other two copies had been that morning. I tried to imagine that I'd taken the other books out for some reason. I was the only one in the store all day so it had to have been me. Time had folded on itself, true, the way time does when you are working alone. But I knew I hadn't moved the books.

'Flora!' I called out to the empty store. 'Not funny. I need that book.'

My stomach hollowed. The soothing music I'd been playing suddenly panicked me and I rushed over to hit the eject button. On the way, I kicked two books lying on the floor. *The* books. Then I tripped, or Flora tripped me, and I stumbled down on the floor. I was on all fours, panting doglike, looking at the braid of sweetgrass on the book's cover. The books were still on the floor where I had not put them. They were a dozen feet from the shelf and in perfect condition. I picked the books up, put one back on the shelf, bagged the other, and set it out on the curbside pickup table.

I ran the scene over and over in my head. Not only

had she thrown down the books, but she really might have tripped me.

Later that night, I called Jackie. When I told her what had happened to me in the store she said, 'Worrisome development.' I hadn't told anyone about the hand on the light switch. It was too awful to admit.

'Worrisome for sure,' I said. 'What should I do about it?'

'Burn sweetgrass.'

'That's Flora's favorite thing. She took to smudging like she invented it.'

'Read the book?'

'Of course I've read the book.'

'She's getting bold. I don't like this.'

'I don't either.'

Jackie didn't have a solution, so I called Asema.

Asema had a lot to say. She told me that it was outrageous that Flora would steal a manuscript that would have added to the primary record of Native history. There is little enough from that time in the voices of Indigenous women. Asema went on talking about how Flora would never admit her theft. She would never talk about the manuscript. But Asema knew how Flora had swiped the papers.

'She came to the store. She'd been pestering whoever answered the phone, or email, because she had
something for us. You know, one of her special things.'

Flora always brought little handmade gifts and
prizes. Useless stuff.

'Remember her herbal sachets?'

Yeah, I remembered.

'She wanted to sell her teas. She was always giving
us some kind of tea or a potpourri mix that was supposed to scent the air. Anyway, she showed up at the
store. I had come across what turned out to be a historical manuscript and brought it in to show Jackie.
I was looking at it in the office and I left to wait on
a customer. Flora went into the office and she must
have seen the manuscript on the office counter.
Damn, Tookie! It was the one-of-a-kind historically
illuminating manuscript a historian waits for all their
life. I could have had an amazing dissertation, but
more than that, it was a work that could have challenged what we know of history in that liminal space
between treaty boundaries on the Red River. All I had
was the notebook I was using to take notes. When I
confronted Flora about it, she wouldn't admit a thing.
I don't forgive her. I never will.'

'Thanks for all of this, Asema. But why won't she
leave me alone and how do I stop her?'

'Honestly, I have no idea.'

I hung up, but I was impressed with Flora's audacity and Asema's unrelenting grudge. And actually those herbal mixtures Flora used to make were kind of nice. If I missed anything about Flora, I missed the rose petals and cinnamon sticks.

AIN'T NO GRAVE

The lights were on, the computers primed like pumps, the card machine ready to accept the numbers that would be spoken into my ear. I made myself a Ghost Managing Playlist. I wanted to turn the tables on Flora and creep her out; the playlist included 'Who Is She,' by I Monster. 'You Can't Kill Me I'm Alive,' by MLMA. 'Que Sera,' by Wax Tailor. 'I'd Like to Walk Around in Your Mind,' by Vashti Bunyan, and so on. After a couple days of the music, I felt better. In fact, I felt scary. I was alone with an active spirit in an enclosed space, all day, but I was serene and powerful. Things were quiet and I believed this time I was protected by the music.

I was putting together a complicated order that had been waiting on a final book. I'd called the customer twice. I was receiving the book, scanning it into our system and preparing to wrap it, when a song began that I knew was *not* on the playlist. Flora cranked up the volume; it was Johnny Cash singing 'Ain't No Grave.'

There ain't no grave can hold my body down. . . .

If you've ever heard Johnny sing this song, you can imagine. My legs went weak. I put my hands on the glass counter for balance. I tried to get control of my breath. I felt her creeping along the edge of the display case until she was standing next to me. She sighed. A low murmur crawled up my neck. Her voice was the low creak of a door.

Let me in.

Come Get Me

COME GET ME

That night, I tried to quit. I called Jackie, who answered with her usual dignified calm. I told her that Flora was trying to talk to me. I told her everything—how when Flora whispered *Let me in* her breath chilled my neck.

'Also, Flora has mildewed,' I said. 'She has that old basement book smell.'

Jackie murmured and coughed but said to go on. So I told her how it had happened.

'I was working behind the counter when Flora approached me. I sensed her slide closer. Her rough silk pants rasped, her bracelets clinked, all the usual. The only new thing was a sifting sound, as if her blood had turned to sand.'

'What happened? Did she grab you? Touch you?'

'The phone rang.'

'Oh good.'

'It didn't faze her.'

The ring had made me start with hope but in that same moment I let down my guard. And no, Flora wasn't about to fall for a ringing phone. Why would she? Her sudden hiss in my ear was a blast of ice. I slipped down the side of the counter, still gripping the top as if there were suction cups on my fingertips. I fixed my eyes on my fingers, my sleeve slipping down my arm. I think my hands saved the rest of me. One hand grabbed the phone receiver and I saw that my caller had been Pollux. He answered redial.

'Come get me,' I said.

It took a while for Jackie to respond. I pictured her face, rapt with concentration, as she always looked when dealing with a troublesome customer. As always, when faced with some difficulty, she asked questions.

'*Let me in.* What would that mean? She was already in the store.'

'I think she wants to possess me.'

There was a grave, kind, Jackie-like silence.

'It sounds like . . . Tookie, it sounds like you need to see a counselor.'

'You mean a shrink.'

'Okay, a psychiatrist or something.'

'If she succeeds, I'll need an exorcist, Jackie. I'm not crazy. Thus my sensible resolution to quit.'

'You can't quit, Tookie.'

'It's a free country. In some ways.'

'No, I mean you can quit, but listen. We applied for a government loan. It's a Paycheck Protection loan. We won't make it unless we get this loan.'

'Won't make it?'

'We're in serious trouble. We have to keep everyone we've got now on payroll. If we stick together, work-wise, the loan will turn into a grant. If not, we'll have to pay it back. Impossible.'

I thought about this for a minute, then said I needed a partner.

⁂

And so I began to work again in blessed companion-ship. Jackie worked in the office and I had the rest of the store. Flora kept her distance. I had read about the strangeness of isolation in the news, but not everybody was alone, or had time to get contemplative. It was a luxury. Now that I was working in peace, with hardly a noise from Flora and Jackie absorbed in her online tasks, I began to feel that I was actually in isolation. Of course, like everything else, I made this complicated.

I became aware of my thoughts. My brain began combing apart the strands of what had happened during the years of my incarceration. The cell in the seg unit was half the size of our store's bathroom. The

walls were painted cinder blocks, perfectly feature-
less. However, after a few weeks, variations appeared.
The nearly invisible imperfections organized into herds
of monkeys, sexy angels, jagged mountains, pastoral
swales. Shadows and shapes emerged. I was amazed at
what was in my brain. How it stepped up to entertain
itself. I saw all that I would never have and would never
be: the silhouette of a mother holding the hand of a
toddler, a woman folded along the body of a swayback
horse, two people pressed together listening to the low
music of wind in a pine grove. It was so fucking sad! I
decided to dive right into that. I cried a thousand tears,
but then, completely against my will, I began to appreciate the tiny window in the far wall. Natural light from
the west changed every day. I waited for the reflection
of a sunset. There was also a small darkened window
in the door above the trap. I could glimpse others on
the row, almost make out their faces, blurred with fury
and yearning. Maybe also wicked lust. Again, I was betrayed by my tendency to stay alive. I fell in love with
a smeary smudge in one of those cells. It was Jacinta.
Later, we became a couple. Once she got out I never
heard from her.

The other businesses in our building were closed, the
streets mostly empty. I wrapped each book in heavy

paper so that it wouldn't get dinged in its box. Usually I wrote a cheerful note on a card, some sort of thank-you. I never admitted this to anyone else, but I'd even draw a little flower or bird if I approved of a book choice. But for some reason, after a few days of work, my notes became more ornate. I crumpled a few and tossed them. My handwriting seemed odd. My script was usually sloppy printed letters joined by cursive loops. I'd stopped developing my handwriting back in high school. Sometimes I still dotted my *i*'s with bubbles. At the bottom of a question mark and exclamation point, a little bubble would appear. Tookie's bubble. People have sometimes remarked that my somewhat childish handwriting does not reflect my persona. But now my handwriting grew emphatic and linear. You could call it commanding. I kept writing miigwech and my *i*'s came out with firm dots, no matter how hard I tried to bubble them. Maybe this was what being in a pandemic brought forth. When everything big is out of control, you start taking charge of small things.

Still, there was something about my new handwriting that creeped me out. I tried to bubble-dot an *i* and my hand objected. Was I possessed? *Let me in.* Was she inside of me now?

I brought my lunch and ate it behind the counter.

One day Jackie came out to join me, sitting all the way across the store.

'I've got a question,' I said, once she'd settled in a chair. 'Has your handwriting ever changed for no reason?'

'All the time,' said Jackie. 'A low-pressure system moving in might cause me to drop my hooks lower. A crisis of confidence will tend to make me overcompensate with spiky capitals.'

'Did you ever try to bubble-dot your *i*'s and have your hand reject your intention?'

'Bubble-dot an *i*? Who does that?'

'Moi.'

'You should really think about changing your handwriting,' said Jackie. She gave me an earnest, teacherly once-over. 'I mean, if you ever quit the store in a sudden blast of sanity, your handwriting could affect how seriously another employer might take your resumé.'

'Oh, Mrs. Kettle. Nobody cares about penmanship anymore,' I said.

'You're wrong.' Jackie continued in her teacher voice, 'Cursive is making a comeback.'

'You wish. It's Flora. I think she got into me.'

'If I was a ghost, I'd take away your bubble dots. It's the first thing I'd do.'

'Harsh.'

'Ugh. I stayed up to all hours,' she said, sliding a book across the floor. Sometimes Jackie resented a perfectly good book because it 'forced' her to stay up all night. I was used to this. It was usually a sign of a literary page-turner—whether spy, sea, or horror—my favorite sort of book. She'd made me read Dennis Lehane, Donna Tartt, Stephen Graham Jones, Marcie R. Rendon, Kate Atkinson. She gave me *The Death of the Heart* and said, 'It's extremely good. Keep it.'

Jackie brought out two cans of lemon fizzy water, sprayed the tops with alcohol, and rolled one over to me.

'Mmm, spiked,' I said.

'So, about Flora's latest tricks,' said Jackie. 'I'm sorry I joked about your handwriting.'

'What if she actually succeeded? Maybe she's inside of me, controlling me, right now.'

Jackie brought her can of fizzy water halfway across the floor, set it down, and knocked it over.

'Oops.'

I watched the patterns the water made crawling across the old wooden floor and sighed.

'All right. She's not in you, Tookie. Flora would have jumped to wipe that up.'

'I suppose you're right.' I stared down at the water.

It was drawn west by gravity. Jackie set her can up-right, then got up and snatched a few paper towels. She bent over and mopped it up.

'Even though this proves you're Tookie, you could help.'

'You're the one who knocked it over.'

'I did it for your sake, to trap Flora.'

'And prove I'm a slob.'

'She's not inhabiting you. We've established that. And not bubble-dotting is a sign of maturity.'

'Hey!'

'You said your writing slanted forward? That's the handwriting of a fearless spirit.'

'That's hilarious. Jackie, what she said was *Let me in.*'

'Tookie, this whole thing is exhausting. Trying not to get sick. Trying to stay in business. What we're living through is either unreal or too real. I can't decide. Anyway, I found something out,' she went on. 'What color were you wearing when Flora spoke to you?'

I remembered well. My hand clutching at the phone and the red sleeve slipping down my wrist. I thought my sleeve would be the last thing I'd ever see.

'Red. I was wearing red.'

Jackie nodded as though I'd told her something she'd suspected all along. She was at her most pedantic when she quoted elders, and I suspected she'd do so even before she did.

'There. I've been told by a couple of knowledgeable elders that you should not wear red at a funeral, or for a year after someone close to you dies. Red is the fire, the doorway to the spirit world. Who knows how long until they are done walking. When the dead see flashes of red as they pass on their journey, they are confused. They think a door is opening and it distracts them from their task, which is to reach a place where we are nothing to them.'

The gravity with which she delivered this teaching made me hesitate, but finally I said, 'That's superstition.'

'Ghosts are superstition. Here.'

She gave me a long-sleeved bookstore hoodie. It was from way back, when the store had opened. I took off my overshirt, a dark red tunic. Red is my favorite color. I guess I'd be attracted from the other side by red. As always, I was wearing one of Pollux's undershirts for warmth. I put on Jackie's hoodie. The fleece was soft, high quality, friendly. I stroked the fabric.

'You know, this is pretty good. How come you're giving it to me?'

'It's nice on you,' she said critically, looking at me from all angles. Finally, she nodded. 'It's a ghost-repelling shirt.'

'Why's it a ghost-repelling shirt?'

'Because I blessed it, smudged it, prayed over it, touched it to my goldfish bowl, washed it in lavender.'

'That's why it smells so good.'

'Also, it's not red. In this hoodie, you're invisible to a ghost.'

'You probably put magic Band-Aids on your kids' scrapes and said the magic lasted for three days. When they'd take off the Band-Aid, poof!'

'Poof!' she said, spreading out her fingers.

'By the way, have you ever been bothered by a ghost?'

I'd finally asked her the right question, because she sat straight up and her eyes flickered. She didn't want to admit it, but yes, she had a ghost story.

'Okay, yes, I had an experience with my uncle.' I asked what happened but she grew vague. I persisted. She decided to tell me. As it turned out, Jackie's was just the first of several ghost stories. It seemed that several people on staff had been haunted and I was about to hear their tales.

'My uncle had been sick for a few months,' said Jackie. 'Seriously ill.'

'What happened?'

She hesitated, took a nervous breath. 'It's embarrassing.'

I waited.

'My uncle was always good to me,' said Jackie. 'He used to take me ice fishing, told me knock-knock jokes while we stared at the dark hole in the ice. He made me pimiento loaf sandwiches with white bread and mayo. I loved him. So when he was fading out I went to visit him up in Duluth. He had no children, but one of my cousins was taking care of him. When I got there, she said she needed a break, had to go to the store or something, so she asked if I'd sit with him. As she left, she told me not to open the curtains or the window. Fine. I sat down beside his bed, held his hand. He was motionless, sickly pale, on the way out, but his hair was still freshly combed and he had a fresh shave. In his day my uncle been handsome and, from what I could tell, devoted to my aunt. After a while, it felt like the room was too stuffy and dim. I forgot what my cousin had said about the windows. I got up, opened the curtains, and cracked the window for a little air. As I lifted the sash a powerful gust surprised me. It wasn't windy outside.

'My uncle sat up, turned to the window, and said, "I knew you'd come!" His face changed. Total joy. Right before my eyes he became himself again—young, delinquent, and deliriously happy.

'"Alvina," he said.'

'Was Alvina your aunt?' I asked.

'Yes, but not the aunt he was married to.'

'Uh-oh.'

'Right. So my uncle was still looking at the window with all that joy on his face. He lifted his arms as if to embrace the curtains.

'"Don't leave a mark on me," he said, and gave this sly little laugh. "You know why." Then he fell back and began to thrash and roll around in the bed. I thought he was going to die and rushed out to call my cousin. I could not get hold of her. However, she had told me not to call an ambulance if something happened. He wanted to die naturally, not hooked up to a machine. While my mind raced and I tried to figure out what to do, things went quiet in my uncle's room. I went back in, expected to find him dead. But he was sleeping peacefully. He was smiling in his sleep.'

'Whew!' I said.

'I went to close the curtains and saw the window was shut.'

'Was the sash loose? Had it fallen?'

'No, it had to have been pushed down. There's more. I went home and the next day got a call from my cousin. She said the home health aide had been giving him a sponge bath and asked if there was something sharp in the bed, or if I could think of why he'd have scratch marks on his back.'

'Like, those kinds of scratch marks?'

'Those kind of scratch marks. I said I had no idea. I thought my cousin wanted to ask me something, but she only stammered a bit and got off the phone.'

I was reduced to making a sort of neutral face, or a mystified face, trying not to blink too much or give a weird smile. I was having trouble adjusting my facial expression.

'I know,' said Jackie.

When I got home after work, Pollux said, 'Wayyyy! New hoodie. I like it.'

I almost told him it was a ghost-repelling shirt but stopped myself in time. When you are haunted, there are no rules. There is no science. You have to do things by instinct because nobody knows how to vanquish a ghost. Most ghost narratives explain away supernatural entities as emotional projections. But Flora had nothing to do with my unconscious. She had ordered me to let her in and was taking me over—penmanship first. I was afraid that my resolve was breaking down. My brain felt loose and spongy. I looked at Pollux, who'd put his hands on my shoulders.

'What's wrong?' he asked. 'Is it that we're having cabbage again tonight?'

I was sad about that, in fact.

'I wish it didn't keep so well,' I said.

I wanted more than anything to tell him the truth and have him close his arms around me. One of the worst things about this was how it cut me off from Pollux, how I had to pretend I was just having a 'blue fit,' which was what he called my depressive moods. Of course, I told him that I was 'just having a blue fit.' He stepped close and locked his arms around me. I put my arms around him, lay my head against his shoulder, and held on for dear life.

PENSTEMON GREEN

Although she only wore black, and her last name was Brown, Penstemon's true color was the deep vibrant green of well-cared-for houseplants. I thought this even before she began to move houseplants from her apartment into the bookstore. She said it would improve the energy, and she was right. There were green leaves all through the store now, even some dripping down the confessional. On the days she wasn't in, Jackie now scheduled Penstemon with me. I was cheered. Perhaps the plants would repel Flora—in spite of her name, Flora had never been good with live plants. Dead plants, yes, for her potpourri mixtures.

She couldn't keep a houseplant going. But Penstemon could. In the same way that one instinctively trusts a restaurant with actual, not fake, personally cared-for plants, the store with Pen's beloved pothos and aloe plants felt intangibly better. By then, we were assessing one another on the basis of the strictness of our quarantines. Pen and I had a talk and agreed that we were taking no risks. We would tell each other if we thought we'd been exposed to the virus.

The phone began ringing intermittently, then oftener, until it was ringing constantly. Which encouraged us, but also presented a challenge. Could we handle this, and was it real? We'd had a few spurts of business through the years, but they never lasted. Sometimes I was in the office with Jackie when she juggled bills, fending off one publisher, promising another, deciding which bills to whittle down and which to leave precariously for later. We'd been on hold with creditors, we'd been frozen out, and time after time nearly shut down. There had been days of two or three customers, all using up gift cards. Mostly, we ran in the red, struggled to pay bills. So we were absolutely unprepared to be loved.

It was also the end of education's fiscal year. We began to get complex multibook orders from schools and libraries that had decided to build significant

Native collections. There were open orders stashed everywhere. With all of this happening in the store, Flora was reduced to rustling or sulking in resentful silence. One day, Pen burned a veggie corn dog in the microwave. The stench was so bad we had to open the fire door in back and wear our parkas as we packed books. Flora stayed away for days. I considered stinking up the store again. But then one afternoon, Pen addressed me from behind one of Asema's masks of (what else) flowered green calico.

'Hey, Tookie,' she said. 'Maybe I'm hearing your ghost too.'

Behind my dull black face mask, I gaped. When I could speak, I said, 'Yes, she's here!'

'That's a relief,' said Pen. 'I thought I was going nuts. I hear this shuffling. . . .'

'Yes, we're haunted,' I croaked.

'Seriously, I'm so relieved,' she said.

I could hardly speak. I didn't want to embarrass Pen by throwing myself on the floor and pounding the scarred boards in relief. So I spoke in a sort of restrained, formal way, I suppose. I told Pen what I heard, where the sounds came from. I didn't talk about the light switch, or about *Let me in*. I didn't want to frighten Pensty. I tried to keep emotion out of my voice and as I did so I saw that Pen's eyes went dull. She seemed to absorb what I was saying like a sponge absorbing dishwater. I stopped.

'You make it sound so clinical,' she said. 'Like it's no big deal.'

'It is a big deal,' I cried out. 'I thought I was the only one. I'm trying to keep a lid on.'

Hysteria bubbled up. Pen's eyes blazed green. Pen was the one to talk to. She had always been the one to talk to.

'Do you remember Flora very well?'

'Of course,' she said sadly. 'The perfect customer.'

'Some would say.'

'So she just couldn't leave the bookstore, huh? This makes it marginally better, except I don't like being alone with a ghost. We have to stick together. By the way, I broke up with Crankyass. He mocked my rituals so he had to go.'

Crankyass had lasted longer than most because of the quarantine. They'd hunkered down together. Now Pen said she was going to take a sanity break. It was too stressful to worry about anyone besides her mom, who was a nurse. She waved her hand in a complete circle. That gesture of hers was pleasing. Pen has signature gestures. The pizza hand, flat palmed and out to the side, like she is going to set a luscious pizza before you, dripping with cheese. Sometimes she illustrates her words with rain-falling fingers or pinches the air like dough, literally grasping for a phrase. When she's thinking, she puts her index finger over her upper lip like a mustache. Of course, now, she indented her flowered mask. After a while she said, 'Can I tell you what's really haunting me?'

'Of course.'

See? Everybody has a ghost story, I thought.

Pen and I agreed to ignore the phones for a few minutes, stepped out the back door, stood outside against the brick wall.

'My mother is an emergency room nurse,' said Penstemon. 'We're close, you know. When this started, she sent my sister and brother to live with our aunt. She now lives alone because she doesn't want to expose any of us. I keep track of her schedule. Every day when I know she's at home I bring a cooked dinner and a bag lunch. I put the food on her doorstep. She comes to the door and talks to me through the glass. Behind her in our house there is a long hall that leads to the kitchen with a sliding door, full of light. I hate talking to her through the glass. Where she stands it is dim and the light behind her is like a halo, like a tunnel leading to "the light." You know, the light you always hear about when someone dies.'

Penstemon paused, fluttered her hand over her heart. Then she blew a breath out and continued.

'I stand there talking to my mother and a chill rises inside of me as we speak. I know how tired she is, how much she wants to reach out and pick up the food I've put on the steps. But I can't stop talking to her because every time we are talking through that door with the light behind her, I think maybe this will be the last time I'll see her. I have to force myself to stop. And when I leave her, I get on my bike and smile and wave goodbye. Then I pedal fast as hell because the pressure sobs are rising up in me and once they start there is nothing I can do to stuff them back.'

We work across the store from each other for the rest of the day, and we hardly speak.

As Pen and I left work that night, she handed me an envelope. 'Read this when you get home,' she said. 'It's either a prose poem or flash fiction.' Of course, I opened the envelope as soon as I was down the street and stood on the corner in the wind to read it.

```
Senior Portrait

Before I broke up with my high school
boyfriend, I framed his high school
portrait. We had gone our separate
```

ways, but I left the picture on my
shelf. We had not parted badly, just
moved on, and had promised to remain
friends. I didn't think about the
picture until one afternoon when I
was cleaning my room in preparation
for going to college. I felt the
prickly sensation of someone staring
at me. I turned around and noticed
the old photograph. Reaching to
take it off the shelf, I noticed a
water drop on the surface and tried
to brush it off. But the water
would not brush away. It was in the
photograph itself. I was amazed to
think I'd never noticed that my old
boyfriend had been crying in his
senior photograph. As we were still
friends, I called his mother's home
to ask him about this, but her voice
on the phone was distraught. . . .
There's been an accident. He was in
the hospital in Fargo, in a coma.
Immediately I drove to see him and
at his bedside I held his hand even
though his new girlfriend didn't

```
like it. The coma lasted four days
and when he emerged from it he told
his mother that he had been weeping
the entire time, knocking at a glass
door, crying to get back into this
life.
```

When I got home after work, I took out the paper again. There had been something about it. Now I realized what it was—typewriting. This wasn't a typewriter font on a computer printout. I touched the letters, some uneven, a couple of blocked *e*'s where the keys had struck ink through the paper. I couldn't compare the writing to Foretelling, but I was pretty sure I'd found the author.

The next day, I asked Pen and she said, 'Oh, you read that?'

'I found it in the cash register drawer under the tray. That was some crazy mind-fucking shit, Pen! Foretelling!'

She shrugged and raised her hands. I knew she was pleased.

'Yeah, I brought it in to show Asema.'

'Why the hell did you write it?' I asked

'It happened after I was working on the collage.' Pen gestured toward the confessional.

'That day you huffed the glue?'

'Heard the voice. And then later, when I got home, I was working on something else when I suddenly just wrote out this thing. It was so strange, like taking dictation, except I wasn't hearing a voice. It's a warning, right?'

'I think so. Do you think Flora was trying to warn us about the pandemic?'

'She would have in real life, I guess,' said Pen. 'And she would be dropping off loads of paper towels and sanitizer.'

'Honestly, this would have been her moment,' I said. 'She was good at scrounging things for other people. Then making them feel all indebted.'

'Maybe,' said Penstemon slowly, 'the reason I can sometimes hear Flora too is because I was in that confessional.'

We turned to stare at the confessional. Someone had screwed a decorative bulb into the electrical socket in the priest's box. When the confessional was in use, the curtains would have been closed and the inside dark. You could hardly expect a priest to hear confessions by flashlight. Pen walked over and pulled the chain. Something seemed to move and she jumped back with a small cry. My heart thumped. The bulb was flame shaped and floated in the dim aperture like the flame on the head of an apostle.

The phone never stopped. The information in my head boiled over. Even though I wrote things down, my *DO* list kept accumulating. I began hearing the phones even after work, as I walked home, as I arrived home, all the time. Now, not only was I haunted at the bookstore, but the bookstore began to haunt me at home. Phones rang in my dreams.

It was exhausting, but also there was something moving about this attention. Louise had been excited by the word 'essential.' As it turned out, books were important, like food, fuel, heat, garbage collection, snow shoveling, and booze. Phones ringing meant our readers had not deserted us and some far-off day they would walk into the bookstore again. Sometimes it was exhilarating to be needed. Sometimes I felt important. Dissatisfaction ordered books on the phone now. He drove a vintage Mercedes-Benz, very classy. His vanity license plate said LAWWOLF. When he picked up his books, I leaned out the door.

'What else you got?' he cried.

I gave him James McBride's *Deacon King Kong*. The next day, he actually called me at the store halfway through, to tell me the book was packed with life and love and he didn't want it to end. Love and life? These were words I had never expected to hear from Dissatisfaction. I was immediately concerned.

'Are you all right?'

He didn't snap back, which worried me even more.

'I liked *The Good Lord Bird*, but this one is even better. It's about human nobility, kindness, craftiness. It's visual, funny. I don't want it to end.'

I stuttered some sort of answer and he kept talking.

'I think it's changing me. I really do. It's hard to change an old hard-ass, which I am. People always thought I was a defense attorney. But hell no, I was a prosecutor. This book brought me back to the old days. I grew up in Rondo and that was a warm neighborhood, full of kindness, pie, elderly folks, kids, craziness, and sorrow. It was a place to belong. All my life I've missed it, but never understood until now. Since they tore through Rondo for I-94, demolished a Black neighborhood in St. Paul with so many people like in Deacon's world, I've missed it. I felt like McBride returned me something personal.'

'What . . . ,' I sputtered, 'are you going to do with all this good feeling?'

'Spread it around, Alphabet Soup! Spread it like jelly.'

Spread it like jelly was what Pollux's grandma used to say when they had a surplus of anything. I'd already made Roland Waring, the name on his credit card, into a sort of relative by giving him a nickname. At one point I'd even told him about his nickname in a fit of frustration when I couldn't come up with a title he hadn't read. He'd said the nickname suited him and that his name for me was Alphabet Soup because I threw out so many titles sometimes I got them mixed up. Now that he'd transformed, I had to change his nickname. Satisfaction wasn't enough. So for the time being I decided to call him Roland Waring. That he could change because of a book brightened me up.

It was the same with a lot of people who called to buy books. Here we were in a global pandemic, and even if challenged they were generally cheerful. Of course, there were a few cranks. There always are. Perhaps not surprisingly, a few were crisis counselors. But if I turned the subject to books almost everyone was eager to talk, which was good with me. I can talk about books indefinitely. Alphabet Soup. I only signed off because there was the pressure of orders to fill.

I could work longer shifts, though, as long as Pen helped me keep track of Flora, who was either branching out or getting careless. Sometimes we raised our eyebrows and glanced toward a sound she was making.

This meant everything to me. It proved this wasn't all in my head. Well, I knew it *wasn't* all in my head. Already, in her methodical way, Pen was making a map of Flora's travels around the store. She was trying to figure out if Flora's repetitive path was meaningful.

'I know one thing,' said Pen. 'She's in and out of the confessional a lot. I'm wondering if there's something to the symbols carved into the door or the pictures glued inside.'

I looked at the carved half door to the priest's box.

'What is that symbol?' I asked.

'It's some kind of quatrefoil.'

'I'll look it up,' I said. But I was more interested in the books that fell, that we retrieved from the floor each morning—*Flora and Fauna of Minnesota, Euphoria,* by Lily King. Maybe those had something to say about our ghost's reasons for not staying dead.

Now as a warning to Flora, the playlist started with *my* Johnny Cash song—'God's Gonna Cut You Down.' Penstemon and I didn't take any chances. We always left the store together. Most of the time I was braver, lighter, more cheerful, but Flora's *let me in* whisper had lingering effects. I didn't like being alone now, anywhere. I was shaky at night and kept the curtains shut. I would wake around three a.m.

with my fists clenched, my feet cramped, my jaws aching. And I was often cold, as though my blood had thinned and I was suffused with dark old winter water. Worst of all, my fatigued nerves sparked at times, little shocks, and I said things that stung Pollux, *Get your fat mitts off me*, and Hetta, *Take your stink-eye off me, little girl*. Tookie, you're better than this, I counseled myself. Rise above. But I am a leaden person. When I jump, I can hardly clear three inches. I wanted to rise above but as Pollux would say, *Wanting ain't getting*.

At least now it was spring.

The Year We
Burn the Ghosts

MAY

White double bloodroot and blue scilla covered yards on my path to the store. The leather knuckles of milkweed were pushing from the earth. Dark hemlocks and pine were tipped with tiny tender green needles. People wandered about like toddlers, bending over to look at last year's dried grass. They watched the sky and examined the tags of newly planted city trees. And the air—it was a clean cold food. Sunlight hit my shoulders at an angle, just that slight burn promising summer. The city closed off parkways so people had room to walk outside and the paths were always full of people dodging one another, stepping off curbs and stumbling into gutters.

MIDNITE COWGIRL

Now the afternoons were still sunny after work, so one day I went home looking forward to the little patio beside our grill. I put my feet on a boulder in the tiny garden, the rest of me sagged into a sagging canvas chair. A travel mug of tea was in the mesh cup holder sunk into the arm of the chair. It was strong black tea and the sun was warm on my shoulders. The day was good. Then Hetta brought Jarvis out and put him into my arms and the day was perfect. Light stirring in the new leaves was suspect to him at first. He frowned at the affrontery. I told him it was normal, that leaves happened every year. He'd get to know them.

Hetta pulled up another chair. Surprise made me wary.

'Sorry I called you an old sow,' she said. Her voice wasn't even forced. She seemed normal, like the leaves.

I cleared my throat, spoke creakily in wonder.

'That was months ago. Or maybe a year.'

Hetta actually smiled at me. 'Still.'

'Okay. What's on your mind?'

'Why does something have to be on my mind?'

'Because why else would you suddenly talk to me?'

And smile, I thought.

Now Hetta was staring into the baby leaves. She had a red cotton scarf knotted around her head, holding back her dark sleek knot of hair. She leaned back and closed her eyes. I kept my counsel.

'There is something. I don't know how to even start.'

Oh god, I thought, is this another human confession about a ghost? But Hetta was talking to me for the first time in forever and I couldn't shut her out. Actually, she was babbling.

'Just pretend like it will all make sense if you start at the beginning,' I said.

'Or maybe I should start at the worst part, at the end, to get it over with.'

'That works too.'

I began rocking Jarvis just a little, jiggling him in my arms. I wanted to talk to him but thought I'd better shut up and wait this out.

'The end of the story has me going crazy with a whip.'

I looked at her carefully, trying not to show too much interest, and said, 'Go on.'

'I was in a film.'

'The one you turned down?'

'Yes, but obviously I took it.'

'Does Pollux know?'

'He can never know.'

'What's the name of the film?'

'*Midnight Cowgirl.* Only midnight is spelled n-i-t-e.'

'I think he knows.'

'How could he? It's not out yet or anything. I just

want to tell you so you can run interference, if I might be so bold as to ask.'

'I'd ask too, if I was so bold as to do the film.'

'I was in a stupid place.'

'Well, I've been in a stupider place. This too shall pass.'

'But it won't pass, Tookie. I will always be haunted by what I did.'

So it was about a ghost, after all. A porn haunting.

'I will always be haunted by what I did, too. Join the club,' I said.

And so we sat there. Two haunted women. And one unhaunted baby trailing clouds of glory.

Later on, when he needed to nurse, I handed Jarvis over. That's when Hetta talked to me about Jarvis's father. As expected, it was Laurent. I hadn't seen him in a while, but who did I see besides Pen, Jackie, family, and masked strangers dodging through grocery aisles.

The ice was broken. Hetta wanted to complain. Although she loved him, Laurent couldn't follow rules. It wasn't a choice, it was just that he was so scattered. Hetta hadn't seen him, but Asema told her how Laurent tried to wear a mask, but it ended up on his chin or draped off one ear. Asema had stopped seeing him at all because Laurent hung around with other people and couldn't seem to stop going to parties and gathering with old friends.

'He's working two jobs. He does house-call tattoos.'

'Enterprising lad. But in this time . . .'

'Should I get him out of our lives? Before Jarvis becomes attached? I know that's awful to say.'

I couldn't answer; I was surprised by a sick twinge. I would have loved to know my father, I mean, not if he was violent. But if he was just an oversocial, foxlike, lurkish tattoo artist who lacked mask etiquette? Yes.

'I guess. I will, you know, get him out . . . ,' she said.

I couldn't tell from the tone of her voice whether she was resigned or relieved.

'Wait,' I said. 'I would have wanted to know my dad even if he was careless, wrote in chicken tracks, made his living by inking people, and was loose with his affections.'

Oops. Hetta blinked and let my words settle.

'Oh god. Did I just say that?'

'Yeah, you did. "Loose with his affections." I suppose you saw him with Asema? At the store?'

'I'm surprised you know about that.'

'He told me. See, we were in an open relationship.'

'Is that where you . . .'

'Yes.' She looked down at the cracked flagstone, shrugged. 'It was all my idea, not his. It wasn't working out, either. Except that I got closer to Asema. She's really careful, for her mom and her mooshum. Plus he never told her about Jarvis and me. That was a rule. So now me and Asema, we're cool. Can I tell you something?'

I gave a nod. A wary nod.

'Don't worry, it's a good thing. I just want to state this. I am over my sexual-adventure phase. Laurent. That stupid movie. Et cetera. Jarvis has taught me there are better things. And also, well, I like Asema.'

'Like like her?'

She nodded, glancing away.

'I have to say, I'm glad to hear that.'

'Wow. Look at you,' said Hetta. 'So normal, so mommish and all. I never thought you could be mommish. And you're such a good grandma, a kookum, a nookomis, or whatever. You like Jarvis so much.'

'Love him, love him, really,' I mumbled. For some reason, all this was making me uncomfortable, shy, ridiculous. I tried to shake that off because I want to be a person who can be trusted with these kinds of words.

BURNING THE GHOSTS

In most human cultures there is a festival of reckoning. We honor our dead with food and flowers. Parade red flags and skulls through the streets or visit graves. We use the smoke of incense and sage. We create careful tableaux of heaven and of hell. Bringing the dead to life again, we let their spirits roam. We remember and trace the signals of their actions on the living. Then we burn them up and set them free and tell them not to bother us. It never works. By the following year they're always back.

Presses were still running, books were being printed. There were disruptions, but I found the idea of book production comforting. We've never had the money to buy multiple copies of all the books we need for schools, or the space to warehouse them. Thus we looked like super-organized hoarders. I wondered how Flora would deal with the lack of floor space—if she'd float above, step into the boxes, or maybe trip, as I had done. To my disappointment, she seemed able to negotiate our complicated space. As long as I was working with someone else, she still didn't speak or even hiss at me. She didn't get near me. But I decided to burn her anyway.

If cremation hadn't worked, how could I expect a punier fire to do any good? Because, I realized, I hadn't burned her stuff. When Jackie had talked about not wearing red, I'd remembered that old-timers gave away the dead person's things or burned them. Maybe the burning came about after all the plagues that hit us. But I was covering all the bases I could think of.

I would make a fire and throw in everything Flora had ever given to me. I went through our house, gathering. There were four containers of potpourri (a bit of a sacrifice). A winter hat she'd knitted out of novelty yarn that made me look like a porcupine. Good riddance. Some holy cards because I'd told her I liked old pictures of saints. A ball of hot pink twine—why? Uggs. She'd ordered a pair too big for her and hadn't tried them on in time to send them back. They had fit me. I'd slopped around in them until I ripped them in a couple places. They would be hard to burn. Some smallish powwow T-shirts. An awkwardly beaded medallion. At first, Flora had beaded like a child, uneven rows and raveling ends, but the medallion gave me a pang. I remembered her lowering the beaded daisy chain over my head. She had given me a tremulous, questing, admiring smile. Her soft blue eyes, whitish cotton-candy hair, pink lips. What had she admired about me? What could I have done? Her standards were impossibly low. I set the medallion on the pile and patted it. Back then, she'd meant well. It wasn't as though she'd waited her whole life to become a slinking, needy, invasive spirit. Maybe she hated herself for what she was doing.

I made a fire outside in the old-fashioned fireplace we hardly used. Nobody else was home, and that was good. I didn't want Hetta to protest burning the Uggs or anything else. The T-shirts were pretty nice. Also, if the items refused to burn, like the book, I didn't want to deal with anybody's supernatural freak-out. When I had my blaze going nicely, I threw in Flora's gifts one by one. They burned. The Uggs gave off a spectacular stink. In the spirit of forgiveness, if not actual forgiveness, I threw tobacco into the fire. Then a large bunch of dried cedar, which made the fire spark up in a sudden burst. I always burned up the cedar left over from Pollux's ceremonies. I loved the fragrant smoke, and how the flames hungrily devoured the branches.

Sitting with the fire made me lonely. It was hard to be isolated by a ghost that I couldn't tell Pollux about. I wondered why he tuned out my ghosts and I tuned out his spirits. Were they not the same? I had always refused ceremonies on principle—to prove that being ceremony-averse did not make me less Ojibwe. It was the same sort of reason Pollux occasionally took one drink—to prove that being Native didn't make him an alcoholic. Actively opposing all talk of ghosts wasn't an identity issue with Pollux, but it did make me wonder why, if he believed in spirits, he didn't also believe in ghosts. I kept sitting there even after everything was ash except the charred soles of the boots. I put more wood onto the fire. The day turned chilly as evening came on and the coals were throwing pleasant heat. After a while, I heard Pollux pull into the driveway. He went through the house and came out to sit with me. He saw the burnt soles.

'Did you fall asleep with your feet in the fire again?'

'Yes,' I said. 'Question. Why do I believe in ghosts if I don't believe in spirits? And why do you believe in spirits but not in ghosts?'

He looked at me, busted eyebrow up, lip pursed, taking me in. Finally he nodded and turned back to the fire.

'It's not that I don't believe in spirits,' he said. 'I don't like it when people say spooks, or even the word ghost. Or the name of a dead person. Especially that. It is disrespectful.'

I leaned in and stared at him like he was a stranger. 'No way,' I said. 'That's the reason you walk away at the very mention?'

'Of course that's the reason.'

'So you're telling me that you believe—let me get this straight—that you *know* that there are ghosts.'

'Not ghosts, spirits. Yes.'

'And here I am, haunted, ever since last November, and haven't dared talk to you about it after you dissed

me. I haven't asked for help. I thought you'd walk away.
You did walk away.'

'So what exactly,' asked Pollux, 'do you mean by
haunted?'

'What I said. Haunted.'

'Literally haunted? As in seeing a spirit?'

'Hearing her, Flora . . .'

'Shhhhhh.'

'See? I can't talk to you. Why?'

'You know I quit being a tribal cop after I arrested
you. You know I wasn't a gung ho officer anyway. So
it's not in me to be a culture cop either. However, I'll
tell you. It's because you say her name. You can't say
her name right out like that. You have to respect the
dead. Also, if she hears her name she might get distracted on the road to heaven, if she's still on the road.
And you don't really want to get her attention once
she's in heaven.'

'Why?'

'She might think you want to join her.'

That shut me up.

'You Chippewas have worked out a way to deal
with this,' said Pollux. 'I learned from Noko. You add
-iban on the end of her name. That way she doesn't
recognize her name and also it means she is in the
spirit world.'

'Why the hell did I not know this?' I raked at Pollux with my glare.

'You're on top of your traditions,' he said. 'I thought you knew and had some reason. I never thought.'

'No, I'm not on top of my traditions! I didn't grow up with traditions! Stealing food was my tradition! I never got to learn about -iban.'

'Geez, I'm sorry. I didn't want to . . . I guess you could say, patronize you.'

I was silent. Get a grip, I was thinking, don't push this any further. He apologized. Mii go maanoo. Just leave it. But I wanted to scream so hard at Pollux that I had to press the back of my hand against my mouth. All of this was not his fault. But.

'Why marry a ceremony man unless I can rely on you to ceremony me out of trouble?' I said.

'I've asked myself that same question,' said Pollux. 'Why marry a bookseller unless you want to buy a book?'

We gave each other the side-eye, then we started laughing. Pretty soon we were upstairs in bed. At some point, dozing off, we heard a car drive up and Hetta's voice out there as she unfastened Jarvis's car seat. She was laughing, with another woman. Asema. Really whooping.

'Guess this is a funny night,' said Pollux.

'Glad we started early.'

We were looking up at the ceiling fan, which I loved. In the grainy half dark its blur calmed me.

'I'm so glad you installed that thing.'

'I did it for you. To hypnotize you. So you'd do my bidding.'

'What's your bidding?'

'You know,' said Pollux.

'I guess I can accommodate you,' I said. 'Just this one time. If you stay real quiet.'

'Ten thousand and one,' he mumbled, after, when we were lying there half asleep. 'I think it's a world record.'

'Definitely a world record. We're on another level.'

'We should get some kind of prize.'

'A plaque with a detailed description. To hang over the fireplace. We'd embarrass Hetta to death,' he said.

'I know. She's pretty innocent, having had a baby and all.'

Uh-oh. I put my hand over my mouth.

'Actually, you're right. She's an innocent,' said Pollux before he plunged into sleep. I hoped what he said meant that he didn't know about *Midnite Cowgirl*. I watched the whirling ceiling fan and let it put me to sleep.

Sometimes as I am waking, between sleep and consciousness, I am afflicted with a wave of crashing sorrow. Where this wave comes from, or why this moment is so bitter and deep, I don't know. It just happens to me. I stay still as though I have a knife in me, afraid to jostle this feeling and make it worse. But I know that it won't go away unless I submit to it. And so I feel it.

This happened to me the morning after Pollux hypnotized me with the ceiling fan. I woke in the grip of sadness and as always I let the dark fill me. Slowly, as it receded, I peered out of my cave of pillows. Pollux was sitting at a little table next to the window. It was one of his workstations, which are scattered through the house and garage. He'd brought this table into our room when Hetta began to inhabit his office. It was the place he worked with the eagle feathers. They were beautiful mottled brown and white feathers, wing feathers, so they curved slightly. Pollux was straightening them out by stroking the spines on a hot lightbulb. He was wearing sunglasses against the glare. Over and over he drew the feather over the glass. This would only be normal in a Native person's house. The feather gradually straightened. It took a long time. I watched him from under my pillows. The light lay on his hair, picking out silver, black, and white strands. The patience of him, the way he was devoted to that feather, worked on me. Again and again he warmed the feather, bent it the opposite direction, pulled it straight, warmed it again. He seemed the picture of human love. I knew the fan was for me. I knew the feathers actually were me—Tookie—straightened by warmth applied a thousand times.

Minnesota Goddamn

SIGNAL EVENT

The public health definition: *An event, usually man-made, in which there is a tremendous 'signal,' often in the form of a disaster, which engenders multiple ripple effects of legislation and landmark legal cases, due in part to a popular outcry against prevailing policies that were inadequate or incapable of addressing the event.*

MAY 25

Monday night, late. Hetta showed her father something on her phone. She was always doing that. Pollux thumped down on the couch and dropped his head in his hands. *Oh no gawiin gawiin,* he said, *oh no. Oh nononono gawiin.* Then I watched it too, the video of a police officer with his knee on the neck of a Black man who cried out and cried out for his mother and then went quiet and then was silent. This happened at Cup Foods in South Minneapolis. Pollux often stopped there to pick up a thing or two on his way back from working on the universe. You can get anything there, and I mean anything, he said about Cup. Now he said, *I was just there. Maybe I could've . . .* I sat down carefully beside him.

Hetta scrolled through her Twitter feed, said, *Bad fucking check maybe? Bad fucking check?* After a while she said there was a plan forming and she was going over to the gathering that would take place tomorrow. She'd take Jarvis.

'I'll keep him safe,' she said. 'I have to be there.' She started to cry. Pollux still had his head down. He'd been that way since the video. I touched his back and he startled. I tried to hold back a wash of derangement. We had all just witnessed a murder and what do you do with that?

Hetta listed every measure she would take, the masks and alcohol spray. Pollux still had his head down, but he was listening.

'Do babies get the virus?'

Hetta shrugged this off, then looked thoughtful. She cradled her baby and sighed.

'I don't want to get him sick.'

'How about if I take care of Jarvis,' I said. 'You leave me some bottles.'

Pollux was still staring at the floor. In the early

days of the American Indian Movement, AIM, they listened to the police radio and showed up with tape recorders wherever there was about to be an arrest in certain neighborhoods, at certain bars. The Minneapolis police regularly took our people down to the river for a beating, and AIM organized to stop that. Now we had cell phone videos.

I stopped circling and tried to sit down.

'Asema just texted me. We're going together,' said Hetta.

'Good. Rule one, have a buddy. Not that I have rules,' I amended. 'I've never been to a march, except Standing Rock, and I was just bringing books.' I tapped my chest. 'Felon. I don't go around cops.' I looked down at Pollux. 'Except this one.'

He didn't lift his head.

'So I can keep Jarvis here in his baby sling,' I said. 'We'll be all right.'

Hetta started talking in earnest, saying people had to mourn. Saying that there finally had to be a reckoning. I was surprised because she'd never reacted this way to anything. Her intensity had been focused on her makeup, her clothes, her friends. But that was before Jarvis, before the reflective isolation of this year, and before getting close to Asema. As for me, once I stopped talking, my thoughts jammed up again. That video of George Floyd dying played over and over in my head.

But would I file it with the others?

Jeronimo Yanez shooting Philando Castile in one annihilating movement. Seven shots. We'll never be clean again, I remember thinking at the time. None of us who let this happen. But what had I done since? A few things. Not effective things.

I thought of Philando's companion, his girlfriend, Diamond Reynolds. *Why did you shoot him, sir?* I thought of Diamond's four-year-old child talking to her handcuffed mother in the backseat of Yanez's patrol car. *I don't want you to get shooted, Mama. I am here for you.*

'Thanks for taking Jarvis, Mom,' said Hetta.

'Sure, honey,' I said.

Pollux stared at each of us in dull wonder, then put his head down again. Hetta went to bed. Pollux and I sat up talking and checking our phones, staying up way too late. We shouldn't have, because it would turn out that nobody in the Cities would sleep for many a night as the city grieved and burned.

I'd dozed off on the couch and when I jolted awake before daylight the house was still. Once, when I couldn't leave my cell, I was extracted by a team of men. So I've been tackled and throttled, the terror of that was in me, and it had struggled to the surface of my skin. I lay speechless in the dark. I'd had the cloth of a man's uniform tight across my face, and it hadn't belonged to Pollux.

It was May 26. Hetta and Asema went to the gathering and march packing water bottles, hats, umbrellas for rain. They came back in a few hours. It had been emotional and cathartic, but they'd left the march before it got to the Third Precinct station. We were sitting together again that evening looking at the live feeds. Things were heating up. We turned away, turned back, and there were fireworks, flash-bangs, tear gas. Then it rained and it seemed like people went home.

HAUNTED CITY

'I can't stay here today.' Hetta gazed steadily at me over eggs and toast. 'We have to stand with Black people because we know. The MPD has fucking done this to Indians since the beginning of this city. No, before that. They practiced on us in the Dakota War and ever since. Look at the goddamn state seal.'

Our state seal and flag: an Indian with a ridiculous spear rides off while a farmer plows his field with a gun propped on a tree stump. Asema was on the latest committee to get it changed so I knew they'd been talking. I'd been going to say to Hetta that she sounded like Asema, but then I thought maybe Hetta was starting to sound like herself. Pollux had gone out early to check in with his buddies, so I was alone when Hetta and Asema got ready to go out again. I had agreed to take Jarvis to work.

'Don't go to the precinct,' I said.

I texted Pollux and he sounded worried. He told me to make sure they used good masks and took water bottles.

'We'll be back early again,' said Hetta. 'Don't worry.'

Hetta took Jarvis from her breast and gave him to me to burp—this meant I'd reached the semipros. I held him on the burp cloth draped over my shoulder and lightly patted him while doing a two-step. Asema drove up in her mother's venerable yellow Forester. Hetta kissed her baby on his head and grabbed her backpack. Pollux had told me to give her his pair of shatterproof goggles in case the police used rubber bullets. Yesterday he'd also tried to give her a bike helmet, but she wouldn't take either one.

'I know you're worried,' she said, 'but it won't be like that.'

She brandished her phone and told me she would text updates. She turned on her location sharing and made sure it was connected to her dad's phone. She even, sort of, hugged at me. Then she gave me a definitive air hug, as if she didn't want to disturb Jarvis. This was close as we'd come to an actual hug, and it gave me a sad glow.

I stood in the window jiggling Jarvis and watching Hetta and Asema spring down the walkway. They'd gone off casually yesterday, but this morning they were dressed for business in track pants and sneakers. Asema wore a white Rage Against the Machine T-shirt with a red fist raised in the middle. Her billed black hat said Birchbark Bookhead. It was overcast and already hot. Hetta was wearing a man's button-down, blue, a white T-shirt underneath. They wore their hair in low knots at the nape of their necks, so they couldn't get seized by the ponytail. Asema had a Sharpie and they were writing on each other's arms. When I realized that they were writing their contact information on their bodies, I went to the door with Jarvis.

'Come back!' My voice was strained and thick.

Hetta smiled at me over her shoulder.

'It's okay, Mom.'

She knew that calling me Mom would completely undo me.

'Nobody's going to get arrested!' Asema shouted.

The two mock-saluted and ducked into the car. I had a terrible feeling as they drove off. I always have terrible feelings when anyone drives off. Throughout my life people have tended to disappear forever. My aunt—diabetic coma. My mother—overdose. My cousins—various accidents, various substances. My lovers—other people. Hetta and Asema will be okay, I thought. It is supposed to be safe to exercise your First Amendment rights in peaceful assembly, but then again there was Standing Rock. We had gone to cook. I'd brought a load of books. I really didn't understand the legal underpinnings of the protest. Truth is, I went because all the people I liked, including Jackie and a person who made really good hominy stew, were going there. Then one thing led to another. Pollux was kneeling when he was teargassed, pepper-sprayed, and hit with a chemical we still can't identify. Since then, he's been short of breath. I needed to talk to him again, so I called.

'Maybe the police will stand down or take a knee,' he said. 'I can't believe how many people are out here.'

I told him to be careful and he said he was social distancing by standing on one side of a table of food, filling chili bowls.

I figured out how to clasp the straps on the baby carrier and wear a baby. We walked to work on the shady sides of the streets. Pollux would pick us up after he fed everybody. The clouds were low and I felt the heat gathering. Jarvis didn't seem to care, but I was glad to reach the bookstore. I unlocked the front door and peered in. Jackie was already working in the office. The air was cool, a relief. I came in and started printing out online orders, checking to see that we had the books.

Hetta said the protests were going to start at Cup Foods again, go east on Thirty-Eighth to Hiawatha, but they'd come home before they ended up at the police station. She'd keep checking in. Hetta kept her word for a while, sent us a few photos she took on the march—a woman in pink tights pushing a baby carriage, a man with a child on his back holding up a sign that said *Justice*. I knew the photos were meant to be reassuring. She promised to double back to the Forester early.

Jarvis drank a sip of water from a bottle, napped for about an hour, then opened his eyes and frowned up at me. Nothing had prepared me for what it felt like when a baby on your chest stares at you from right below your chin with a look of intense disappointment. His expression told me that by not being Hetta I had failed him in every way. I reached into the baby bag, pulled out a chilled bottle, ran hot water over it to warm it just enough. I did not remove Jarvis from the carrier, although his tiny mouth turned down and his brow furrowed in despair.

'I know it's terrible, little one,' I said in my most tender voice. 'But I am Tookie. And I've got your mom's milk.'

'You shouldn't growl at a baby. And what you said sounded creepy.'

Jackie came out of the office. She wore one of those blue paper masks that were hard to get. Her hair was swirled on top of her head in a beaded clip. Her eyes were made up with swoopy eyeliner and her brows were strong and full. I marveled that she fixed herself up just to be alone.

'Aww, can it, boss. Can't you see I'm a frickin' novice?'

'You're doing great. You're a natural,' she said as Jarvis's face fell into utter abjection. When he opened his mouth to wail, I gently inserted the nipple of the bottle. He was suspicious, then outraged. He wanted to bluster, but tasted a drop of milk and in his surprise agreed to be fed. He finished the entire bottle and pressed his head against my heart.

'Shouldn't you change his diaper before he falls asleep?'

'He's got one of those high-tech diapers on,' I said,

although he was heavy in the bottom and I could feel a patch of damp.

All right. I'd smell of baby pee. But I'd passed my first test as a solo grandma, with a no-previous-child handicap too. I'd fed a baby and put him to sleep. Who could argue? I was less than awful. I curved my hand around Jarvis's tiny body and sat back down at the computer.

There was nothing from Hetta.

By late afternoon, I'd changed his diaper thrice, fed him his second bottle. I took him up to the play loft for exercise and we rolled around together on the floor. Jackie looked on, but she was too scrupulous about the virus to touch him. Jarvis now gave startled belly laughs when I shook my head and flung my hair around. I did that, over and over, and every time I got a laugh. Then out of the blue, he started whimpering. I exhausted my bag of tricks but his whimper only grew more intense. If he'd even squeaked before, I'd simply turned him over to Hetta. His face crumpled and he began to roar. Now there was something so wrong that I was paralyzed. Maybe he'd swallowed poison. Maybe he had a twisted intestine. Maybe there was a pin sticking in him. Where? I checked him all over, ever more frantic. I couldn't find the source.

'Jackie! What do I do?'

'Babies cry! Just hold him and jiggle him.'

Jackie put her hands up and shut the door to the office. I heard the fan go on full blast.

Twenty minutes by the clock, an eternity in my nerves. The violent agonies of my grandson entered my heart and my chest squeezed around a red lump of misery. Jackie peeked out once and told me she used to sing. I started a song without thinking, *You can have it all, my empire of dirt*, and Jackie said maybe don't sing. She closed the door again. Eventually, Jarvis simmered down and then I felt his tiny body relax and go heavy. However, if I sat down, he stirred. I had to keep moving and this became a problem. I couldn't use the computer unless I swayed back and forth. I spent the last hour of work packing boxes, two-stepping in place. It was exhausting. No wonder Hetta was so skinny.

After work, Pollux met me coming out the door, and together we strapped Jarvis into his highly engineered baby seat. It looked like something from a space rocket.

'I wish I had one of these,' I said. 'I'd go to Mars. Have you heard from Hetta?'

She had texted Pollux in the beginning but we hadn't heard from her for a few hours. It was six now. As we drove he told me how he could tell that she'd left her phone somewhere, probably in Asema's car. Neither of us had Asema's location.

'The march is at the Third Precinct now.'

'They said they wouldn't go that far.'

I examined my phone again. I didn't want to bug Hetta because I wanted her to trust that she could leave her baby with me and not be harassed. Jarvis was awake in back, but quiet. He'd guzzled his last bottle with an air of reserved acceptance, keeping a watch-eye on me.

We got home, settled Jarvis into a contraptiony lounge-bed that bounced and had an archway decorated with dangling toys. Hetta had tapped into a post-baby equipment exchange. New things kept appearing.

'Dial Hetta's number again,' I said. 'I'll thaw a packet of milk.'

After six calls and an hour or so she answered and I could hear her say *I'm okay don't come get me.*

'On their way back to the car now,' he said.

I wanted to slump over and take a nap, but I was standing up again and had a baby on me. Pollux put his arms around me from behind. He looked over my shoulder, startling Jarvis.

'Maybe he thinks I've grown an extra head.'

'A big ugly one,' said Pollux.

Jarvis broke out a gummy smile of joy and gazed long at Pollux. I could feel Pollux working his eyebrows up and down.

'Babies love me,' he said. 'I don't know why.'

'You're a giant baby with caterpillar eyebrows. What's not to love?'

He smoothed his eyebrows with his fingers.

'I'd look more like a baby if I shaved them off.'

'Oh Pollux, your one beauty.'

'If only I could have given you a little papoose like this one.'

'Aren't we still trying? I might have a rogue egg or two left in me.'

'Hush your mouth,' said Pollux. 'Little ears. I'll help you get out of that thing.'

Pollux unhooked the baby carrier from behind. I held on to the baby and Pollux lifted the carrier away from my body. He cradled Jarvis, jounced around with him, sat down in the easy chair to jiggle him while I fixed us beers and peanut butter sandwiches. I found some weird peach jelly and brought it out, on the side. Pollux was looking at his phone and said he'd have to go meet up at Pow Wow Grounds later on. I opened my mouth to argue, but the tension in his eyes when he saw the sandwiches stopped me.

'I'm gonna make pancakes when she comes back,' he said, taking a tiny bite of the sandwich. 'Pancakes with smiley faces. The way she likes 'em.'

I wanted to tell Pollux that as far as I knew Hetta hadn't eaten smiley pancakes for years, but I held my tongue. His face was quiet and he was closed in, the way he got when he was worried.

THE BOULEVARD

Hetta curled around her baby. She was home. He fit perfectly against her body. He was her source of primal joy. Why had she left him? Her arms and legs were watery and weak with spent adrenaline. She shifted closer to her baby on the foldout bed. She really needed the nursing endorphins. She really needed a diazepam of some kind, any kind. She really needed her heart to stop galloping, her ears to stop buzzing, her head to stop headaching. She'd taken a long shower and changed into clean clothes, then stripped them off and showered again. Her eyes still hurt, her face burned, her throat. She was worried tear gas would get into her milk.

For most of the way it was a regular march. She saw a woman in brown tatters with a hand drum, fake Indian, singing *Waa naa waa.* Asema reached over and snatched away her drum.

'What are you?' laughed Hetta.

'I'm the drum police!' said Asema. She put the drum in her pack and kept walking. They paced beside a poised lady with gray hair, wearing a red sheath dress, holding hands with her masked balding husband in a suit and tie. The march went on and on, gathering, snaking, and folding until the crowd formlessly collected itself near the end.

As they marched across the railroad tracks and up the street, Asema became alarmingly energized. She surged forward and started running down the pavement, then through a parking lot toward the Third Precinct station. They got separated for a while, and Hetta tripped, went sprawling across a grassy strip of boulevard. Her milk came down and wet the front of her shirt. Someone was rolling away from underneath her. There was a man in dangling earrings and a ripped cowboy shirt helping her up. A woman in hot-yellow overalls and blond dreads to her waist jumped to her feet and bent forward, hoarsely calling. There were explosions, then smoke. A person running through tear gas like a deer suddenly collapsed. All the people with children had peeled off a mile ago and Hetta wished she'd gone with them. Ahead of her, Asema with her hands held up high disappeared into a cloud. A girl in a hijab, maybe twelve years old, darted forward and kicked a canister back at the police. Something so excruciating it didn't register as pain streamed into Hetta's eyes and lungs. Tear gas went for the moisture on her sweaty skin, her nipples. Someone turned her over and poured water over her face and eyes. Please! Hetta gasped and pointed at her chest. Someone was gasping, gagging, panicking, lost. It was herself. A storm of legs around her, ferocious noises, thuds, screams. Someone pulled her to a clear place and she returned to her body.

Through flooding tears she realized that person was Laurent. He held her head with steady, tender hands and tipped water into her eyes. A pair of swimming goggles was pushed up his forehead and his swatch of hair stuck straight up. He was wearing long sleeves and gloves. His bandanna was down around his neck. He pulled out another one, blue, and dabbed Hetta's face.

'You okay now?'

'No.'

He smoothed her hair back and tipped more water on her face. Hetta grabbed his wrist and blinked at him.

'Asema's still back there,' she said.

Laurent kissed his finger, touched it to her nose, and was gone. Hetta had loved when Pollux did that but always hated that gesture when she saw it in movies. Why? Patronizing? Like she was a little kid. And yet she clung to the blue bandanna.

Asema finally came back through the cloud. Together they staggered across a parking lot and found another grass boulevard, farther from the precinct.

No Laurent. Hetta poured water from her pack over Asema's eyes. Blinking up through the trickles, Asema gasped that she was going back to fight. Hetta threatened to slug her. *Fuck, you promised!* Asema didn't want to leave, but Hetta made her leave. They started walking back to the Forester, debating whether they should try to get a Lyft, but because of Covid deciding it was too risky.

Their feet swelled. Their armpits burned. Their skin. The walk seemed endless. Hetta wetted the bandanna and tied it around her neck. She regretted the Chucks because no arch support. Pregnancy had wrecked her feet.

'Fuck 12,' Asema kept saying. 'They fucking shot shit at us.'

At last they'd reached the car and made it home. And now as she lay with her baby waiting for sleep, a mixture of images surged up and diminished. Her mind flickered with sound and color, then went gray. She startled. The crazy scenes from yesteryear that started up whenever she was half asleep—bad hookups, drunk customers, stalker dates, a controlling boss, a sadistic boyfriend, and her own curiosities that cost her so much—bulged into her mind, then collapsed. Laurent sneaked in but she channeled the word ambivalence. She took the ten deep breaths her sleep app recommended and at last she sank and was covered with cottony snow. Jarvis. *My little love, I will never leave you.* The pictures of the past mixed with today's pictures flashed like raindrops in streetlight. She felt coldly the squalor and drama of all she'd raged against, caused, or suffered in her life.

MAY 28

Asema woke panting with ire. She texted Tookie that she'd be late for work, then realized it was three a.m. She stumbled into the shower. The last of the itchy grime of the march flowed away and she began to mourn. She had felt them, the dead, very close. A grandmother from Leech Lake had called George Floyd our relative and she had prayed for *our relatives who long ago were brought to this land against their will.* During the march Asema had been overwhelmed by the radiant warmth of other people. Fury shot through her stomach when she saw the riot-geared police. They made themselves look inhuman, invulnerable, faces behind shields, anonymous armor. The very sight of how they got themselves up like storm troopers meant to Asema that they were cowards so she was more furious than scared. But at first she hadn't realized they were shooting marker rounds, tear gas canisters, rubber bullets. She ran to the front line and threw her hands up to shield the others before she understood what was coming at her. The canister had landed at her feet. She stumbled as she tried to move away from the boiling chemical smoke.

Then, after she had tried so hard to do everything right—the sanitizing, the masks, the spraying down of groceries, the distance, everything—in a moment she ripped off her mask, fled, coughed out, and sucked in other people's breath. And now she was scared. She had been among hundreds of people. Now she'd get the virus.

Asema went outside and sat down on the dark back stoop, three wooden steps that led down to their little vegetable garden. Last year the squash vine had grown from its dirt box out across the mowed weeds and scuffed earth that made their lawn. It was a homey sort of lawn. A useful lawn. There was a fire pit, a rickety charcoal grill, a new lattice arbor, a metal shepherd's crook holding a bird feeder with a lone sparrow on it. There were lawn chairs made of sagging woven plastic. A scratched picnic table. The cheerful cantina lights. Birthday parties, graduations, baby showers. There was the residue of joy in their tattered yard. Around six a.m. she walked six blocks over to the memorial and helped arrange scattered bouquets along the wall where an image of George Floyd was being painted. Farther on, closer to the precinct, there were people out sweeping up glass, picking up trash. She grabbed a broom and started sweeping too.

NIGHT

We stayed up watching familiar places burn. Every so often one of us would murmur as we recognized a box store, grocery store, restaurant, liquor store, pawnshop. There was scene after scene of people silhouetted against flames. Hetta was texting Asema, who was not answering. There were all sorts of people out there now. Black white brown. Ordinary. Sorrowful and infuriated. Hetta said people were seeing white-supremacist action. The fires were across town but close by there were fireworks, sirens, helicopters, the incoherent roar of conflict, pops of gunfire, engines revving, tearing through streets, motorcycles, more fireworks and shots, sometimes near and sometimes far. There were lights up and down our leafy street of 1970s and '80s ranch-style houses, some expensively renovated. There were a few older, smaller, idiosyncratic wood-frame houses, like ours, that must have been hand-built during the 1930s.

'There's a fire truck,' I said.

We were using our laptop and phones to try and figure out what was happening. On one screen, there was a constant replay of the night before, when a giant white man in bizarre black headgear appeared. He carried a sledgehammer, smashed the window of an AutoZone. A slim Black man in a pink shirt tried to stop him, then followed him through the parking lot across from the police station. We saw a half-constructed apartment building with affordable housing units collapse, and more silhouettes of people dancing in the flame light. Was that Laurent?

'I think it's him,' Hetta said.

Hetta faced Jarvis toward the screen.

'See? It's Daddy,' her voice thunked. 'And to think,' she muttered, 'I'm the one who taught him how to start a fire.'

'You really think he's starting fires?' I asked. 'He's more into earnest scratchings and hammocking. Anyway, I thought you were getting skinny shanks out of your life.'

'Me too, but sometimes I look at Jarvis. Am I enough?'

'Of course you're enough,' said Pollux. 'But unless

this kid is an actual wiindigoo I wouldn't cut him out of your baby's life.'

I knew the two of them had to be thinking of Hetta's mother, dead now, like mine. Hetta's face cleared and she said, 'You two would have made good parents together.'

'What do you mean "would have"?' said Pollux. 'We're here with you. Plus you never know, we might be still trying.'

'Oooh, I can't handle this!' Hetta laughed.

'Not to worry, child, we're ever platonic,' said Pollux. 'Sometimes we hold hands in bed, but just to fall asleep.'

'That's the only picture I need,' said Hetta. 'I can think of you as romantic, but in an abstract way. I know you go way back, maybe to when you were kids, so I like to picture a pleasant friendship. But really . . .' She paused. '. . . how did you decide to get together? I mean, you've told me that story about meeting in a parking lot a hundred times now. But what came before?'

'Before?'

Before. I found myself at a loss. Where to start? And Pollux seemed equally uncomfortable. He eventually said, in a low voice, 'I guess you could say that we had a professional relationship.'

'Professional on your part, at least,' I said.

I put my hand on my chest and closed my eyes. I have a dinosaur heart, cold, massive, indestructible, a thick meaty red. And I have a glass heart, tiny and pink, that can be shattered. The glass heart belongs to Pollux. There was a ping. To my surprise, it had developed a minute crack, nearly invisible. But it was there, and it hurt.

Our voices grew hushed. We were watching a live stream from Unicorn Riot. Last I'd looked, the police had been shooting tear gas and rubber bullets down off the roof, into the crowd. Now police cars in an orderly, jaw-dropping line started moving slowly out of the Third Precinct parking lot. Pollux put his hand up to his face and said he'd never seen anything remotely like what was happening now.

'You don't leave your base. I don't know what's going on.'

The police were still pulling away in a motorcade, down the street. Soon came the scenes of shattering glass at the police station, people walking through drifts of paper inside the precinct, water pouring from sprinklers, a lawless exuberance. I looked at Pollux. The action on the screen was reflecting on his face. They were fucking up the station! I carefully hid my expression as I bent toward the laptop. I was trying to contain a surprise bubble of exultation bobbing in the anger I have always tried to keep bottled up. Fury lived in me under pressure. Now it all started going off inside my body liked popped corks; the rage-champagne and feral glee were foaming out.

I slowly got up and slipped into the kitchen. Then out the door and down the steps. I lowered myself onto the grass and pretty soon I started rolling around. I sat up a minute, panting. Looked both ways, but no one was watching. I threw myself back down and kept rolling the shit off myself—assault by COs, offhand blows, shoves, kicks, contempt. All of the times I was treated like a piece of nothing-dirt by a cop or someone in a uniform. More bubbles brimmed up in me. Some were tears.

After a while I went back into the house. The mood was dark. There was nobody stopping anybody from doing anything at all now. To Pollux and Hetta, it was like a crack had opened in the earth. *Is this good old Minneapolis? Can this be Minneapolis?* Hetta kept saying.

'It's Minneapolis Goddamn,' said Pollux.

'Down by the river Minneapolis,' said Hetta. I'd told her about the interrogations there.

'I know it's a fucked-up town, but it's my fucked-up town,' said Pollux.

'It's freaking me the fuck out,' said Hetta.

Only Jarvis and I were taking this well.

'People are fed up though,' said Hetta, watching her Twitter feed.

'Those little restaurants had great soup,' I said. 'Too bad George Floyd won't taste any.'

'The police are maxed out,' said Pollux, ignoring me. 'The firefighters are maxed out. Some of those places are just gonna burn. It's gonna be hard for everybody who lives around there to even buy a toothbrush. Elders with no rides live there, but fuck, you know, people have had it.'

His last sentence was sarcastic. Pollux turned to us. 'That's not all righteous anger out there,' he said. 'Some of the looters are pros. It happens all the time. And the fires are taking everything now.

'You're not working tomorrow,' said Pollux to me. 'Right?'

'We're playing it by ear,' I said. There was a sentence people were chanting all over the world now. I can't breathe. I wanted to run out the door again.

'Did you board up the store?' asked Hetta, still scrolling. 'Uptown's looted. There's action on Hennepin, I mean the store's not that far away. . . .'

'No.'

'Mom, you can't go to work.'

She called me Mom again, I thought, coming back to earth, and this time she didn't want anything.

Suddenly Hetta jumped up and threw her phone down on the couch.

'Abolish the police,' she said, looking hard at Pollux. He'd been dozing and put his head up slowly, blinked at her.

'You don't know what you're saying, my girl. I mean, the police *are* abolished for the moment. You like what's happening?'

'In a more just world this wouldn't be happening, Dad. They teargassed Asema and me. They're killers. They keep on and keep on killing Black people, brown people, *our people*, Dad.'

'Okay, sweetheart,' said Pollux. He could hardly see straight he was so tired. 'We got a good police chief in Arradondo, I know their union chief's—'

Pollux kept talking as though he could reason this away. 'They're still hiring from outside the city. This Chauvin, he was from some burb.'

Hetta was burstingly mad. She screwed her lips shut and panted through her nose, seethed, then barked loudly. 'I'm sure you would have stopped Derek Chauvin. Three other cops were there. One even Black. But I'm sure you would have stopped Derek Chauvin.'

Pollux scrubbed his face with his palms. Rubbed

his eyes with the heels of his hands. Shook his head like he was coming out of a dream. His voice was too gentle.

'I hope I would have. But you never know what you're gonna do until you're in that situation. Until the world is a better place, we need cops, daughter.'

Hetta lowered her head and stared at him from under her brow. Her lower lip drooped. Her eyes were black slash marks.

'Were you in that situation? Ever? Were you, Dad?'

'Hetta, I was a words cop. I was out with AIM patrol last night. Frank Paro's in charge now. Clyde Bellecourt just appointed him a couple weeks ago. Really good man. This is community work like you want, right? We don't carry guns, most of us. Well, I don't know . . .' Pollux paused with a troubled stare. 'After all this, some of us might have to. But we try to talk it out. Smooth it down. So on a possible fake bill this would not happen.'

'Did you hurt anybody?'

'Hetta. Not like that.'

'But like what?'

Pollux got up and left the room. We could hear the refrigerator open, shut. Drawers rattled. Water gushed. Soon we smelled coffee.

'He's gonna come back out here with a plate of sandwiches or something,' said Hetta. 'But he's not gonna buy me off with a couple slabs of cheap ham.'

'He can buy me off,' I said, 'if there's cheese.'

'Or even mayo,' said Hetta. 'You come cheap, like the ham. But he's my dad. He's gotta level with me.'

'Mustard. But it's too late for this,' I said. 'We shouldn't go there. We'll be sorry in the morning.'

'It is morning,' said Hetta. 'And when has being sorry in the morning ever stopped you?'

I had to think for a while.

'Never,' I said.

Pollux came back with a plate of sandwiches and three coffee mugs looped in his fingers. He went back into the kitchen, brought out the coffeepot, poured us coffee, and went back. I lifted a piece of bread to peek and nodded. He'd loaded the sandwiches.

'Let's eat these before he comes back,' I said.

'I'm not touching a goddamn bite.'

I lifted one, brought it to my mouth, but before I could chomp down Hetta spoke.

'How did you two meet? That professional thing? Not really an answer.'

'Oh, wasn't it?' I put down the sandwich. I had become extremely hungry. 'Your dad arrested me,' I said. 'Now can I eat my sandwich?'

Hetta gaped. 'Well fuck yeah. Eat that piggy.'

I grabbed the sandwich and stuffed my mouth, glaring at the computer screen where a young man was narrating flames and mayhem, bottles flying past his head. The Third Precinct station was now enveloped in golden fire. What if Moon Palace, or even Uncle Hugo's, or Dreamhaven bookstore burned? Hetta might say books were just property. Stores too. That sure, every small enterprise was somebody's dream but George Floyd had lost his dream. It didn't fit together so neatly when it got this personal. All I could think of was pages curling in waves of flame.

Pollux came back into the room. For a while, Hetta didn't speak. Pollux and I chewed our sandwiches slowly, as if in a state of intense deliberation. I was mesmerized by the destruction. Hetta didn't touch her sandwich. I willed Jarvis to cry so Hetta wouldn't get back into my business. 'Was that Jarvis?' I said. 'I thought I heard him.' But Hetta had her baby monitor on her phone.

'Nope,' said Hetta. 'Baby J ain't gonna save you. Now let's go back to the arrest where you met my dad.'

Pollux turned his eye on me.

'None of your fucking business.' I picked up Hetta's sandwich and took a bite. 'Sleep well, beautiful people.'

I walked up the stairs with the sandwich. In the bathroom, I threw it away. What a waste. And Pollux will see it, I thought, looking at the sprawled thing lying grossly on some tissues and drain hair.

Let him see it, I thought, turning out the light. Neither Pollux nor Hetta could possibly understand what I was feeling now. As for the sandwich, it might seem a small thing to have done. But Pollux and I ate everything, even the coldest french fry. And we never wasted food made with love. So the sandwich was a glaring signal. I drew the covers down. Rolled in. But no sleep. My brain was a lamp shining in a dark street. In that circle, I saw my arms stretch across the table at Lucky Dog. I saw my fingers open, ready to wind with his fingers, but instead he cuffs me up. Well, he didn't use cuffs, to be real about it, he used a zip tie like you'd fasten on a bag of garbage.

MAY 29

After an hour or so, I woke in the dark and realized that Pollux hadn't come to bed. For a fuzzy moment I thought of going downstairs to fetch him, probably from the couch. But then I understood he was gone. I could feel his absence from the house, but I did nothing. Sleep took me away again, for a long time. The next morning I felt like I had a hangover. An old-time hangover as from the days of yore. I felt like someone was shooting off a space blaster in my head, and Jarvis was bawling.

Pollux had left a note to say he'd gone out last night. He owned a sidearm. It was so locked away that I'd only seen it once. But I remembered it, a Glock 19. I jiggled the door on the small gun safe but couldn't tell if it was in there. However, the shotgun, which he kept in a case of molded plastic and which I had seen, was nowhere to be found. I had a sick feeling about how I'd left him downstairs and the sandwich in the trash.

Hetta was in her room with her screaming infant and I was glad. But it went on for a while and I was sorry, so I knocked on the door. During my sleep a switch with a lot of complicated settings had been pushed to a different bar. It was a bar that connected me to Hetta in spite of it all. Or because.

'I sue for peace,' I said, holding out my arms for the baby. Instead, Hetta put her arms out and did her air hug. 'I'd hug you but I was out there with the germs,' she said. 'Peace.'

I put a cup of hot coffee on the little table beside her bed. Jarvis was still crying and a fog came in, rolling over me, erasing all time before now like a dream with only the sharp edges poking out.

'To tell you the truth, I can't remember half of what

happened before I met your dad again by the kayaks,' I said. 'Sometimes I think I went mental.'

'Who wouldn't,' she said. 'I can tell you loved him. Love him.'

'Yeah,' I said. 'And then there were my years of free room and board.'

I walked outside to drink my coffee on the back steps.

Pollux. I loved him and he put me away. No, he just arrested me, I thought. Judge Ragnarok, I mean Judge Ragnik, put me away. My brain wheel started spinning on its old track. How I'd been used by Danae and Mara. What became of me after that. Only this time I decided that I acquitted, if I can use that word, I think that eventually I acquitted myself pretty well. I mean, there was the initial fuckup, then the next fuckup where I tried suicide by paper. After that, I decided to let paper save my life.

That I was lucky to have been arrested by Pollux may have occurred to me. That he'd argued his colleagues into letting him take me in may have occurred to me. That I would have resisted arrest and could have been beaten or hurt or worse was also perfectly true. But this was a time of reckoning and I was reckoning really hard along with everybody else. Along with my furtive joy, I was pissed off at Pollux, even knowing that for years he'd tried to make up for setting into motion my lost decade, which nevertheless taught me all that books could not.

Pollux startled me when he walked in late that morning. I saw no signs of weapons but he'd probably stashed them in the garage. His hair was in strings, his eyes were red, his mouth was set in a tense line. He walked past me, saying he would have to shower and put on a new mask. Now, in addition to my systemic resentment, I wanted to belt Pollux for having walked—old, asthmatic, achy boned, precious, armed for bear—onto Lake Street. Yet he was safe. I stepped toward Pollux in relief, but he waved me off. I asked what had happened, but he just looked into the air. He started up the stairs. Halfway up, he turned around and told me that Migizi had burned.

Migizi has been in existence for over forty years. A communications organization, it contained the history of urban Indigenous people in this city. So it was as I feared: a library had burned. Migizi's building was brand-new, a triumph for the community. The first night, it served as a triage center for people recovering from being teargassed or injured during the protests.

The second night, the AIM patrol had successfully defended it from vandalism. But on the third night embers from another fiery building had landed on its roof and burned it to the ground. Pollux had gone out when he got a message. It was a long night and a disheartening dawn. He burned sage, tried to comfort people, but he felt that he had failed. He didn't want to see or talk to anyone, not that day.

Popcorn and Arson

MAY 30

I was worried about Dissatisfaction—I mean, Roland. He hadn't ordered books for a while. I knew he lived somewhere in South Minneapolis, where I'd delivered books to Flora. Jackie was at the store filling orders. I found Roland's number on an orders list, and called him. He answered on the second ring.

'Who is this?'

'Tookie. Bookstore lady.'

'Oh, Alphabet Soup.'

'Right. How are you?'

'How do you think?'

I heard intense sadness in his voice.

'I have sons his age, that George. I keep dreaming about him. I'm not myself, bookstore lady.'

Everything I thought of saying got stuck in my throat. Roland gave a scratchy, furious laugh.

'But you don't wanna hear this. What'd you call me for?'

'Maybe you don't have a damn thing left to read?'

He laughed again but this time there was relief in it.

'You'd be right,' he said.

'Where do you live?'

'Why?'

'Delivery.'

'What've you got?'

'Trust me.'

'Trust is not my thing. But okay.'

He lived fairly close to Moon Palace, one of the bookstores I'd been worrying about, although it was still standing, precariously untouched, in the middle of the destruction. I was surprised and asked him why he didn't shop at Moon Palace.

'I do. Like to spread around my business.'

I said nothing. But he was old and maybe lived on a fixed income. I was moved that he used his finite cash to buy books. But then I remembered his LAWWOLF vanity plate and that he was a prosecutor. Still flush. Whatever. He was in fact a customer in dire need. I would rescue him with books.

I filled a couple boxes and drove down Franklin Avenue to Pow Wow Grounds, which had become one of the organizing spots for Native people. The building is bright gold with a baby blue stripe and windows trimmed in red. It's a cheerful, proud, friendly building that contains an Indigenous art gallery and a neighborhood organization as well as a coffee shop that at various times sells chili, frybread tacos, frybread pizza, wild rice soup, and different types of pie. I parked in front of a mural. The centerpiece was an Indigenous woman with a red handprint across her mouth—that image is about silence and violence against us ikwewag—but then there is a magic flow of water from her braids that feeds animals, dancers, city people, the night sky, and the phases of the moon.

The parking lot was jammed with cars. A champion reader, artist, and philosopher named Al works there. I parked, brought in a box of books, and was about to also leave a pint of precious hand sanitizer when an intimidating man, rock solid, Asian, packing a well-secured gun, walked in with gallons of the stuff. He put the bottles of sanitizer down like a sacred offering and walked out. I took my time arranging the books on the inside counter by a Little Free Library. Al walked by and said when this was over we had to talk about Alain Badiou.

'Sure,' I said, 'after I look him up.'

He waved and went behind the counter. People came and went. The gallery was filling with stacks of bottled water, food, diapers, fire extinguishers. Pollux was in the parking lot, talking to his buddies. I walked out and saw that he had his giant Crock-Pot going on a foldout banquet table. It fit a couple of roasts and I knew he'd scored bison from a Sisseton guy. I was stabbed with such a pang of longing. It was hard to walk away. I went out to the street, got into the car. Then I rolled down the window to smell the rich sauce on the sullen air. Pollux saw me. As I watched him walk toward me, hands alert at his belt like a gunslinger's, my pang of longing became a physical ache. I have always loved seeing Pollux from a distance. He has a loose walk, like he's ready to brawl. I know he isn't, wouldn't, but the walk of an old boxer trained to be light on his feet is a beautiful thing, even if he's got a few pounds on him. I couldn't help it. His walk drew me back out of the car.

'What are you guys up to?' My voice was neutral, giving him an in.

'I'm taking another shift with the patrol tonight.'

'The hell you are.' Alarm choked me. 'You took your damn shotgun out there. You could get killed. You've got a baby and your daughter at home. Not to mention me. And your bum lung. What if you get sick?'

'Who you calling Bum Lung? It's all outside. I'll mask up. And don't worry, I just gave that shotgun away. Plus I'll keep my distance.'

'You damn well *will* keep your distance.' I was mad I'd let my guard down. 'And so will I.'

Without another word I got into the car, intending

to peel out. But I was parked in already and had to edge back with Pollux guiding me. It wasn't the dramatic exit I'd hoped for and Pollux knew that. He was trying to keep a straight face as he beckoned me this way and that. I suspected that he might be getting me more stuck, but at last I edged through. By the time I pulled out, I was more upset for him than for myself.

'Be careful,' I shouted. He was already strolling away and I'd forgotten to get on his case about the other gun. 'Pick your battles, Tookie,' I counseled myself. And kept driving.

I took a route that skirted the worst of the burning, but here and there I passed through a rancorous brume. Roland Waring's house was a cream stucco bungalow surrounded by a chain-link fence made opaque by green plastic strips woven through the metal. He had his Little Free Library, a tiny house on a sturdy post with window doors, a blue one painted with circles of clouds and jammed with books. I phoned him from the curb and Roland emerged. He was slower, thinner, maybe even fragile. He was using a cane. I'd never seen that. A fluffy brown and white dog went before Roland as he made his way down the steps, gripping the railing. The dog was like his personal attendant. I lifted the latch on the gate and brought the box of books to the steps. Roland bent down and picked up some titles, nodded, put them back. His dog gave me a careful assessing look and moved in front of Roland, guarding him. When Roland took his checkbook out of his shirt pocket, I told him there would be no charge. We had a standoff with him shaking a check at me and me refusing to step up and take it. At last I told him Jackie insisted. He has a lot of respect for Jackie's recommendations. He put the check and checkbook back in his pocket. I was about to say goodbye when he asked, 'How are you?'

It took me a moment. He'd never addressed me as a person he might like to know.

'I'm all roiled up,' I said. 'What about you?'

'Everybody's asking how I am.'

'You asked me first.'

'I'm . . .'

He flung his hand out, waved it around as if he was searching the air for words. Then he found his old self.

'What are you, a social worker? Don't worry. My daughter's down the street.'

He picked up a copy of *The Charterhouse of Parma*, held it in his hand like he was weighing it, and finally said that he'd never read it. I pointed out the translation by Richard Howard. I'd pulled out all the stops and added everything to the box that might appeal. I'd broken Roland Waring's rule on nonfiction, and added *White Rage*, which he handled gently.

'Grab a lawn chair, sit down,' he said. 'I'll spray my mitts with alcohol and pour you a glass of cold iced tea.'

'That would go down nicely,' I said.

'Listen, Gary,' he said to the dog, 'this book lady's all right. Relax. Stay out here and get to know her while I get some tea.'

The dog was medium sized, the type of dog I'd seen in movies herding sheep. It was different from other dogs I'd encountered. It didn't bite me and didn't even seem to hate me. Gary watched me with a neutral interest. I decided to talk to it the way Roland had.

'Gary, I'm going up on the porch now,' I said.

I brought a couple of folded lawn chairs down off the porch and set them in the grass. The dog stood up, motionless. When Roland came out with the tea, I took my glass from him and we sat down together.

'So, how's the store?' he asked.

Not only had he never addressed me except when looking for a book, but we had never had a conversation outside the bookstore, or a conversation not about books.

'We're haunted,' I told him.

Firecrackers and bottle rockets were going off a few streets over. Now and then a helicopter ripped apart the air. I hadn't actually slept. My eyes burned, my thoughts were muffled; I was in tough shape, but so was Roland. The ibuprofen wore off and a band of pain started squeezing my head again.

'Haunted?' he said. 'The whole damn city's haunted.'

'I mean literally. There's a ghost in the store.'

'I'm not talking figuratively either. When I cast my mind over the city I see lines, lines, lines. Red lines. Blue lines. Green lines. Red for the way they kept white neighborhoods white. Blue for—'

'I know. I'm married to an ex-cop.'

'That must be complicated right about now.'

'It's not easy.'

'Helluva thing.'

We nodded and frowned into our glasses of iced tea. Swirled the cubes.

'So what's gonna happen?' I asked.

'Let me consult my crystal ball.' Roland held up an imaginary magic sphere and peered into its depths. 'It says there will be more of this, everywhere and for a long time. It says this is another beginning. I've seen a lot of them.'

'I believe that.' I waited for him to go on, but he only said, 'Times like this, people become more human, anyway. Mostly, that's a good thing.'

I asked how long he'd had Gary.

'Six years. She was up and down the block, a stray that people fed. Finally, she settled on me. Strange thing though, she looks just like the dog my family had when I was a little kid. That's why I call her Gary. She even has a piece of her ear chewed off, see?' Roland carefully showed me the nick. 'Just like the old Gary.'

Gary narrowed her eyes and panted in pleasure as Roland scratched behind her ears. She seemed to be grinning at me like she knew me.

'You know what?' said Roland. 'I wasn't really a prosecutor. Just messing with you.'

'Are you messing with me again?'

He laughed. I looked down at Gary.

'You're the first dog that ever smiled at me,' I told her. I reached out my hand but drew it back. I'd been fooled too many times by fake smiles and sharp teeth.

THE HOUSE

Roland lived close to the house that my mother and I lived in when we ping-ponged between the reservation and the city. The house was still there. It is always still there. It is a gray clapboard place with six tiny apartments carved out inside. Cheap rent, livable. There was a blanket tacked over one window, cardboard where an attic window was broken, and a couple of air conditioners sticking out of a couple of upper-floor windows. I parked in the alley to see what was happening with my old window. My second-floor room was a closet. But it had a square of glass with diamond mullions in the top panel. It even opened. At night I could hear the city breathing all around me, in and out as though we lived in a giant animal. I'd traveled in that room. Done homework. Developed my bubble/dot distinction. I could slip in and close the door to get away from Mom and her friends. The room had a lightbulb with a string, like in the confessional. I had two shelves, a tiny table and stool, a pallet on the floor. I had a pillow and a quilt. I had everything I needed.

I caught the school bus at the end of the block. After I got my homework and tests back, I would bring them to Mom. Lay them on the table. F or A+. She never noticed. Rarely spoke. I'd watch her on the day she cashed her disability check. Slip away with her cash or pick through her drugs. She wandered in, she wandered out. Sometimes she didn't speak a word for what seemed like months. The window looked exactly the same. When my feelings were too much for me I used to wrap myself in blankets and lie in my closet waiting for the feelings to pass. At one point, I decided to become a person who didn't feel so much. I stand by that decision, though it didn't work.

※

On the way back, I passed streams of people with signs, packs, water bottles. I passed squad cars and squadrons. I passed burnt-out stores with walls like broken teeth. Uncle Hugo's was gone. Smoldering. My stomach dropped and my eyes began to sting. I passed a woman with a shopping cart full of children. Down another street, a giant armored and armed Humvee rolling forward. I turned to get out of the way. Pockets of peace, then full-out soldiers in battle gear. I got a cold, sick feeling. Minneapolis had been caught by surprise, but now the response had hardened. I passed a church with people milling about on its steps. Around back of the church there was about an acre of full grocery bags to hand out. I passed two teens sitting on a curb, toking up, their signs tossed down. I passed people painting vibrantly colored pictures on the boards over store windows. I passed tents, I passed liquor bottles in the gutter, I passed small devotional shrines. There were messages to other people taped to trees. Flowers hanging off fences. I had to swerve to miss a car parked in the middle of the street, a Confederate flag stuck to its bumper. Mostly, I passed people going about their normal business, planting their gardens, flower beds, watering their lawns. I passed a popcorn store that was open and I stopped to buy popcorn. The popcorn smell modified the smell of spent tear gas— sour, musky chalk. I got stopped by a cloud when I was nearly home. It was a cloud of emotion. I came to a halt and tried to breathe my way through the mist. It was cleared by the loud curfew alert on my phone. I was tired and flat-out sad. If only it would rain.

MAY 31

But it did not rain. Night. Journalists tased, arrested, teargassed, beaten. Journalist with an eye shot out.

'What the fuck are you so afraid of?' Hetta screaming at the police.

We talked about the National Guard.

'They're not all bad though,' Hetta said, surprising me. 'Asema told me at the capitol protest that this National Guard commander or whatever took a knee in front of everybody. He said he was there to protect our right to assemble and then he moved off, I mean, way off, and it was fine.'

Pollux came back from his shift. I made sure he stashed his weapon. 'I don't like it,' I said.

'Me neither. There's way too many guns out there. I'm gonna lay mine down and make frybread. That's my true calling.'

'And my true calling is to eat frybread,' I said. But he had already closed the door to the bathroom and was taking a Hetta-length shower. He came down in fresh clothes and his mask. We were all avoiding one another's germs at this point. Pollux told us that a couple nights ago AIM patrol had caught some tow-head Wisconsin boys trying to rob a liquor store.

'They came down hard on those boys,' he said to Hetta. 'You could call it cruel and unusual.'

'Dad? What'd they do?'

'Made them call their moms.'

'So, like, it was *Hi, Mom, come get me I got caught looting*?'

Pollux squinted into the air. He was sprawled on the floor and now carefully draped his blue AIM patrol T-shirt over his head. We were awake for yet another night, trying to figure out the tweet storms. People were alarmed by the National Guard telling them not to be alarmed by UH-60 Black Hawks here and there. It was three a.m. and we were lying on the floor, using all the couch pillows, lights blazing. 'Listen to this,' said Hetta. 'It's bullet points from the MPD. We're supposed to have an escape plan? Oh my god. Cell towers might go out! Get out your garden hose. Keep an eye out for water bottles full of gasoline! Hose down your roofs! Your fences! Empty the books from Little Free Libraries?'

We were now manic. Every time our laughter guttered out, Hetta would say *Hi, Mom?* or *Empty the books* and we'd groan and start again. How did we get to our cherished little book boxes from the horror of a full daylight police murder? I said it seemed that around the central fact of any tragedy there swirled a flotsam of extrania like the twenty-dollar bill that led to the police call at Cup Foods, the broken taillight that led the police to stop Philando Castile, the hunger for eggs and a farm woman's fury to defend those eggs, an incident that started the Dakota War, the *let them eat grass* phrase that has kept it in memory ever since, the sudden route change of a driver that enabled the assassination of an obscure archduke, an act of defiance that averted a nuclear war during the Cuban Missile Crisis. So many other occurrences. For instance, said Hetta, the glass of root beer that led to Jarvis.

'Stop right there,' said Pollux from under his shirt.

'Or us,' I said. 'Why were you in the Midwest

Mountaineering parking lot that day?' It was like me to press on the bruise. I wanted to slap myself. He tried to keep it light.

'For socks,' said Pollux. 'I like their wool socks.'

In love as in death and mayhem, small things start a chain of events which veer so out of control that sooner or later an absurd detail intrudes, bringing the trail of events back for us to ponder. Pollux shook off the T-shirt and propped himself up on one elbow.

'So you're saying that we wouldn't be here, all together, if not for socks? No, no, it was fate!' said I.

'It was feet! And all the rest of me,' said Pollux.

'Please stop right there,' Hetta yawned. It was a fake yawn. She was keeping the lid on too.

I jumped up and ran into the kitchen with a general notion that made me reach deep into the lower shelf of the refrigerator. My hand closed around the tube of chocolate chip cookie dough I'd bought at Target. It was still good. Sometimes you do the right thing, Tookie girl, I said to myself. I turned on the oven, sliced the dough into rounds and placed them on a cookie sheet. I put the cookies in the oven and walked back into the living room to wait for the timer. It pinged, waking me after ten minutes.

'What's that?' called Hetta.

'Cookies.'

Hetta stumbled toward me and this time there was no air hug. She wrapped her arms around me. I forgot about the distancing. I didn't know what to do. This was new. My arms floated for a moment's indecision then lowered themselves to hold her.

We finally slept at dawn and woke to an innocent spring afternoon. Pollux was sleeping next to me. In spite of it all, I was glad.

'What time is it?' said Pollux.

'Noon o'clock.'

We lay still, messed up by the tense nights and the strangeness of waking to a full-blown day.

I didn't have to work, so we wandered around the house, in and out, disoriented. Hetta was in touch with Asema, who was out with Gruen marching down I-94 and then I-35, which was closed off.

'I'm getting some scary posts,' Hetta said. Then she jumped up from the couch, shouting incoherently. Jarvis squalled in shock. I ran to her. She pointed to the screen of her laptop where a semi truck sped onto 35 North and plowed straight into a wildly scattering crowd of protesters. I turned away, whipped right and left, as if to deny what I'd seen. I ran outside and plopped down on the stairs, put my head in my hands and squeezed my eyes shut. Pollux stayed with Hetta and Jarvis. They watched as the scene re-solved and after a while they called me inside. Un-believably, no one was killed, or even hurt. Even the driver, who was pulled from the truck, was all right. He'd been punched, but then defended by protesters when it turned out he spoke very little English. He was shaken up, but basically okay. The barriers were just going up as he took the on-ramp and he'd been utterly confused.

Hetta's thumbs feverishly pummeled her phone.

'They're okay. Gruen was closest, but they dodged and the truck stopped. They're gonna keep marching.'

The horrifying but miraculous footage played on a loop with different angles as news stations uploaded new videos from bystanders. In one video, a lithe young man in a gold T-shirt with a black mask leaped onto the cab and grabbed the windshield wipers, trying to stop the truck. He was so light, acrobatic. He'd landed like a grasshopper.

'Look,' said Hetta. 'It's Laurent. I'm sure, it's him.'

We played the video over and over until eventually, it seemed to me also, the leaping man with the long insectlike legs could only be Laurent.

'What's going on with this guy?'

'He was meeting up with Gruen and Asema,' said Hetta, toneless with exhaustion. 'He's gonna fight this

out. He gets like this. He'll never quit. He's probably
been out there all night.'

MAY 32

The Cities were boiling with emotion. Small towns,
county seats, other cities all over the world were boiling with emotion. Every morning now Pollux went out
with a janitor's broom, dustpan, and bucket, to shovel
glass. It seemed penitential. It also seemed kind. After
cleaning up he went to smoke his pipe in a ceremony he
swore followed public safety rules. We were slammed at
the bookstore. Everyone who wasn't out on the streets
wanted to read about why everyone else was out on the
streets. Orders kept coming for books about the police,
about racism, race history, incarceration. Penstemon
was drooping. The orders piled up on the book table.

'This must be a good thing?'

'It's a good thing? I mean, we're getting information
to people?'

'That's our mission,' said Penstemon.

'Oh god, I'll get this phone call. You keep packing.'

All day there were police, medevac, news, and
private-security helicopters overhead chopping our
thoughts. Occasionally a pickup truck flew by and

I glimpsed a Gadsden flag. The parkways around us were still closed down so people could walk around the lakes safely distanced, and these pickups kept getting lost in the tangle of streets, buzzing around like hornets. All around the city on those boards protecting windows, more art was springing to life and now a group of minority artists were planning to warehouse it all together. Hetta and Jarvis had joined me at work. I was glad daylight was coming through our windows. Glad we hadn't boarded up. Anyway, how would we even score plywood in this town?

As I worked away, I listened to Jarvis and Hetta. I'd never heard laughter so musical, like bells, yet I could also feel how my heart had cracked like a windshield, the minute split traveling slowly through the glass. I should do something. I should get it repaired, I thought. The crevice was edging deeper. Everything seemed to be cracking: windows, windshields, hearts, lungs, skulls. We may be a striver city of blue progressives in a sea of red, but we are also a city of historically sequestered neighborhoods and old hatreds that die hard or leave a residue that is invisible to the well and wealthy, but chokingly present to the ill and the exploited. Nothing good would come of it, or so I thought.

The Circles

MAY 34

Another bright, hot morning. Asema texted everyone to say that grandmothers were putting out the call for us to work with our tobacco, sing healing songs. Now jingle dancers were gathering at the George Floyd memorial.

'Break out your dress,' said Hetta.

'How did you know about that?'

'Dad told me he had one made for you.'

'I was at fighting weight then,' I lied. 'It doesn't fit me now. Maybe you could wear it and I'd go with you.'

'You'd let me wear your dress?'

'Of course I would. It's super-traditional, like an old-timer dress. It's not sequins and glitter like the girls are wearing now.'

'I don't know how to dance, but I could pick it up.'

'Asema's a dancer.'

'Of course she is,' Hetta sighed.

The dress was at the back of my closet on a high shelf. I stored it flat in a cardboard box so it could breathe. There was wild bergamot and sweetgrass underneath it in a pillowcase. Pollux had seen to that. I actually was about the same weight now as I'd been when Pollux gave me the dress. If I put another hole or two in the belt it would cinch around Hetta's waist. I still hadn't danced in it. Jingle dresses are alive and you have to be a certain kind of person to wear one with sincerity. I was not that kind of person. I even thought maybe that was why Flora kept coming for me. Maybe I would never be the kind of person who could wear a jingle dress and carry an eagle feather fan.

I lifted the dress from the box and shook it. The dress rattled in a friendly way. There was an under-skirt with rows of jingles at the bottom, and the top half of the dress which could be lifted up so that you didn't have to sit on the metal cones. Maybe if I wore the dress it would change me. But if Hetta wore the dress maybe it would change us both.

THE HAUNTING OF POLLUX

Pollux was sorting through boxes of donations at Pow Wow Grounds, making up family food bags that weren't all boxes of macaroni and jars of peanut but-ter. There was still a significant stack of fire extin-guishers. At night, the patrol carried them in the pickup truck. So much macaroni. So much peanut butter. As he packed, Pollux imagined the peanut butter with vinegar and hot sauce, studded with onion tips and mushed with a tad of garlic, maybe a squirt of soy. Could be good on noodles. Spaghetti if you didn't have ramen. There was a ton of spaghetti and he considered including a handwritten recipe. As he sorted, he did more recipes in his head until the repetition got to him. He went outside, sat down in the shade against the outside wall, took off his mask, and breathed. Pollux was still trying for balance after the night Hetta had grilled him. He didn't feel like Tookie was all there for him either. Also, she was right about small things becoming big things. He thought about clothes.

A uniform. It was only fabric, but it was powerful. He had been warned but he hadn't listened. The first time he walked in the door puffing out his chest, clad in his blues, which weren't blue, but were black, his grandma said something. His grandma supposedly cut a mean hard swath when she was young. Time had worn her contradictory edges off, but not by much. She was angular yet round. Her eyes were sharp but her gaze usually rested soft on Pollux. Her nose was pointed but her cheeks were velvet. She wore harsh bright polyester blouses but her skin was tender suede. She would hug Pollux or pat him and say, 'It'll be all right, my boy. You just wait and see.' But when he walked in the door in that uniform she said, 'Watch out.'

'For what?' said Pollux.

'For when that uniform starts to wear you,' said his grandma.

Pollux laughed and gave her a hug. He couldn't see that happening. Not at first. But her words stuck inside him, like she meant them to. Little by little, maybe a year or two after he'd started working as a tribal cop, he felt this enter him. Once, he had heard a man who'd survived Canadian Catholic residential schools say that the school nuns and priests 'left a crooked thing to lurch inside of us.' What entered felt to Pollux like a crooked thing. Sometimes it lurched. The way he'd hear his voice scratch out an angry order. The simple weariness that gave way to cynical weariness. The impatience with stupid stuff people did that froze his heart. The anger that led to a violent refusal to feel. Then to even connect with his people. And the things he saw, the beaten women stuffed in cupboards, the children blue with cold hiding under the porch, Dad bleeding through the floor, the old people tossed aside for their cancer drugs, the car accidents and the accidents on purpose. The things people did to one another and to themselves wore him down. Still, he did not believe his uniform had ever held contempt. It was more exhaustion, wasn't it? He was not a saint.

He finished sorting and drove miserably down the boarded-up streets.

That crooked thing. Pollux was haunted by image after image. People kneeling, beaten. People singing, beaten. Mothers, beaten. Fathers, beaten. Young, beaten. Old, knocked down or beaten. If you approached the police, beaten. If you ran away, kettled, then beaten. Pollux had known good people, seen lives saved by his fellow patrol officers. So who was doing the beating? The uniforms or those inside them? How was it that protests against police violence showed how violent police really were?

At home, a lonely pang shot through Pollux when he saw that Hetta was wearing the jingle dress he'd given Tookie as a love gift. He held out the fan he had finally finished. The handle he'd carved was covered with smoked deerhide. Elegant fringes hung off the end of the handle. Each feather was wrapped at the base and reinforced with tightly wrapped red embroidery floss. The fan was elegant, regal, and each feather was perfectly straight.

'You hold it first,' he said to Tookie. 'You can let Hetta use it, but the fan's for you.'

She took it gingerly, held it awkwardly. He thought maybe there was a tender thank-you stuffed in her throat.

He cradled Jarvis as they left, watched the two of them walk to the car. Tookie didn't know it but sometimes when she walked she prowled. He tried not to look at the way she shifted her hips. She stirred his heart. Ah, it was still all there. He looked down at Jarvis.

'You're in for it, little man,' he said.

THE CIRCLE

We were in the van together, me driving along in my favored black jeans and black T-shirt. Hetta sitting carefully in the passenger seat with the skirt of the jingle dress pulled up behind her and the front tucked up around her waist so the jingles wouldn't poke her butt. Under the dress, she wore a racerback T-shirt and a tiny pair of shorts. The dress clattered gently whenever I stopped at a light.

'God damn, this is beautiful,' she kept saying, stroking the appliqué work. The dress zipped down the front. The colors were rust, bronze, and ivory. Two sides of a scarlet heart-shaped flower met at the zipper.

There were lavender tulips and green leaves. Pollux had given me a piece of art.

The interior of the car was cool and our sunglasses fogged up. Driving a car was still dreamlike and strange. It seemed like we were rushing through the air but we were only going twenty-five. We crossed I-35 and then pulled around onto a side street to park. We sat in the car making the most of the cool air before we got out. We opened the doors and the heat closed down on us. I'd promised to wear a germ-blocking mask, one of Pollux's special ones. Breathing through it made me mildly dizzy. I was hyperventilating, but I kind of liked the sensation. I carried a canvas bag with two water bottles. Jarvis had outgrown his newborn diapers and I had the leftover 0–3 months organics in a bag. My wallet was in my jeans, which were cooking my legs.

Hetta was tall and dignified, gracious even in a mask, with red-wrapped braids and dramatic eye makeup. She wore rawhide-soled dance moccasins. The jingle dress transformed her into a visibly sacred being. Walking beside her with water bottles and a bag of diapers, I felt like the attendant of a young queen. As she passed along the street, people called out to her, to me, as if they knew us. There were tables loaded with packages of food and sundries for the taking as we neared the square. I added the diapers. There were flags—BLM and Pan African flags, AIM flags, rainbow flags. At the center of the square, stacks of plastic-wrapped flower bouquets were arranged in a circular altar. More bouquets were banked against the wall where his portrait was painted. Hetta hopped over the bouquets into the circle and stood with the other dancers. She looked nervously back at me, then grinned and waved. Asema tapped me on the arm. Her hair was braided with silver ribbons, her dress was neon blue satin with orange flowers, acid green leaves. It was lavish with silver-crusted braid down her arms and up her throat. It looked suffocating.

As people crushed in toward the circle, I eased out and made my way to the edge of the crowd. There was a sturdy wooden bench in a gas station parking lot. I climbed up, stood there, found a tiny breeze, and took gulps of air from the side of my mask. From where I stood, I could see Hetta and Asema together. They were figures from a story where Ojibwe women danced medicine. When they lifted their eagle feather fans, their hopeful grace swept over me. My vision was misty from sweat dripping off my eyebrows. I wondered if this was a thing regular mothers felt looking at their daughters from a distance, finding them perilous in their magnetic beauty, which makes no distinction in which screws and nuts it attracts. And in fact, as they started dancing and the drum was in the third push-up of a heart-stirring song, one appeared. There he was. Iron filings in the shape of a person. Laurent.

He was standing against a lamppost, limp as a belt, his eyes narrow and hot, his hair sticking up in a burnished shock. The moment I saw him, a plan formed. I thumped down off the bench and busted my way over to him. Got to within an arm's reach. Knocked him on the shoulder. He uncrossed his arms, looked at me in surprise. He didn't recognize me but followed when I gestured away from the square.

'I'm Tookie, from the bookstore,' I said. 'Where Asema works. Could you give me your address? I have something to send you.'

'Oh yeah, I couldn't place you. Sorry, I don't have an address.'

'Could I send it to a friend's house? A relative? Perhaps your parents?'

He gave me an address in Bloomington and volunteered their names. I asked for their phone numbers but he said he'd have to ask them first. He was getting a mite suspicious.

'It's okay,' I said. 'I liked your book, the one you gave me. Reminded me of something. I just wanted to return the favor.'

In reality, my intention was to hire a lawyer and

serve Laurent with papers, put him on notice that even a chicken-scratch hammocker had to pay child support. Like so many authors, mention of his book warmed him up. He smiled a modest smile and waved his hand as though he was accustomed to such praise. Perhaps my face changed. My voice faltered. I couldn't help think of Pollux pretending to read step-by-step instructions to . . . oh Pollux. I wanted to laugh but it was too hot. I caught myself against a fence.

'Are you all right?'

Laurent gripped my elbow and steered me into a yard with a tree. He asked a group of people out front, sitting in lawn chairs, if he could lead me into the shade. They were all kindness and made room for us, even brought a chair and a cup of water. I drank the cup of water. I let the bag with the heavy water bottles slide to the ground.

'Thank you, Laurent,' I said in a formal way. 'You should go back there. Watch them dance. Please tell them where I am.'

I wasn't okay yet. Maybe it was heatstroke. They would be worried when they couldn't find me and I really didn't want to be there with Laurent. He moved away from me, holding out his arms as if I might fall out of the chair. His fake concern ticked me off.

'Beat it. I'm not gonna keel over. Scat.'

'I'll just stay a minute,' he said agreeably. 'As long as we're here, I'd like to plead my case.'

'Your case? What case would that be?'

True, he'd helped me just now. But I didn't owe him. I was not won over. Hetta was wrong: My goodwill does not come cheap.

'My first edition sold out. I need to find a real publisher, and I thought you might be able to help, being you work at a bookstore and all.'

I examined him more closely. Maybe after all he was just a chucklehead.

'I'll tell you what,' I said. 'I'm not just the bookstore lady, I'm Hetta's mom.'

He frowned and shook his head.

'She said she didn't have a mom.'

'Well, now she does.'

He gave me a shy look from under his eyelashes. I thought it was done with calculated charm.

'That changes things,' he said. 'Now I have an entirely different case to plead.'

'Which is what?'

'Please tell Hetta to stop ghosting me.'

'Why would I do that?'

'For the little guy, of course, for Jarvis. He needs a father. Or maybe not now, but I know he'll need a father real bad someday.'

Laurent kept talking, now openly, perhaps believably miserable. His earnest dejection was smothering me. 'At first I panicked, maybe she told you. I mean never, I never expected her to have the baby! I met her and I fell in love with her on the set of this movie I was hired to edit. But then, see, her role in *Midnite Cowgirl*—'

'*Midnite Cowgirl?*'

'Just destroyed me. The mustang. Don't ask. One night while I was working on the edit, I suddenly went berserk and deleted every scene and every copy of a scene that had her in it. I double-deleted all the deletes. They'd already paid her in cash. I made it look like a mistake. Skipped town. I dodged around in Cali, ended up doing a little stunt work, then fighting wildfires. I moved back here to live with my folks, hoping Hetta would come back too. And she did. She did!'

Laurent grasped at me, his fingers clenched like claws, and I stepped back. What lovely eyes he had, dark like a shady woodsy trail, beaming with goodwill and innocence. He ignored me when I told him to shut up.

'Then I found out she had the baby, which, or who, I am 96 percent sure is mine. I'll take a test, but I'd support the baby no matter whose it is.'

He stopped talking for a moment, took a deep

breath. I was too paralyzed by his captivating speech and tender gaze to get up and walk away. I'd have done anything for my own father to claim me like this.

When Laurent spoke again, his voice was shaking. 'My soul left my body when I met Hetta. I am totally a hollow person now. But that's okay, it means I can accept my son. I know my soul is safe with Hetta. I am working for Wells Fargo.'

We were silent for a while. The drum was still going. I broke down.

'Did you tell all this to Hetta? I mean, about the movie?'

'Not yet.'

'Then tell her. Maybe she's not avoiding you. Maybe she's sick about that movie. Maybe she thinks you would, like, blackmail her with it or something. You wouldn't do that, would you?'

He honestly looked stunned. 'How could I? Everything she did is totally wiped. I made sure of it.'

'All right, Laurent. Last thing. What's a rugaroo?'

His face changed, and when I say that I mean visibly changed. For a blink, for a fraction of a moment, he was something else. Not an animal, not a person, but I say this in awe: somethingfuckingelse. Then he was himself again.

'Please be on your way now,' I said, covering up the quiver in my voice. 'I will take this under advisement.'

I drank a lot of water, then put my mask back on and entered the mash of people. Waves of emotion swept through the crowd. I found myself between a Black woman dressed in turquoise, and a Red Lake woman in T-shirt and jeans like me, both of whom had nearly lost their sons to police beatings—down at the river. The women grasped my hands. From their palms into my palms there poured a sorrow beyond reckoning and I struggled briefly to let go. But they held on and so I was pulled into the circle. An elder announced that the jingle dress dance was meant to heal people and whoever needed healing could come forward. People moved in from every direction. They held one another up. It was beastly out there. My head was ringing and I was afraid I would fall to my knees. Suffering opened around me. Another woman screamed for her son, yet another for her daughter. I realized that the women whose sons had been beaten, merely beaten and left alive, were weeping with gratitude. How's that. There was the rattling music of jingles, the drum, the boiling sun. It went on and on. I stood behind Hetta as she danced in place. What flowed over me was not easy to feel and I resisted, but then a ripple of energy caught me up and spread, became wider, powerful, deep, musical, whole, universal: it was the drum. My hip pained me on the side where I came down hardest. I kept dancing. I saw spots and lights, nearly fainted, but still I danced, on and on.

Walking back, I thought again of those words a child raised with love would say to a mother loved beyond reckoning. *I don't want you to get shooted.* Like the children at the school where Philando Castile worked in the lunchroom, this girl loved him, and she loved her mother. Before her eyes he'd been murdered and her mother, not the murderer, was the one cuffed and sitting in the back of a squad car. I thought of Zachary Bearheels, possibly schizophrenic, tased seven times and dragged by his ponytail. The face of Jamar Clark. And . . . oh no, here it came. The image of a big teddy bear of a boy, Jason Pero, fourteen years old, Bad River Ojibwe, who was having an emotional crisis and called the police on himself. Deputy Brock Mrdjenoich shot him dead. Paul Castaway . . . Indian after Indian and Black after Black and brown after brown person, and other people, white people, men, women, shot for being off medications, or running while Black, or having a taillight out or just knocking on the windshield by mistake. Jaywalking, a box of cigarillos. I thought of Charles Lone Eagle and John Boney slung in the trunk of a squad car and dumped at a Minneapolis ER by Officers Schumer and Lardy, who hardly got their knuckles rapped. You rarely hear about police killings of Indigenous people, though the numbers are right up there with Black people, because so often it happens on remote reservations, and the police don't wear cameras. So I was thankful, however shattering the truth, for the witnesses with the cameras.

An Abundance of Caution

THE PROFESSOR

It was the golden hour on a day of reprieve from the crushing heat. A cool breeze thumped down tiny green apples from time to time. The National Guard was gone and people displaced during Covid and the uprising were camped out or looking for shelter. On the way here we'd passed dozens of tent clusters. Still, the city was deep and green. Now we sat on opposite sides of Asema's tiny backyard. Pollux and I had old blue metal chairs. Asema sat in a tippy aluminum lawn chair with red plastic webbing. When the sun slanted in from the west, the spindle leaves of a locust tree danced and glowed. In a ragged garden, yellow squash blossoms blazed under spotted leaf umbrellas. Heavy-bottomed bumblebees and arrowing dragonflies lifted in and out of the deep scarlet flowers of Monarda. A curious baby hummingbird paused in midair before my face.

I held my breath. I was being given a valediction. The hummingbird vanished and I closed my eyes to trap in my mind the iridescence.

'Goodbye, little god.'

Asema poured us glasses of cold water flavored with mint stalks and sliced lemons. She was being careful— using a piece of paper towel to grasp the handle of the jug. She reassured us that the glasses, on a tray, were just washed in hot water. We reached forward and grasped the bottoms of the glasses. Tipped them toward our mouths.

'A hummingbird remembers every flower it has ever sipped from,' said Asema.

'I remember every beer I've ever drunk with you,' Pollux said to me.

I did not respond. We were trying to get back to the easy transparent love but every time we got close I stirred up the mud. I was tired of making things worse.

'This goes down good,' said Pollux. He bent his leg and rested his ankle on his knee. This meant he was self-conscious. But our bookstore historian had asked us over for a reason. She was trying to get back to the regular business of life, and work on her dissertation. Asema wanted to talk to me about the book, the one I'd buried. The book I'd told her had killed Flora and nearly killed me. I hadn't wanted to come over. The heat had lifted and the day was so blessed, so beautiful. I didn't want to touch even one syllable of that book. But she had bribed us with a kettle of early sweetcorn.

'So,' she said, after our paper plates were set aside, heaped with gnawed cobs. 'About the book.'

'Aw, please,' I said. 'The book of doom. Let's just forget about it. Why go back there?'

'Because I think that I may have some answers for you.'

'Asema, mii go maanoo, for godsakes just let it go.'

'Tookie, it's just a book.'

'It killed Flora and it nearly disintegrated me.'

I could feel Pollux fidgeting, rolling his eyes. I could feel him frowning into the distance.

'I mean, Flora-iban,' I said.

'Where's the book now? I'll read it and see if I die,' said Asema.

'I don't have the damn book! I buried it.'

'Oh yeah. Buried it.'

Asema stretched her hands out and leaned forward in her precarious chair.

'You told me you had buried a dog. I knew you hadn't. You don't even like dogs enough to dig a hole.'

'I do like dogs. Maybe not enough to dig a hole, but enough to . . . I tolerate dogs, even though they hate me. And I burned the book.'

Beneath the flickering leaves, her face became intent and composed. Uh-oh. The day was ruined. Asema assumed an air of false authority, steepled her fingers beneath her jaw, and smiled.

'You didn't burn it,' she said. 'That's a lie.'

'Half a lie,' I said.

Asema ignored me. 'Furthermore, I have a confession to make.'

Pollux glanced at me.

'Absolved,' I said. 'Let's move on.'

'I kept thinking about that day we sat in your downed tree, what you said. I went to your house when you were gone,' said Asema. 'I went to the place you told me you had buried the dog. I pried up the sod, then the dirt. It took me a while, but I got the book out.'

I choked on my rage, but I didn't do more than kick the leg of an old table.

'God damn. You went behind my back.'

'I know and I'm sorry,' said Asema. 'I couldn't leave it alone. But I did find something.'

The golden hour had softened me up for huge emotional reactions, but Pollux touched my arm and brought me back. I tried to gather myself.

'I don't forgive you. Or I do forgive you. But I'm still pissed.'

'Okay, I'm sorry. I was afraid of that.'

'But not afraid enough to respect my decision to get rid of the book?'

'I'm worried about you, Tookie.'

I was now too upset to speak, so I rattled on anyway

about how Kateri had passed the book to me and me alone and how I was the only one with the authority to destroy it. I told Asema about how the book had nearly killed me after it had killed Flora. At last Asema said, 'I do respect your what—your decision. But you weren't getting rid of the book. You were only burying it. And also, most important, it was my book.'

'Yours? It was mine!'

'Tookie, that book belonged to me first. Flora stole it from me. More important, it belongs to history.'

She said this in a pious voice, irritating me.

'I'm all ears, Professor Asema.'

'Just listen, Tookie! I go looking for primary sources,' said Asema. 'Driving down from Winnipeg, I saw a sign for a farm auction and stopped. There was a box of old ledgers. I was the only one who bid on it. When I got home, I started looking through the bound ledgers and journals. Usually there are entries, accounts, notes on merchandise or debts. But the writing hardly ever takes up the whole notebook. One of the journals looked empty at first, but about a quarter of the way in some writing began. As I read the journal, I realized it had to have been written right after what is called the Riel rebellion, you know, the early war for Indigenous land rights in Canada.'

Asema was really going to make an excellent professor,

I thought, and settled back in a resentful huff. She was just getting wound up. She began to pace on the cracked cement and beaten grass. All she needed was a pipe and elbow patches on a tweed jacket.

'The policing of Indigenous people by white people on this continent goes back to the creation of occupying military forces bent on wars of extermination in both the U.S. and Canada.' She narrowed her eyes. 'It was the bluecoats, the cavalry, the RCMP. Then Indian agents or the military chose tribal members to police their community. Once the Bureau of Indian Affairs was formed, it was BIA cops.'

Next to me, Pollux leaned back in his chair and folded his arms. I could feel him turning off, but Asema powered on. 'Now with jurisdictional issues on reservations it's a mixture—federal, tribal, local, and state police. Or here in Minneapolis, it's the MPD and a history of legacy attitudes stemming from the Dakota War.'

'Way to go, Asema!'

I got up to take my leave, giving slow, ironic claps. Asema made an earnest hushing motion and spoke over me.

'After the defeat at Batoche, the Cree, Ojibwe, and Michif people scattered and lots of people crossed the Medicine Line to live around the Sweet Grass Hills of Montana, or the Turtle Mountains, or around Pembina, near the Red River. The manuscript was written by a young woman, probably Oji-Cree and French, who fell ill, was rescued by a white farm family, but then kept as a sort of servant. As I read on, I realized that she was held against her will, basically enslaved.'

Asema picked up a wooden spoon and began to slap her hand with it as she walked back and forth. Oh my god!

'Do I get credits for listening to this?' I groaned and glanced at Pollux. But now he was listening.

'There were accounts of brutal treatments our young woman suffered when she tried to run away. This was difficult to read, filled with details of what was done to this woman. Some of it was so harrowing that I could only take in a few lines at a time before putting down the book.'

She stopped talking, put one hand over her eyes in a childish gesture I'd never seen her use. She appeared to be struggling. She threw down the spoon.

'What did you do?' asked Pollux, softening toward his daughter's friend.

'After a bout of reading I would stare for hours at nothing, unable to lift my hands or move, unable to feel agency, unable to decide whether to stand up and make myself a cup of tea or wander outside or maybe to the refrigerator and make a sandwich. I was aware that I had these choices and that also confused me. It helped to remember that I should burn sage and make an offering each time I picked up the book.'

Asema gathered herself, patted her chest as if to restart her heart, and went on talking. 'This woman was named Maaname, which is a clan name referring to a creature, half woman, half fish, a character in our teachings. Her zhaaganaash name was Genevieve Moulin. Eventually Maaname freed herself and went to live in a small settlement along the Red River. Last time I was there, Pembina was composed of a few houses, big green trees, a bar full of suspicious citizens, a struggling hotel, and a historical society with a soaring tower that contained all sorts of wonderful memorabilia of those times. I stopped there the same day I bought the old journals. But when Maaname lived there almost a century and a half ago, it was a rowdy place and she was young. A woman who seemed kindly took her in, fed her, then drugged her and forced her into prostitution. This woman who ran the brothel became Maaname's nemesis. She was a true sadist. She broke the girl's bones, carved a sign onto her breast, burned the soles of her feet so she couldn't run away, and so terrorized her that ultimately a client of the place took pity on her. A third time she was abducted, but this time by a man with a redeeming characteristic or two. He married her to his son and moved them to Rolette, North Dakota, where they worked the father's land for twenty years, at which time they inherited it. Maaname, now known as Genevieve, had learned to read and write during her captivity and this was the account she left. And now, listen, if what you say is right and something in the book killed Flora, I know what it was. It was on the last page Flora laid her eyes on, the one that was bookmarked.'

'You read the page? What did it do to you?'

'Nothing. Flora stole this manuscript, a woman's testimony, because she hoped it would validate her assumed identity. I can't forgive her for that. She essentially removed a vital piece of history. But as if to punish her, the book killed her.'

'What words? What sentence?' asked Pollux.

'A sentence that contained a name.'

'A name can be very powerful.' Pollux spoke slowly. Maybe he felt about names the way I felt about ghosts.

'I think, as you will see, that what caused Flora's death was Flora's name,' Asema said. 'I think it shattered her to learn where her name originated, and with whom.'

'Flora's name,' I whispered.

Yellow spots formed before my eyes; my brain went blank. Then I stood up and wandered into a room in my head I'd seen before. Everything in the room repelled me with an unyielding force that grew stronger and stronger until I was catapulted into my body, from which there was no escape.

I slumped over and fainted. As a staged escape, it was perfect. Except that I was actually unconscious. Moments later I opened my eyes. Asema was trying to pour water between my lips and Pollux was fanning me with his shirt.

THE MEETING

This was a ragged time, brutally hot, crime prone, lush. A comet passed over us. The buildup of boxes and books on the floor increased. The sailboat table was taken over with curbside pickup bags. We were selling many copies of very few titles. Only Penstemon made it her business to witness the passing of the comet, which would not return for 6,800 years. Now, our staff was sitting in lawn chairs on a plot of grass shielded from the sidewalk by a wall of arborvitae. We popped open cans of flavored seltzer water.

'What I hate is, when people talk about the vaccine, they say the cavalry's coming,' said Asema. 'Don't they get they're talking about genocide?'

'Everybody here will agree with you one hundred percent,' said Gruen.

'Let's circle the wagons,' said Jackie, as we distanced our lawn chairs.

'Let's circle the wagons *and* have a powwow,' I said.

We were filling school orders from all over the country. We try our best to vet our books and decide which Native books were good to carry, and we talk teachers and librarians through the process.

'Do we have enough money to warehouse the most popular titles?' asked Penstemon.

'Wait, first can we raise a can of cold fizzy water to our customers?' Asema grabbed a new can from the cooler on the grass, popped it, and everyone toasted the number of curbside and online orders we were still receiving. Everyone was strung out. Although people couldn't browse and discover surprises, we were still selling books and had decided to hire. Our volume had perhaps canceled out the extra costs in work hours and materials, but we were still paying storefront rent. We weren't sure we'd survive as a mail-order bookstore. School sales had come to our rescue, but would they carry us through?

'Still, it's so nice to have people care about us,' Jackie marveled.

'It is a miracle,' said Gruen. 'Our space, it rocks with friendship.'

Asema and Penstemon air-hugged him from across the circle.

At the time, Gruen's country had contained the virus. Our country had fanned its spread and Americans were now banned from crossing borders around the world. Now Gruen was trapped in the United States with a bunch of pariahs, in a city slashed with fire and ash, in a country led by a filthy old con artist. He had been kettled and arrested on a Minneapolis bridge. He was cheerful even in this faltering republic.

'Feel the love!' he said, draining his can of coconut fizz.

'I feel like we're at a crossroads,' said Jackie.

I didn't want to talk about the crossroads. I was already overloaded. I got up and pretended to need something from the store, but when I reached the store I saw Roland's dog, Gary, sitting on the steps. She grinned at me. I stopped and looked at Gary, expecting that Roland had brought his dog to pick up books. But Gary seemed to be alone on the street. She was alert and calm, sitting there as if she was waiting to see me. 'Hello, Gary,' I said. 'Where's Roland?' With that recognition, it seemed Gary had enough. She got up and began to trot away. I followed as she sped up and turned a corner. When I rounded the corner a few seconds later, she had disappeared.

This bothered me for the rest of the day. A conviction lodged itself: Gary had come to deliver a message. Eventually, I dialed Roland's number but he didn't answer. I immediately pictured Roland collapsed in his house, helpless, and decided to drive over to make sure he was all right. The city was hot and sticky, the air soupy. Another police shooting of a Black man in Kenosha had brought people out into the streets. The catalyst this time was a birthday party. On the way to Roland's I saw very few people. It was as though the part of the city I drove through was under some sort of spell. Maybe the spell was air-conditioning. However, the dense, humid calm made me uneasy. I felt like exploding with anxiety myself as I drove along in the empty silence. I reached Roland's street and pulled up in front of his house.

Well, I thought, it's still there and it looks tranquil. I stepped out into the hot, wet blanket of air and walked up the steps. Before I reached the top step, a woman opened the door and greeted me with a surprised look.

'I'm Tookie, from the bookstore. Is Mr. Waring home?'

The woman clutched her blouse. 'I'm his daughter,' she said. 'I just got back from the hospital. Roland's there. It's not Covid,' she said when she saw my face. 'It's a heart incident.'

'Is he going to be all right?'

'He got a stent. The doctors are just keeping him now for observation. He's okay.'

The energy drained out of me and I lowered myself to the steps. She came down and sat with me. From the corner of my eye I could see her wipe her face, but she was silent. At last I told her that I'd driven over because Roland's dog had come to the bookstore.

'Maybe you're looking for Gary,' I said.

There was an odd silence.

'No,' she answered after a bit. 'A few hours after we took Dad to the hospital, Gary died right here. That was a couple days ago. She's buried in the backyard. You must have seen a different dog.'

'It was Gary. I saw the nick on her ear.'

There was another odd silence. Then we each lifted our burdensome sweating bodies off the steps, said good-bye, and parted ways. Halfway home, I pulled over. Pollux's grandma had once told him dogs are so close with people that sometimes, when death shows up, the dog will step in and take the hit. Meaning, the dog would go off with death, taking their person's place. I was pretty sure that Gary had done this for Roland and then visited the store to let me know.

❋

In the rest of the world, things did not calm down—
things continued to falter. By sheer repetition our
highest elected official was wearing false grooves into
people's brains that they interpreted as truth. Port-
land protesters were grabbed off the street by anonymous officers, thrown in vans for questioning. It was
learned that cats live in a state of chronic schizophre-
nia. There was this sense as we approached fall and
the election that we were traveling down a steep slope
toward an unknown fate—maybe there would be relief, or maybe things would get worse. The numbers
of deaths ticked over and continued to grow. Our
country crept along beneath a pall of sorrow. There
was a continual hum of panic. Everything felt syn-
thetic. Everything was constantly rearranging. Here,
some of the city parks were homeless encampments.
Some were lawless, run by sex traffickers. Other
camps were valiant and heartbreaking attempts at self-
policed utopias. Pollux made his special potato salad
with bacon and hot pickles. I noticed that my hair was
growing thin on one side of my head. Pollux blamed
my heated right brain. Hetta decided yet again to stay
and live with us, *out of an abundance of caution.* We
kept using that phrase ironically because people in

government kept using it to cover up their fear or incompetence. Jarvis started to gnaw on a teething ring. Hetta allowed Laurent to visit.

They were sitting outside in the yard, on a strip of grass under the kitchen window, which was open. I heard them talking and tiptoed to the window to eavesdrop.

'Is he really mine?' Laurent asked.

'Are you serious? What's your grandpa's name?'

'Oh.'

'Would I name a baby Jarvis for any other reason? Plus, look at his hair.'

Laurent began to apologize in every way possible. I've never heard a man apologize so fervently. This went on and on, so I could only assume that Hetta was eating it up, or at least accepting what he said. Laurent also professed his love for Hetta and handed over what he said was a stack of love letters. Apparently they were written in the language he'd discovered. There was the sound of ruffling paper.

'How am I supposed to read these?'

'Just glance at the letters and cross your eyes. The meaning hovers.'

'Take them back.'

'I'm just kidding. If you want, I'll translate them. By the way, I deleted your part in *Midnite Cowgirl*, entirely. It's gone. I went through every file, got rid of any scene you were in. I mean, for sure by now they've found out. But they don't know where you went and I've hidden my tracks.' There was only a sly pause. 'I'm good at that.'

I couldn't tell how Hetta reacted, but after a while there were snuffling sounds, low cries, a soothing murmur from Laurent that changed to a lower register. Listening in on Hetta weeping and the two making up made me (even me) ashamed to listen. So I sneaked away.

MY HEART, MY TREE

Flora laid low, faked me out. I went back to work one morning.

I wasn't supposed to be alone, but Jackie had decided to work from home. She texted me on the way to the store, and I debated whether to work without her. We were too far behind and would flounder if I bowed out, so I persuaded myself it would be fine. Besides, the store was cool and the street was already an inferno. If only I had used an abundance of caution! I had a moment of discomfort as I entered the store, but there hadn't been a whisper or a hiss out of Flora for at least a month. Nor had she hidden books from me, although she still occasionally knocked a couple of books off the shelves. Earlier, I'd become accustomed to her shuffling and sliding. I had decided to accept her comings and goings as background noise. The store's activity had seemed to pacify or neutralize Flora's resentment. I played ever stronger ghost-repelling music. I wasn't feeling the pall of her regard. I wasn't worried. Had no hint, no intimation. When a large delivery arrived, I worked calmly, entering books into the system and setting them in piles. The task required deep-level concentration but the music kept me going. I lost track of Flora until I walked across the floor to shelve the books I'd entered. About halfway across the store, right next to the sailboat table, she pushed me over.

The books falling from my arm cushioned me. I caught myself before my face hit the floor and I slowly tried to rise. But then, but then . . . Something lowered onto my back, pressing me down. I gave in to the sensation without a struggle. It wasn't terrible. Warmth bloomed under the steady pressure and my heart slowed. I was a bird in a blanket, a swaddled baby. When I pushed up against the heavy substance, it gave way and I knelt on the floor. Once the pressure was gone it felt like nothing had happened. I lay back down on my stomach and stretched out, numb and forgetful. Unperturbed. Later for perturbance, I thought.

Then she tried to enter me.

I felt the shark-fin edge of her hand sink into my back. The shock of it didn't register as pain until her fingers flexed beneath my shoulder blades and gripped me from inside. Then, oh god. She was prying at my body. She was pulling my shoulders apart. She tried to press aside my spine. I fought against her hand like a fish on a hook. We struggled and I lost. She was sitting on me and she had weight, force. She used one hand as a wedge. Snaking her other hand in alongside it, she enlarged the opening in my back, pressing, twisting, tearing me open and going deeper until both hands found my heart and tried to wring it like a rag.

My heart, my beautiful fire.

My heart, my tree.

I closed my eyes and in the blackness my tree crashed down, flailing forward. My branches caught and lowered me until I was floating just over the floor. There, as if I were on a table before her, Flora opened the rest of my body carefully, unzipping me like a wet suit. She flopped me to the ground and tried to shove her feet down to the bottom of my feet, her arms to my fingertips. She tried to rear up inside of my torso and push her head through my neck so that she'd be able to see through my eyes. But I didn't go limp like a body rag. I wasn't an empty wet suit. I am quite solid. There just wasn't any room, no matter how she squeezed and jostled. There was just too much of me, the way there always has been. I am, and will always be, too much Tookie.

When I didn't come home or answer the phone, Pollux used my extra key and found me on the floor. I was snoring, so he knew right away that I wasn't dead. Maybe drunk. Maybe the pandemic stress and all else that was happening had snapped my resolve.

'What resolve?' I asked later, as we walked home. Nobody was out. It was a stifling evening. The leaves hung sullen in the lifeless air.

'Your resolve to . . . well, not a resolution, just the convention where you don't drink on the job.'

'I never did drink on the job, my love.'

'Of course, don't know why I even said that, I was just . . .'

Pollux stopped mumbling and fetched a sigh. I knew he kind of hung on the fact I'd called him *my love*. Actually, I'd meant it ironically, but the words had come out shaky and true. He threw his head back. Sweat dripped from his brow and our fingers were sloppily joined. It was like holding hands underwater. I could feel my sweat trickling down my back, streaming down my neck, running down my legs. I could not control it. I'd never sweat that way before and I was embarrassed.

'I'm dripping. It's awful.'

'It's me,' said Pollux. 'I'm sweating worse.'

My hair was soggy, my face covered in beads of water. Water rolled off my brow and the salt stung my eyes.

'Look at my back,' I said, turning away from him and tapping my shoulder. 'See if there's any blood. Pull my shirt up.'

'Out here in the open?'

'I don't care who sees.'

I knew I'd been ripped apart and blood should have been pouring out of me, but I could feel only drips. Pollux lifted my shirt.

'You're sweaty,' he said. 'And you've got these weird marks, creases, and dents. Were you sleeping on a coil of rope?'

'I was on my stomach,' I said in a croaking voice. 'Pollux, I used -iban. I put tobacco out. I did everything you told me. I fought Flora, blessed her, played music. But this afternoon she tried something else.'

Pollux was silent as we hotly sloshed along. He was waiting for me to go on, but I was afraid that I'd sound even crazier than I'd sounded before. I was afraid that this would be the tipping point and Pollux would have me committed, or just as awful, he might just stop believing me.

'You wouldn't commit me, would you?' I asked.

'It depends,' he said, trying for a wan joke.

'I'm serious.'

'No, no, never!' Pollux eagerly professed this and tried to sling his wet arm around my wet shoulders. His arm slipped off. 'What happened? Come on, you can tell old Pollux.'

'Good ol' Pollux,' I said. My voice was either sad or weakly sarcastic or both.

We'd stopped on the sidewalk in the middle of the bridge where we'd usually pick up a slight breeze. The trees below us had been scraped off the earth. I stood before him and tried to find the words, tried to make the sounds come out of my mouth, tried to tell him. But a tangle of thorns filled my lungs. I couldn't take a deep breath. I wheezed and he put his arms around me.

'Tookie?'

I tried. I held my breath, beat my hands on my head, growled, laughed. But it was useless. I was just as alarmed as Pollux when it began. His arms tightened as the first sob burst out of me. Another. Tears splattered my hands. I could feel my nose swelling, eyes sinking. My skin went fever hot. Pollux held on to me. At least he knew exactly what to do—nothing. I grew younger and younger until I was a giant leaking child who sagged in his arms, then socked him, hard. He did not fight me. He did not throw me over the bridge. I thought someone would pass and see us struggling, but the super-heated road was still. Pollux drew my head to his heart and smoothed my hair.

'Tookie.'

He kept repeating my name like a mantra and let me convulse until the madness passed out of me and I was simple again. He took a bandanna out of his pocket and I put it to my face. The cloth was already damp. I took his hand like the docile creature I am not and I let him lead me home.

Tookie, oh Tookie, thought Pollux. My magic menace.

Tookie had been doing so well. Pollux had been hoping she wouldn't foam up, boil over, start tossing molten lava in the dark. He never knew exactly what he'd done besides the obvious, but so much was his fault. Tookie had been relatively calm for a long time. He'd begun to feel the tension, the aliveness, the shakery, the clenching and unclenching of her fists, even though she held it together. This was the difficulty of living with Tookie. It was easier to live with her after she fell apart than to dread when it would happen. The first time she'd cracked, so long ago, Pollux had failed her. Through the years she'd been in prison, he'd been afraid to get in touch with her. He'd been ashamed of himself. Then the fateful day and a life of surprising love. Most of the time. The last time Tookie had cracked, Hetta wouldn't speak to her for a year. But maybe? Maybe Tookie had done some inner work she never talked about. Maybe Pollux's prayers had grown stronger. Because this was the longest either one of them could remember her holding it together. Furthermore, instead of falling into a frenzy of anger she had, for the first time ever, at least that Pollux could remember, cried on his shoulder.

Rugaroo

PILLOWS AND SHEETS

I couldn't get back on the bus and travel around the city tasting soup during pandemic times. I also couldn't go back to work, not at all. Penstemon had told Jackie that she heard Flora too, so when I told Jackie what had happened she hired a college student taking classes from home and divided my hours among the rest of the staff, without comment. She was a compassionate juggler. So I was on leave. There were two ways to handle my nerves—stay in bed forever. Or not. My body loves inertia. My brain loves oblivion. So there was really no choice. I did have a scolding inner voice that tried to tell me that, after I'd been locked up and isolated in my life, it was extremely wrong to voluntarily confine myself with a bunch of sheets and pillows. But it was a safe nest of tangled hugs! I wrapped and unwrapped. Plumped and squashed. Then collapsed. Even Pollux gave me space after I told him that I needed to wrestle with my demon. What man in his right mind is going to come between a woman and her demon?

Or maybe he wasn't a demon. Maybe he was just someone who taught me who I am.

Budgie's real name was Benedict Godfrey. His was an elegant name, suited to a British aristocrat, a name that deserved a Sir or Lord before it. He went by his initials, BG, and eventually BG became Budgie. Even if he'd been dressed in coat and tails instead of his usual black baggy metal band T-shirts, BG would still have been a colorless person, measly as I've said, with pitted skin and a lipless sneer. He was scarred from getting regularly beaten up and had a rotten disposition. The only positive thing I ever heard him say, somewhere from the depths of satisfaction in his nowhereness, was a drawn-out *yeaaaahhhhh*. Budgie wore long-sleeved shirts beneath his T-shirts either because of tracks and bruises or because he was always cold. His ass was so skinny and hips so rickety that his jeans puckered inward in all the wrong places. One summer a few of us went out camping by a lake poisoned by some kind of brain-eating algae. We built a fire to get high around, and I commenced staring at the heavens from my camping chair. Then it happened. A poignant plucking ornamented a song of outrageous tenderness. No words because to use words would take away the meaning. It was the sound of the stars. Only wolves are supposed to hear the stars. By then, I didn't know if I'd become a wolf or was violating some sacred rule. I began to shiver apart into molecules of dark air but I was not afraid. I was riding spiderwebs and moonbeams. I was infinitely soothed. I swirled a million miles up and a million miles back and then the music stopped, a can rattled, and I heard the guitar player, *yeaahhhhhhhhhhh*.

I hated Benedict Godfrey for messing with my vibe. But it was for love that I threw him in the cold truck and was thus betrayed. Now I saw that both of us had been betrayed. For Danae and Mara had treated his body like a shipping box. I guess the question is: How much do we owe the dead? I supposed that question was my devil.

But I'd lied about what I was doing. I couldn't fight. I'd lost my will to struggle. I had decided to become a slug.

No thinking. No extraneous motion. No talking, at all. I made an epic trip to the kitchen twice a day. Brought back a tray of whatever. Didn't even, couldn't even, hold Jarvis. That's how bad it was. Until one day Hetta barged in.

'Get up,' she said. 'I know what happened. Dad told me. Do you think you're the only one dealing with ghosts and shit?'

'No,' I mumbled from my nest. 'Everybody's got a ghost they want to tell me about. But mine tried to get inside of me.'

'Me, me, me. It's fucking always fucking you.'

I wasn't even going to dignify that. I turned over, made a cozy lump of myself, shut my eyes. Hetta charged around the bed and shook my shoulder. I pushed her away. I did it gently, but I made sure she knew I wasn't going to move. Then she did something underhanded, something devious, something she knew I couldn't bear. She knelt beside the bed and began to weep. Having been overtaken by tears on that bridge, I was vulnerable. I felt the pressure rise in me like steam.

After a good long while in which she didn't let up and I understood she wasn't faking, I turned to her and patted her shoulder. I asked her what was wrong. The sobs she was belting out weakened. She gulped, snorted, gave a despairing honk, started crying again. I kept patting her shoulder. Finally she said to me in a wee little thready voice,

'Tookie, I don't know what's real anymore.'

'Okayyyy . . . ,' I began, then stopped myself. I tried again. 'Explain?'

'Laurent was here. He started giving me this, I don't know, this *mad crazy garbage*.'

'What about?'

'Some heritable illness, something that gets passed on in his family, something he says I should know about.'

I sat up like I'd been shocked by a live wire.

'Something that would affect Jarvis?'

'Yes!'

She started in again, crying. I begged her to try and calm down so I could figure out what was going on. I reared up out of the covers, in my dizziness saw sparks and lights, for I was used to being horizontal. I tried again and managed to crawl over and sit beside her in my bed-lump hair and my baggy, ripped, cheap Target trauma pants. I was reporting for duty.

'All right. Slow down. Let's go back over this, using more words. Whewww, breathe, slow, okay.'

'He said that he's a rugaroo. He said that it runs in his family. That it's even what that book he gave you is about, his memoir or whatever.'

'The one that's written in a dead language?'

'His ancestors' language. He dreamed in this language all his life. Then for about a year, every so often, when he woke up from those dreams he wrote down a few sentences in this language, this script. He says this book he gave you was dictated to him by a part of himself that channeled his family history.'

I picked up Hetta's hand and held it. 'Don't worry. I'm pretty sure Laurent's deluded although . . .'

'What?'

I had just remembered how his face had shifted

slightly the last time I really talked to him. Then at Lyle's how he'd tried to push *Empire of Wild* like it was the Holy Bible. That book included a loathsomely attractive Rugaroo. Was there something to this?

'Let's get him to come over and read the book to us. We'll find out what he's talking about.'

Jarvis piped up from below, a thin wail. Hetta ran downstairs. I kept sitting on the side of the bed. Suddenly without thinking it through I was on my feet, striding over to my dresser, pulling out my favorite black jeans. The next thing I knew they were on me, and a black long-sleeved T-shirt too. I was walking down the stairs, abandoning my oblivion, back in whatever game the world was playing with me, with us.

THE STORY OF THE RUGAROO

We set up the reading outside in the yard. Pollux, me, Hetta, baby in Hetta's lap, and Laurent across from us. With a chillingly earnest expression on his face, he removed it—*Empire of Wild*—from a tawny leather bag. He held the book across his heart for a moment.

'Finally,' he said, 'a book that speaks for my People—'

'Yes, the author's Métis,' I jumped in, 'like you.'

'She may be one of us in other ways as well.' His

voice was soft as fawn suede. 'Though I wouldn't venture to say.'

He put the book down and withdrew his own book carefully from the melty-soft bag. He opened his book, smoothed the page with a finger. He licked his lips and stared at the pages as if the print was moving.

'Why don't you not read it.' I had to get this over with. 'Why don't you just tell us in your own words about this heritage of yours?'

Laurent put down his book and said in that case he would set the scene. Would we like to know about the Métis?

'No,' I said. But he'd already started. His voice was warm and resolute. It was hard not to feel reassured, but my feelings had switched so instantly that I tried to shake myself out of it.

'Over generations . . .'

I reeled my hand around. He sped up.

'We made our way along rivers, selling furs, getting blind drunk, and marrying pretty Indian women, until we reached Manitoba. Once we took to the Plains, my friends'—his eyes sparkled—'we were another generation! We changed our bark canoes for horses and rode down the buffalo. When the buffalo dwindled and were mostly reduced to bones littering the prairies, we turned to farming, took up allotments, or bought land wherever we could. For we're adaptable. That is our genius. Also, we're a devoutly religious people who love wild parties. We jigged, played the fiddle, talked to the saints and the Virgin Mary, believed in the devil, God, and the Rugaroo.'

I put my hand up. 'Let's cut to the family stuff. When did it start?'

'With my great-great-grandfather Gregoire,' said Laurent. 'He was fathered by a man in an elegant black suit who came to a wedding celebration, which in the old days could last for as long as a week. Every night, this man appeared in the doorway with his fiddle. And could he play! He also danced. Métis men were known for high kicks. This man could float into the air and slap the ceiling with the sole of his boot. And he was entirely charming. He paid attention to every woman, spoke seductively to the grandmothers, who nearly perished laughing. He played bone games with the children, drank and boistered about with every man. And of course he joined the fiddlers, played wild songs that snared their emotions, made them weep, scream with joy, dance outrageous jigs.'

I couldn't help it. God help me. I was avidly listening to Laurent. And next to me, Hetta. I could feel the tension of her breathless concentration.

'Here's where my great-times-three-grandma comes

in. She was the sweetest, kindest, meekest, dearest woman of them all. Berenice was known for her mild forgiving dovelike gaze. Every night this stranger came to the wedding. At midnight, he laid away his fiddle and always led Berenice to the dance. As the week went on and they danced every night, the old ladies noticed a bit of hair had sprouted up around his neck. Fur trimmed his boots. It seemed, perhaps, that his brow was lower and his nose was broader. His teeth were a bit whiter, and sharper. You'd think there would be an outcry, you'd think he would be chased away, or captured, but he was so companionable that nobody wanted to insult him. It wasn't until the last night of the celebration, right at midnight, that they knew for sure.'

'Knew what for sure?' I sneaked a glance. Although Hetta was rocking Jarvis, her lips were slightly parted and her eyes were fixed on Laurent, rapt with interest. He leaned forward and used his hands like a storyteller.

'As the wedding celebration was ending with the maniacal sobbing of the fiddles and the crazed dancing of the entire wedding party, the handsome stranger put his fiddle in a case with straps. He slung the case around his neck, tossed his head up, and started howling. You could see now that his teeth were very long and sharp, fangs really. Right before the dancers' eyes, his hair turned into a thick white pelt. His back split the suit jacket. He'd cast such a profound spell that even when he carried Berenice out the door, nobody stopped them. They say she clung happily to the Rugaroo and laughed, insisting that everyone must let them pass.'

'I can't believe those buffalo hunters didn't go after them,' said Pollux. He, at least, was not impressed.

'Yes of course. A few family members tried to follow their trail. But the two were untraceable, far off in the bush. They stayed away for one entire summer. Her family mourned her and gave her up for dead, then lambasted the Rugaroo and insisted she was still alive.

'At last one early dawn the Rugaroo deposited Berenice back at her parents' door. Berenice wept and moped for weeks, insisted that the Rugaroo hadn't harmed her at all, and at last realized she was pregnant.'

Laurent stopped, looked up at us, wide-eyed.

Hetta stared back at him with a goofy little mystified smile on her face and I thought, *Oh, no.*

Pollux was still trying to tolerate this, his face was calm but his feet large in gray runners were jiggling. He was tugging on his hair. I grabbed his hand before he pulled out his ponytail.

'What happened then?' he asked in a strangled voice.

'A fearless husband was found for Berenice. The child was born with the ignorant blessing of the priest.

When the baby was baptized, the water sizzled off its brow. But the bleach of Berenice's goodness and the priest's godliness expunged the stain and the boy, Gregoire, grew up to be a good person, hardworking, faithful, pious. It seemed that the power of Berenice's kindly soul had expunged any rugaroo ways. Gregoire danced but never played the fiddle, married one quiet woman, and stayed at home with her for the rest of his life.'

Laurent addressed Pollux with a respectful nod when he said this. Then he paused meaningfully, as much as to say, *Your protectiveness for Hetta is noble and I share it! I'm not like the first Rugaroo. I'm like Gregoire!* Then he resumed.

'Gregoire left behind some medicinal knowledge taught to his mother during the summer of her abduction. Only when Gregoire died, thrown off a fast horse at the age of fifty-six, did the trouble manifest.

'As people did in those times, a carpenter built the coffin. People brought food for the wake and his family and friends sat with his body in the house. Around midnight of the first night, his eyes flipped open and he gave a heavy moan. This thrilled his wife, who grabbed his arm and tried to sit him up—but he was not alive and it was obvious that his body was being forcibly possessed.

'An old Michif lady grabbed a cast-iron skillet and struck the head of the corpse. Then she spilled the vial of holy water that she carried upon her person at all times across its heart. The body sighed, closed its eyes, and went back to being dead. However, during the early morning hours the body vanished entirely. The family problem was thereby revealed. From then on, it just kept happening. This refusal to stay dead was handed down. There were eight children. This tendency manifested in several of them. One uncle actually got out of his grave and ran away. He never made it out of the graveyard, but still . . .'

'This sounds horrible,' cried Hetta in excitement.

'After many generations, here's where I come in,' Laurent said. 'I was born in a coffin.'

Now I was upset. The spell was broken. Born in a goddamn coffin? But Hetta was looking at Laurent with wild intrigue. She wasn't put off in the least. Her eyes were incandescent. It was like she'd had a revelation.

'And then what?' she breathed.

'My mother was a bit actress and had a part in a community theater production as the wife of a vampire. She was onstage, ready to rise from her coffin, when she went into labor. It happened so quickly there was no time to move her. Someone closed the curtain, but the birth was a sensation. They changed the title of the play to *Birth of a Vampire*. My parents and me, as the vampire baby, acted in it for a while, then moved on to other adventures. They've always loved the hospitality industry and their sports bar is very popular.'

Laurent paused as if to see if we were still with him. Hetta was practically swooning with joy now.

'This is so deeply goth,' she said. 'Are you dangerous on the full moon?'

'I have cravings,' said Laurent.

Hetta actually seemed to blush.

Laurent went on to tell Hetta that this rugaroo gene came here from the Old World and was introduced to Métis or Michif culture via the French werewolf, the loup-garou. He said that the tribal people who intermarried with the French took it upon themselves not only to improve the looks of the voyageurs, but to indigenize their cryptids and hybrids.

'So the rugaroo became someone like me,' said Laurent. 'I am loyal, brave for the most part, honest, kind for the most part. I've never really had violent tendencies, but I thirst for justice. I'm excitable and have a ton of physical stamina. Besides working at Wells Fargo, I'm studying plant medicines. I play the fiddle and I also advocate for our relatives, the wolves. The only thing that's different about me, really, is that I've decided my true vocation is writing in this ancient language and I don't know if I'll stay dead when I die.'

'Oh Laurent,' said Hetta, moved to happiness. Actual happiness, I think. 'If you'd only told me this from the first!'

'I thought you might reject me,' said Laurent.

'No way,' said Hetta. 'This is the coolest thing I've ever heard. Our baby is . . .'

'A savage immortal. That's what they called us way back when.' Laurent bowed his head.

'I don't know if you're really dad material,' said Pollux.

'Maybe you have this wrong.' Laurent looked up and held his own in a long gaze with Pollux. 'I'm totally in love with Hetta but she's totally in love with someone else. So my role at this point is to support them and support my son.'

I batted at my head. 'Am I hearing things?'

'He's very evolved,' said Hetta, with a giddy smile. 'Dad and Mom know how I felt about Asema. It's okay. That's over. She never succumbed to my charms.'

'Unbelievable, that she wouldn't,' murmured Laurent.

'Maybe I should stick with my baby's father, at least for now,' said Hetta.

'At least for now,' I muttered, and grabbed Pollux by the shirt. We left the scene. Whatever happened next was not for us.

Hetta and Laurent took off for a couple hours. I was on the babysitting docket. Jarvis had discovered my face. He studied each of my features. When they added up to his satisfaction, his eyes sparked, his smile burst out, his arms jerked around, he kicked his fat apple feet. It bewildered me to be a source of human joy. I could hardly bear it when he landed in my arms and gripped my finger with his fierce little fist. I held him.

'What are you?' I asked.

He wouldn't tell.

'Are you perhaps a tiny baby rugaroo?'

He blinked at me with one ascertaining eye, the other shut, so it seemed that he was trying to wink.

'What's going on?'

It was Pollux, chomping into an apple that he'd lightly peppered. That's how he ate apples. Held the pepper tin in one hand so he could get a jolt in every bite.

'I'm just wondering if Laurent bequeathed his slippery fox ways to his son.'

'A baby. He's pure. Leave him out of this!'

'You know anything about rugaroos?'

'Yeah. From Grandma. Though she was scareder of the wiindigoo.'

'So there really are people who refuse to stay dead.'

'I guess, and reanimators.'

'It's a thing?'

'More common than you'd suppose, though less common now with medical science.'

'Did you ever, you know, have experience with a reanimator?'

I asked this cautiously, trying not to imply there was anything to it but ordinary science. Pollux peppered himself a huge bite of apple. Jarvis sneezed. I looked reproachfully at Pollux and he moved his pepper hand away from the baby.

'Not a personal experience. The scariest reanimation I ever heard of was a cute little girl.'

I said I didn't want to hear it.

'She came out of the earth ponytail first.'

'Pollux, I'm warning you.'

'Just science.' He shrugged.

Luck and Love

THE FRYBREAD HOUR

As the season turned there was a sense of slipping downhill. We skied weightlessly through the days as if they were a landscape of repeating features. The air cooled and I went back to work because we got busy filling panic orders—it seemed everybody dreaded another lockdown and they needed books. We had to stagger shifts in the tiny space. The store was a hive of intense activity from seven or eight in the morning to nine p.m. We'd never done such a thing before. Working those full-day staggered hours with other people kept me safe from Flora.

For Pollux and me during this time, the one complete refuge from care, sort of a communion ritual, centered on frybread. Around 11 a.m., one day a week, we made our way to Pow Wow Grounds. Sometimes we unfolded our camp chairs in the parking lot. If we didn't have long to wait, we might street park and stay in the car. People wandered up, stood around shuffling their feet, sat at an outdoor table, or leaned against the wall. You could hear bursts of laughter ricochet between conversation bunches, people of all ages.

There would be a stir of expectation at noon. Then someone would see the gray van driven by Bob Rice, and people would laugh and watch as he drove up. An elder would yell, 'It's about time!' or 'What took you so long?' More laughs. Bob would pull up and unload the frybread. A line would form. The holy moment had arrived.

We got out. Bought our frybread and extra for whoever was working at the store. Sometimes, with all the fixings, Indian tacos. We might eat right there. Maybe in the car. The frybread was golden, and light, as if you'd dropped a round piece of cloud in hot fresh grease. Yet it was dense enough to hold the taco toppings if you bought it that way.

Sure, it's not good for you, but Asema says it's grandma food, 'bad for the arteries but good for the heart.' She'll eat it any day, she says, instead of her other vice—those neon red-hot Cheetos that make your fingers look dipped in blood.

Made by hand. Made with love. Still, frybread didn't really bring Pollux and me back together. We'd have that moment, but it would fade.

When it really turned cold, I caught the disease of un-fixed dread. I was weary, bedraggled, and my brain had stalled back in November 2019, when Flora died and did not leave. Our house had become crammed with cardboard boxes, grocery bags, random sup-plies. Again we were buying things that might become scarce, more pasta and frozen vegetables, diapers, salted nuts, ketchup. Books I'd brought home overflowed the shelves and crept in stacks up the walls. I had stopped wearing anything but three pairs of black pants that I rotated through the week, and an assortment of gray and black T-shirts that I wore with a black jean jacket. Worse, I had broken the shoestrings on the boots I liked and started wearing plastic clogs. I am not a clog person—they remind me of corrections facilities—but I didn't have the heart either to buy the right shoestrings or in general to alter my circumstances.

Pollux and I figured we'd used up our luck during the protests, so we were extremely careful about our ritu-als of isolation. Still, sometimes a moment occurred when one of us thought we'd been exposed, or had the virus. A surprise greeting, a panting runner at your shoulder, an old friend showing up with his mask on his chin. Ceremonies. Pollux had never worked in politics, *but look what happened*, he said. He went out with a team to register Native voters up in White Earth. One day he got tired and forgot to wear his mask in the car. Another day he forgot his phone and borrowed one from a stranger. Then there was the funeral. A woman who did traditional funerals died. Pollux took over. We were losing our elders, our jokers, our beloveds, our tradition keepers. We were all coming loose at the seams. Anyway, he got exposed.

One morning, he said, *Get away from me.*

'What's going on?'

'I'm not all right.'

His cough was slight, his fever low. It appeared that if this was Covid he had a light case, so we left him alone in his room. He spoke through the door, telling me that he felt only halfway sick. His voice was mopey but strong. I brought his food to the door and picked it up with gloves, put his dishes directly into the dishwasher. Toast, broth, noodles, juice, and once he ate a homemade chicken potpie. He always put the juice and Gatorade bottles and tray back out, empty. He was too miserable to drive himself in for testing and refused to get in a car so I could drive him. We talked through the door about what he needed and he went to sleep. Then one morning, about five days after he'd been isolated in his room, he phoned me. He told me his head was spinning. He said there was a golden star quilt hanging on our bedroom wall. (There wasn't.) He told me that all night he'd watched it billowing in and out like it was breathing. The closet was halfway open and there was a clothes iron on a shelf. He said it had a face and the eyes kept winking at him. He had to catch his breath between sentences. I barged into his room.

His eyes were sunken, his gaze confused, his face gray and sweaty. He kept rolling his eyes to the ceiling, and frowning as if he saw something up there.

'Do you know what mammatus clouds are?' he asked. 'There's going to be a tornado.'

'You're going to the hospital,' I told him.

'Get Hetta to take me in,' he gasped.

'You're coming with me,' I said. 'Hetta is Jarvis's one and only.'

I didn't say to Pollux, because you're my one and only. I could have, but I didn't. Because I am a stubborn grudger and I cannot let things go. Pollux's breath was ragged and shallow. *Catch me, Tender Sasquatch,* he said, wavering as I walked behind him out to the car. His laugh became a cough. I put my arm around his back, grabbed his elbow, helped him in. It had suddenly gotten cold so I bundled him in a wool blanket. With the windows down, both wearing masks, we drove to the nearest emergency room, twenty endless minutes away. I drove quickly but very carefully. I was numb, vigilant. Pollux was struggling for air by the time we got there. A nurse in protective headgear, bagged shoes, a billowing yellow gown, met us. *You look good in yellow,* he wheezed at her. *You should wear it more often.* She wheeled him in, said *Here, tough guy,* and immediately put a pulse oximeter on his finger. It dipped into the 80s.

The nurse pushed him down the Covid corridor, where the ER doctor would order oxygen and admit him. Just like that. So fast. There was too much to feel. Pollux wouldn't let me touch him. He wouldn't look at me. I watched the nurse wheel him away. When she paused to hit a flat knob on the wall beside the door, I stumbled forward, threw out my hand, called his name. The door opened with a click and hushed sigh. Pollux turned as the nurse wheeled him through and flashed our sideways peace sign. *You're hot, but later. The door is shut. Leave.* I could not move. I stood there as people in face shields and masks and gowns and shower caps flowed around me. The doors were a scorched brown color. I stared at the seam between the doors. A mysterious line. Then I ducked back into the room we'd been assigned.

Everything was hollow. I rocked back and forth, sitting in a chair, arms crossed.

'What do I do now?' I asked the nurse who came in to give me the test. It was a saliva test and I didn't have any spit. It took forever to fill the vial and half the time I missed and got my shoe.

'You wait outside for the results of the first test. We'll call you. Then go home and isolate. Take good care of yourself,' said the nurse. 'We are surging again.' Her voice was dull with fatigue, but kind.

'Can I see him?

The nurse had round hazel eyes, thick brows, and her hair was in a net. There was not much of her to see, and I didn't want to stare at her photo ID in plastic. The nurse promised that once Pollux was settled, his care team would be in touch. Pollux would communicate, or staff would communicate, by phone or FaceTime. She took my information meticulously. They would take care of him. They would do everything possible. I nodded and nodded. I went out to the car, which was in short-term parking across from the emergency entrance. I plugged in my phone and drove slowly around the hospital to charge it up. Then I entered the long-term parking garage. I drove the spiral to the top floor and found the least visible parking spot. There was always a sleeping bag in the van. I pushed my seat back and made it as flat as possible. Then I unzipped the sleeping bag, tucked it around my body, and lay back with my eyes closed. After another hour, my phone rang and it was Pollux.

'They got me all set up,' he said. 'I'm gonna be okay. This O2 is good stuff.'

'You're on oxygen?'

'Out of an abundance of caution.'

I could hear him take a gulping breath.

'Don't joke.'

'Don't sleep in the parking lot.'

'How'd you know I was in the parking lot?'

'Have we been married five years?'

'Actually, I'm on the top floor of the parking garage.'

'Go home. You've gotta keep your strength up and not get sick.'

'I tested negative,' I said, though they hadn't called me yet.

'Thank you,' he whispered.

I heard him holding back a gasp, a cough. His voice thinned to a thread.

'Dang,' he said. 'I'll be okay. I love you. Gotta go.'

He hung up before I could say I love you too. I waited in the hum of absence, dialed him back, no answer. I texted him five red hearts. I never used emojis, considering them beneath my dignity. Maybe this would mean something. How pathetic. I stayed there staring through the windshield at a redbrick wall.

❀

I followed Pollux to the Covid hospital in St. Paul, in a warehouse-style district that included other hospitals. At night it was hard to tell whether people lived in the area or were there only as the ill and those tending to the ill. The parking garages were lighted, the hospital entrances, the windows of a pizza place, Thai restaurant. But nobody walked in the streets. Outside those squares of radiance there was a depth of darkness I rarely saw in the Cities. Anything could be out there. I found a parking spot. I guess I was one of those things.

I knew I couldn't see him in person, or be with him, or hold his hand, or smooth his lumpy brow. But parked near the hospital, I was closer to Pollux than I was at home and I could imagine that I was doing something. I stared at the hospital windows, lit by a chilly radiance. For hours I watched people's heads pop into view, swerve, vanish. I knew the floor he was on, but had no idea which way his room faced. I'd scrolled through enough stories of other coronavirus families, relationships, cases. I knew what it meant when your loved one could not communicate. Soon I was asked to leave my spot. I gassed up, bought a bag of Fritos and a bottle of water. I chose a different way out of the all-night parking lot and then returned. I wasn't leaving until I found out more. I pulled up the sleeping bag and closed my eyes. But I didn't sleep. I just tried to breathe. My phone rang.

'Mrs. Pollux here,' I said.

The woman who spoke had a young clear voice. She sounded like a precocious teenager.

'I'm Dr. Shannon. Just calling to update you. Your husband's still on supplemental oxygen and we are proceeding cautiously. It's much too early to know if he's improving, but he's a strong man, and he's in fairly good health. He said to tell you not to sleep in the parking lot.'

'Well, tough shit,' I said. 'I'm staying.'

'We won't know more for a while.'

'I'll be here.'

'It's not safe, Mrs. Pollux.'

'It's safer for me than being away from him.'

The doctor didn't answer for a long time and when she did her voice was clogged. 'I'm sorry,' she said. 'I know. I had a close relative here.'

'Did they live?'

'No.'

'Oh hell, doctor. Keep a close eye on Pollux and keep calling me. He's my lucky star. He's my . . .'

I hung up and slumped over and tried to live.

QUESTIONS FROM TOOKIE TO TOOKIE

Awake in the wee hours of the morning, staring at my breath-fogged windshield. Longing to stretch out, as on an endless bus ride. Stuck in my aching body, numb ass, frozen feet.

What are you?

A juicy roast dwelling in the awareness of time.

Can you stop being angry at Pollux?

He cuffed me up at the Lucky. I was tried and sentenced. He didn't visit. He didn't care that I was transferred or that I broke. He wasn't there when I was freaked out, had sickening dreams, didn't want to leave my cell. He was living his good ol' Pollux life when I became a plant.

Was he responsible for your vegetative state?

Not exactly. I mean, he said he prayed for me. But he was living his life without me!

He may have enjoyed life without you. But like dressing up in fruit, was that so terrible?

Yes.

Did you think about him? Did you write to him?

Sometimes, to the first question. No, to the second. I was trying to survive day to day under the burden of my sentence. I suppose I was haunted even before Flora.

Haunted by what?

Dread and fear.

Of what?

Of what happened.

Continue?

To be locked away. To be forgotten by normal people. To be subject, to be ruled, to be watched, to be the one to eat the leftovers of a thriving nation. To walk on lines of tape, to remember Lucky Dog baked potatoes and the night sky with equal teary longing.

Why, after all that, be bothered by a ghost?

Why indeed? I have proved that I'm too much! I shall accept her. As I was able to accept the mashed rutabagas.

And Pollux? Will you accept that when he did his job he also failed you? Can you forgive him for that?

RAINBOW

The nights turned cold. My breath began to freeze on the windshield. One early morning someone knocked on the window of the van. I turned the car on but couldn't roll down the window. I had parked on the roof of the garage. Rain had poured down, then froze. The window was sealed shut by clear ice. I tried to open the door but the door was stuck. The person outside said to keep trying. I threw myself against it. Panic bubbled in me but my guardrails held and I was able to force my way out. It turned out the person knocking was a pleasant young woman in a rainbow mask. She'd just parked, seen me in the driver's seat, the car covered in a clear shell. She was checking to see if I was all right. After I reassured her, I got back in and started the car. I'd warm it up to clear off the windshield before starting home. I sat there, rubbing my hands together, tapping my frozen toes, waiting. The way Rainbow Mask had knocked. The way she peered into the windshield covered with glassy transparent ice. Rainbow Mask. She vanished as though she'd been a visitor from another dimension. That plus the way I'd broken out of my car—it was though I'd fallen through the ice into a different world.

From that perspective, I returned to my self-interrogation. It occurred to me that Pollux must have been watching over me in his own way. Those years I was in prison, he'd been looking after me the same way I was looking after Pollux now—helplessly, from the outside. He always said he'd prayed for me. Maybe sleeping in various parking garages near Pollux was a form of prayer. I knew he'd worked to get me pardoned, too. And after I got out of prison, I am pretty sure Pollux tried to keep an eye on me. Maybe that meeting in the Midwest Mountaineering parking lot wasn't fate. He'd taken himself there on purpose. Maybe it was feet.

I drove over to the Indian Health Board in Minneapolis. The testing center is set up in the parking area beneath the building. I pulled my car up and waited in my parking spot while the gowned, capped, gloved, masked, and face-shielded medical people reached into the windows of cars with swabs. They were graceful. It looked like they were pollinating flowers, though I didn't feel like a pollinated flower as I drove out of the parking garage. I was just a woman with a tested nose, tired and grimy, whose relationship had been complicated by reality, and who would give anything to sit beside my husband in the hospital and hold his hand.

In October the sky recedes to a backdrop. The brilliance on earth gathers. The trees are incendiary. Crowns of gold and carmine. Walking is like floating in a dream. Pollux loved the changing leaves. We had our special routes where sugar maples lined the streets. There is generally a spate of cold, windy rainstorms and the leaves start dropping. I'm a little sad when the shapes of the trees are revealed. This year when the leaves disappeared I took it personally—Pollux was still fighting. The doctors were still saying that he was holding his own, which I know meant that he was not getting better. It seemed that he and Covid were in a standoff. From one day to the next I hung on, but I could feel his fingers slipping through my fingers. All of a sudden he took a slide. There was a call from the hospital. I listened. Said I understood. My hand was shaking so hard I dropped the phone. Hetta reached toward me.

'He had a directive that stipulated no ventilator,' I told her. 'He never told me, just brought the paper in with him. He's still on oxygen but he's worse.'

We held hands and cried, abject, sobbing in crags and crevasses of fear. After a while, we decided to be brave and we set up a time to see Pollux. An hour later, our favorite nurse, Patrick, held an iPad. The spectral image of Pollux, gray as silt, swam toward us. I tried to power up my love to a blaze that would project through the screen. I could tell that Hetta was also trying, calling *Daddy*. We had vowed no tears. Jarvis showed off his new tooth. We said everything we could think of and tried to make useless jokes. His eyes were wide and helpless. We could see him struggling to breathe. Patrick cut the visit off and told us it was time to prone him. Hetta leaned toward me on the couch and I caught her. It was me, trying to comfort her. My pats were awkward, my voice scratchy and strained. But Hetta didn't pull away. Pollux on a screen had looked ghostly. We all do. We look like special effects ghosts in sixties B movies. But I desperately, wrenchingly, wanted Pollux to be solid with his solid warmth. I wanted his big hands, the hunch of his shoulders when he laughed, his skeptic glare, his square head, and his big tough body in my arms.

Unaccountable feelings bound me to Pollux. There were things about him that he never showed to other people—tenderness, but also things he knew I understood. In his boxing days, how to hit a man so the blow lifted him off his feet. In his street-fighting days, where to bite a man's finger so he lets go of you and his arm is temporarily paralyzed. In his first marriage, how he blamed himself when his wife died of an overdose, the circumstances eerily the same as my own mother's overdose. His guilt was like mine. When young, he'd been joyous, but also hungry. He'd loved his uncle who taught him the ceremonies he practiced now. How sometimes just from looking at him, people thought he was raring to fight and tried to get the jump on him. How he had become gentle and tried to keep things balanced, not with rules or force, but with song.

LILY FLORABELLA

I dropped by the bookstore because I couldn't keep walking in circles. I was trying to take my mind off the fact that I was useless to Pollux. I was desperate enough to try clearing things up with Asema.

'I need to talk to you again,' I said to her. 'This time I promise I won't pass out.'

Asema took a cautious breath. Penstemon was working in the back of the store. I could hear the tape gun make a slick snicking sound. She smoothed down the tape with her fingers and set a package on the pile.

'It's about Flora-iban.'

We were scattered apart in the store, and I realized that I couldn't remember when, outside of our house, I'd last talked with two people at the same time.

'She's still hanging around, I take it?'

'Worse.'

Flora's attempt to enter my body seemed an age ago and also yesterday. Such was the warpage of time in this era.

'All right,' said Asema. 'We were going to call you anyway because I deciphered more of the manuscript Flora stole from me. I think I've figured a few things out. I've already run them by Pen.'

We agreed to meet in the park by the bookstore

where we could keep talking outside and I left. First, I swung by my house and I picked up my mail. I put on a black flannel shirt that belonged to Pollux. It was my security shirt, and yes, I'd started wearing his clothes as a way to have him with me. Except his pants were tight in the ass because he had one of those skinny Anishinaabe man asses. So it was his shirts and his jackets that I wore. I went to the park, sat down on a bench, and flipped through mail, waiting for Pen and Asema.

'What've you got there?' Asema was standing beside the bench.

'Coupon pack. Bill. More voting stuff.'

I stepped over to the trash can to throw out all but the water bill—for Hetta's endless showers.

'Oh no, you don't,' said Asema. She came up behind me and snatched away the voting packet.

It had warmed up enough to sit on the grass, take off our jackets, and sit on them in the fading sun.

'So tell me.'

Asema slid a conspiratorial look at Pen, who narrowed her eyes and looked amused. They were both wearing their hair in twining braids, a mädchen look that wrapped up and over their heads, charming and incongruous.

'Okay, Tookie. We knew our customer as Flora LaFrance. But Flora was only part of her second name.

She held on to LaFrance from her brief first marriage to Sarge LaFrance, who owned a Subway franchise up near Spice Cake Lake.'

'Passing that place on the interstate always makes me hungry,' I said.

I was nervous and pulled Pollux's heavy shirt around me. Asema ignored me and kept talking. I folded my hands and stared at her in concentration.

'Flora was the youngest of six children from a wealthy family. She was adopted, so she grew up with questions. She knew her biological mother's last name. That was all. Her adoptive family was old money, at least by Midwestern standards, and made their fortune in lumber, first-growth timber, forests that had covered northern Minnesota and belonged to the Ojibwe. In other words, she was adopted by the descendants of the timber barons who cheated and killed us. But moving on. Flora grew up in a house made of primeval pine and quartersawn oak. She went to Catholic school and attended St. Catherine's, after which the old money ran completely out. After she'd married and divorced the Subway owner, she decided that she had to work with Indigenous people, then she got overenthusiastic and wanted to be one. A friend who knew Flora's biological mother's name gave her that antique picture of a woman with Flora's name written on the back of the photograph. What a sign, huh? The woman in the photograph looked a bit like Flora, if you squinted hard, and she was of an indeterminate ethnicity. The photo woman was probably in her midforties, wore a black dress buttoned up the neck, and a carefully placed limp web of shawl. It was the kind of knitted triangle worn by women of all sorts around that time—Indigenous and white. This photograph was a great solace to Flora.'

'I know. She showed it to me. Several times, I think.'

'Did you see her name written on the back of the picture?'

'No, I didn't.'

'Me neither, but I wouldn't have recognized that family name anyway. She had the photo copied and put into an antique frame for herself and for Kateri. This image was her touchstone, and from it she spun an identity—at first of course she was Dakota. Then things became confused and she made some people mad, so she amended herself to Ojibwe or Anishinaabe, and then as she clarified her confusions, she told everyone she was the descendant of the woman in the picture, who was probably of mixed bloods, and who made it somehow through the harrowing years of the Dakota War and its aftermath. Then of course she became vaguely Métis. At last, she stopped casting about and left her identity vague.'

'Right.'

'And I've already told you that Flora stole the book written about the woman who . . .'

I put my hand up to stop Asema from saying the name, but I was too late.

'The woman's name, the *white* woman's name, was . . .'

I put my hands over my ears but Asema didn't notice. Pen, however, did notice, cocked her braid-circled head, and frowned keenly at me.

'When Flora read this name, she understood that she was not descended of a Métis woman, but of a white woman. Perhaps at first she hoped the woman in the picture was actually Maaname, or Genevieve Moulin. I think she hoped this woman was her ancestor. But the portrait was of the white woman who kept and controlled Genevieve. This woman was known for keeping other women locked in a bedroom. This woman ran what was called "a house of commercial affection." She rented out these women's bodies and was known to have covered up or perhaps committed several murders. She was known as the Nightbird Butcher. She was the woman who left her sign on Genevieve's body and cruelly enforced her transformation. Her name was written out in the book with descriptions of what she had done. Flora read the name. It was the same name as the name on the back of her photograph. At that instant, Flora's identity turned upside down. Everything that she'd concocted about herself turned out to be its opposite. And don't forget that Flora was a devout Catholic. To find she'd modeled herself on a woman of cruel appetites who tortured helpless girls, this was unbearable.'

I held up my hand again. What she was saying filled me with an agitation so extreme I wanted to jump out of my skin. Maybe the extreme discomfort I felt was a normal reaction. But I needed to shift the story, so she wouldn't say the name. I brought up the other thing.

'Say, you two! Something else happened that I haven't told you about. It happened a couple of weeks ago, the last time I was at work. I was alone. And this time . . .'

I couldn't form the words, could hardly frame the thought. I tried again.

'Flora tried to . . . she tried to . . .'

I turned away. I was all jammed up. My heart was fluttering and knocking in its cage of ribs.

'What did she try to do?' asked Penstemon.

In a rush I got it out. 'She tried to unzip my body and squeeze herself inside of me.'

Asema folded her arms in frozen concentration. Penstemon stood up slowly and looked down at me in alarm. She was dressed in black from neck scarf to socks, all in black, spectral black. At some point she sat back down and muttered, 'It makes sense.'

'How does it make sense?'

Penstemon flipped back a widowy scarf.

'Are you in mourning? Why can't you wear a damn color?' I asked.

'Oh this'—she looked at her clothing—'It's what I always wear, Tookie. And speaking of . . . just look at yourself.'

'You're too young to be so grim,' I said, but it was true I was also dressed in black.

'A wannabe,' said Penstemon. 'She wanted to *be*. Flora wanted to exist inside of a Native body. But a certain kind of Indigenous body, big and tough. She wanted to be recognizably Indian so badly that she spent her life trying to engineer an identity. But she knew, on some level, that none of it was real. Thus, her desperation.'

'I can see that,' I said. 'But what I don't get is this—when she couldn't kick me out of my body, why didn't she try yours, or Asema's.'

'There's a reason,' said Pen. 'And I think . . . don't take this wrong. I think maybe you're more porous.'

I looked at my arms. Strong from Marine-style push-ups. I turned my hands over. I seemed so solid, but in my life there had been so many times I'd been on the verge of dissolving. So close to it that I'd looked up and copied down a word.

> **deliquesce**. 1. To melt away or disappear as if by melting. 2. *Chemistry*. To dissolve and become liquid by absorbing moisture from the air. 3. *Botany*. a. To branch out into numerous subdivisions that lack a main axis. b. To become fluid or soft on maturing, as do certain fungi.

I had looked up the word because it applied to what happened to me when I dissolved at times, 'as do certain fungi.' I told Penstemon about the word and admitted that there was something to what she said. Pen took a breath, gave me a relieved smile, and went on talking.

'Flora knew there would be a reckoning, that someone, maybe Kateri, would figure out that she'd pulled together elements of other people's lives to fake her own. The thing is, most of us Indigenous people do have to consciously pull together our identities. We've endured centuries of being erased and sentenced to live in a replacement culture. So even someone raised strictly in their own tradition gets pulled toward white perspectives.'

'For sure,' said Asema, 'white realities are powerful. And most of us have to pick and choose between our family and tribal traditions to find ourselves. She knew we struggled, she knew we were sometimes tentative, she knew we sought our own sense of belonging. She knew that some of us have to make a choice every day to hold on, to speak our language, to dance, to pay our dues to the spirits.'

What she said hit me hard. She had just described Pollux's life work. He did make that decision every day when he woke up, burned cedar and sweetgrass, put out offerings, went off to keep the universe ticking along.

'Excuse me,' I said. 'I have to send an urgent message.'

I walked over to a tree and pretended to look at my phone. I closed my eyes and focused my thoughts as tightly as possible and sent them to Pollux. *Just live, just live, and I'll be there for you. You're needed here to keep things going and I'll help you.*

Walking back to the benches, I heard Penstemon say, 'I really believe that to live inauthentically is to live in a sort of hell.'

'She seemed happy enough though,' said Asema.

'How could she be?'

I had witnessed Flora's tension, her zeal to correct mistakes in other people. I remembered how once she had told me I couldn't talk about being 'Indian' or 'Aboriginal,' but should always say 'Indigenous.' I'd told her that I'd call myself whatever I wanted and to get the hell out of my face. Now I saw Flora's pedantry as a form of desperation. It was true that she was constantly on high alert. Always offering her latest proof. Always scared she'd be laughed at. She studied us out. In fact, it crossed my mind that she might have tried to go to Ojibwe heaven and been turned back. That alone would devastate.

'She just tried so fucking hard,' I said. 'And for all that, still, I only liked her when she acted white, I guess, like when she was reading Proust.'

'You read *Swann's Way*,' said Penstemon. 'You told me. So how can that be white?'

'Point taken.'

'Remember when she took up beading?' said Asema, a bit sad.

'She brought her beadwork in to Jackie, but her earrings sagged; she beaded too loose,' said Penstemon. 'But you know? She got better. She got perfect. But then she forgot to put the wrong bead, the spirit bead in. Only the Creator's perfect, right? Maybe she insulted the spirits.'

'She made me a medallion,' said Asema. 'And she did a lot of good things, you know, threw herself into helping young people. Adopted Kateri, not legally. Kateri was a teenager, after all. Kateri chose her.'

'And loved her,' I said.

'Right. We can't tell Kateri about this.'

'Of course not.'

We looked out over the lake. The sun was shards of brilliance.

'It's a poem out there,' I said for some reason.

'You should write it, Tookie. It's yours.'

'Oh for godsakes, Pen. Don't patronize. I'd rather get rid of Flora's ghost. I mean, I can't work alone. I can't even go into the store alone.'

'I've thought of something.'

'What?'

'One time you said something about the most beautiful sentence in the human language,' said Pen. 'As you know, I'm big on ritual. Maybe she needs one. What you're really referring to is the meaning of the sentence, in any language, right?'

'I suppose I am.'

'Then I know what she wants to hear.'

The Most Beautiful Sentence

Who but an NDN would know that some days truth is a ghost who shouts in the voice of no one in particular and other days it is a secret nostalgia poured into the coffee cups of the living?

—BILLY-RAY BELCOURT,
NDN COPING MECHANISMS: NOTES FROM THE FIELD

EGO TE ABSOLVO

I went into the store the next morning. Penstemon was shelving stacks of books and pulling books to fill more orders. She told me she was now thinking of tattooing her body in protest of blood quantum rules. Red lines would divide her eighths of Ho-Chunk, Hidatsa, Lakota, and Ojibwe. A blue line, her Norwegian area.

'Where would you put that blue line?'

'Around my heart. I really love my mother.'

'I am touched,' I said. 'But this idea's even worse than literary idol Mount Rushmore.'

I started to print out packing labels. Pen asked me if I'd ever looked up the quatrefoil symbol on the door of the confessional.

'No, I didn't. Of course I forgot.'

'Well, I did and it's cool. In heraldry the quatrefoil is a stylized four-petaled flower. As a Christian symbol, the petals are supposed to represent the four evangelists. But the quatrefoil is also an Indigenous symbol, Mayan, Olmec. It represents the four directions, the opening of the cosmos. And get this: It is considered a passageway between the celestial world and the underworld.'

Penstemon's face was bright with revelation. She and her rituals, her passion for symbolism.

'Maybe we could take off the door of the confessional, burn it, and see if destroying the portal stops her,' I said.

'If our plan doesn't work, let's try. Maybe not burn it, Tookie. But you know, it could be that the portal only works one way. Maybe Flora came through it by mistake and was trapped in the bookstore. Maybe we could coax her to use the front door.'

'Coax,' I said.

Pen shrugged. 'Yeah, how would that even work? I can't even coax Flex Wheeler to pick up his socks.'

'You're dating Flex Wheeler? Funny, that name rings a bell. . . .'

'Bodybuilder. My current boyfriend's real name is Kenneth. He's a Ho-Chunk and I just call him Flex because he lifts weights.'

'You like him?'

'Maybe. So far it's just long walks and Zoom dates, but there's always a pair of socks in his background, draped on a chair or something.'

'I consider that a good sign. A sock man. Lucky.' I caught my breath at the pain of thinking of Pollux.

Around eleven a.m., her usual time, Flora began rustling in Fiction. Penstemon looked at me, made Thriller claw hands, and we stopped talking. I texted Kateri and Asema, 'She's here.' A short time later, Asema showed up. Then Kateri paced in and stood frowning with her fists shoved in her jacket pockets. Her hair was growing out in a wavy shag. She was grounded and calm. We spread out into the aisles of books. Flora was messing around in the Cookbook section—I was pretty sure ghosts missed the taste of food. I'd have been sad if Flora wasn't trying in a sense to devour me. I looked at Asema, expecting she'd heard Flora's loud shuffle, but her face was blank. Kateri shook her head no. They couldn't hear Flora's footsteps, the tinkle of her bracelets, the slippery sounds of Flora's shawl or her silky pants swishing as she walked. Penstemon pointed out Flora's path. Asema strained forward, but she couldn't tell that Flora lingered now in Memoirs and Politics. Kateri didn't hear Flora browsing Native History and pausing at the sailboat table. Flora seemed to waver before the confessional. I'd left the gate open.

Flora entered the confessional. I nodded at Asema, stepped forward, and pulled from my pocket the piece of paper that Penstemon had given me because she thought Flora needed to be forgiven. She'd written out the words of absolution. *Indulgentiam, absolutionem, et remissionem peccatorum tuorum tribuat tibi omnipotens, et misericors Dominus. Amen.* I read words out slowly in Latin that was probably painful to hear, until I reached the crucial ending. Then in firm tones I said, *Ego te absolvo.* There was a suspension, a silence, a weighty sense of consideration. Then together we spoke one of the loveliest sentences in the English language.

Go in peace.

Nothing. She was still there. Sad, scorched, mildewed, alone. I squeezed my head between my hands to keep my bursting thoughts from overwhelming me. There was something. There had to be a key. I'd try anything.

'Wait a minute,' I said. 'I do know her favorite sentence. Listen!'

I had talked about Proust the day before, and in fact once I'd memorized a sentence that I knew Flora loved as I did.

A little tap on the window-pane, as though something had struck it, followed by a plentiful light falling sound, as of grains of sand being sprinkled from a window overhead, gradually spreading, intensifying, acquiring a regular rhythm, becoming fluid, sonorous, musical, immeasurable, universal: it was the rain.

Nothing. But I could feel her listening the way you feel it when an audience draws near.

'It was the rain.'

I spoke in a louder voice. She was definitely hanging on my words. My thoughts zinged around in my brain, touching here and there in the past. I came across a place that felt soft and painful; I stayed there and found some words that had been stuck in me. Words I thought now, in desperation, she might need because possibly she was haunting me out of a sense of entitlement. Maybe she needed the same thing the bone lady kept referring to. She needed me to be *so grateful.* I set my jaw and tried to focus through my resentment. It wasn't easy but I put it out there.

'All right, Flora. I give up. You saved my mother. You did a lot.'

Wait, it struck me. *Maybe I owed Flora everything.* She'd kept my mother sober, drugless, probably even well hydrated, while she was pregnant with me. Possibly, I owed Flora points on the IQ test I took that apparently (Jackie told me later) it was thought I'd somehow cheated on. Possibly I owed Flora my love of books, my words, my survival. But did I have to thank her? And was a bullied thank-you a real thank-you? And since this thank-you was coerced, could I coerce Flora back? Or fool her?

'Miigwech aapiji, Flora.' I pitched my voice in that special register that expresses something true, however grating, or sells something broken. 'Thank you for saving my life.'

There was a listening pause, a small sigh, a delicate rattle of wooden beads. Asema's eyes opened wide. She, too, heard Flora leaving the confessional. I'd left our front door, the blue door, open. The floor creaked near the entry. The air changed. Her footsteps paused. And then there was a hushed murmur, a thin whoosh, as she went out into the world.

'Shall I close the door?' asked Kateri.

As she stepped forward, the wind rose and slammed the door violently shut. The blow reverberated, shaking the windows and the books in the windows. The crash of the door nearly finished me. Kateri laughed in surprise.

'Happy trails,' she said.

'What was that about?'

Still laughing, hand on heart, Kateri croaked this out.

'I used to run around the house slamming doors, with Mom, for fun. She always said that's the way they got the ghosts out. I think this means she's happy.'

TOOKIE'S RETURN

After Flora left, I opened the gate to the confessional and took out the portable sound system, which was stored where the priest had rested his feet. I set aside the sign that said *Do not enter. Our insurance doesn't cover damnation.* I sat down on the bench with its sagging maroon leather cushion forever dented by a priestly ass.

I cannot remember reading Flora's full name in the book as I read the simple sentence that killed: *Her name was Lily Florabella Truax.* But Penstemon and Asema were right. I am permeable. Even recalling that name, now, I began to float apart, dissolving as though my cells were being seized by a room of hungry air. When I came back to myself, I knew. I had carefully kept myself in a cloud of unknowing, but now I understood. Lily Florabella.

My mother slammed me to the floor when I was eight, because I tried to stop her from going out the door. She slammed me down like an all-star wrestler. Knocked my wind out. Left me lying there. She stepped over me as she began her daily hunt for oblivion. I never forgave her for that, but it is the only moment I can remember of real violence. It was her nothingness, her being lost in space when I was right there with her. But other than her sudden, shocking, all-star wrestler move, there isn't one instance I can point to that hurt more than any other. There was just so much loneliness. I'd taken a pink eraser to my childhood and blurred the pain.

Compared to other lives, people I knew in prison and people I grew up with, my life was not so hard. I make a big deal of having fought dogs for food, for scrounging stuff and stealing food, but thanks to our neighbors and relatives, there *was* food. Nobody grudged what I took and often they handed me more. And although my mother didn't love me, she didn't hate me either. Yet, I grew to hate her.

You can't get over things you do to other people as easily as you get over things they do to you.

As her addictions weakened her and she became increasingly confused, I became strong and cruel. Sometimes I used the force of my entire body to yell at her because I knew how to break her down. I could make her sob, deep ugly wrenching gags that shamed me. I couldn't stop. Maybe I just needed to have some effect on her, even if it hurt her. My heart was empty. I could get at her tiny soft seed. Carve out the pith. I had no way to punish my father, whose crimes were supernumerary. Every hour he was absent from my life was an offense. Instead of blaming him I took apart my mother.

In fact, I'd slapped her hard, pushed her down on the gritty linoleum floor, told her she was shit, then bugged out on the day she overdosed.

When I came back hours later, I opened the door and stood beneath the jamb. There was a low whistle coming from somewhere. It chilled my blood. I knew it wasn't good. We didn't have a teakettle and it was not a windy day. The whistle only stopped when I found my mother in my closet. She'd crawled into my heap of blankets and rocketed off this earth within the one aperture that was mine. I remember finding her there, so dead, yet no harder to reach than when she was alive. Instead of feeling sad for her, I wanted to wash my blankets. I am probably porous because it costs a lot to not be aware. When I get stuck circling back to how I shoved her to the floor, it seems like the shame strengthens rather than fades with time.

Then one day, maybe it's gone.

My mother did tell me that she'd stayed clean while she was pregnant. That was something. She could have ditched Flora and gone on a nine-month drinking binge. That's true.

My mother's name was Charlotte Beaupre. When she was between usings, she had light brown eyes and the kind of dark brown hair that looks black after six p.m. When she was using heavy, her eyes sank back in her skull and you didn't want to look in there. We never talked when she was using or drunk but between those times she might say, 'Shut the fridge' or 'Cereal,' which meant I was to go to the corner store because we ate a lot of cereal. She didn't care what kind, but I caught a faint light in her eyes once when I bought Count Chocula. So I kept on getting it although it tasted like barf and took a lot of stamps. There's not much else to say. She wore no jewelry, had no favorite possessions. If she watched TV it could be anything. How can the person who gave you life and kept you more or less with them by some profound miracle of oversight leave such a scarce impression?

I put her ashes in the Mississippi River not because she ever noticed the river or gave the slightest indication she wanted that, but because it was a way to think of her as she'd always been, wordless and inert, pulled along by a strong, hidden current.

My name is Lily Florabella Truax Beaupre, named after the woman who helped my mother, the woman who became my ghost.

Flora had flung down books with my name. I accept the name, but not as I accepted the mashed rutabagas. I'm still Tookie; she's still Flora. And now she was gone, perhaps fooled when I'd deviously thanked her, or perhaps because of Marcel Proust or maybe the words of absolution in Latin had worked. There was a sliding sound. I'd heard it when her blood had turned to sand. I waited, but that was all. It didn't seem that she was coming back. I opened the door and walked out of the sin box. Stained, tainted, human, I stood in a beam of weak autumn light.

Souls and Saints

DARK OF THE YEAR

October 31, Halloween, the day that demons roam.
November 1, All Saints', the day the saints triumph.
November 2, All Souls', the day for souls in purgatory.
November 3, Election Day, all and none of the above.

HALLOWEEN

Hetta found a length of gutter pipe in the garage.

'Look at this, Tookie!' She was gloating. I was glad for some distraction from our fear over Pollux.

'It's an old drainpipe,' I said.

'No, it's a pandemic candy funnel.'

She and Asema used it to deliver candy into children's candy bags. I hadn't imagined there would be many trick-or-treaters this year, but there were astronauts, tigers, a girl wearing a picture frame, and a ton of superheroes. Earlier, three girls from the neighborhood had come to the store dressed as the Brontë sisters. Bonnets, capes, long sweeping dresses, shawls, the works. When they left, Jackie had turned to me and said they made her glad to be alive.

'Isn't that a bit of an overstatement?' I'd asked.

'No,' said Jackie.

'I'd really have been excited if they'd included the mad wife in Rochester's attic.'

'They're still little girls,' said Jackie. 'When they're tweens they'll all be her. So enjoy.'

I watched the trick-or-treaters for a while, then left Hetta and Asema to their funneling. The Halloween candy was tinier and more intensely wrapped every year. I headed for the hospital, where my plan was to eat thumb-size KitKats and wave at a window that I imagined was my husband's room. Sometimes late at night the hospital emitted thin streams of mist from the cracks along its windows and between the bricks. They took the shapes of spirits freed from bodies. The world was filling with ghosts. We were a haunted country in a haunted world.

I moved into the backseat and pulled up my sleeping bag. It was blue, puffy, beloved, a bit sour. But I was too. Although I was taking breaks as often as I could, I was still becoming a sour ball with arms and legs. I'd wake in the morning with numb arms, stiff legs, and a raging headache. My self-care was minimal. So what.

I was surviving, even if on candy, coffee, and boxes of power bars. It was getting so I welcomed the aches and shooting pains. These were signals that I was alive, emphatically alive. Yes, I was cold, grubby, wrecked. But I was also possessed of a rare, bizarre, yet ordinary gift. Before this year I'd have wanted to hand it over to Pollux. But the truth is I wanted this locked box full of treasure. I wanted this life for myself.

ALL SAINTS' DAY

It was again that time of the year when the veil between the worlds is thin. However, this year the veil had been ripped asunder. It was gone. After Pen told me about the quatrefoil she kept talking. She told me that in the medieval view there were rifts, holes, tears in space and time through which demons and human evils can erupt. Hatreds boil through the cracks. Even one person of a certain magnetism in this time can seize the energy and cause a maelstrom to form around each sentence they utter. One person can create a giant hurricane of unreality that feels like reality.

'That's what's happening,' she said. 'Just look around.'

I didn't have to. I felt like I could see everything—hatred, valor, cruelty, mercy. It was all over the news and in the hospitals and all over me. Watching and waiting for word of Pollux had turned me inside out.

I saw the families in parkas at the windows, holding up their love signs. I saw the old paper hearts, curled, the new paper hearts, still vivid. I wore fear like a cape. Fear was my sack pants, my black runners. I always carried along Pollux's dim brown plaid man shirt and favorite old jeans. Every day I got an update. Pollux was back to holding his own again. One day improvement, the next day worse. I tried not to shift my thoughts with every new voice on the phone. I'd never known Pollux to be afraid for himself, but he'd never been so helpless. For a while in my life I'd lived with the certainty that I would be held in love, and now I was sleeping in a parking lot. For a while in his life, Pollux had been held in love, and now he was marooned in a hospital bed on the other wide of a wall.

ALL SOULS' DAY

On All Souls' morning I got to work early, before Jackie. I took a deep breath before I unlocked the blue door to the bookstore. I let my breath go as I stepped inside. The store was quiet, but the silence wasn't ominous. Peace reigned. A clear blue light. The scent of sweetgrass and books. Yesterday it seemed that Pollux might be better. Today, no word. The door to the confessional was open, and I'd started to like the little perch, so I sat down.

On this day of souls, the millions absent in this world were leaving the between place, the limbo, if that existed. I thought of the people packed into narrow sleeves of earth. I sat there waiting. Surely not for Flora. Surely I had not become codependent with a ghost. No, I was waiting for her *not* to be here on the anniversary of her first visit. Not to slide step in her 1,700-degree shoes. I was waiting for my own heart to beat at a normal tempo. For my breath to ease. For my stomach to settle. I sat there in the peace for a long time with no god, no music, no ghost, no fellow worker, no Pollux.

Or maybe there was a god. Mine is the god of isolation, the god of the small voice, the god of the little spirit, of the earthworm and the friendly mouse, the hummingbird, the greenbottle fly and all things iridescent. In that quiet perhaps one of my tiny gods told me that I should drive back to the hospital parking lot.

I looked at my phone. There was no message. I looked at my email on the store computer. Nothing. I called the numbers I'd been given and there wasn't any news. I shut myself down, locked up the store, and drove. Left the car parked on the street and ran to the front desk of the hospital, pulling up my mask. The attendant saw it in my eyes and picked up the phone.

'Yes, please, Pollux . . . please doctor, please nurse.'

I could hear the sounds of purgatory. The scrape of a chair, a staticky bustle, then a voice.

'Hello, Mrs. Pollux. We've been trying to get in touch with you.'

My knees buckled. I went to the floor with the phone.

'Your husband is off the oxygen, breathing on his own. We think he's ready to come home.'

'What did you say?'

'Here, you want to talk to him?'

I stuttered out a yes and then Pollux was on the phone.

'Stop sleeping . . . in the . . . parking lot.'

'Pollux.'

'Come get me.'

After I was veiled and shielded, there was a copious amount of paperwork. One nurse told me how to take care of Pollux at home. Another nurse told me not to baby him. Let him walk around and so forth, build up his lungs. Both warned me to be careful and take his oxygen levels constantly. Pollux came down in an elevator in an actual bubble and then a shrouded nurse wheeled him to the entrance. I could tell he was skinny from the drape of the gowns he wore over his clothes. I opened the side door of the van and she helped him into the backseat. He had an oxygen tank for emergency breathing and a box of inhalers. I told the nurse that I'd strap him in and as I bent over him to grab the buckle, he rasped, 'Trouble's back.'

'Life's been kinda boring without you,' I choked.

I slid the side door shut tenderly and went around to the front. Three nurses waved us off. I coasted down the circular hospital drive and paused at the end to adjust my rearview mirror so that I could see Pollux. He was looking straight at me.

As I drove up with him, I saw that Hetta and Laurent were waiting at the door. Between us all, we plucked him out of the van.

'I'm weak as a kitten,' he said.

'Your fur is kind of lopsided,' said Hetta, pushing his ponytail behind his ears. He was able to walk slowly to the steps with one of us at each elbow. Laurent walked behind. He had a bag of swamp tea in his hand.

'Are you back there in case I suddenly drop?' asked Pollux.

'I guess,' said Laurent.

'Good.'

He rested after each step on the front stairs. I put my arms around him. Together, we toddled into the house. Hetta had taken off the back pillows and made the couch up as a bed. He tumbled down, out of breath, then recovered and let himself be propped up enough to breathe easier. The oxygen tank was at his side, but he waved it off.

'Being home is medicine.' His voice quavered. He drank some swamp tea and then he slept for nine hours. He was breathing easily in his sleep so I didn't wake him. I set up the comfortable chair next to the couch and sat there, holding his hand, tracing his scarred knuckles.

BONES

Election Day was perfectly warm. This was my first vote. I'd been shamed into it by Hetta and Asema, but really, Pollux had threatened to go himself if I didn't vote. So I went. I'd put up with the process, whatever it was. I'd always said that voting was for people who hadn't been where I'd been or done what I'd done. But maybe in fact I was just lazy. Asema and I walked over to the local school gym and I felt the strength drain from my legs again. Pollux! I didn't collapse, but I felt weak and ready to surrender. Getting out of the hospital was only a step. Nobody could tell me what came next. At one point, I sat down on a park bench and looked at my feet, in hot purple runners trimmed in black. I gazed at my feet the way you fixate on something familiar when your life is changing. I moved my toes up and down. My feet calmed me by obeying me. *He's breathing on his own.* Now that's a beautiful sentence. Last night I had slept on the extra couch pillows, on the floor beside Pollux. When I woke and reared up over Pollux he was still there.

'The hell.' I was looking through my pockets, pretending to be upset. 'My license, I forgot my license.' I gave Asema a smile of fake regret and rose to walk away. 'Oh well, see you later. Next time.'

Asema grabbed my arm.

'You gave me your voting card, remember? You're not getting out of this.'

I walked along, still looking down at my shoes. We reached the line and took our place. Asema told me she needed to talk to me about her latest findings, but before she could go on the woman in front of us turned and pounced.

'You're from the bookstore!'

We turned. I couldn't place her at first, then Asema said, 'You're the bone lady.'

She was dressed in rust orange this time, but she was indeed the woman who had cornered us last fall and talked about her great-aunt's science project—wired-together human remains that she stored under her bed.

'I just dropped off a box at your store,' she said. Her eyes were bright and shiny. She wore an orange plaid bucket hat. We nodded and turned away and I felt a chill along my shoulders. I turned back.

'Is it bones?' I asked.

The bone lady nodded, her eyes beaming. 'I hope you're grateful,' she said with a coy wink.

❈

Asema tiptoed into the store as though she was the grave robber. A cardboard box that had once held a sun lamp was in the office. Asema rocked the box and the bones shifted.

'I'm dying to see what's inside,' I said.

'Groan,' said Asema. She opened the box and peered

in. 'Yep, bones.' She stood there, blinking, her hand at the back of her head.

'Are we grateful?' I asked.

'Only if she gives the land back.'

I went out of the office and when I came back, I found Asema using a fork to hold up a scrap of blue. Before I could stop her, she torched it with her lighter. The blue ribbon flared and vanished. There was nothing to say. Next, Asema burned some sage and brushed the smoke over the bones; she twisted braids of sweetgrass among the bones and ripped open a package of bear root and laid the pieces inside before she closed the box. She asked me if I thought Pollux would know what to do about the situation. 'I mean, if he feels well enough, maybe he could ask one of his friends,' she said.

'He just got out of the hospital,' I said. 'And you want me to ask him what to do with human remains.'

'But when he gets well, he'll be unhappy if we do the wrong thing,' said Asema. I knew she was right.

Pen had made a chocolate cake for Pollux. It was the size of a pillbox hat, moist and dense. I carried it home wanting like a bear to stop and eat it with my paws. He was sleeping again, his face pinched and defenseless. But when he woke around noon, he looked slightly better. His voice hit some of the old notes. I made him some toast, then some scrambled eggs, then toast and scrambled eggs together. I decided that he was a lot better and I told him that a white woman had dropped a box of bones off at the store.

'People bones?'

'Probably from a burial mound.'

'I know a guy who can handle this,' said Pollux. 'He's done some burials and repatriations. If you give me my phone, I'll call him.'

Pollux was sitting up on the couch now. I gave him the phone and he talked for a while.

'He says the bones shouldn't stay in the store overnight. He says it's kind of an emergency and he'd come get them himself, but he's old, doesn't like to drive.'

❊

Asema volunteered to drive the bones out of the city and asked Hetta to come along with her. They set out in the dark of late fall, with the box of bones in the back of the van. I waved them off with Jarvis in my arms, then went back to Pollux. We made Jarvis an arena with pillows and Pollux watched him crawl around and drag himself up the side of the couch. I fixed a cup of tomato soup and a grilled cheese sandwich for Pollux.

'No jalapeños?'

'Not yet.'

'I wish you'd put on a nurse outfit.'

'Scrubs? Sure.'

'I was thinking more retro.'

'Not yet for that, too.'

He ate half and asked for more swamp tea and also music. It never occurred to me to follow the election results, and Pollux said we wouldn't know for a while anyway. Jarvis and I danced, Pollux nodded from the couch, we reminisced about our favorite diner breakfasts, we checked in with a real nurse, we walked Pollux to the bathroom and I plumped up his pillows. Pollux sang a phrase of song before his voice gave out. He ate a small wedge of cake.

The evening had turned cool and Jarvis was absorbed by a freakishly responsive toy that sang, cooed, purred, gurgled, or spoke when he touched it. I wanted to make a fire, but I couldn't remember ever making one before. I was a city Indian, mainly, then my hobby of getting massively wasted in various ways had taken over, then of course I'd been surrounded by concrete for a decade, until at last I met up with a Potawatomi. I decided to ask Pollux for a lesson.

He was propped up well enough to see the fireplace

and tell me what to assemble from the kindling box and the little pile of split wood. More was on the back porch.

'Strip the birchbark off that piece,' he said. He directed me to put down a loose layer of sticks on the grate, along with strips of birchbark, then top with a few thin chops of kindling. 'Put a couple nice dense splits in back. Make sure the flue's open.' He told me to crush up some newspaper. I mashed a couple sections.

'Not like that,' he said. 'Take one page at a time and crunch it into a ball, not too tight. That's good. Now shove them beneath the grate. Stick a scrap of birchbark in the papers and put a match to that.'

The fire blazed up and caught all the way to the biggest log. He told me which pieces of wood to add and where to place them.

'Flame follows air. Air's the food of fire and fire is always hungry.'

'Like you.' My back was turned.

'Yeah,' he said. I could feel him grin.

I followed his instructions until a nice bed of coals collected under the grate. I sat back.

'Now watch,' he said. 'Your fire's gonna start going out.'

It did. I turned to him.

'What'd I do?'

'You let the logs burn long enough so they made a space between them. You gotta keep the fire new. Every piece of wood needs a companion to keep it burning. Now push them together. Not too much. They also need that air. Get them close, but not on top of each other. Just a light connection all the way along. Now you'll see a row of even flames.'

The flames popped out. Picture perfect.

'God damn. I really love you,' I whispered, sitting back on my heels.

We fell into a dreamy assonance. I drifted on the couch cushions down on the floor, attached to a warm baby limpet who was nearing his first birthday. Pollux's breathing evened out and grew deeper. He was asleep. I stared at my husband's face, the new cheekbones of a skinny man, his surprising beauty, and I decided to live for love again and take the chance of another lifetime.

Jarvis awakened. We regarded each other in the calm light. He was on the verge of his first steps. Walking is a feat of controlled falling. Like life, I guess. But for the moment he was still a baby. Omaa akiing. He sighed in delicious boredom. His eyelids quivered as they shut. He smiled at some inward secret. Ah, my chubby traveler. You entered this world at the crossroads. Together, we straggled through a year that sometimes seemed like the beginning of the end. A slow tornado. I want to forget this year, but I'm also afraid I won't remember this year. I want this now to be the now where we save our place, your place, on earth.

Ghosts bring elegies and epitaphs, but also signs and wonders. What comes next? I want to know, so I manage to drag the dictionary to my side. I need a word, a sentence.

The door is open. Go.

TOTALLY BIASED LIST OF
TOOKIE'S FAVORITE BOOKS

Ghost-Managing Book List

The Uninvited Guests, by Sadie Jones

Ceremonies of the Damned, by Adrian C. Louis

Moon of the Crusted Snow, by Waubgeshig Rice

Father of Lies, by Brian Evenson

The Underground Railroad, by Colson Whitehead

Asleep, by Banana Yoshimoto

The Hatak Witches, by Devon A. Mihesuah

Beloved, by Toni Morrison

The Through, by A. Rafael Johnson

Lincoln in the Bardo, by George Saunders

Savage Conversations, by LeAnne Howe

The Regeneration Trilogy, by Pat Barker

Exit Ghost, by Philip Roth

Songs for Discharming, by Denise Sweet

Hiroshima Bugi: Atomu 57, by Gerald Vizenor

Short Perfect Novels

Too Loud a Solitude, by Bohumil Hrabel

Train Dreams, by Denis Johnson

Sula, by Toni Morrison

The Shadow-Line, by Joseph Conrad

The All of It, by Jeannette Haine

Winter in the Blood, by James Welch

Swimmer in the Secret Sea, by William Kotzwinkle

The Blue Flower, by Penelope Fitzgerald

First Love, by Ivan Turgenev

Wide Sargasso Sea, by Jean Rhys

Mrs. Dalloway, by Virginia Woolf

Waiting for the Barbarians, by J. M. Coetzee

Fire on the Mountain, by Anita Desai

Sailboat Table (table by Quint Hankle)

The Voyage of the Narwhal, by Andrea Barrett

Complete Stories, by Clarice Lispector

Boy Kings of Texas, by Domingo Martinez

The Marrow Thieves, by Cherie Dimaline

A Brief History of Seven Killings, by Marlon James

There There, by Tommy Orange

Citizen: An American Lyric, by Claudia Rankine

Underland, by Robert Macfarlane

The Undocumented Americans, by Karla Cornejo
    Villavicencio

Deacon King Kong, by James McBride

The Dutch House, by Ann Patchett

Will and Testament, by Vigdis Hjorth

Every Man Dies Alone, by Hans Fallada

The Door, by Magda Svabo

The Plot Against America, by Philip Roth

Fates and Furies, by Lauren Groff

The Overstory, by Richard Power

Night Train, by Lise Erdrich

Her Body and Other Parties, by Carmen Maria Machado

The Penguin Book of the Modern American Short Story,
    edited by John Freeman

Between the World and Me, by Ta-Nehisi Coates

Birds of America, by Lorrie Moore

Mongrels, by Stephen Graham Jones

The Office of Historical Corrections, by Danielle Evans

Tenth of December, by George Saunders

Murder on the Red River, by Marcie R. Rendon

Leave the World Behind, by Rumaan Alam

Ceremony, by Leslie Marmon Silko

On Earth We're Briefly Gorgeous, by Ocean Vuong

The Unwomanly Face of War, by Svetlana Alexievich

Standard Deviation, by Katherine Heiny

All My Puny Sorrows, by Miriam Toews

The Death of the Heart, by Elizabeth Bowen

Mean Spirit, by Linda Hogan

NW, by Zadie Smith

Being Mortal, by Atul Gawande

Americanah, by Chimamanda Ngozi Adichie

Firekeeper's Daughter, by Angeline Boulley

Erasure, by Percival Everett

Sharks in the Time of Saviors, by Kawai Strong Washburn

Heaven, by Mieko Kawakami

Books for Banned Love

Sea of Poppies, by Amitav Ghosh

The English Patient, by Michael Ondaatje

Euphoria, by Lily King

The Red and the Black, by Stendahl

Luster, by Raven Leilani

Asymmetry, by Lisa Halliday

All the Pretty Horses, by Cormac McCarthy

Middlesex, by Jeffrey Eugenides

The Vixen, by Francine Prose

Legends of the Fall, by Jim Harrison

The Winter Soldier, by Daniel Mason

Indigenous Lives

Holding Our World Together, by Brenda J. Child

American Indian Stories, by Zitkala-Sa

A History of My Brief Body, by Billy-Ray Belcourt

The Falling Sky: Words of a Yanomami Shaman,
    by Davi Kopenawa and Bruce Albert
Apple: Skin to the Core, by Eric Gansworth
Heart Berries, by Terese Marie Mailhot
The Blue Sky, by Galsan Tschinag
Crazy Brave, by Joy Harjo
Standoff, by Jacqueline Keeler
Braiding Sweetgrass, by Robin Wall Kimmerer
You Don't Have to Say You Love Me, by Sherman Alexie
Spirit Car, by Diane Wilson
Two Old Women, by Velma Wallis
Pipestone: My Life in an Indian Boarding School,
    by Adam Fortunate Eagle
Split Tooth, by Tanya Tagaq
Walking the Rez Road, by Jim Northrup
Mamaskatch, by Darrel J. McLeod

Indigenous Poetry

Conflict Resolution for Holy Beings, by Joy Harjo
Ghost River (Wakpá Wanági), by Trevino L.
    Brings Plenty
The Book of Medicines, by Linda Hogan
The Smoke That Settled, by Jay Thomas Bad Heart Bull
The Crooked Beak of Love, by Duane Niatum
Whereas, by Layli Long Soldier

Little Big Bully, by Heid E. Erdrich

A Half-Life of Cardio-Pulmonary Resuscitation,
    by Eric Gansworth

NDN Coping Mechanisms, by Billy-Ray Belcourt

The Invisible Musician, by Ray A. Young Bear

When the Light of the World Was Subdued, Our Songs
    Came Through, edited by Joy Harjo

New Poets of Native Nations, edited by Heid E. Erdrich

The Failure of Certain Charms, by Gordon Henry Jr.

Indigenous History and Nonfiction

Everything You Know About Indians Is Wrong,
    by Paul Chaat Smith

Decolonizing Methodologies, by Linda Tuhiwai Smith

Through Dakota Eyes: Narrative Accounts of the
    Minnesota Indian War of 1862, edited by Gary Clayton
    Anderson and Alan R. Woodworth

Being Dakota, by Amos E. Oneroad and Alanson B.
    Skinner

Boarding School Blues, edited by Clifford E. Trafzer,
    Jean A. Keller, and Lorene Sisquoc

Masters of Empire, by Michael A. McDonnell

Like a Hurricane: The Indian Movement from Alcatraz
    to Wounded Knee, by Paul Chaat Smith and Robert
    Allen Warrior

Boarding School Seasons, by Brenda J. Child
They Called It Prairie Light, by K. Tsianina Lomawaima
To Be a Water Protector, by Winona LaDuke
Minneapolis: An Urban Biography, by Tom Weber

Sublime Books

The Known World, by Edward P. Jones
The Buried Giant, by Kazuo Ishiguro
A Thousand Trails Home, by Seth Kantner
House Made of Dawn, by N. Scott Momaday
Faithful and Virtuous Night, by Louise Glück
The Left Hand of Darkness, by Ursula K. Le Guin
My Sentence Was a Thousand Years of Joy, by Robert Bly
The World Without Us, by Alan Weisman
Unfortunately, It Was Paradise, by Mahmoud Darwish
Collected Fictions, by Jorge Luis Borges,
     trans. Andrew Hurley
The Xenogenesis Trilogy, by Octavia E. Butler
Map: Collected and Last Poems, by Wisława Szymborska
In the Lateness of the World, by Carolyn Forché
Angels, by Denis Johnson
Postcolonial Love Poem, by Natalie Diaz
Hope Against Hope, by Nadezhda Mandelstam
Exhalation, by Ted Chaing
Strange Empire, by Joseph Kinsey Howard

Tookie's Pandemic Reading

Deep Survival, by Laurence Gonzales
The Lost City of the Monkey God, by Douglas Preston
The House of Broken Angels, by Luis Alberto Urrea
The Heartsong of Charging Elk, by James Welch
Selected Stories of Anton Chekhov, trans. Richard Pevear
    and Larissa Volokhonsky
The Sound of a Wild Snail Eating, by Elisabeth Tova
    Bailey
Let's Take the Long Way Home, by Gail Caldwell
The Aubrey/Maturin Novels, by Patrick O'Brian
The Ibis Trilogy, by Amitav Ghosh
The Golden Wolf Saga, by Linnea Hartsuyker
Children of Time, by Adrian Tchaikovsky
Coyote Warrior, by Paul VanDevelder

Incarceration

Felon, by Reginald Dwayne Betts
Against the Loveless World, by Susan Abulhawa
Waiting for an Echo, by Christine Montross, M.D.
The Mars Room, by Rachel Kushner
The New Jim Crow, by Michelle Alexander
This Is Where, by Louise K. Waakaa'igan
I Will Never See the World Again, by Ahmet Altan
Sorrow Mountain, by Ani Pachen and Adelaide Donnelley
American Prison, by Shane Bauer

Solitary, by Albert Woodfox

Are Prisons Obsolete?, by Angela Y. Davis

1000 Years of Joys and Sorrows, by Ai Weiwei

*Books contain everything worth knowing
except what ultimately matters.*

—TOOKIE

If you are interested in the books on these lists, please seek them out at your local independent bookstore. Miigwech!

Acknowledgments

As for the dictionary . . .

In 1971, I entered a contest sponsored by the National Football League. The author of the winning essay on the topic 'Why I Want to Go to College' would receive a scholarship for several thousand dollars. One hundred runners-up would receive a dictionary. I was a runner-up. My dictionary, *The American Heritage Dictionary of the English Language*, 1969, came with a gold-stamped letter from the president of the NFL, J. Robert Carey, thanking me for my interest in Professional Football. As it turned out, my true interest was in Professional Writing. Although I didn't know at the time how important words would become for me, I carried this (heavy) clothbound dictionary to college, to a summer at the Blacksmith House coffee shop in Boston, back to North Dakota where I was a poet in the North Dakota State Penitentiary, and in schools throughout the state. The dictionary returned with me to the East Coast, where I worked at the Boston Indian Council. It stayed with me through marriage, was there when I brought my daughters home as newborns, became a comfort to me through difficult times, and collected newspaper clippings, pressed flowers, pictures of William Faulkner, Octavia Butler, and Jean Rhys, bookmarks from vanished bookstores, and other mementos within its pages. It was the dictionary I consulted for this book.

So first of all, I want to thank this dictionary. Next, I want to thank Terry Karten for making daunting decisions to help this book along and for believing I could write it. Most of all, Terry, thanks for sharing with me your critical thinking. Trent Duffy, I have exhausted superlatives. Thank you for literally reading between the lines and for using your formidable skills to improve this book. Jane Beirn, I so appreciate your unerring guidance and your friendship over many years.

Andrew Wylie, thank you for supporting my unbearable need to write. Jin Auh, for your cool intelligence, your friendship, and your reliable good cheer under trying circumstances, thank you. I'm so glad you came to the spooky tarot reading in the basement of the bookstore.

To my first readers, Pallas Erdrich, Greta Haugland, Heid Erdrich, Angie Erdrich, Nadine Teisberg, I am in your debt. You helped me see this book for what it could be. You extended my understanding. Thank you, Persia Erdrich, for checking the Ojibwemowin; Kiizh Kinew Erdrich, for giving me insights into my young characters and for jingle dancing; and Aza Erdrich Abe, for creating the stately, striking, original cover.

George Floyd's murder blew open a city's consciousness in a way that I hope means an ongoing reckoning. This book is just one fictional character's attempt to figure out what was happening at the time. I want to thank the many journalists who were arrested or harmed for doing their job covering the protests here and, presently in northern Minnesota, on Line 3. Thank you also to the many people who talked to me about occurrences in this book, including Heid Erdrich, Al Gross, Bob Rice, Judy Azure, Frank Paro, Brenda Child, and in particular Pallas Erdrich, who kept track of all that happened and also gave me insights into customers and bookselling (all my daughters and many of their cousins have worked at the store). Also, Pallas, thanks for listening to endless plot variations and for troubleshooting during a fraught year.

Thank you to everyone who has ever worked at Birchbark Books or entered our blue door. Enormous thanks to our present staff and those who got us through 2020, including Kate Day, Carolyn Anderson, Prudence Johnson, Christian Pederson Behrends, Anthony Ceballo, Nadine Teisberg, Halee Kirkwood, Will Fraser, Eliza Erdrich, Kate Porter, Evelyn Vocu, Tom Dolan, Jack Theis, and Allicia Waukau. I'd like to especially thank Nathan Pederson, whose work as buyer gives the store its distinctive outlook; whose work as web technician gives the store extraordinary reach; and who appears (fictively) only once in this book, as Nick.

I would like to acknowledge the Women's Prison Book Project Collective here in Minneapolis.

In *The Sentence*, books are matters of life and death, and readers reach through unknowable realms to maintain some connection to the written word. So with the bookstore. From the very beginning, people gave unstintingly of themselves to the project, and for the past twenty years one book lover after another has worked passionately to keep the bookstore going or support it as a customer. There aren't enough thanks for what this means.

To everyone's amazement, Birchbark Books is doing fine now. If you are going to buy a book, including this one, please visit your nearest independent bookstore and support its singular vision.

Yours for books,
Louise

About the Author

LOUISE ERDRICH, a member of the Turtle Mountain Band of Chippewa, is the author of many novels as well as volumes of poetry, children's books, and memoirs of early motherhood. Erdrich lives in Minnesota with her daughters and is the owner of Birchbark Books, a small independent bookstore. Her most recent book, *The Night Watchman*, won the Pulitzer Prize. A ghost lives in her creaky old house.